AN AFTERNOON PICNIC

Asher set the basket down and helped Caramarena spread the quilt. The last thing he needed right now was this little tête-à-tête.

Caramarena lowered herself to her knees, then curled her legs underneath her and opened the basket.

All of her hair was neatly arranged on top of her head. As Caramarena began pulling food out of the basket, Asher wanted badly to pull the pins from her hair and let it fall.

"Please feel free to untie your cravat, Mr. Millhouse, and unbutton some of those buttons. It makes me hot just to look at you stuffed so tightly into that shirt."

She didn't look at him as she made this astonishing statement. There was nothing Asher would have liked better, but he'd die of heat stroke first.

"I'm fine, Miss Cantrell, but thank you for thinking of my well-being."

She looked up at him and smiled pleasantly. "Please yourself, Mr. Millhouse."

Asher returned her smile. If only he could.

Sultry Nights

Charla Cameron

PINNACLE BOOKS
WINDSOR PUBLISHING CORP.

PINNACLE BOOKS

are published by

Windsor Publishing Corp.
475 Park Avenue South
New York, NY 10016

First printing: June, 1992

Printed in the United States of America

Prologue

Northwest Florida: 1848

Damn, this Florida heat was killing him, Asher thought as he watched the woman he'd just spent less than half an hour with. Sweat glistened on the breasts of the whore as she slowly pulled her dress on. She stopped for a moment at her waist before letting the wrinkled satinet skirt fall to her feet, and Asher knew she was trying to renew his interest in her with that provocative movement.

"You sure you don't want another one before I go, sugar?" she asked in a husky voice.

Asher strained to see her pretty face in the dim candlelight as he sipped the expensive whiskey he'd abandoned earlier in favor of the woman. She was well-trained in the art of pleasing a man, but in this heat she just wasn't worth it. He'd wait until he returned to England, where the weather was more conducive to paying for a whole night with a woman. He shook his head and watched a pout form on her thin lips. It wasn't his style to disappoint a woman, but tonight he'd had enough.

"Maybe next time," he said. He laid his head back against the wall and stretched his legs out their full length, feeling not a thread of embarrassment at lying naked before her.

She smiled and ran her hand down her side as she took a slow steady breath. "You know where to find me when you're ready."

Asher nodded and she turned away. He almost let her leave the small room without asking his usual question, but habit made him speak up. "Wait," he called and she swung back around, a hopeful look in her questioning eyes. "I'm looking for a man—an old friend of my father's. John Cantrell. Did you ever hear of him?"

Closing the door, she walked closer to the bed. "Maybe. I'm not sure."

Her dark eyes gave her away. Asher was certain she knew the name. His heart started beating wildly. Could it be after fourteen years of searching he'd found the man he sought on the banks of the Apalachicola River? Damn! And he'd almost let this woman get away.

Asher swung his legs off the bed and set his drink on the small table, the amber liquid sloshing in the glass. He picked up his breeches and dug into the pockets, bringing out a handful of coins. He dropped the pants to his feet and extended his open palm toward her. "You can have one for every question you answer."

The woman stroked her lips with her tongue and let her gaze wander from the coins to his face. With the back of her hand she pushed her long tangled hair away from her face and sniffed. Asher knew that she was trying to decide if she could trust him to pay for the information.

"Have you ever heard of John Cantrell?" he asked again, watching her closely. This time she nodded and Asher lifted his palm a little higher. She slowly reached for a gold coin, and once her fingers closed around it she quickly snatched her hand away and held it tightly to her breast.

Asher remained calm on the outside but felt as if his heart were going to beat out of his chest. Sweat beaded his forehead and ran down his cheek. "Do you know where I can find him?"

She nodded again and quickly grabbed another coin, never taking her eyes off his face, poised as if ready to run should he renege on his promise.

"Where will I find him?" Asher swallowed hard and held his breath.

She rubbed her lips with the tips of her fingers and watched him. Asher knew she was pondering whether or not to tell him. Once he knew where to find Cantrell the money would stop. She must have decided to take her chances because she drew a deep breath and said, " 'Bout thirty miles up the river. He has a big plantation called Live Oak. He's been there ever since I can remember." She grabbed another gold piece to add to her bounty, but this time Asher caught her wrist with his other hand. She gasped and terror filled her eyes.

Asher smiled to ease her fear. "Take the rest and get out of here. You earned it," he said and let go of her. She gave him a slight, trembling smile before grabbing the money and fleeing out the door.

Asher ran both hands through his dark brown hair, then picked up his drink and stretched his naked body out on the rumpled, damp sheets. Damn, what good luck!

He needed to think and plan. Even though everyone said he took after his mother in looks, he couldn't show up at Cantrell's door; the man might recognize him as George Worthy's son. Maybe he should grow a beard. He rubbed his lightly whiskered chin, thinking he already had a good start. He'd need a letter of introduction, too. There were plenty of men who owed him favors who could take care of that. He smiled. And his last name. Cantrell would surely recognize that. It was better to just use his middle name. Yes, Asher Millhouse. He'd drop Worthy for now. When the right time came, Cantrell would know who he was.

A low chuckle rumbled in his chest. He lifted his drink in a mock salute. "To you, John Cantrell. May you rot in hell with my father."

Chapter One

Whatever else Caramarena Cantrell was, she was her father's daughter, Asher thought, watching the young woman give him yet another beautiful smile as he sat across the dinner table from her. She was trying to win him over just as John Cantrell must have won his father's friendship.

Asher had decided to visit the sultry west coast of Florida looking for new business for his shipping industry. It was luck that he'd found the man he had been searching for, the man who'd betrayed his father more than twenty-five years ago.

"I read over your letter of introduction this afternoon and it seems to be in order. Live Oak has been doing business with Mr. Shock for many years. We're pleased he sent you our way."

Asher shifted in his chair. When he agreed to stay for dinner he hadn't expected Cantrell's daughter to be so interested in him or his business with her father.

"I'm sorry to hear your father's not well and couldn't join us for dinner after inviting me to stay."

"Papa's not feeling well."

At the sound of the soft childlike voice both Asher and Caramarena turned their attention to the other young lady at the table. Caramarena reached over and patted her sister's hand. "That's right, Bunch. We'll go

9

up later and say good night to him after you've finished your dinner."

Caramarena turned her attention back to Asher and smiled at him again. "Don't you worry about that, Mr. Millhouse. We expect anyone who visits Live Oak to stay the night. The nearest boarding house is thirty miles back down the river. We couldn't ask you to come and go each day until Papa decides whether or not he wants your ships to take his cotton and turpentine to England."

"Papa's not feeling well," Bunch repeated, and Caramarena reached over and took her sister's hand, squeezing it affectionately.

Asher continued to eat his duck and rice and the delicious bread while he watched the sisters. He put Bunch's age at about fifteen or sixteen and her sister closer to twenty. Bunch was a very pretty young lady with an oval face, dark green eyes and honey-gold hair. Caramarena was a beautiful woman with the more dramatic heart-shaped face and light green eyes, her hair a lustrous golden brown.

It was clear to him that Bunch's mind wasn't quite right, and Asher was impressed by the patience with which Caramarena treated her younger sister. There were no undertones of irritation in her voice or manner when she spoke to Bunch and no hint of embarrassment at Bunch's deficiency either. He knew a family in London with a son who was simpleminded, as Bunch appeared to be, and they kept him locked in a room. Certainly they would have never allowed him at the dinner table with guests in the house.

"How often do you come to America, Mr. Millhouse?" Caramarena asked.

"Every year. I usually sail with the first ship in the spring and return with the last in the fall. The best way to keep our business prosperous is to call on our clients, listen to their complaints and keep them happy. This is my first trip to Florida's west coast, although I've been tempted to stop many times on my way to New Orleans."

And this would probably be his last trip, Asher thought, as he recalled the bright, sunlit, humid days and the sultry, insect-riddled nights. Remembrance of the bug bites he'd sustained reminded him of how the heat made the newly grown beard itch. He had the urge to reach up and give it a good scratching. Instead, he pulled on his tight shirt collar.

"Papa's not feeling well," Bunch said again.

Caramarena turned to Bunch. "Do you want to go up and see Papa before you have dessert?" she asked, and Bunch nodded. "All right, I'll get Kissie to go with you." She looked at Asher and smiled. "Please excuse me for a moment, Mr. Millhouse."

"Of course," he said and stood while she left the table.

Asher watched as Caramarena left the room in a rustle of petticoats over pale yellow lawn. Her shoulders were slight, her back straight, and her waist small, he noticed as she walked gracefully from the room. Suddenly he had the urge to see that beautiful mound of shiny hair cascading down her back, swishing back and forth as she moved.

Asher shook his head. The last thing he needed was to become enamored of Cantrell's daughter. Caramarena was beautiful and charming, and her smiles told him she found him attractive. He had to keep reminding himself that he was here because of Cantrell and for no other reason.

He looked over at Bunch, who remained quiet. Her hands folded in her lap, she stared straight ahead. He wondered if he should speak to her. When Caramarena had introduced them at the beginning of dinner she had greeted him politely, but she'd had little to say throughout the meal.

Asher heard Caramarena's footsteps and mentally chided himself. He had to be careful or he'd find himself caught up in the lives of these two women and for-

11

get that he was sitting at the table of the man he meant to destroy.

Caramarena walked in from the warming room, where the food was held after being brought up from the cookhouse. "Kissie will be waiting for you at the bottom of the stairs, Bunch. She'll take you upstairs to see Papa. Don't forget to say good night to Mr. Millhouse."

Asher rose, took Bunch's offered hand, and planted a polite kiss on it. "It was a pleasure to dine with you, Bunch."

"Thank you," she said with a shy smile, then quickly left the room.

Caramarena watched Bunch go, then turned to her guest. "Thank you for allowing me to disrupt your dinner, Mr. Millhouse. I do apologize."

"No apology necessary, Miss Cantrell," he answered, looking directly into her eyes. "Your sister is not only beautiful, she's also charming."

The sincerity Caramarena heard in this man's voice lifted her spirits. She'd found that most people were uncomfortable around Bunch. She gave him a big appreciative smile. "Do sit back down, Mr. Millhouse. I asked the cook to bring in dessert. Are you finished?"

"Yes, thank you. The duck was excellent." He helped Caramarena with her chair before returning to his own.

Caramarena folded her hands in her lap and said, "While we're waiting why don't you tell me more about yourself?"

Asher pulled on his tight shirt collar and wished a breeze would blow through the open windows. The skin under his beard was itching like hell, but he'd be damned if he'd break down and scratch in front of this beautiful woman. In London August nights were cool and comfortable. This place was hot as hell.

"There's really very little to tell. My two brothers and I have managed Three Sons Shipping since my father's

12

death fifteen years ago. Parker and Winston take care of the paperwork at our office in London and I travel with the ships, always on the lookout for new business."

"I see," she said, picking up her water glass and taking a drink as an idea started forming in her mind. "And what does Mrs. Millhouse think of your traveling so much?" She knew it wasn't the proper thing to ask, but if Mr. Millhouse had a wife she needn't take her idea further.

He smiled and Caramarena's breath caught in her throat. He was very handsome, and not as old as the beard suggested. The closely trimmed facial hair hid his features, and she hadn't taken the time to look past it. Now she saw that his eyes were a warm shade of blue, his skin textured to a light golden brown from the sun. His teeth were straight and white and his lips full and generous, giving him a breathtaking smile. Caramarena also liked his British accent. It was heavier than her father's but just as warm and pleasing.

"There is no Mrs. Asher Millhouse. That's one of the reasons my brothers do the paperwork and I do the soliciting."

She pondered his statement for a moment. "So your brothers stay in London because they have families?"

"That and the fact they don't enjoy sailing to the many ports I usually visit."

"Ah—here comes the dessert. I do hope you like blackberries and cream." Caramarena picked up her dessert spoon and watched it sparkle in the candlelight. Mr. Millhouse wasn't ready to settle down. Just maybe her idea would work.

"Very much," Asher answered, although he wasn't certain he'd ever eaten blackberries and cream.

They remained quiet while the dinner plates were taken away and a crystal bowl of berries was left in their place.

When the server finished, Asher decided it was his turn to ask questions. He'd spent about twenty minutes with Cantrell earlier in the afternoon but failed to obtain any concrete information from him. Cantrell had been polite but quiet, letting Asher do most of the talking. Asher had had to push his shipping business and didn't have the time to talk about Cantrell's past.

"How many years has Live Oak been in your family?" he asked as he scooped up a spoonful of berries.

Caramarena laid down her spoon and daintily wiped her mouth with her lace-trimmed napkin. Watching her, Asher felt a tightening in his groin. Why should such an ordinary act as wiping her mouth make him react in such a primitive way? He'd already admitted she was beautiful, charming and attractive. Now he had to stop thinking about her as a woman. He was here to transact a business deal, and he couldn't let anything or anyone interfere.

"My father bought it when he was a young man back in the early twenties. He came from your country." She smiled. "Because he has no family left in England he's never returned. He's considered America his homeland for many years now."

The orphan story was as good as any, Asher supposed, but he knew for a fact that Cantrell had left an elderly aunt when he fled London. His father had kept in touch with her for years while she clung to the hope that one day she would hear from her runaway nephew. The only thing she ever admitted receiving from him was a note when he left saying that he'd gone to make his fortune in America.

Asher looked around the large, high-ceilinged room. The beautiful dining table and matching chairs were genuine Duncan Phyfe originals. Lustrous brass candelabras sat on small tables in each corner of the room, their candles filling the room with soft yellow light. The carved and gilted frame of the mirror hanging above the fireplace added grandeur to the spacious room. A bitter chuckle rumbled low in Asher's chest. John Cantrell hadn't come to America to make his fortune but to spend the one he'd stolen from George Worthy.

Asher looked back at the lovely Caramarena and knew that he didn't want to ruin her life as well as her father's, but it couldn't be helped. If he was successful in financially destroying Cantrell, Bunch and Caramarena would have to go down with him. Asher tightened his lips. Why should that bother him? Had Cantrell thought of his father and mother and their young son when he'd absconded with the greater portion of George Worthy's wealth, forcing him to forsake his family to rebuild his business?

The blackberries were suddenly bitter in Asher's mouth. He and his two brothers had vowed on their father's deathbed to find John Cantrell and destroy him. He couldn't let the two beautiful sisters soften him.

Asher put his spoon down and pushed the half-eaten berries aside. The torridity of the night added to his anger. He stuck his finger down his collar and pulled on it but found no relief from the tightness of the fabric or the heat. How could Caramarena sit there and look so fresh when the heat was killing him?

"Does your father manage the plantation or does he have a manager?" he asked.

Caramarena dabbed at the corners of her mouth again. Asher wished she would quit bringing his attention to her mouth. It made his breeches uncomfortably tight, and he was too damned hot already.

"I suppose I could be considered Papa's manager. Mama died when Bunch was born, leaving Papa without a son. My two older sisters were never interested in how and what it took to keep a plantation this size going. I have to admit I wasn't interested at first either, but Papa wanted one of us to know, so he kept working with me until the whole system started fitting together. Now I know what supplies to order for the main house as well as how to take care of the slaves and their needs. I know how to manage the household and business accounts and how to give our overseer, Mr. Wulpher, a dressing down should he need it."

She gave him a confident smile and Asher accepted it with a nod of approval. "Well, I've been a guest at some of the finest plantations in Virginia, the Carolinas, Georgia and Mississippi. But this is the first one I've visited where the owner's daughter knew so much about the business of the plantation."

"Excuse me, Miss Cara."

Caramarena turned to see Ivy, the middle-aged woman who'd been their cook for many years, standing in the doorway of the warming room. "Yes, Ivy?"

"Is it time for me ta serve de coffee?" she asked in a high-pitched, timid voice as she ran her hands down the front of her clean apron.

"Heavens yes!" Caramarena exclaimed. "I forgot about coffee. But bring it into the drawing room. I think it will be cooler in there. And Ivy, go upstairs and ask Kissie to join us."

As hot as it was, Asher didn't want coffee. And this damn beard was itching and driving him crazy. It was only ten days old. He didn't know what he'd do in this heat when it grew fuller. He could hardly wait to get up to his room and splash cool water on his face and neck. And he was ready to get out of his shirt, cravat, waistcoat and jacket and lie naked on the cool sheets. How did one learn to tolerate this heat?

"If you don't mind, Miss Cantrell, I think I'll decline the coffee tonight and go up to my room."

"Oh, not at all, Mr. Millhouse," Caramarena said, hoping her voice didn't reveal her disappointment as she rose from her chair. "I should have realized you were tired from your journey."

"Please give my regards to your father. And thank you for a wonderful dinner."

Caramarena offered her hand and was taken aback when he paused before grasping her fingers and placing

16

a brief kiss on the back of her palm. "Good night, Miss Cantrell."

Feeling thoroughly rebuffed, Caramarena watched Asher Millhouse, with his strong legs, broad shoulders and dark brown hair that fell just below his collar in soft waves, disappear up the stairs. Most men would have jumped at the chance to spend a few minutes in her company without her father present. Well, it was clear she hadn't impressed Mr. Millhouse.

But he had impressed her.

"Miss Cara, Ivy says you needs me ta come right away," Kissie exclaimed as she hurried down the stairs, her long slender legs pumping in excitement.

Caramarena pursed her lips and folded her arms across her chest, drumming her fingers on her elbows. "Oh, never mind, Kissie. I was going to ask that you chaperone Mr. Millhouse and me while we had coffee, but he declined to join me."

Kissie hurrumphed as she stopped in front of Caramarena. "What kind a man will miss de chance ta have coffee wid you?"

Caramarena let her shoulders drop for a moment. "The kind that isn't interested in me." Suddenly she grabbed the slave's arm and pulled on it. "Come into the parlor with me, Kissie. I need some advice."

Caramarena led Kissie into her favorite room in the house. The walls were painted a golden color and the brocade drapes matched. The two Sheraton sofas and side chairs were covered in a gold-striped satin. A gilt-framed painting of the four Cantrell daughters hung over the fireplace. When the late afternoon sunlight poured into the room it would glow and remind Caramarena of the stories she'd heard about heaven, where the streets were paved with gold.

"Whats you got on yo' mind?" Kissie asked in a puzzled tone as she scratched behind her ear.

Caramarena plopped down on one of the sofas and drew her eyebrows together in a frown. "I've decided

17

that Mr. Millhouse would make a perfect husband for me."

Kissie rolled her dark, thickly fringed eyes heavenward, balled her hands into fists and stuck them on her slim hips. "God bless my soul and give me de patience wid dis chile. You done lost yo' mind, Miss Cara."

"Stop that nonsense talk and listen to me, Kissie!" Caramarena sat very straight with her hands folded demurely in her lap. "I need your help."

"No sir. No sir," she shook her head adamantly and pursed her full lips. "I ain't gonna help you plan ta marry dat stranger. No sir. Not me."

"Stop shaking your head and listen to me. Papa won't tell me what's wrong, but he's not getting any better. He grows weaker every day. I haven't had time to think out all the details, but I need a husband to give me an heir for Live Oak. Bunch will never be able to marry, and Catherine and Charlotte's sons will inherit their husband's land. If I don't marry and have an heir to take over Live Oak when Papa's gone, who will?"

"You gonna run dis place, Miss Cara," Kissie interjected fiercely, her fingers outlining her tapered waist.

"And to whom will I leave it? Think, Kissie. I need an heir — and a husband who will let me live at Live Oak and continue to manage it. I'm afraid Catherine and Charlotte will want to sell Live Oak if anything happens to Papa. I couldn't bear to lose this place." Caramarena rose from the sofa and rubbed her hands together. "I know I vowed never to marry when Philip left me." She took a deep breath, remembering the pain of being jilted when she was seventeen. It still hurt. "It appears the only acceptable way to have a child is first to have a husband, so I must forsake my vow. I've got to be in a position to keep Live Oak if the worst happens." She looked into Kissie's worried eyes and continued. "Mr. Millhouse is handsome, wealthy and he lives in England."

"How's dat make him purfeck. 'Pears ta me if he marries you he'll take you across de water with him." Her big rounded eyes held fast to Caramarena's.

"No, that's really what makes him perfect. He'll see that I need to stay here and take care of Papa, Bunch and Live Oak, and he can continue his travels, or go back to England to take care of his business." Caramarena glanced away from Kissie and added. "He can come back here every year or so and—leave me with child."

"You don't know what you saying, chile," Kissie said in a soft, husky voice.

Her sincerity touched Caramarena but she fought it with anger. "Yes, I do! And don't call me *child* anymore. I'm a grown woman of twenty. I should have been married years ago."

Caramarena was ashamed of her outburst the minute it was over. Kissie had been her nanny, her confidant, her companion and friend since her mother died fifteen years ago. Caramarena had no right to be sharp to her. She took a deep breath. "I'm sorry, Kissie, I didn't mean to yell at you, but I don't want to be talked out of this. I need a husband and I've decided Mr. Millhouse is the one I want. Will you help me?" she implored.

Kissie didn't appear the least bit perturbed by Caramarena's scolding. She cocked her head to one side and asked, "What you want me ta do?"

Caramarena smiled when she saw she was forgiven. "Unlike most men who visit Live Oak, Mr. Millhouse didn't seem to notice I'm a woman. I've got to do something to make him notice me, to want to marry me. I smiled at him, but he seldom returned it. My dress is lovely and Lacy did a beautiful job with my hair, yet he wouldn't agree to spend a few minutes alone with me."

"You sho' he ain't got a missus?"

"Well, he said he didn't. Oh, Kissie, I know he's just the kind of husband I need."

Kissie hurrumphed again. "What man's gonna want

19

a wife like you wanna be? He's gonna want you with him same as dat other man you planned ta marry. Ain't no man wirth his bread gonna let you lives here and hisself somewhere else."

"I've got to try," she said, suddenly feeling desperate. "I have to find a husband who will either live at Live Oak with me or allow me to live here and take care of Papa and Bunch. Mr. Millhouse admitted he travels most of the year. Besides, what would be better than a husband who would only come home once a year for a few weeks, leave me with child and be on his way again?"

Much to Caramarena's chagrin Kissie started laughing. At Caramarena's scowl Kissie picked up her clean apron and covered her mouth, but her shoulders kept shaking with laughter.

"Don't laugh at me," Caramarena said in an irritable tone, paused then asked, "What's so funny anyway?"

"God bless my soul, I can't tell ye. You gots ta find out fo' yo'self. Oh, chile, you ain't a woman yet. Not if'n you want a husband once a year."

Caramarena wasn't pleased that Kissie thought her plan was funny. She decided she wouldn't get any more out of her tonight, but she felt sure Kissie would help her when the time came.

"We'll talk about this later. I'm going up to say good night to Papa and tuck Bunch into bed. Give me a few minutes, then send Lacy up. And don't forget to tell Ivy to divide the leftover food with the others. Be sure every lamp and candle are out before you go home."

"Yes'm, Miss Cara. You knows you can count on me. I gone ta take care of everything same as always."

"I know." Caramarena rubbed her forehead. She hated being so irritable with Kissie, but now that she was devising a plan, she wanted it to work. She smiled and said, "Good night, Kissie. I'll see you in the morning."

Caramarena lifted her skirts and hurried up the

stairs. She felt a strange tremor when she walked past Asher Millhouse's door and knew it must be because she planned to manipulate his life to fit her own needs. It wasn't right, but Mr. Millhouse was just the man she needed. If she were married and living at Live Oak she felt sure Catherine and Charlotte wouldn't worry her to sell the plantation and move in with one of them.

Farther down the hall in her father's room she found him asleep on his pillows. Bunch was curled up on the foot of his bed, her stuffed lamb held tightly in her arms. Bunch had changed into a nightgown so Caramarena decided not to disturb her sleep. Before leaving the room she checked the windows, pulled a sheet over Bunch, gave both of them a kiss on the cheek and blew out the candles.

As she walked back to her room Caramarena pondered the plan that had entered her mind tonight and the possibility of simply asking Mr. Millhouse to marry her. Maybe he would accommodate her if she explained she needed a husband only to give her an heir for Live Oak, and he would be free to continue his travels. Would he be interested or would he be like every other man and want her to leave her father and Bunch and make a home with him?

She opened the doors to her balcony and walked out to stand by the rail. She often came out at night to cool off before going to bed. Tonight there was no breeze. Only humidity and the familiar sounds of night birds, crickets and frogs.

Caramarena sighed as she looked up into the starry night. Taking care of the plantation and Bunch was her responsibility now that her father was ill. She wouldn't let them down. She'd never met a man she'd give up her family for. She had to have a husband who would allow her to live at Live Oak. She had to.

Chapter Two

Asher hurried down the stairs the next morning, once again fully dressed with stiff collar and cravat, waistcoat and jacket. If he had to stay in this climate very long he'd wear collarless shirts and leave them unbuttoned. He stopped in the hall and looked around. At the end of the long foyer two gilt-capped Corinthian columns flanked the front door. The cornice was gilded as well.

For the first time Asher let himself wonder how much Cantrell had paid for Live Oak. Surely the six thousand pounds he stole would have only made a down payment on the house and land. He was probably still carrying a mortgage that had to be met each year. Losing an entire year's harvest was bound to put him in trouble if not ruin him completely.

As he stood and pondered how he could get Cantrell to sign with his ships, Caramarena entered his thoughts. She was beautiful, but that wasn't the only thing that attracted him. He knew dozens of beautiful women. She was actually intelligent. He'd wanted to stay and talk to her last night but knew the futility of encouraging the way she made him feel. He'd come to Live Oak to ruin John Cantrell, not his daughter.

Caramarena was sure to marry well. Considering her beauty and intelligence, he wondered why she wasn't already married. But it was easy to console himself with thoughts that Caramarena would soon marry and take her lovely sister Bunch along with her, leaving Cantrell to rot in hell.

Suddenly Asher was anxious to complete his business and get away from Live Oak and Cantrell's daughters. He had to put distance between himself and Caramarena and Bunch if he was going to destroy the plantation. He had to put aside the tender feelings that were developing for the two young ladies. If he stayed much longer he was afraid he'd start caring. That would never do. Once Cantrell signed the papers, he'd leave, and when Live Oak's harvest was completed his ships would take the cargo on board. He'd make sure it never reached its destination, so Cantrell couldn't be paid. If his plan worked, it would bankrupt Cantrell.

Some time during the night it had cooled off enough for him to fall asleep. And sometime during the night he'd stopped thinking about Caramarena, how her beautiful lips moved up and down and how small her waist was, how he wanted to see her hair flowing about her shoulders, how he wanted to touch her and kiss her and how he wanted to lie with her and make her his.

Hell, he had to get away fast. If he believed in magic spells he'd think Caramarena was working one on him. No woman should be on his mind as much as this one was.

The upstairs maid told him that breakfast was served on the verandah, so he opened the front door and stepped outside. He thanked God it wasn't hot yet. Cantrell was sitting at a round table reading a paper and looked up when Asher opened the door.

"Come join me, Mr. Millhouse." He put the paper aside and motioned with a frail hand for Asher to take a seat. "I like a man who's up early. Pour Mr. Millhouse coffee, Ivy, and give him some of your biscuits and a dish of those peaches you cooked in sugar."

Asher glanced at Ivy, the woman who'd served him last night. She was short and quite a bit heavier than the woman they called Kissie, and Ivy's glance had been a little more subtle than Kissie's had been. Kissie had openly stared at him when he first arrived.

Ivy was obviously in charge of the kitchen but he wasn't sure what Kissie's title was, or of the one they called Lacy. It appeared they were Caramarena and Bunch's personal maids because they were always near one or the other.

Kissie was a beautiful Negress with round expressive eyes and full lips. She had a straight back and proud shoulders. Her skin tone was more of a light chocolate rather than a dark coffee color, and her voice had a husky pitch.

As Asher sat down at the table he turned his attention to Cantrell. In the natural light of day Asher could see the planter wasn't a healthy man. He was thin and pale, and his cheeks and eyes were sunken inward as if he were near starvation. For a man who must be in his late fifties he still had a full head of brown hair with scant signs of gray. His cheeks were clean-shaven, but a neatly trimmed beard ran along his jawline and chin. Asher wondered how the frail man before him now could ever have been cold-blooded enough to steal six thousand pounds.

Asher mentally shook himself. The accident that Cantrell wasn't well was a matter of indifference to him. He couldn't let it cloud his judgment of the man.

He only hoped Cantrell lived long enough to know that George Worthy's sons had bankrupted him.

"I also like your plan to pay one-fourth more than our current shipper pays. Insurance gets more expensive each year," Cantrell was saying as Asher turned

24

his attention back to the older man.

He cleared his throat. "You'll not find a shipper these days who pays more than we do. And our sea-going vessels are some of the finest and fastest made. As Mr. Shock stated in his letter of introduction, we treat our customers fairly. That's why they stay with us and that's why we've done so well." Asher felt an unwelcome twinge of guilt. This was one client who wouldn't be satisfied when their business ended.

"How's you dis morning, Mr. Millhouse?" Ivy asked as she set a heavy-laden plate in front of him.

Asher was surprised that the slave greeted him. Usually they didn't speak unless they were spoken to. "Very well, thank you, Ivy. And you?"

"Jes fine," she answered. "Can I gets you anything mo'?"

Asher looked down at his plate and saw three large golden-topped biscuits, a thick slice of ham and a quartered orange. In a separate dish she'd added cooked peaches. He looked back at her and smiled. "No, thank you, this is more than enough."

The food looked delicious and the dark rich coffee was smooth and very hot, just the way he liked it. He cut into one of the biscuits and covered each half with butter before adding the peaches.

While he ate Asher was tempted to ask Cantrell about his life in London, but decided any mention of the city might put him on the alert, so he refrained from saying anything. He was too close to closing the deal and he didn't want anything to stop him now.

The door opened and Bunch walked out on the verandah. A smile immediately came to Asher's face as he rose from his chair. If he'd had a sister he would have wanted her to look just like Bunch. Her honey gold hair was pulled back from her face with a pink ribbon and fell in shining waves down her back. Her morning dress was pink with white bands of satin around the short puffy sleeves and waist. Her bright eyes glowed with innocence. She appeared the perfect picture of goodness and loveliness.

"Good morning, Papa." Bunch smiled at him, then bent and placed a kiss on his cheek.

Cantrell patted her arm affectionately. "Guess who I found at my feet when I woke up this morning?"

Bunch giggled. "Me!" she said enthusiastically and clasped her hands together under her chin.

Cantrell laughed too, then asked, "How's my beautiful daughter this morning?"

She looked down into his eyes. "Very well, Papa. Thank you," she curtsied, walked over to Asher and extended her hand to him. "Good morning, Mr. . . . Mr. . . ." Suddenly her eyes widened, and a look of fear clouded her expression. She snapped her head around to her father.

"Millhouse," he said patiently.

Bunch turned back to face Asher, the fear gone as quickly as it appeared. "Mr. Millhouse."

Asher kissed her hand tenderly and gave her a big smile. "Good morning, Bunch. How are you today?"

"Very well, thank you," she replied as if she'd rehearsed the phrase many times.

"Caramarena is not an early riser like the rest of us," Cantrell offered as Asher helped Bunch with her chair. "She'll stay up to all hours of the night going over ledgers, checking behind me and Mr. Wulpher. I may have done wrong in teaching her so much."

"One can never have too much knowledge, Mr. Cantrell," Asher said, feeling he should make a response.

Caramarena did know more about the plantation than a lot of planter's sons he'd met on his many trips to the southern East Coast of America. Suddenly a picture of Caramarena lying in bed, arms stretched toward him flashed through his mind. Damn, he thought, she had to be working some kind of spell on him. He couldn't remember a woman disturbing him the way Caramarena was.

Cantrell's cup clattered when it hit the saucer, causing Asher to glance up. He noticed the older man's frail hands were trembling. He'd also noticed his eyes looked dull and pierced with pain, but no other outward signs of weakness showed.

When Cantrell saw that Asher was watching he quickly dropped his hands into his lap and said, "I've decided Caramarena should be the one to show you around the plantation today and let you see how we operate here at Live Oak. She knows this place as well as I do. You might want to take a look at the turpentine you'll be shipping if I sign with your company."

It was on the tip of Asher's tongue to say that he didn't need to look around the damn plantation. He'd seen plenty of them in his lifetime and was more than vaguely familiar with the system and how it worked. The only thing he needed was Cantrell's signature on the shipping papers that were lying on his desk. Once Asher had that he would be on the next boat down the Apalachicola River. Then he could take his time and decide just what fate would befall Cantrell's cargo. He'd also spend a little time celebrating. Maybe he'd find a woman who looked like Caramarena and stay the whole damn night with her. He'd do some card playing, drink a little whiskey and then head for cooler climates.

Asher pushed his breakfast plate away. Dammit, he didn't want to spend the afternoon riding around the plantation in a buggy with Caramarena. She'd made it clear last night that she was interested in him and he was trying very hard not to show his interest in her. Every time he thought about her his manhood tightened and wanted to spring to life.

What he needed was exercise. On the long voyages, he always had someone he could fence or box with. He'd been idle for too many days and it was beginning to show. He needed something to test his strength. As soon as he was finished with Caramarena for the day he'd go for a long swim. He was sure he'd need it, just as he needed to leave this man.

"Mr. Cantrell, while I wait for your daughter do you mind if I walk the grounds?"

"Not at all, Mr. Millhouse. I should have suggested it. Why don't you go down to the stable and have Cypress saddle a horse and take a ride?"

Asher's thank you stuck in his throat as he excused himself from the table. His father had spent his younger years rebuilding his business, working day and night, neglecting his family. When George Worthy did come home he was so tired all he did was snap at his wife and beat his three sons because of the frustration John Cantrell had left with him. All the time his father suffered John Cantrell was happy on Live Oak with slaves to do everything for him, having the easy life because he'd stolen George Worthy's inheritance.

With each step Asher took away from the main house, with each crunch his boots made on the ground, his anger grew. His father had been a tortured man who had vented his anger on his wife and children. Now Asher intended to go to any lengths to see that John Cantrell was tormented in his last years.

A few minutes later Asher rode out of the barn at a trot. As soon as the house was out of sight he dug his heels into the flanks of the horse and let him run. He wouldn't rest until Live Oak was destroyed.

By early afternoon Asher Millhouse Worthy was

ruing the day he laid eyes on Miss Caramarena Cantrell. True to her father's word she was extremely knowledgeable about the plantation, but what had his insides in knots was simply her presence. It didn't matter that their shoulders rubbed together in the confines of the small carriage, or that her soft skirts brushed his legs with every movement, or that her lips were sometimes so close to his he felt her breath. It didn't matter that he had trouble taking his eyes off her face, or that she smelled as sweet as a rose, or that her voice was soft and her laughter lilting. It didn't matter that every time the carriage stopped he grasped her small waist and helped her to the ground, or that every time he took her warm fingers in his and helped her into the carriage. If none of those things had happened he still would have wanted her. A gnawing emptiness was growing inside him. Caramarena was bright and alluring and he wished like hell he'd spent a week with the whore in Apalachicola. But would it have done any good? No. He'd still want Caramarena.

After visiting the slave quarters, which were better than most of the ones he'd seen in the South; the fields, which were in full season for late August; and the turpentine and sawmills that Cantrell had added five years ago; Cypress stopped the carriage under a large live oak tree whose branches, heavy with Spanish moss, formed a green canopy. Once again Asher slid his fingers around Caramarena's waist and helped her down.

"You run along and have your meal, Cypress," Caramarena said. "But be back in an hour."

"You's shore you wants ta leave you here with him?" Cypress nodded in Asher's direction, seeming not to care that Asher heard every word he said.

Cypress wore a battered gray hat and his clothes hung loosely on his slim frame. But even though the man was thin, Asher could see strength in the slave's arms and hands, and he saw hesitation in his eyes.

Caramarena looked at Asher and gave him a knowing smile before turning back to their driver. "Cypress, I couldn't be in safer hands if I were here with Papa."

He glanced around as if looking for someone to agree with him. "I don't know. I don't think Mr. John's gone like dis. He 'spects me ta takes care of ye."

"Cypress, I don't want to hear another word from you. Now go before I change my mind and have you stay and miss your meal."

The tall, lanky man handed a picnic basket to Asher, but was still reluctant to leave. His gaze locked with Asher's.

Caramarena reached back into the carriage for a quilt and walked further under the shady canopy of the oak's heavy branches. She turned back to Cypress. "You can leave now."

After a final pleading look to Caramarena he relented and said, "Yes, Miss Cara."

The view was lovely, Asher had to admit. The trees separated just enough to show the rushing waters below. Along the Apalachicola River was an excellent place to set up a plantation, as many planters had. Most of them resembled Live Oak, built with the front of the house facing the river so that anyone on the passing boats could view the magnificent homes with their tall windows and grand columns. Because the houses were so close to the river they were elevated five feet on stone pillars; when the river flooded the houses were spared. Each house had its own landing and docks, and boats would pull up and receive passengers or cargo and then take them down river to the towns of Apalachicola and St. Josephs.

Asher set the basket down and helped Caramarena

spread the quilt. The last thing he needed right now was this private little picnic. His desire for this woman was already running high. He had a feeling he was going to be hurting before this little tête-à-tête was over.

Caramarena lowered herself to her knees, then curled her legs underneath her and straightened her ivory-colored skirts before opening the basket. Asher had no choice but to join her.

Unlike Bunch's hair this morning, all of Caramarena's hair was neatly arranged on top of her head and Asher felt as if he'd been cheated out of something that should have been his. Caramarena was pulling food out of the basket, and he wanted to pull the pins from her hair and let it fall.

"Please feel free to untie your cravat, Mr. Millhouse, and unbutton some of those buttons. It makes me hot just to look at you stuffed so tightly in that shirt."

She didn't look at him as she made this astonishing statement. There was nothing Asher would have liked better, but he'd die of a heat stroke first. Maybe she wanted someone to show up and find him half-dressed. That surely wouldn't make her father happy and could very well ruin his business with the man. No, as much as he'd love to untie his cravat and unbutton his shirt and as much as he'd like to pull the young woman into his arms and kiss her, he couldn't. He was too close to trapping Cantrell.

Under the shade of the tree the heat wasn't unbearable, so he politely declined by saying, "I'm fine, Miss Cantrell, but thank you for thinking of my well-being."

She looked up at him and smiled pleasantly. "Please yourself, Mr. Millhouse."

Asher returned her smile. If only he could. Asher wondered if her father was deliberately throwing

31

them together or was it just that Caramarena was that innocent and naive? It puzzled him. All he knew for sure was that he wished Caramarena had been anyone else's daughter.

On one of the plates Caramarena laid sliced bread, a piece of cold chicken, cheese and several smoked oysters and handed it to him. She laid two oranges and a flask of wine on the blanket between them.

"Do you like your home in England, Mr. Millhouse?" Caramarena asked, then popped a small oyster into her mouth.

"What an odd thing to ask," he answered. "It's like my asking you if you like Live Oak."

"Not really. You did indicate you prefer traveling to staying at your office in London."

"But it doesn't mean I don't like my home." He tilted his head and looked into her eyes. "Why do you ask?"

"I was just thinking that a man is seldom asked to leave his home."

"I don't know what you're referring to," he said and took a bite out of the cold chicken.

"Well, when a woman marries she is supposed to leave her father's home and go to her husband's house. Men seldom, if ever, marry and move into their wives' homes. Isn't that correct?"

Asher laughed lightly. "Yes. I think it started with the beginning of time. Somewhere in the Bible it says something about a woman forsaking her father and cleaving to her husband."

Caramarena looked beyond the tree-lined bank to the water for a few moments, then asked, "If you married a woman who had a beautiful home with many acres of land, would you live with her there if she wanted you to?"

Asher's chicken went down hard. He wanted to put a stop to this conversation immediately. He was flattered that she was interested in him and possibly wanted to marry him, but she was Cantrell's daughter and he couldn't let this conversation go any farther. He picked up the flask and took a long drink. The wine was smooth, good. He stuffed the cork back in the leather pouch and looked at Caramarena.

"You're not being very subtle, Miss Cantrell."

Caramarena lowered her eyes, wishing she knew more about how to deal with difficult men. "Whatever do you mean, Mr. Millhouse?" She shored up her courage and looked him in the eyes. "Surely you don't mind if I ask simple questions? It's natural curiosity. It wasn't my intention to make you uncomfortable."

Asher gave her a point in this little game they were playing. She'd easily turned the tables on him. "No, not uncomfortable. Just surprised that you speak your mind so easily."

"Good," she said with a bright smile. "Then you won't mind answering my question."

"Yes, I do mind." He laughed when he saw that surprised her. "But since you are so willing to ask questions maybe you like to answer them as well. Why aren't you married, Miss Cantrell?"

Caramarena watched Asher take another bite of chicken. He was definitely a difficult man, but she found she liked the challenge he presented. She really didn't want to tell him why she, too, wasn't married. But as they ate and she continued to watch him, she thought that maybe she did want to talk about it.

Caramarena's smile faded and all the hurt and bitterness of rejection filled her as if it had been only yesterday that Philip had sent her that damning letter, cancelling their wedding.

"Why the long face, Miss Cantrell? I hope my question didn't make you uncomfortable. That wasn't my intention." he said, echoing her words, before biting into the soft bread.

Caramarena picked up one of the oranges and sank her thumbnail into the soft flesh of the peel. Yes, she did want to talk about it. It was time to release the bitterness and forget the past.

"I was betrothed once. Three years ago, to be exact."

Asher took another drink, then wiped his mouth with the back of his hand. He wouldn't have been so crass had he known she'd been engaged.

"What happened?" he asked, keeping his voice low.

She didn't look at him but kept her gaze on the river as her fingers worked the orange. The strong scent of the orange reached him. It was potent, heady. He watched Caramarena pull the skin away from the fruit, leaving a thin white sheet of flesh covering the juicy meat inside. He liked the way the orange fit into her hand, the way her fingers closed around it, and he found himself reaching over and picking up the other one and palming it, feeling its weight, feeling its texture, while watching Caramarena.

"I was prepared to leave Papa and Live Oak and go with him to his home in Tallahassee, but I couldn't bear the thought of leaving Bunch. At first Philip agreed she could come live with us, but later went back on his word."

Her thumbnail went deep and penetrated the tender outer skin of the orange. Juice spurted from the center and coated her thumb and forefinger with its nectar. Asher wanted to lift her hand to his lips and suck her thumb into his mouth. He wet his lips. The scent was so piercing, he almost had the taste on his tongue.

"What happened then?" he asked and realized his voice wasn't natural; it was throaty, husky.

"A week before the wedding, I told Philip I wouldn't marry him if I couldn't take Bunch to live with me. Papa tried to talk me out of it, saying that he and Kissie could take care of her, but I think he knew I couldn't leave her."

At last all of the outer skin was gone and she broke open the ball, making two halves. Again juice spurted out, and Asher's stomach muscles contracted. He watched as she tore off a section and carried it to her lips and bit into it. The golden juice ran down her fingers but she didn't seem to notice. Asher's manhood was in a hard cramp. God, she was killing him. He'd never watched a woman eat an orange before, and he had had no idea it could be erotic, so damn sensual. He wanted to reach over, grab her and lick every trace of orange juice off her.

"So you called off the wedding?" he asked, his voice still husky.

"No, I wasn't that lucky," she broke off another wedge and bit into it.

Oh God, how much more could he take? He was aching to kiss her, to taste that tangy sweet flavor on those lips, to thrust his tongue into the warm recesses of her mouth and enjoy the pleasure he would find there.

"I believed he'd give in to my wishes. The day of the wedding I received a letter telling me he released me from our betrothal. It wouldn't have been so bad had not the guests already started to arrive."

"I'm sorry," he offered, but knew it wouldn't help. Damn, what kind of man would give up Caramarena and Bunch? He'd gladly take Bunch for a sister if it meant having a wife like Cara. . . . What the hell was he thinking?

"So was I — for a time. Now I know it was for the best. I would have never been happy with Philip."

Caramarena put the rest of the orange aside, picked up a napkin and started wiping the juice off her hands. What a waste, he thought. He wanted to pull each finger into his mouth and suck the nectar from each one, he wanted to run his tongue over her lips and into her mouth until all taste of the orange was gone and he was left tasting her alone.

Asher couldn't move. If he did he would reveal his swollen manhood. He had to get away from this woman, away from Live Oak before he went crazy and did something stupid—like kiss her.

Caramarena came out of the trance she'd been in while she spoke of the past. She didn't usually talk about that incident in her life and didn't know exactly why she'd confided in Asher, except that the time seemed to be right.

"Well, enough about my life." She brightened, thankful that Asher had let her talk without passing judgment. "Now I've answered your question. Answer mine."

He brushed his hair back, then ran a finger down the tight collar of his shirt. "I've forgotten what you asked."

She knew that wasn't true but decided not to take him to task. Smiling indulgently she asked, "Under certain circumstances would you move into your wife's home?" She rephrased it a little this time.

Much to his surprise Asher answered truthfully. "I wouldn't be against considering the possibility."

His answer satisfied her. She smiled. "Tell me, what questions do you have about the plantation?"

None, he wasn't trying to buy it; he only wanted the rights to ship its harvest. "I believe you took care of everything this morning."

"Did I mention that because we have so much arable land one slave is required for every twenty acres? We have very little in woodland, wetlands or gardens."

He laughed and shook his head. "You really love this place, don't you."

"Yes," she said, pride showing in her eyes. "I can't

imagine ever leaving it. Even though our summers are very hot, our winters are mild so it evens out and makes for a wonderful place to live."

Asher's chest tightened and he looked away. Guilt ate at him. His plan was going to deprive her of her home. In the distance Asher saw Cypress coming and breathed a sigh of relief.

"Tell me," he said, changing the subject. "Is Bunch a pet name?"

She smiled warmly. "Yes. I forget how it must sound to outsiders. Her name is Carolina. I was four when she was born and still couldn't talk very well. All I could see when she was born was a little pink face peeking out of a bunch of blankets. So I would always ask to see 'bunch.' My two older sisters also started calling the little bundle of blankets and baby Bunch and before long Carolina was forgotten. I'm sure she wouldn't answer if you called her Carolina."

"The name Bunch suits her. She's very lovely."

"You like her?" she asked, her heart warming at his nice words about her sister. This was another reason he would make a perfect husband.

Feeling more at ease with Cypress on his way, Asher decided to tease Caramarena and lighten the tension. "Oh yes, very much. She doesn't talk as much as someone else I know, which makes her very pleasant to be around."

Hurt registered in Caramarena's eyes before she quickly looked away and started putting the leftover food back in the basket. This surprised Asher. His teasing had hurt her feelings. That wasn't what he'd intended. He didn't want to hurt Caramarena.

"I'm sorry Cara, I shouldn't have said that."

She looked up at him, her eyes bright with anger. "Please, don't call me Cara, Mr. Millhouse." She took a deep breath, picked up the orange peels and threw them in with the food. "And as for what you said—

there is never anything wrong with speaking your mind."

"Will you stop putting the food away and listen to me? Look at me." When she didn't he grabbed her wrist and her gaze flew to his face.

"Bunch is a lovely young lady, but I could never be interested in her—as a woman. I admit I'm interested in you. Right now there's nothing I want more than to kiss you, but I'm not going to." Asher glanced away. He shouldn't have admitted that. But now that he had he needed to explain. "It's not only that big buck over there giving me the evil eye for holding your wrist; I don't want to botch this deal with your father. Kissing you could do that. Caramarena, if Cypress was the only thing standing between me and you, I'd take him on. I want your father's business."

Her tongue came out and wet her lips and Asher felt his groin tighten again. Her lips were so damn tempting. He let her go and sat back on his heels.

Caramarena softened. So he did want to kiss her. Relief washed over her and made her feel better. He wasn't indifferent to her. Her heartbeat quickened. He wanted to kiss her, and that was a start. He was simply afraid of spoiling his business with her father. She could understand that. After all that was the reason he came to Live Oak in the first place. But it wouldn't get her what she wanted. She'd have to find a way to make him change his mind about her.

She looked into his eyes. "You want the business with my father more than you want to kiss me?" she asked.

It was difficult to admit and right now, feeling the way he did, he wasn't sure that it was true, but he nodded confirmation anyway.

"Thank you for being honest, Mr. Millhouse."

Caramarena stood up and called for Cypress to come and get the basket.

Later that afternoon Caramarena walked out to the cookhouse, where Kissie was helping Ivy cut up a chicken. Even though the cookhouse had six windows the room was unbearably hot when Ivy was preparing dinner.

"Kissie, I'd like to talk with you outside, please."

"You sound worried," Kissie exclaimed, wiping her hands on her soiled apron as she followed Caramarena. "Is it Mr. John?"

"No, no, nothing like that," she answered as they stepped outside. It was near sundown. Dusk was settling over the sky, and the worst of the heat was fading with the light. "As far as I know, Papa will be joining us for dinner. Let's take a walk."

"It dat Mr. Millhouse, ain't it?" Kissie complained as she tightened the black kerchief she wore on her head.

"Yes. Oh, Kissie, I'm more sure than ever that he is the man I should marry. He told me he likes Bunch and today he even admitted that he would like to kiss me but he won't because he's afraid Papa will find out and then not give him Live Oak's business."

"I knows he be a fool if'n he don't wanna kiss yo' purty lips, Miss Cara."

Caramarena laughed lightly. "You're so sweet." She sighed wistfully and turned somber eyes upon the older woman. "Kissie, you've been married twice."

"Yes'm, I has," she admitted as they walked past one of the rose gardens

"Did you love them? Your husbands?"

"I sho' did," she answered firmly. "And dat de only reason ta tie yo'self to a man. Fo' love."

Caramarena stopped, bent down and smelled the sweet scent of a dark red rose. She inhaled deeply before they continued walking. "I tried love. It didn't

39

work. Now all I need is a man who will give me a son." She folded her arms across her chest. Her long skirts swooshed against her legs as darkness inched a little closer. "Papa and Mr. Millhouse are in the office now finishing the paperwork. Tomorrow Mr. Millhouse will leave on the first boat that passes and with him will go my chance for the kind of husband I need."

"You didn't love that man you planned ta marry. He weren't strong enough fo' you." Kissie shook her dark brown finger at Caramarena. "And I's tellin' you another thing. Dat mans with yo' pa ain't wirth his bread if'n he'd rather have yo' pa's business than a kiss from you."

Caramarena stopped and pondered what Kissie said. Now that she'd decided she must marry, she would have liked it to be for love. But with her father's failing health, she couldn't wait forever. And if she were truthful with herself she had to admit that she did find Mr. Millhouse appealing. She had wanted him to kiss her today. Surely if they were to marry it wouldn't be so bad.

"You may be right, Kissie, but whatever the case, I've decided Mr. Millhouse is the man I want to marry, and I need your help to make it happen."

"No sir." Kissie shook her head and stuck her hands on her hips. "No sir. I done tole you I ain't gonna help you ta marry no stranger."

"You've got to. I've been thinking. I remember when Martha Blankenship was caught on the sofa with William Davenport and her papa forced William to marry her. I want you to help me get Mr. Millhouse on the sofa."

Kissie's eyes rounded and her mouth fell open. "You wants me ta hold him fo' you whiles you jump on top of him?"

Caramarena laughed. "Oh, Kissie, of course not.

40

You've had two husbands—tell me what to do so that Mr. Millhouse will break down and kiss me long enough for Papa to catch us."

"Dat all?" Kissie wiped her forehead with the back of her hand and whistled huskily.

"Well, I guess. I don't know how to go about this, Kissie. Just tell me what to do," Caramarena urged her.

"Well, if'n it was me and I wanned to kiss a man I's just reach up and do it."

"I can't do that."

"Den why ask me what ta do?" Kissie threw up her hand in disgust and started to walk off.

"All right," Caramarena cajoled and Kissie stopped. "This is what we'll do. After dinner tonight we'll serve coffee in the gold room. Papa will go to his office for his pipe. While he's gone you stand in the doorway and when you see Papa coming wave to me and I'll reach up and kiss Mr. Millhouse. Then Papa will insist we get married."

Caramarena could see Kissie thought the plan wouldn't work. "What's wrong with it?" she asked.

Kissie slowly scratched behind her ear. "I think dat Blankenship girl was doing more'n kissing."

Caramarena was afraid to ask for details. "Stop blubbering on about Martha and tell me if you think it will work." Caramarena heard the desperate plea in her own voice.

"Dat depenz on how yo' papa feels bout dat stranger kissing you."

Caramarena sank her teeth into her bottom lip. "I guess you're right. But for now it's the only chance I have." She turned around and headed back for the house. There was no time left to woo the handsome man or to think of a better plan. This one had to work. It just had to.

Kissie ambled back toward the cookhouse, deep in

thought about Miss Cara. She didn't want to see her marry a man who didn't love her. Kissie wanted her to find a man who would put sparkles in her eyes and roses in her cheeks, a man who was strong and would take good care of her and Live Oak. Kissie wasn't so sure Mr. Millhouse would ever do that. She had a feeling he was hiding something. But what?

As Kissie rounded the corner of the building, arms slid around her waist and cupped her breasts, startling her for a moment. "Lands a mercy! Cypress, I ought ta hit you wid a board. Scaring me like dat." There was no anger in her voice as she turned into his arms, a big smile on her face.

Cypress kissed her briefly, then pushed her up against the wall and pressed his body close to her. "Who else gonna cuddle you like dis?" he asked.

A smile broke on Kissie's face. "You better let me go befo' somebody see us."

"I don't care ifs they do. I couldn't wait till night ta touch ya." His hand left her waist and slid up her full breast and cupped it, squeezing ever so gently.

Kissie smiled, enjoying his touch, his caring, his wanting her. "You'd mind if'n Mr. Wulpher strapped you to a tree."

Cypress pressed her harder. "You wirth it, Kissie. You de softest woman I ever touched."

Kissie felt warm all over. If only her sweet Cara could find a man who would say such things to her, make her feel this wanted, this loved.

"You a fine woman, Kissie. When is you gone marry me?" he asked in a raspy voice.

Kissie touched his cheek affectionately. "I told you I done had two husbands and I don't want no mo'." But she let her hand slip down his pants and ran her palm over his hardened member, making him moan softly.

Cypress chuckled lightly. "Jest give me time. I gonna change yo' mind." He bent his head and kissed her lightly, then pulled away from her. "I gots to get away from you. I be waitin' fo' ye tanight afta you finish at de big house."

He winked at her, then turned away, his long stride quickly putting him out of sight.

Kissie stayed by the cookhouse for a few moments, and remembered the first time she married when she was thirteen. Oh, how she loved that man. But the old master sold him a few months later and the new master didn't want to buy his young wife. Her second husband was a good man but she never loved him like the first. Although she cried when the fever took him a few years ago.

Now Cypress wanted to marry her. Was she too old? She had passed forty several years ago. A smile swept across her face. No, she wasn't too old; she was just having too much fun letting Cypress pursue her. She'd give in when she was ready.

Chapter Three

Caramarena was quiet all through dinner. After concluding the paperwork with Mr. Millhouse, her father had decided to have his dinner in his room, something he'd been doing a lot lately. All of her nervousness and shoring up her courage to throw her arms around Mr. Millhouse and kiss him had been for nothing. Her father would not be around to catch them in the act. And tomorrow Mr. Millhouse would leave. She wouldn't get the kiss she wanted or the husband she needed.

Mr. Millhouse made several attempts at conversation while they ate, but her short answers left little doubt that she didn't want to talk. Not only had she been looking forward to the security of marrying Mr. Millhouse, she'd wanted him to kiss her. She didn't know why exactly. Philip had kissed her and she didn't remember it as being anything special. But she felt different when Asher Millhouse looked at her and touched her. When he'd lifted her down from the carriage today, his hands had been warm, strong and strangely comforting. He didn't smile often, but when he did it sent her heart fluttering. She would be sorry to see him go.

Asher felt like the cad and deceiver he was. The papers he wanted so desperately were signed and tucked safely away in his coat pocket. He was so protective of them he wouldn't leave them in his room for fear something would happen. Dammit! He hated like hell what he would be forced to do to Caramarena and Bunch. His grudge against their father had nothing to do with them, yet they would suffer for it.

He watched Caramarena. She was too quiet tonight, he thought. He must have really hurt her this afternoon when he indicated he liked being with Bunch more than with her because Bunch didn't talk as much. If only she knew what she'd been doing to him just minutes before that. He'd never look at an orange again without thinking of Caramarena. And as he remembered how much he wanted to kiss her when she was eating that orange, another thought crossed his mind. The papers were signed. He had rights to ship John Cantrell's harvest and his turpentine. Cantrell was in his room because he wasn't feeling well. Why not have coffee in the drawing room with Caramarena tonight and end the evening with that kiss he'd wanted so badly? Yes, dammit, he'd do it. He'd taste the passion he sensed deep within her.

A few minutes later Caramarena asked Ivy to bring in coffee, but she didn't suggest the drawing room, so Asher spoke up. "I was hoping we'd have coffee in the drawing room since I missed the opportunity last night," he said in a low voice, meant to entice her to agree.

Caramarena eyed him warily before giving in. "Of course, if you'd like." She turned to Bunch, who was finishing a tart. "You'll join us, won't you, Bunch?"

Bunch shook her head, and her honey gold curls danced on her back. She made an ugly face. "I don't like coffee."

Caramarena smiled at her. "You don't have to drink coffee. Just stay and talk to us."

45

"He wants to talk?" She pointed to Asher.

"Yes, he'd like to talk to you. Isn't that right, Mr. Millhouse?" Caramarena turned to Asher and gave him a questioning look.

"I'd be very pleased if you'd join us, Bunch. Your father told me today that you have a rabbit. Maybe you'd show him to me before I leave tomorrow." Asher spoke in soft tones, but he really didn't want Bunch tagging along—not this time.

Bunch drew her brows together, her dark green eyes sparkled. She shook her head furiously. "Bunny's mine. You can't have him. He's mine!" she screamed.

Startled, Asher started to speak but Caramarena spoke first, laying a gentle hand on Bunch's shoulder. "Calm down, Bunch. Mr. Millhouse doesn't want to take Bunny with him. He only wants to see him."

Bunch pushed her chair back, knocking over her water glass as she scrambled to get out of the chair. "I want to see Papa," she demanded, lifting her chin defiantly.

Caramarena and Asher rose also. "All right, I'll take you to Papa," Caramarena said in a soothing tone. "Say good night to Mr. Millhouse."

Suddenly Bunch threw her arms around Caramarena, burying her face in her sister's shoulder. "No, he wants to take Bunny," she mumbled. "I don't like him. Make him go away, Cara."

"Bunch, raise your head."

Caramarena spoke in a sharp tone which surprised Asher. He wanted to tell Caramarena not to be so harsh with Bunch when she was upset but Bunch's head popped up. Not a single tear shone in her eyes.

"Mr. Millhouse does not want Bunny." Caramarena's voice was firm. She held Bunch's arms tightly. "Now turn around and say good night to him."

Bunch looked at her sister for a moment longer, then turned and smiled at Asher, politely holding her hand out to him. "Good night, Mr. . . . Mr. Mill-house."

Asher took her fingers and kissed her hand affectionately. If he hadn't seen and heard her display of temper, Asher would have never believed it. He started to reassure her he didn't want her rabbit but decided it was best not to mention Bunny's name again. "Good night, Bunch."

She turned her clear, innocent eyes on her sister. "Papa's not feeling well."

"I know." Caramarena's voice was soft once again. "I'll take you up to Papa." She looked at Asher. "Mr. Millhouse, will you excuse me while I take Bunch upstairs? I'll join you in the gold room in a few minutes."

"Of course," he said and stepped aside to let the two sisters pass. He watched as they walked away, Caramarena holding her sister's hand. Both were lovely but so different.

The skill and love with which Caramarena handled Bunch impressed him. His chest tightened. No, he wouldn't think about what would happen to them when Live Oak fell. He was sure Caramarena would marry and take Bunch with her. Caramarena was beautiful, intelligent, and softhearted, and if he were any judge of women she'd be passionate as well. Any man would be fortunate to have her for a wife. If need be, when the time came, he'd see that Caramarena made a good marriage.

A few minutes later Caramarena rubbed her forehead as she walked down the stairs. Bunch didn't get upset as often as she used to but Caramarena still never knew what might set her off. If Mr. Millhouse had asked about her rabbit at another time Bunch would probably have wanted to take him to see it immediately and insist he hold and cuddle it. She took a deep breath as she reached the bottom of the stairs.

The only thing she could do was apologize for Bunch's behavior, just as she always did and hope that Mr. Millhouse wouldn't think badly of her sister. Caramarena lifted her dark green skirts and headed for the gold room.

"Mr. Millhouse, I do apologize for Bunch's little display of temper and for leaving you alone for so long." Asher was standing by the open window, so she walked over and joined him.

He looked down into her eyes and smiled. "No apology is necessary."

Caramarena smiled back at him, grateful that he understood. "Thank you."

"Here's de coffee, Miss Cara. I told Ivy I's gone bring it to you. You needs me to chaperones anyways."

"Thank you, Kissie. Let's sit here by the window, Mr. Millhouse. The chairs aren't as comfortable as the sofa, but it's cooler."

Separate chairs weren't exactly what Asher had in mind. He also wasn't happy to see Kissie plop down on the small settee and glue her dark eyes on them. He ran a finger down his shirt collar, trying to stretch it. The only advantage to sitting in the chairs was the one Caramarena mentioned, a welcome relief from the heat.

"Go ahead and be seated, Mr. Millhouse, while I pour coffee."

Asher placed a hand on her arm and her gaze flew to his face. "Why don't we wait a few minutes on the coffee."

"All right." Caramarena felt breathless. He wanted to spend some time with her. But why now? Why now when he would be gone on the first boat that passed in the morning? Caramarena took a seat in the lyre-back side chair.

"I suppose you still plan to leave tomorrow,"

she said, keeping her eyes on his face as he settled into the chair beside her.

"Yes. My captain is probably wondering what happened to me. I hadn't expected to be gone this long. And I'll need to prepare for the load of turpentine we'll be taking on board."

"Will you be sailing directly back to England?" she asked.

He nodded. "I've already made stops along the Eastern Coast and decided not to sail on to New Orleans this late in the season."

"I see," she said, knowing that she was going to miss him, but not understanding why. She shouldn't be disappointed. It hadn't been right for her to want to trap Mr. Millhouse in the first place. She should be ashamed of herself for planning to deceive him.

Asher had the feeling that Caramarena still hadn't forgiven him for his blunder earlier in the afternoon. Surely that was the reason she was so quiet, so somber. Before he left, he wanted this woman to know just how much he'd wanted to kiss her and just how long he was going to think about her after he was gone. First, he had to think of something to get Kissie out of the room so he could apologize again and smooth things over with her.

"Do you think Kissie would mind getting me a glass of water?" he asked. Pulling on his collar had become a habit. "I'm still not used to the heat."

"Oh, certainly." She turned around. "Kissie, Mr. Millhouse would like a glass of water. Have some fresh water drawn from the well so it will be cool. You should also go up and check on Bunch and make sure she has on her nightclothes and is in her own bed. Last night she fell asleep on Papa's."

"Yes, Miss Cara," Kissie said and ambled from the room.

Caramarena realized how easy it would have been

to trap Mr. Millhouse into marriage tonight if her father had been well enough to join them for dinner.

When Kissie was out of sight Asher said, "I want to apologize again for what I said this afternoon. You don't talk too much. In fact I'd rather have you talking than being as quiet as you have been tonight."

Caramarena smiled, touched that he was so concerned about hurting her feelings. The truth was he had, but she'd gotten over it quickly. He had no way of knowing that statement had nothing to do with why she was so quiet. He had no way of knowing that if her father didn't get any better and she was left without a husband or a child her sisters could force her to sell Live Oak.

"I told you I don't mind your speaking your mind to me, Mr. Millhouse. We're not as formal here as in some other homes. We make allowances for various things. For instance, you need not wear your cravat when it's hot enough to make you faint."

Asher chuckled lightly. "Were you disappointed I didn't loosen this today?" Asher reached up and untied his cravat.

"Certainly not," she insisted. "I was only concerned for your comfort."

"In that case, since it's so hot tonight you won't mind if I take this off." He laid the brown silk cravat on the arm of the chair, then unbuttoned three buttons on his shirt.

"No, of course I don't mind," she answered, a catch in her breath. Caramarena was mesmerized by Asher's movements. She knew she should have looked away when he unbuttoned his shirt, but she couldn't. She wanted to watch him. The intimate act made her stomach flutter and her heartbeat increase.

Asher knew he didn't have much time before Kissie came back, and he desperately wanted to kiss Caramarena just once. She was different from any woman

50

he'd ever known. His need to touch her was far more powerful than he had expected. Damn, he couldn't go back to England without one kiss. Asher reached over and caressed her cheek. God, it was so soft. She didn't flinch. He liked that.

"Caramarena," he said in a strained voice. "I can't leave without kissing you." He rose from the chair and took her hands, pulling her up with him.

"Do you mind if I kiss you?" he asked.

No, she wanted him to kiss her, even though she knew nothing would come of it now. Her plan couldn't work with her father upstairs. Trembling inside, she lightly shook her head and watched as Asher's face came closer and closer until their lips met. His lips were warm, soft, pleasant.

Asher raised his head and looked into her eyes. She didn't know how to kiss. Oh God, she was such an innocent. He should back away right now and leave her, let someone else teach her how to open her lips and enjoy a man's kisses and touch, but the challenge was so exhilarating, so stimulating, that he couldn't give up the chance. He wanted to be her teacher.

He slid his arms around her waist and pulled her close to his chest. Through her clothing he could feel her trembling. "Do I frighten you?" he asked.

She swallowed hard. "No," she answered. She liked the way he held her, the feel of his arms around her. She liked this new feeling he was creating inside her.

Slowly, Asher bent his head again and placed his lips on hers. "Close your eyes and open your mouth, Cara," he whispered against her lips. "Not that much. Yes, that's better. Now press your lips to mine. Oh God yes, that way."

Asher slipped his tongue into her mouth. She tasted of oranges. Heat swept through Asher's body and his manhood shot to life. He couldn't remember the last time he'd been aroused so quickly. He wanted to fill her mouth with his tongue, fill her body with his, but knew he had to be gentle. She was no seasoned whore. God, she was beautiful. Wonderful. Her innocence and vulnerability heightened his desire, making her overwhelmingly exciting. What he felt was so intense, he was afraid of frightening her and making her pull away from him. He didn't want her to go. Not yet.

He lifted his head and whispered. "I know this sounds absurd but you taste of orange."

She looked up at him, her light green eyes searching his face. "Is that bad? I had a slice of Papa's when I took Bunch upstairs."

Asher pulled her closer still, wanting to feel her soft breasts against his chest. He smiled. "It's very good. You don't know how badly I wanted to kiss you today while you were eating that orange, how I wanted to lick every trace of the fruit from your lips and fingers."

Caramarena didn't blush easily but his words sent flaming color to her cheeks. She cleared her throat and said, "Thank you for teaching me how to kiss," she said softly.

"Didn't your fiancé ever kiss you?" Asher asked as he rubbed his hands up and down her back, loving the feel of her.

"Not the way you do. I like the way you kiss," she whispered, hoping he would kiss her one more time before he let her go, before he walked out of her life forever.

How could such an innocent say the very thing needed to set him on fire again. Asher groaned and pressed his lips to hers. She responded quickly this time, returning the kiss.

His lips left hers and traveled over her cheeks and down the soft column of her throat. She was so sweet-smelling. She felt so damn good in his arms. The soft moans of surprise she made excited him even more. Oh damn, she didn't know what she was doing to him. The heat of the night was nothing compared to the heat in his body. He should turn her loose, but instead his lips slipped further down to the base of her throat. He hooked his fingers under the edge of her dress and slid it off her shoulder as his lips and tongue explored the newly exposed skin.

He should stop, he thought, somewhere at the back of his mind. This wasn't part of his plan. He should look at her as the enemy and have nothing to do with her. Her fingers lightly played through his hair and he knew he didn't want to stop the desire that was building inside him. At this moment, he wanted everything she had to give. His lips found the swell of her breast and Asher thought he was going to explode.

"Oh, Cara—Caramarena, you're driving me crazy," he said as his lips traced a pattern across her heated skin.

A murmur of protest rose in her throat but it was a soft sigh that left her lips. Asher was taking her breath away. Surely she was going to faint from the sheer pleasure of his touch and kisses. Philip had never kissed her like this, had never touched her like this, had never made her feel this way. Her head fell back, giving him further access to her neck and shoulders. She knew what she was letting him do wasn't right, but she didn't want him to stop. It felt too good.

"I can't breathe," she managed to whisper.

"Me either," he answered huskily and slipped the sleeve of her dress off her other shoulder, letting his gaze wander over the crest of her heaving breasts. None of the many experienced women he'd been with had ever made him feel this exalted. He bent his head and let his tongue glide over the soft swell of her breasts, loving, absorbing the taste of her.

"Great God almighty! What are you doing to my girl?"

"Damn!" Asher swore as he jerked away from Caramarena and looked into the wild eyes of John Cantrell. He quickly glanced at Caramarena, who was frantically trying to straighten her dress. "God damn!" he swore again and ran his hands through his long hair. How could he have let this happen? What a fool he'd been!

Suddenly there was a clamor of banging doors and running, shuffling feet. Asher tensed. "What the hell's going on here?" he asked.

Cantrell stepped aside, and two large bucks plowed through the doorway and charged Asher. He heard Caramarena scream as a big black fist shot toward him. He ducked and the punch missed its mark but as he straightened another one centered on the left side of his jaw with a crack. Asher groaned and fell backward, knocking over a chair as the two men pounced on top of him.

Chapter Four

Asher struggled to break free of the two dark men who hauled him unceremoniously to his feet. Strong fingers gouged into his flesh and tightly gripped his flexing muscles. His jaw ached from the blow. His breathing was deep and labored. Rage burned inside him to think that John Cantrell would send his slaves to attack him.

Sweat rolled into Asher's eyes and he blinked several times to clear his vision. His gaze focused on Caramarena, who stood with her hands clasped together in front of her chest, fear, shock and something else he couldn't define on her face. Out of the corner of his eye he saw John Cantrell leaning against the door frame, his cotton robe slightly parted. Behind the two, Asher saw Kissie. As their eyes met, a satisfied smile spread across her dark face, emphasizing a full set of white teeth.

Goddammit, she had the nerve to smile at him! Obviously, she'd gone upstairs, roused Cantrell from his sleep and told him of the passionate embrace. She was probably the one who ran for the big slaves, too.

"Mr. John, let me breaks his neck right now, and throw him in de river," Cypress said. "Won't no one ever knows what happened to him."

"No!" Caramarena screamed, swinging around to

face her father, her eyes wide with shock. "Papa, tell them to let Asher go. He's not going to run away."

"Go upstairs, Cara, I'll handle this," he answered angrily and straightened his robe, knotting the belt tighter.

"No, Papa. I'm not leaving."

"I can explain everything," Asher broke in, not knowing what Caramarena might say. But as soon as he said the words he didn't know what in the hell there was to explain. Dammit, he'd wanted to kiss her, and he had. He wanted more than kisses, too, but he knew it was best not to tell Cantrell that.

The color had drained from Cantrell's face, although Caramarena was still flushed. His newly grown beard hadn't been kind to her tender skin. If she was worried about what her father might do, he'd better be worried, too.

"Let him go, Cypress. You too, Jank," her father finally said in a tired voice.

Jank turned him loose and stepped back, but Cypress didn't make a move until Caramarena spoke. "Let him go," she said, taking her gaze off her father and appealing to the slave.

The Negro's hand closed tighter around Asher's arm. "I don't likes him messing wid you, Miss Cara. I take care of him fo' ye, right now."

Cantrell shook his head. "I can still take care of my own house, Cypress. I'll thank you to remember that. Turn him loose. Cara's right, Mr. Millhouse isn't going to run away."

Asher jerked free of the slave and straightened his shirt. What a hell of a mess he'd gotten himself into, all because he wanted a kiss. He knew better than to play around with Cantrell's daughter. He looked over at her and saw she was worried about their predicament, too. He threw another glance at Kissie, who was standing in the background grinning from ear to ear. Why was she so damned pleased with herself, he wondered? Anger tightened his stomach muscles.

"Papa, we were just kissing," Caramarena said in their defense.

"Hush, child. You don't have to say anything. You are an innocent and this man is knowledgeable in the ways of the world." He turned cold eyes on Asher. "You couldn't stop with my business, could you? You had to have my daughter as well."

For a brief moment Asher felt as if Cantrell knew his real identity, and an eerie feeling washed over him. He brushed his hair away from his forehead and looked hard at the sick old man.

"Caramarena is right. It was only a kiss."

"A kiss that left her dress off her shoulders. Don't tell me it was only a kiss!" His voice shook with anger as his hands turned into fists at his sides. "If I gave the word Cypress could have you strung from a tree in a matter of minutes and there's not a sheriff around who'd blame me for your death."

"No, Goddammit!" Asher started toward Cantrell but was quickly jerked backward as the slaves grabbed him once again. He struggled against their strength but knew the futility of trying to best the two men. Kissie had known which slaves to send to the house.

"You had no right to touch her!" Cantrell said, his voice still angry and shaky. "You are a guest in my home. It would serve you right if I let Cypress hang you."

"Papa! No!" Caramarena pleaded again. "Stop this kind of talk. You're getting yourself worked up for no good reason. Nothing happened."

Asher could have told the old man that Caramarena was besotted with him and had been after him ever since he set foot on Live Oak. But he knew that would only fuel Cantrell's anger. He had to start thinking of something that was going to get him out of this, not into more trouble. He had no intention of swinging from a tree because of a kiss, no matter how tempting the woman was.

" 'Pears ta me if'n a man's caught kissing a proper young lady likes Miss Cara he's supposed ta marry her."

Everyone's gaze flew to Kissie, who had spoken quietly. Caramarena's hand flew to cover her mouth as she gasped. Had Kissie carried through with the plan they had devised earlier in the day? *Oh, no!* She must have seen them kissing and ran upstairs to tell her father. Caramarena winced. She had wanted to be caught kissing Asher, but she had no idea it would cause this horrible scene. Threats on Asher's life wasn't part of her plan.

"We don't need any comments from you, Kissie." John added a stern look to his rebuke, and she stepped back into the shadowed hallway. "I'll handle my own household." He turned angry eyes upon Asher. "Much as it grieves me to have to say it." He stopped and shook his head before going on. "I have no choice but insist that you marry Caramarena."

"I'm not marrying anyone," Asher said in his own defense, but as he said the words an idea came to him. His pulse raced. Why not marry Caramarena? What better way to destroy Live Oak than from within the family? With Cantrell sick, he could easily take over the managing of the plantation and in less than a few months squander the entire estate, leaving nothing but the land to burn up in this godforsaken heat.

Asher heard his name and quickly gave his attention back to what was going on in the room.

Caramarena grabbed the lapels of her father's robe. "You don't mean what you're saying, Papa. You've got to stop this before it goes any farther."

"Lets me break his neck fo' ye, Mr. John," Cypress said again.

Caramarena was tired of all this talk of hanging. She stepped away from her father and turned angry eyes upon Cypress and Jank. "Stop that kind of talk this instant! I don't want to hear you say that again. I was not harmed in any way and there is no need for you to want to kill this man." She scolded him firmly.

Caramarena's stomach was quaking with fear. Her father seemed to be sinking into the woodwork, he leaned so heavily upon it. She took a deep breath, for the first time realizing how this incident had taken its toll on his strength.

"I'll marry her." Asher glanced from John to Caramarena as he continued. "You're absolutely right, Mr. Cantrell. I behaved as a common scoundrel and it's only right I make amends by giving your daughter my name."

An uneasy fear crept up Caramarena's back as she looked into Asher's eyes. He was challenging her. Why? Did he expect or want her to plead to her father not to make them marry? If only he knew that this very afternoon she was trying to plan this very incident he wouldn't be soliciting her help in this matter. This idea was fine when she was planning the scheme, but now that she was caught in her own trap she wasn't so sure. The decision had been taken out of her hands, and she wasn't certain she liked that.

"A forced marriage is not what I wanted for you, Cara." Her father fumbled with the front of his robe, his hands trembling.

She swallowed hard and took both his cold hands in hers. "I know, Papa. We can't settle all this tonight." She bent closer to him and whispered, "We'll discuss this later. You need to get back to bed."

With the expulsion of a tired breath and the wave of his hand Cantrell murmured, "I'll make my final decision tomorrow. Cypress, lock Mr. Millhouse in the smokehouse."

"Dammit, Cantrell, I've agreed to marry her. I'm not going to run away."

Cypress grabbed a handful of Asher's hair and yanked his head back. "You watch how yous speak to Mr. John or I gone pop yo' neck where you stand."

Cantrell whirled, pointing a shaky finger at him. "You say another word and I'll see to it you don't live to see sunrise."

"Don't get so upset, Papa. It's not good for you," Caramarena soothed. "Come, let me help you back upstairs. I can see you're not feeling well."

She took her father's arm and he leaned heavily on her. She wasn't happy that this unpleasant scene had taken so much of his strength.

"Help me with Papa, Kissie," she said, and Kissie took the old man's other arm. Caramarena turned back to Cypress and Jank and said, "If anything happens to him tonight, I'll see to it that you two will be the ones swinging from a tree."

Rage burned deep in Asher as the two women led Cantrell away.

Cypress pushed him and Asher stumbled forward. He swung around with a ready fist but stopped when he saw a smile on the dark man's face.

"I's hopin' you gone ta give me a reason ta teach you some respect fo' Miss Cara."

Asher looked at both men, although Cypress was the only one he was worried about. He was as strong as any man Asher had ever fought. He wouldn't mind trying to take him if it were one on one. But with the other buck itching to get at him, too, Asher decided not to try them. He lowered his arm and turned, heading for the door, the two slaves at his heels.

The night air wasn't cool but it was better than the hot stuffy air inside the house so Asher welcomed it.

He took a deep breath and pushed his sweat-soaked hair back with both his hands. He unbuttoned his shirt as they walked. Cypress stayed behind him. The slave they called Jank walked ahead of him to lead the way.

Asher cursed Cantrell under his breath, vowing to let nothing stop him from destroying Live Oak. But that kind of thinking led to thoughts of Caramarena. He remembered the innocent passion in her eyes as he showed her how a man loves a woman and the satiny feel of her skin. He moistened his lips and found the taste of her sweet mouth still on his. The desire she had aroused flared within him again. He had to be careful. Caramarena was a lovely young woman. If he should consummate the marriage and get her with child it would be difficult to walk away from her when he destroyed Live Oak. An annulment would be the only solution. Damn, what rotten luck! He was going to marry one of the most beautiful and intelligent women he'd ever met, but there was no way he could take her to his bed.

The drying sweat made his beard itch, and Asher scratched it as he ambled behind Jank. Yes, if he played his cards right, as Caramarena's husband, he could earn her trust and gain control of the plantation. But how to stay away from her at night would be a problem. She was a very desirable woman. Maybe he should keep up the pretense that he didn't want to marry her in order to stay away from her. Yes, he would make it clear he was only marrying Caramarena to save her reputation.

Asher rubbed his bruised cheek and touched his swollen lip. Anger resurfaced, but he quickly replaced it with a light chuckle which shook his shoulders as he planned Cantrell's downfall. Marriage to Caramarena would seal John Cantrell's destiny.

A push from Cypress let Asher know he'd slowed

down too much, so he picked up his pace again. Another thought crossed his mind, as the smokehouse came into view, giving him a moment of satisfaction. The first thing he'd do when he took over charge of Live Oak would be to sell Cypress and Kissie.

Upstairs, Caramarena helped her father into bed. He trembled with weakness as she covered him with the sheet. She was angry with herself. Upsetting her father had not been part of the original plan. She should have had some thought for his health before she spoke to Kissie about this scheme. She'd never forgive herself if this made him worse.

While she lowered the flame on the lamp she turned to Kissie and said, "I want you to follow Cypress and make sure nothing happens to Mr. Millhouse. I don't want him harmed in any way. And give him some cool water to drink. He's not used to this heat."

Kissie nodded. "Yes'm, Miss Cara. I gone see to it right now."

Caramarena turned back to her father. His breathing was labored, his color almost as pale as the sheet that covered him. For a moment she wondered if she should send Cypress for Dr. Johnstone. Not that the doctor had been able to do much for him.

She sat down on the edge of the bed and took hold of his hand. "Papa, are you feeling better now?"

"Yes, I'm better," he agreed, but Caramarena could see he wasn't.

"Should I send for the doctor?"

"No, no. I'm not going to die yet, Caramarena. It's just that the least exertion takes all my strength."

"Why, Papa?" she pleaded. "What is wrong? Why can't Dr. Johnstone help you to get better."

"Don't worry, Caramarena. He's doing all he can."

"Well it's not enough. If you're not better by morning, Papa, I'm going to send for him with or without your permission."

John Cantrell smiled. "I always knew you'd be the one daughter who could take charge for me. I'll be better after a night's rest. I promise. Now stop trying to change the subject. I was not happy to find you in such a compromising position tonight."

She lowered her lashes over her eyes. "I know. I'm at a loss for words to explain how it came about."

"Well, no need to worry about that now. It's over." His head rolled from one side of the pillow to the other before he looked into her eyes and said, "Caramarena, I know the damning words came from my own lips, but I have to take them back. I can't let you marry a man who will take you all the way to England. What would Bunch and I do without you to look after us?"

Caramarena carried his cold hand to her lips and kissed it. She didn't want to tax his strength further but she had to make him understand why she wanted—needed to marry Mr. Millhouse. Bending closer to him, softly she said, "Papa, I want you to listen to me. I want to marry Mr. Millhouse. I wouldn't go to England and leave you and Bunch. Papa, hear me out," she said when he opened his mouth to stop her. She squeezed his hand again. "I don't want to leave Live Oak. I want an heir for it. I want to live here with my children."

"I could name five men who would marry you tomorrow, Cara, but you've never shown any of them the slightest attention."

"That's true, Papa and every one of them would want me to leave you and Bunch here and live at their home. I won't do it." She took a deep breath and let go of his hand. "Although Mr. Millhouse was a gentleman and agreed to marry me, we both know he

63

doesn't want to. That's one of the things that makes him perfect for what I have in mind."

With his elbows John Cantrell scooted himself up on his pillows. "What are you trying to tell me?"

"I'm saying if Mr. Millhouse doesn't want to marry me, he won't be interested in taking me back to England with him. He can leave me here to take care of the plantation and return every year or two and give me a child. He will have his freedom to continue his travels, and I will have what I want."

John smiled weakly. "You expect him to just fall in with your plan to live here? How confident you sound."

"You've made it so he doesn't have a choice. He will save my honor and marry me, and his business will take him away. Don't you see how perfect this will be? I can have it all. A husband, a child and Live Oak."

"What about love?"

Caramarena felt a warm pressure in her chest. "I'll be marrying for love, Papa. Because I love you and Bunch and Live Oak and don't want to leave, I'm willing to marry a man who will go about his own life and let me stay here and take care of you." She rose from the bed, lifting her shoulders as she went. "And when Mr. Millhouse gives me a child, Papa, I won't be lacking in love. I'll have everything I want."

"For you, a child just might be enough. Only time will tell." A weary smile brightened his face for a brief time. "I would like to see you married before I'm gone. All right, Caramarena. We'll make the necessary arrangements tomorrow. Now go. I'm tired."

She reached over and kissed his cheek. His eyes were already closed. "Thank you, Papa," she whispered, but she knew the night wasn't over yet. Caramarena still wasn't sure how the whole thing happened, but it appeared she was going to get her wish. She put out the lamp and quietly left the room.

The moon was a big silvery ball hanging in the dark sky as Caramarena walked toward the smokehouse. She wouldn't sleep until she talked to Mr. Millhouse. She didn't blame him for hating her. His anger was understandable. She'd feel the same way if she were in his place. She wouldn't like being forced to marry a man she didn't want. A twinge of guilt nagged at her because she had set up the plan with Kissie, but she easily dismissed it because she'd assumed the plan could not be carried through when her father didn't come down for dinner. She'd kissed Asher Millhouse for the sake of the kiss, nothing more, but the chance she'd been given tonight was too good to pass up.

As she approached the smokehouse she saw two dark figures wrapped in each other's arms, and she slowed her pace. After a moment she realized it was Cypress and Kissie locked in a passionate embrace. They were so engrossed in each other they hadn't heard her. She felt funny inside, watching them, but at the same time she was mesmerized by the passion and hunger she sensed between them. Was that the way she and Asher looked earlier in the evening when he'd kissed her? Heat rushed up her cheeks and her hands closed into fists. This was private and not the sort of thing that should be witnessed. She took a few more steps, then loudly cleared her throat. They parted quickly.

Kissie stepped in front of Cypress, shielding him. "I's sorry 'bout this, Miss Cara, it's all my fault. Don't be mad at Cypress for kissin' me. He didn't wants to. It's all my fault," she explained in a rush of words.

Cypress pushed Kissie aside, shaking his head and holding out his hand as if to protect her. "No, Miss Cara. It's my fault. I wuz the one kissin' her. She didn't wants me ta do it."

Caramarena smiled and rubbed her forehead. She'd had no idea that Cypress and Kissie were sweet on each other. Out of all the slaves, these two were her favorites, and she wasn't unhappy to see them together. Not only that, she was impressed by the way they protected each other, each so willing to take the blame.

"Both of you calm down," Caramarena said. "Unlike you and my father, I'm not upset about a few kisses. Cypress, I want you to unlock the door. I need to talk to Mr. Millhouse."

"I can't lets you in there wid that man, Miss Cara." Cypress drew each word out slowly, the whites of his eyes shining brightly against the darkness.

Caramarena was in no mood to argue with him. "You can and you will." She turned to Kissie. "Did you give Mr. Millhouse fresh water?"

"Yes'm, I sho' did," Kissie answered as she clasped her hands together behind her back and started swaying back and forth.

"Thank you." Caramarena picked up the lantern that sat by the door and held it up to the lock. "Now unlock the door, Cypress," she ordered once again.

Cypress looked at Kissie and she nodded. Reluctantly he pulled a ring of keys from his pocket and, finding the one he wanted, unlocked the door.

"Wait out here for me."

"I can't lets you go in there wid that man, Miss Cara. Yo' papa'll have me whupped fo' sho'."

"How many times has Papa ever had you whipped, Cypress?" she snapped, her patience with the slave running out. She took a deep breath and calmed herself. "Don't worry. I'll take care of Papa if there's a problem," she said firmly but softly. "You wait here."

"I don't think yo' papa gone like dis," she heard him complain as she opened the heavy door and stepped inside, pushing it shut behind her.

Asher rose from the far corner of the room when she walked inside. His bare, chest gleamed with sweat in the harsh glare of the lantern light as he walked toward her. Even with his hands tied behind his back, he walked with a proud swagger. He lifted his bearded chin defiantly. Her stomach quaked and her insides trembled. Her skirts felt heavy around her waist. This man didn't really want to marry her but was agreeing because he was a gentleman. He didn't have to know it was what she'd wanted all along.

She moistened her lips and cleared her throat when he stopped a few inches from her. "Mr. Millhouse, I'm sorry about what happened earlier this evening."

He gave her a sardonic grin, his eyes squinting in the harsh light. "Are you really sorry we kissed, Caramarena? You were so warm and responsive in my arms. It's a shame to be sorry for something that pleased both of us so much."

Her back stiffened and she was immediately angered. She set the lantern on a salt box and lifted her shoulders. "I was referring to the fact that Papa caught us and the fight, Mr. Millhouse. Not the kiss."

"Come now, Caramarena. I should think we'd be on first names after all that's happened."

"All right, Asher," she said, thinking she liked the way his name sounded on her tongue. She swallowed to ease the dryness in her throat. "I know marrying me wasn't in your plans, but—"

He chuckled, a deep knowing sound that chilled her.

He tossed his head to sling his long damp hair out of his eyes. "A wedding isn't quite as festive as a hanging—but what the hell—either one means a noose around my neck, and makes your father happy." He laughed again.

Renewed anger surged through her and the sound

67

of his laughter seemed to crawl all over her. Did he think she was enjoying this? It was impossible to be nice to this man in his present mood. He didn't know when he'd gotten off easy.

"Your insolence is not appropriate since I'm trying to be nice to you."

"Don't do me any favors, Caramarena." The teasing quality left his voice and his eyes.

She didn't care for his cynical manner, even though she understood the reason for it. She had to keep reminding herself that he was being forced to marry against his will. His anger was natural. She folded her hands in front of her skirt. "Would you prefer hanging to marrying me?"

"Hell no!"

Asher threw back his head and laughed again when he saw that his loud bellow had startled her. She quickly regained her composure, determined not to let him get the best of her. A close look at him showed a reddening bruise under his left eye, and his bottom lip was swollen and puffy. His hands weren't even free to brush the hair from his face. No wonder he was in such a disagreeable frame of mind. He wasn't being treated like a gentleman.

She softened. "Asher, I know this isn't what you wanted but it will—"

"Save your dignity, Caramarena. I'd hate to see a beautiful woman like you beg. I've already told your father I'd marry you."

Caramarena's temper snapped and before she knew what was happening she reached up and slapped him, a hard solid contact that jerked his head around, and a loud ringing sound that reverberated across the darkened room. She was instantly horrified by her own actions but refused to let it show. Instead of covering her mouth and running from the room, she stood her ground and even managed to lift her chin a little higher.

"I had no intention of *begging* you." The words came clear and concise with just a hint of haughtiness. Thank goodness, she'd saved her dignity.

His eyes held hers, an easy smile enhancing his handsome face, spreading across his lips. "Didn't you?"

As Caramarena studied him she realized he was goading her to do exactly what she'd done moments before—attack him. How could she even think of marrying this man? How?

He had the nerve to chuckle again, but she refused to let it rile her this time. She took a deep breath. "I didn't intend to *beg* you for anything. As you just stated. You've already agreed to marry me."

The simple answer seemed to soften him. "In that case, I deserved the slap. But Cara, the first one is free. If it happens again there's a price."

She believed him. "I'd like to explain—"

"Please, Caramarena, go to bed. I'm tired. We'll discuss this in the morning." He turned away from her and started back toward the far corner of the room.

Caramarena felt terrible. In fact, she felt very small and shallow. She'd never slapped a man in her life, and she wasn't happy that this man was the first. She moistened her lips and called to him: "Asher." He faced her. "I'm not going to let you stay the night in the smokehouse. We have never treated guests at Live Oak in such a manner and we're not going to start tonight. You're free to go back to your room."

"How very kind of you."

The teasing quality had returned to his voice and that irritated her anew. She picked up the lantern, jerked the door open and stepped out. "Cypress, untie Mr. Millhouse," she said. "He'll be spending the night in his room."

69

"You sho' you wants me ta do dat?" he asked.

"Yes," she said through tight lips. "And don't start with those questions again. Just untie him."

"Whatever you say. I's gone walk back to de house wid you," he offered as he worked on the knots.

"That won't be necessary. I'll be perfectly safe in Mr. Millhouse's care. Isn't that right, Asher?" She turned cold eyes upon him.

"I give my word I won't touch you," he said, a smile playing on his lips.

Why was he bantering with this woman? His lip was swollen and cut and hurt like hell. He felt like an iron smith's hammer had hit him in the head and the damn beard was itching. When his hands were free Asher winced and rubbed his wrists. Cypress hadn't intended for him to work the ropes free during the night.

Without meeting his eyes, Caramarena handed him the lantern and started toward the house. Maybe he'd been a little hard on her, considering that he'd already decided it would suit his purpose to marry her. He rubbed his burning cheek. She was surprisingly strong for a woman so slight.

Asher looked back at Cypress and said, "I owe you one," before taking off after Caramarena.

Kissie watched Caramarena and Asher walk away and sighed regretfully. Well, she'd given Miss Cara what she wanted, but she didn't think she was going to like that man. He had some bad blood running in his veins. She might not have done the right thing tonight in going after Mr. John when she saw Miss Cara and Mr. Millhouse wrapped in each other's arms.

"I don't like dat man," Cypress said when the two figures faded from view.

"He don't like you either," Kissie responded in a matter-of-fact tone.

"You's right. Guess he don't like me putting a little color to his pale cheek."

"It'll be sore for days," she answered as she scratched behind her ear.

Kissie looked at Cypress and a low rumble of laughter started in her chest. Cypress joined her.

"He sho' is white," Kissie added between gusts of lusty laughter.

"Yeah, I hears dey don't got no sunshine where he come from. Po' shame." Cypress wiped his eyes on his sleeve.

When the laughter died down, Kissie said, "You best be careful, Cypress. If'n he marries Miss Cara, he could talk her into selling you."

"You right again, Kissie." He nodded. "He may be white, but he's strong under all those clothes he wear. We both best be careful of dat man."

"Oh, Lord have mercy on mah soul," Kissie exclaimed. "I hope I did de right thing tonight. Miss Cara sho' want ta marry dat man bad."

Cypress pulled her into the circle of his arms and stroked her back. "You always do the right thing, honeybee."

"Hush yo' mouth, you lying darkie." She pushed at his chest but not with any real strength.

"You gonna let me stay da night wid you?" he asked, pressing his lower body against her. His hands slipped down to cup her buttocks and bring her up tight against him.

"Not tonight," Kissie answered, but the feel of his hardened member made her want to change her mind. She ran her hands up his broad chest, over his wide shoulders and down his back. He was mighty tempting. She pushed out of his arms before it was too late. "I's tired, and I gots me some thinkin' to do."

"What's you gonna think about? Thinkin' won't do nutin' but get you in trouble."

Kissie started toward her small one room house; Cypress fell in step beside her. "I been in trouble befo'. I gots ta think 'bout Miss Cara and dat man she wants ta marry. Don't make no sense ta me. She don't need no man. Not Miss Cara."

"Don't worry your purty head none about Miss Cara, Kissie. He hurts her and I'll kill him sho'."

Kissie stopped and looked up at him, her big eyes shining. "Jest don't do it befo' she get wid child, or I's gone kill you," Kissie said sternly, then smiled.

Chapter Five

Asher lightly touched the tender bruise under his left eye. Damn, it was sore. His fingers slipped down his bearded cheek to his neck and rubbed the tense muscles. The heat and tight collars had made his neck almost as sore as the bruise.

Asher splashed more water on his face and looked into the mirror again. After a stiff lecture to himself for kissing a woman he knew would get him in trouble, he'd finally slept. He chuckled ruefully. He could have had any whore in any town, but no, he had to have a kiss from the tempting, the forbidden Caramarena Cantrell. If he hadn't told himself he couldn't touch her, he might not have wanted her so badly.

August was a pleasant month in London with its cool temperatures, but here in this godforsaken place the heat and insect bites were enough to drive a man crazy. It was hot when he went to bed and hot when he woke up. He had to do something about lighter clothing. His summer wools were fine for home but not along the sultry banks of the Apalachicola River. When he went into Apalachicola to speak with his captain, he'd find a shop and be fitted for some lightweight cotton clothes.

He patted his neck with a dry cloth, then slipped his arms into his shirt. Since he'd had more time to think about it, he realized what a perfect setup it was for him to marry Cantrell's daughter. He could still carry out his plan to have Cantrell's shipment lost at sea and make it look as if Cantrell had masterminded the plan to get money from his cargo and the insurance company.

Marrying Caramarena meant he would have to winter in Florida. He could handle that—the temperature had to be cooler then than in the summers. As soon as they were married he would find a way to get to the account books. With Cantrell sick it should be easy. No use in Caramarena continuing to do a man's work when she'd have a capable husband. Come spring, he would sail back to London leaving Live Oak without a penny in the bank, no money coming from this year's harvest, either. There would be no way to save Live Oak. It was a foolproof plan. And of course, John Cantrell would know the name of George Worthy before he sailed.

Asher felt a strong sense of guilt when he thought about Caramarena. This had nothing to do with her. Why couldn't she and Bunch have been conveniently married like Cantrell's other two daughters?

If he didn't take Caramarena to bed it would be easy enough to get an annulment. But then what would he do? He couldn't leave her penniless and without a home. He'd have to see Caramarena and Bunch settled in another house before leaving—and arrange for them to draw a monthly allowance. With the annulment Caramarena would be free to marry again.

Asher shook his head. He didn't expect her to easily accept his plan. And he wasn't exactly happy with the idea that this would put his own life on hold for a year or so. He sighed. Why lie to himself? He had no plans for the future. Elizabeth was the only woman he'd ever considered marrying, and he'd waited so long that she'd finally married someone else. Marrying Caramarena wouldn't upset any of his immediate plans, and it was apparent Caramarena was more than agreeable to the marriage.

He stepped into his trousers, and immediately wanted to strip them off again. If he didn't get lighter clothes soon there wouldn't be anything left of him for Caramarena to marry. One other thing was for sure, he thought as he pulled the breeches over a sore hip. He'd get rid of the big buck and the woman called Kissie. She was smart and Cypress was strong. Asher didn't want or need slaves watching every move he made.

Asher hurried down the stairs and out to the front porch. He was surprised to find only Bunch sitting at the round table on the verandah. "Good morning, Bunch," he said. "How are you this morning?"

"Very well, thank you." She rose and extended her hand which he promptly kissed.

He wrinkled his nose when he was assaulted by the strong odor of lilac. Bunch had been into the perfume bottle and hadn't been judicious in her use of it. Looking down into her smiling green eyes he said, "You look lovely."

"Thank you," she answered, glowing from his compliment.

Asher felt a little sad to think this young woman would never know a lover's touch. Such a waste, he thought.

"How's you dis mornin'?" Ivy asked as she started heaping a plate with fluffy eggs and fried potatoes.

"I've been better," he mumbled under his breath, wondering why the slaves at this plantation felt they had the freedom to speak to guests. It was apparent the slaves on Live Oak were treated very well, unlike some he'd seen in his many travels around the South.

"Papa's not feeling well," Bunch said and retook her seat.

Asher looked over at her pretty face and smiled. "I'm sorry to hear that, Bunch. Does that mean he won't be joining us for breakfast?" He pulled out the chair opposite her and sat down. The verandah was shaded and thankfully there was a slight breeze. Birds chirped in the nearby trees, and in the distance Asher heard the voice of a darkie singing a sad tune.

Ivy placed a filled plate and a bowl of orange slices in front of him, and he immediately remembered how good Caramarena felt in his arms. How sweet her lips tasted with the flavor of orange upon them. He shook his head and picked up the cup of strong black coffee. He pushed the bowl away. He didn't want to ever taste the fruit again.

"Cara's sleeping," Bunch announced, rather than answer his question.

"Mr. Cantrell's having his breakfast in his room dis morning. But he be down soon," Ivy offered from her position at the serving table. "And Miss Cara, she won't be up for another hour. She's a late one."

Asher didn't want to think about Caramarena being in bed. He had to keep those thoughts far from his mind. He picked up his knife and fork and folded his eggs into the white gravy on his plate, then sliced the thick piece of ham.

"Cara's teaching me to sew," Bunch said, looking at the piece of white material lying beside her plate. "Would you like to see what I made?"

Asher was startled that Bunch offered conversation, and even more that she wanted him to look at her handiwork. She was usually quiet when Caramarena wasn't around. He laid down his fork and said, "I'd be delighted to see it."

Bunch pushed her chair back and walked over to hand him the sampler. Her honey gold hair bounced on her shoulders. She was lovely in her rose pink dress with its folds of lace and ribbons on the skirt.

76

He took the sampler from her and looked at it.

"I did it all by myself." Her voice was full of pride, and a smile beamed across her face.

Looking at the uneven stitching of a simple flower, Asher once again felt sorry for Bunch. Fate had not been kind in giving her the face and body of a lovely woman while leaving her with the mind of a child. "It's beautiful," he said in a husky tone. "You're very good with a needle."

The beaming smile stretched farther across her face, and she looked over at Ivy to make sure the woman had heard his praise. Ivy gave a nod of approval.

The door opened and all three turned to see John Cantrell step out onto the porch. The first thing Asher noticed was that Cantrell's color was a little better than it had been last night. As usual he was impeccably dressed and his thinning gray hair was combed into place. When his gaze fell on Asher his brows drew together and his lips set in a grim line.

"Good morning," he said, nodding at Asher while Bunch rushed to his side and reached up to kiss his cheek.

"Mr. Millhouse thinks it's beautiful." She held the sampler up to her father's inspection.

He graciously took the time to study it before smiling at her and saying, "He's right. It is." Bunch clutched the material to her breast, cradling it like a babe. Cantrell patted her cheek affectionately and said, "Go up and check on Caramarena for me, dear. If she's awake, tell her I'd like to speak to her. Would you do that for me?"

"Yes, Papa." In a whirl of flying pink skirts, Bunch opened the door and disappeared inside.

Cantrell turned to Ivy. "You, too." He waved his hand at her. "Go find something to do inside. I want to speak to Mr. Millhouse alone."

Without comment, Ivy followed Bunch, and Asher pushed his plate aside and rose. He had no one to blame but himself for the predicament he found himself in. Had it not been for that damning kiss last night, this morning he'd be on his way down the river and in a few days sailing to England. He felt sure Cantrell was going to insist again he had to marry Caramarena. What Cantrell didn't know was that he'd already decided to do it. That in fact, it would fit into his plan very nicely.

When the door shut firmly behind Ivy, Cantrell turned cold eyes upon Asher. "I see Caramarena took pity on you and allowed you back in the house last night. I expected as much."

Asher didn't respond to his statement. He rubbed his sore jaw and continued to stare at the man.

"You abused my hospitality and my daughter's honor, Mr. Millhouse; however, I won't see my daughter's reputation ruined because of your dishonorable action. Since Caramarena would rather marry you than see you hang, I have to insist you marry her." Asher started to speak but Cantrell shook his head and held up his hand in protest. "You have no say in this matter. It's unfortunate for you, but around here we have our own kind of justice."

Asher tensed. He'd already decided to marry Caramarena, but he didn't like Cantrell thinking he could make him do it if he didn't want to. He didn't want anyone telling him he didn't have a choice. He would have loved to tell the old man that he welcomed the idea of marrying his precious Caramarena and bedding her, too, but he had to play his true feelings close to his heart. It was best to make the two Cantrells think he was marrying against his will.

"Your daughter's honor wasn't violated last night. Believe me, nothing happened between us but a few harmless kisses," he stated firmly.

"One of the slaves witnessed Caramarena in a state of undress. That would be talked about among the community, and I can't let that happen." Cantrell walked over to the edge of the porch and leaned against the large Doric column. He seemed to weaken as the moments passed. "This is what I've decided. You must marry Caramarena within the week. However, I don't expect you to give up your current life. After the wedding you will be free to go back to England and leave Caramarena here with me. All I ask is that you honor her by giving her your name."

Shocked, Asher walked closer to him. He hadn't thought about the possibility of Cantrell giving him freedom to leave without Caramarena. He wondered if he'd talked with his daughter about that. He didn't have the feeling she'd want him to sail on his merry way once they were married. In fact, she'd been agreeable to the marriage right from the start.

Asher hid his surprise and grunted. "Just my name?" He laughed bitterly. If he could tell this man his true name, Asher didn't think it would be a name Cantrell would want his Caramarena to take in marriage.

"A small price to pay," Cantrell said. "As I said, you can retain your freedom and sail back to England on the first available ship for all I care."

This Asher would have to think about. He was fairly certain Caramarena wouldn't like the idea of her husband having the freedom to return to England without her. Now that he'd been given the choice to leave, he had to weigh the possibilities. If Cantrell wanted him to go there had to be a reason.

"What will be my dowry if I agree to this wedding?" he asked, walking over to stand in front of the older man.

Cantrell seemed to think for a few seconds. "Half

79

of the cargo of turpentine that will go aboard your ship."

Asher stiffened. "No." He had to keep all of that in Cantrell's name for his plan to work. "I want five thousand dollars on the wedding day." The sooner he could deplete Cantrell's bank accounts, the quicker he could be on his way back to England with his father's honor avenged.

Cantrell thought about it for a few seconds, then said, "Very well. Consider it an agreement."

Their eyes locked together. Finally, Asher nodded. "I have to go into Apalachicola before the wedding. I need clothes and I have to speak to my captain."

Cantrell pushed away from the pillar. "The slaves are loading the first shipment of turpentine right now. They should be ready to leave in a couple of hours. You can go with them."

"I'm surprised you're going to let me out of your sight. What makes you so sure I'll return?"

Cantrell looked back at Asher as if he were dense, then said, "Caramarena."

The old man was no fool, but he was wrong. It wasn't that Asher didn't want to bed Caramarena, but there was no way in hell he was going to. He wouldn't get caught in that trap. He ran down the steps and followed the path to the river. He wanted to let the overseer know that he'd be going with them downriver. Another thought nagged him as he strode along. Why had Cantrell given him permission to leave without Caramarena after the wedding? He hadn't expected that. And he was sure Cantrell hadn't expected him to stay at Live Oak, which he fully intended to do.

Asher chuckled. This could prove a very interesting winter.

Caramarena stepped off the front porch, picked up

the skirt of her fawn-colored dress and headed toward the dock. Her father had just told her that he and Mr. . . . he and Asher . . . had agreed to the marriage and a dowry. Her heartbeat quickened. Maybe it was going to really happen. Bless Kissie's soul for making their plan work when it looked as if all would be lost. Caramarena made a mental note to do something special for her.

As she neared the dock, she saw Asher talking to Mr. Wulpher. The slaves were busy loading barrels onto the river boat. Asher and Mr. Wulpher made an odd couple, she thought. Asher was tall and well-built with thick brown hair that fell neatly to his collar, while the overseer was short, balding and heavyset.

She walked up to the two men, a smile on her face. "Good morning, gentlemen."

Mr. Wulpher took his hat off and held it in front of his white, collarless shirt. "Good morning to you, Miss Cara," he responded politely.

Caramarena turned to Asher and at once saw the ugly bruise under his left eye. The puffiness in his bottom lip was still apparent, although the cut looked better. She had the urge to reach out and comfort him.

"You look ravishing as usual, Caramarena," Asher said, his voice low and husky.

His blue eyes mocked her, his words challenged her. She lifted her chin. "And I see that you are still determined to give yourself a heat stroke."

He laughed. "Not for long. I was just telling Mr. Wulpher that I intend to accompany him into town and be fitted for lighter clothes. I'll need them now that I'll be staying in Florida for a time."

Caramarena kept her shoulders and back straight. "There's no need for you to see anyone in Apalachicola about new clothes. We have the best seamstress in this area right here at Live Oak. I'll see that she's in your room in an hour with fabrics and to measure you."

"Thank you. I'd be happy to have her make the clothes, but alas, I still have to go into town. I must speak to my captain and send a letter to my brothers telling them the latest news."

"By all means, Asher." She said his name with silky sweetness and smiled up at him before turning to Mr. Wulpher.

"How many runs do you expect to make?" Caramarena asked.

"Three should handle all the barrels, Miss Cara. Mr. Millhouse was just telling me that three hundred should fill his ship."

"I see. Well, since Asher will be traveling with the shipment to see his captain why don't we let him oversee the loading onto his ship and you stay here to be sure the other two hundred barrels are brought down to the dock. You know the workers don't get as much done if you're not watching their every move."

Mr. Wulpher looked at Asher, then twisted his hat between his hands. "Will that be all?"

"Yes. Now go find Cypress and tell him that I need to see him on the front porch immediately."

"Yes, Miss Cara," he said politely, nodded to Asher and turned away.

Asher chuckled under his breath. "When you said you knew how to manage this plantation you meant it, didn't you?" His eyes swept across her face. "How long have you been running the day-to-day operations?" he asked.

Caramarena took the time to really look at him, and she wondered what he looked like without the beard. She supposed he wore it because of the amount of time he spent at sea. It would have to get tiresome shaving every day, she thought.

She softened a little because his tone of voice told

her he was impressed. "Almost a year. Of course Papa still signs all contracts and actually handles the business. Usually, Mr. Wulpher and the slaves deal directly with me."

"And they don't mind?"

"Why should they?" Her chin lifted and her gaze drifted over to the dark men struggling to load the barrels onto the large boat. "I'm a much easier taskmaster than my father was in his younger years. I haven't had to whip a slave yet, but I wouldn't be opposed to it if the need arose."

He smiled and rubbed his cheek. "I'm sure you wouldn't."

Caramarena looked away from him. Why did he have to remind her of what passed between them last night? Slapping him was a horrible thing for her to have done.

"I was angry," she explained, but the smirk on his face wouldn't let her leave it at that. "You deliberately tested my temper," she added, trying to lay the blame on him.

"My hands were tied last night." He reached out and cupped her chin. She tried to pull away but his fingers dug into her flesh and held her firmly.

He lowered his head as if he meant to kiss her. "Rest assured it could never happen again, Caramarena."

His voice was soft but she knew he meant every word. She didn't want it to happen again either. She wasn't happy that she'd slapped him. It was uncalled for. And he was right, he had been as defenseless as she was in his arms. Even though he held her now in anger, his touch still warmed her.

"M-my father told me you had agreed on a dowry."

His grip loosened and his touch became more of a caress than a vise. "A small price to be sure. But I must take responsibilities for my actions. I knew the possible consequences when I kissed you." He turned her loose and stepped away.

Caramarena cleared her throat. "We'll make the wedding a week from today. That will give me time to have a dress made, invite the guests and have the food prepared."

"I can hardly wait," he said dryly.

Caramarena knew he considered marriage to her a prison sentence. She felt a twinge of guilt. She wouldn't want anyone trapping her into marriage, forcing her to marry someone she didn't want. She wouldn't even consider doing it to someone else if it weren't so perfect for her plans.

Instead of rubbing her chin as she wanted to, she said, "If you don't mind, I'd like to send Cypress into town with you. I'd like him to deliver the wedding invitations. There's only time to invite a few friends. I'm afraid there's not even time for my sisters, Catherine and Charlotte, to make the trip down."

"Do we have to be in *that* big a hurry, Cara?"

She ignored the teasing glint in his eyes. "I'm just following Papa's instructions. I'll make sure Cypress meets you here." She turned to walk away but Asher grabbed her arm and whirled her around to face him. His hand was warm upon her skin. His fingers sent a tingling sensation up her arm. Their eyes met and for a moment, she was sure she felt him tremble.

"Am I to be his caretaker?" he questioned, letting her go.

Caramarena touched her arm where he'd held her. "Cypress is more than able to take care of himself, but naturally he will be under your supervision."

"Why do I get the feeling you're sending him along to make sure I don't sail away with my ship?"

Caramarena gave him a long look. "I assume you are a gentleman and a man of your word. You have agreed to marry me, and that's what I expect from you. I'll send the seamstress to your room immediately. She should have time to fit you before the boat sails."

She turned and walked away. She had too much to do to mince words with Asher Millhouse. She needed to write the invitations for Cypress to deliver, and she had to tell Bunch about the marriage before someone else did. She also had to reflect on the way Asher Millhouse made her feel.

Later that afternoon Caramarena watched the boat carrying one hundred barrels of turpentine, Asher and Cypress down the river to Apalachicola. It was strange but already she missed his handsome smile, the way he challenged her at every turn. And there was something slightly forbidding in knowing that this handsome stranger who had come into her life only three days ago was now to be her husband.

Caramarena shook her head. She couldn't spend her time daydreaming about Asher. She had too many things to take care of. She had to record today's transactions. Then she had to speak with Fanny about her wedding dress. She needed to talk with Ivy about the food and tell her sister about the marriage.

"Wuz you asking for me, Miss Cara?"

Caramarena looked up to see Kissie lounging in the open doorway. "Come in, Kissie. Have you been avoiding me today?"

"Yes'm, I guess so."

"Why?" she asked.

Kissie walked on into the room with its richly paneled wood and heavy velvet draperies and stood before her mistress. "I expects you mad wid me about last night."

"For kissing Cypress? I told you. That doesn't bother me. I'm happy if you're sweet on Cypress."

"Yes'm, I's glad to hear that, but I's talking about me getting your papa when I sees you kissing dat English man."

Caramarena rose from her chair and walked around the desk. "Why would I be angry with you? You know I was hoping—wanting something like that to happen. If you'll remember we planned it yesterday afternoon."

"Yes, I do, but—" Big dark eyes stared at Caramarena, and Kissie fiddled with the black kerchief that covered her hair.

"But what, Kissie? What's bothering you?" Caramarena had never known this woman to be at a loss for words. Kissie always knew what she wanted to say and didn't think twice about saying it.

"I's not sure he da man you wants ta marry," she finally said. "Dat man gots a mean streak."

Caramarena felt relief and smiled. "Oh, Kissie, I don't think he's mean. I'd be just as angry as he was last night, if I'd been beaten up and thrown in the smokehouse for kissing someone. Asher had a right to be furious and he may be for a long time. There are many reasons why he wouldn't want to marry me. He doesn't know me or love me. I'm really a stranger to him. His home is in England. I can't blame Asher for being angry."

"Dat may be so. I don't like you sending Cypress off with him. He don't like Cypress."

Now they were getting down to the real reason Kissie was pouting. Caramarena smiled. "Well, Cypress doesn't like him either. I think those two will be watching their backs on this trip. Don't worry, Kissie. I don't believe Asher would do anything to hurt Cypress."

"I sho' hope you right, Miss Cara. Cypress is a good worker. Dey don't come no better."

"I know," she said and returned to her chair. "Kissie, I want you to know I'm grateful you went and roused Papa from his bed last night. And I understand your reservations. But this marriage is what we need at Live Oak. Without a husband who will let me stay here, Live Oak would be sold when Papa—" she looked away. She hated to think it, but she knew her father wasn't getting any better. He knew it, too. That was the reason he wanted her to marry Asher Millhouse. "If Papa dies. As long as Live Oak is home for me and Bunch, I don't think Catherine and Charlotte will insist on selling it."

Kissie picked up the tail of her apron and moved closer to the desk. "Don't worry 'bout your papa. He gots a long life ahead of him yet. The old age is creeping up on him, dat's all."

Caramarena smiled, knowing Kissie didn't believe what she said. "I hope you're right."

"And I hope you right in marrying dis man," she mumbled, wiping the end of the desk with her apron.

"It will work out, Kissie. I'm going to make it work." She took a deep breath and rose from her chair again. "I need to talk to Bunch. Do you know where she is?"

"I seen her in de gold room, playing."

"All right. Go tell Fanny to wait for me in my room."

"She's busy making yo' man some new shirts and breeches."

"Never mind that for now. Tell her we need to talk about my wedding dress." She turned at the door and added, "And, Kissie, please refer to Asher as Mr. Asher from now on."

When Caramarena found her, Bunch was sitting in a high-back rocker, cradling a baby doll in her arms and humming a lullaby that Caramarena used to sing to her. Love for her sister filled Caramarena's heart as she stood at the door and watched. Bunch reached down and kissed the doll's hard cheek, then returned to humming. The thought of Bunch holding a live baby sent a warm flush over Caramarena's cheeks. Surely Asher would get her pregnant before he left for England. Then she and Bunch would have a real baby to hold and love and kiss.

She walked quietly into the room and knelt down in front of her sister. "Your baby's so quiet. Is she asleep?"

Bunch nodded. "She's asleep."

"Let's lay her on the sofa. I want to talk to you about something."

When the blanket had been lovingly tucked around the doll which lay between the two sisters, Caramarena took a deep breath and said, "Bunch, I'm going to marry Asher Millhouse."

"Marry him?" she asked, her big blue eyes staring blankly at Caramarena.

Nodding, Caramarena smiled and took her hand. "Just as Catherine and Charlotte have husbands, Asher will be my husband."

Bunch's eyes widened. "You're going to leave me?" Her bottom lip trembled.

"No, honey, no! I won't ever leave you. I'll always be here to take care of you and Papa. Mr. Millhouse is going to let me live here. I won't go away."

"Do you promise?" she asked.

Caramarena nodded. She picked up the doll and placed it in Bunch's arms. "Mr. Millhouse will give me a real baby. One that really cries and needs feeding. You can help me take care of him. Would you like that?" she asked.

"Today?" Bunch asked, her eyes lighting with joy.

Caramarena laughed. "No, it takes longer than a day to make a baby. But maybe by next spring." Bunch made a face as if she didn't comprehend that distant a future. "I know that sounds like a long time

88

to wait, but it takes several months to make a real baby."

"Mr. Millhouse will give you a baby that really cries?" she asked again.

"Yes. And you don't have to call him Mr. Millhouse any more. You can call him Asher. Would you like that?" Bunch pursed her lips and nodded. "After we're married he'll no longer be a guest but part of the family. We won't have to be so formal around him. You'll like that, won't you?"

Bunch nodded again and cradled her doll to her chest. "I don't like trying to remember what to do when we have guests in the house."

Smiling, Caramarena retied a bow on the sleeve of her dress. "I know. But you do a good job. I'm always so proud of you."

Bunch laughed, then hugged and kissed the doll.

Chapter Six

When the riverboat landed at the dock in the port of Apalachicola, Asher reminded Cypress to meet him back at the dock at dusk, then sent him on his way to deliver the wedding invitations. Rather than spend the night in a room in town, Asher decided to stay on board his ship, *Sandor* and sail back with the riverboat to Live Oak tomorrow when it brought the next shipment of turpentine. He needed the evening to write a letter to Parker and Winston, telling them he'd found John Cantrell and his plan for destroying Live Oak.

For now he wouldn't tell them that he was marrying Cantrell's daughter. He would have to explain that in person when the time came. With Parker, his oldest brother, the less you said the better. He read too much in the least comment.

While the slaves loaded the turpentine he went below with Captain Simon Barclay to his cabin in the forward section of the ship. Simon was a soundly built man with a mass of unruly red hair, who usually held a pipe between his teeth.

Following Simon down the narrow hallway, Asher couldn't help comparing the small space to the spacious hallways and floor to ceiling windows at Live Oak.

"I was going to give you a few more days,

then come looking for you," the captain said as he opened his office door and stepped inside.

Asher followed him, taking his jacket and cravat off as he went. The small room was dark and stuffy and smelled of stale pipe tobacco. He thought it odd that it had never bothered him before today. Why did he keep having visions of the large, bright rooms at Live Oak? He'd been on this ship more than he'd been off it for the last fourteen years. This was his home, not a mansion built on a bluff overlooking the river.

"Leave that door open if you want," Simon said as he walked behind his desk to sit down. "Damn, it gets hot as hell here."

"So you've noticed, too," Asher commented, and shut the door. "I have things to say that I don't want others to hear." Asher threw his jacket over the chair and rolled up the sleeves of his shirt.

"You going to tell me how you got that shiner under your eye?" Simon asked.

"No."

Simon's eyes narrowed and he laid his unlit pipe aside. "This sounds serious. What's going on? Trouble?"

"I'm getting married," Asher said flatly.

"Here? In this hellish heat?" Simon laughed heartily, his round belly jumping with each gusty burst. "What in God's name are you going to do that for?"

"Don't play with me, Simon, I'm in no mood for it. For now let's just say I'm marrying the daughter of a business associate and leave it at that. You'll be sailing back to England without me."

Simon settled down and leaned back in his chair, causing it to creak from his weight. "Parker's not going to like this. You getting married without letting him know ahead of time. I imagine Winston will have a thing or two to say as well."

"I expect they'll have many things to say when the

time comes, but this isn't what we need to talk about right now. I have something more important to discuss with you."

"No need to worry about your favorite ship. I'll take care of her same as always."

"I've no worry on that account, Simon. It's something else." He was stalling and knew it.

"I can't imagine what. Go on. Tell me." He picked up his pipe and started stuffing it with tobacco from a tin canister.

Simon could be ornery but he was always faithful. Asher was sure he could trust his captain with this mission. "First, I have to demand your silence on this."

"Done," was all he needed to say.

"The cargo that's being loaded right now is never to reach England."

"What?" He looked up from stuffing the pipe, his eyes searching Asher's face.

"Just listen for a moment." Asher had never asked Simon to do anything illegal before, and he wasn't in the habit of reneging on his business deals. "I have a plan, but will admit it's not a good one. The thing I want you to do is pick the man you trust above all others. Do you have one on board?"

"Right. Buford's been with me longer than you have."

Asher smiled. Buford was the man he'd hoped Simon would suggest. "This is what you're to do. Send Buford to Charleston. By stagecoach. That way he'll arrive a full month before you, and he'll probably need that much time."

"Saints alive, stop all this prattle and tell me what you've planned." Simon let his pipe drop to his desk and scooted his chair closer.

"All right. I want Buford to reach Charleston before you dock for supplies. While there I want him to hire some men to steal the *Sandor*'s cargo."

Shaking his head, Simon pushed his chair back. "The heat's gotten to you, son."

Asher moved to the edge of his seat and placed both hands on the desk. "Simon, I'm serious."

"But you've never done anything like this before. What am I to think of this madness?"

"We've sailed together for fourteen years. There's good reason. You know I wouldn't ask something like this of you if it wasn't important."

"I've been captain of *Sandor* for close to twenty years. I've never lost a shipment."

"Exactly. The insurance investigators will have no reason to suspect any wrongdoing on your part."

"I don't like this, Asher. Hiring men to steal our cargo. Too many things can go wrong. It's too risky." He shook his head again.

"No!" Asher's fist came down hard on the desk and Simon flinched. "This shipment must never reach London. I agree it's not a foolproof plan but it's the best I've come up with. I want you to send Buford to Charleston. Have him hire some men for the piracy and tell him to be sure he lets the name Cantrell slip."

"*Cantrell*. By all that's holy, you've found Cantrell! Why in God's name didn't you say so." Simon leaned back in his chair and laughed. "You've been looking for him since you started sailing with me. How long did you say it's been?"

"Too long," Asher responded.

Simon shook his head. "I watched your mother turn from a lovely young woman to a bitter shrew while your father slowly drove himself insane. All because John Cantrell, his friend and employee, stole all his money."

A knot grew in Asher's stomach as Simon continued to talk. He didn't like being reminded of the past.

"You would have saved yourself a lot of wind if you'd simply told me you'd finally found Cantrell. I'm surprised that pirating his cargo is the only thing you want to do." Simon picked up his pipe but it never reached his mouth. His eyes widened and his mouth gaped, showing teeth aged with a yellow stain. "That's not all you intend, is it? Hell and damnation! Asher, you're going to marry his daughter!"

Asher rose from his chair and rubbed the back of his damp neck. The humid air caused his shirt to cling uncomfortably to his skin. He knew how sordid this whole thing sounded to Simon. Now that it was out in the open he somehow felt as if he were losing his honor in order to avenge his father's. He needed some fresh air. He turned back to the captain. "Well? Are you going to help?"

"Done."

Asher walked back to the upper deck and looked out over the water. The sun was already hanging low in the western sky and the gulf breeze cooled his heated body. He wouldn't be a gentleman if he didn't have second thoughts about what he had to do, he told himself. A faraway look crept into his eyes as he was transported back in time. He didn't remember his father before the bitterness settled in. He was the youngest son, so he was at home when his father called him to his deathbed. Parker and Winston were already running the business. He'd never forget the withered old man grabbing his hand, making him promise to find John Cantrell and destroy him. Parker and Winston came in only long enough to make the vow as well.

George Worthy had worked like a madman to re-build his business so he'd have the money to search the world for Cantrell. But by the time he had the money, he didn't have the health, so he placed the burden on his sons' shoulders. Asher had made a promise and he'd keep it. He'd ruin Cantrell and Live Oak. He just didn't like what he was going to have to do to Caramarena and Bunch.

He felt a hand on his shoulder and turned to see Simon beside him, an understanding expression on his face. "Come below and have a drink with me. It will do you good."

Asher shook his head. "Not now. I have to go ashore and pick up a slave. Have a pallet placed in my room for him."

Simon laughed. "Are you going to start the South's ways and travel with a slave?"

"Don't test my temper, Simon. I'm in no mood for it."

Simon cleared his throat. "Very well, I'll get one of the men to row you to shore."

"No. I'll do it. I need the exercise."

The Apalachicola River flowed into the clear blue water of the Gulf of Mexico. Rowing to shore was made easy by the gently rolling waves. The physical work of rowing felt good, but by the time he made it to shore Asher was tired. He was going to have to find something to do at Live Oak to keep from getting soft. He'd seen too many men lose their strength from lack of exercise once they settled into the easy life — like that of his brothers, sitting behind a desk all day.

It was sundown by the time he reached the dock and climbed up the ladder to the pier. He looked around in the fading light but didn't see Cypress anywhere. As he suspected, the slave hadn't arrived. It surprised him that the dock was deserted. He would have thought it was still early enough for it to be bustling with activity. He walked down the wide-planked pier to where the buildings started, anger growing inside him because he had to wait for the slave. This gave him another reason to want to sell the slothful man once he controlled Live Oak.

A few minutes later the sun completely disappeared in the western sky, leaving dark shadows of purple and brown along the hazy horizon. He contemplated leaving Cypress to find his own bed for the night.

Asher leaned against a post as full darkness descended upon him and thought about Caramarena. Would she be all right once he had the marriage annulled and set her up in another house? Once she knew the whole story, would she forgive him for what he had to do? Asher shook his head. He knew he was taking a lot for granted, but his vow to his father left no other alternative.

Asher scratched his beard, grateful for the setting sun and the night's breeze to cool him. He didn't like the idea that Caramarena would hate him. And he didn't like the idea of upsetting Bunch's little world either. But John Cantrell hadn't thought twice about George Worthy's family when he'd absconded with the money. Maybe if he explained to Caramarena what her father had done and how he believed he was bound by honor and a vow to avenge his father, she would understand and forgive him.

Asher snapped the twig he held in his hands. What was he doing thinking such fanciful notions about Caramarena? He would do best to keep her as far away from his thoughts as possible. Forming an attachment of any kind to her would only make the break harder. And there would have to be a break.

The sound of footsteps and muted voices caused Asher to stand up straight. His gaze darted from one corner of the dark buildings and alleyways to the other, but he saw no one. After a moment two men rounded a corner and came into view. One of the men pulled notes out of a wallet and threw it away, then divided the money with the other. Asher's back stiffened and his hand made a fist. These men meant trouble and he had no weapon. What the men didn't know was that he also had no money. It was back at the ship in his jacket pocket. Now he knew why the dock was deserted. It wasn't safe to be out here after dark. He would have realized that if he hadn't been so preoccupied.

One of the men spotted him and stopped. He spoke to his friend in low tones, but Asher didn't have to hear them to know what they were saying. Asher took the time to size them up. Both were shorter than he. One was of a strong and sturdy build; that one worried him. The other he figured he could take care of after a few blows to the head, but the stocky one would be more difficult. He also had to assume they would come after him with the knives probably hidden beneath their clothing.

Sweat ran down the side of Asher's bruised cheek and reminded him he'd been in a fight with two slaves just last evening, leaving his ribs sore as hell. He wasn't looking forward to another confrontation. The two men started toward him. If he got out of this alive he was going to personally kill Cypress.

"Pardon us, sir, we were hoping you might direct us to Canal Street. We seem to be lost."

Asher knew it wouldn't be wise to tell them he was a stranger in town. Strangers were easy to get rid of because there would be no one asking questions about a missing person. "No," he said, trying to appear uninterested in the two.

"You alone?" the thinner man asked.

It was a dumb question and Asher and the other man knew it. "I'm waiting for someone who's late," he said hoping to stave off any attack. But he knew better as soon as the stocky-built man stepped back and the faint glint of steel caught Asher's eye.

The man lunged for Asher, jabbing the knife toward him. Asher grabbed the man's wrist and forced

97

his arm up and away from his chest. The man's face reddened in the moonlight as he strained against Asher's strength. Out of the corner of his eye Asher saw the other man reaching for his knife so he brought his knee up into his attacker's crotch. The man doubled over and groaned before falling backward as the thin man made a swipe at Asher. The blade caught him across his midsection.

Asher didn't have time to worry about how bad the cut might be. He pushed the burning pain out of his mind as the man made another wide sweep for his chest. Asher whirled and kicked the knife out of the attacker's hand.

From behind him the stronger man grabbed Asher under the arms and locked his beefy hands across Asher's bloody chest. His partner picked up the knife and came at Asher again. Asher kicked the man but not before the blade sliced down his leg. The searing pain blurred his vision long enough for the man to come after him again.

Suddenly the slight man was drawn up short and yanked back by a black arm hooked around his neck. Asher watched long black fingers cup the man's chin. The man's head was given a hard jerk; bones snapped. The knife fell from the robber's quaking hand, and he slid wide-eyed to the ground.

Cypress looked down at the dead man. The grip on Asher loosened. He took advantage of his assailant's shock and turned, hitting him with a hard right to his jaw. The man stumbled backward and Asher caught him with a blow to his left eye.

Cypress joined the fight and finished the man off with a hard right to his midsection, then one to his jaw. Again Asher heard bones cracking. Blood covered the man's face. His eyes rolled back in his head, and he fell to the ground in a bloody heap.

Two minutes after the fight started one man lay

dead and the other out cold.

Asher didn't know what part of his body hurt worse. He sensed the cut on his side was deeper than the one on his leg, but he felt blood running down his leg into his boot. With the back of his hand he wiped blood from his lip, burning his skinned knuckles. "You're late," he said in a breathless voice.

Cypress remained calm. "Yessir, I knows I is."

"You ever seen either of these men around?" he asked and winced as the pain in his side increased.

Cypress shook his head, the whites of his eyes standing out in the darkness.

Asher looked around. No one seemed to have witnessed the killing. He wiped sweat out of his eyes with the tips of his fingers and damned himself for getting caught up in this situation with the slave.

He looked at Cypress. "They'll hang you if they find out you killed that man. There's no self-defense for a slave."

"Yessir, I knows dat. But I couldn't let him kills Miss Cara's man."

Asher felt a chill run up his back. So he now had a new title. Miss Cara's man. If he didn't hurt in so many places he'd laugh. Another thought struck him. This was his opportunity to get rid of Cypress. All he had to do was call in the authorities and Cypress would be done away with promptly. This was what he'd wanted.

He watched the big black man looking so gentle, standing there knowing that his fate rested in the hands of a man he'd beaten up just the night before. Asher wondered why he wasn't running away or pleading for his life. He liked the fact that he wasn't doing either. Cypress had accepted the consequences when he made the choice to help him. Asher took a deep breath and winced. Cypress had saved his life— he could do no less for this giant.

"Let's get the hell out of here before someone stumbles upon us and does to you what you just did to that poor soul."

He held his side and started running down the pier, the slave's steps right behind him. Blood and sweat ran down his neck and dripped onto his shirt. Asher picked up the oars but Cypress grabbed them out of his hand.

"Let go. I'll row," Asher barked.

"No sir. Dat's my job. Besides, you bleedin' likes a butchered hog."

Asher let go of the oars and sat back while Cypress sliced smoothly through the water with the oars, carrying them away from the aftermath of the scene they'd left behind. He hoped the other man lived, but he also hoped it was too dark for him to recognize Cypress again. Asher had spent enough time in the South to know that he'd be hung without question for killing a white man. That he'd saved Asher's life wouldn't count.

Asher knew it was pointless to try and tend his wounds until he reached the ship. He hurt in too many places to try and distinguish one from the other. Simon would have him patched up in no time, he told himself. And he could sure use a stiff drink.

When they pulled up to the ladder hanging on the side of the ship Asher turned to Cypress and said, "You're never to mention this incident to anyone."

"I gots to tell Miss Cara," he said.

"No," Asher said firmly. "It's best that no one else know about this, including Caramarena. If anyone questions you about this you are to say you don't know anything about it."

"Yessir."

Asher took a deep breath. "All right. Now help me get up the ladder."

The man coughed. Blood ran out of his mouth and slid down his cheek to drop onto the dirt. He held his jaw with one hand and his ribs with the other as he groaned from the pain that engulfed him. He heard booted feet running down the pier and knew the darkie and the white man thought he was dead like his brother.

A minute or two later he heard oars splashing in the water. So the two were headed for the big ship that was anchored out in the harbor. He coughed up blood again and tried to turn his head and spit it out. The bastards had broken his jaw and several ribs. He probably had a punctured lung, too. Damn he hurt!

If he lived he'd find out what ship they boarded. Then he'd find the black son of a bitch that murdered his brother, and he'd kill him. Spit and blood mingled in his mouth choking him. He'd kill the white bastard, too.

Chapter Seven

Caramarena sucked in her breath one last time as Kissie pulled on the ribbons of her corset. "That's tight enough. Any more and I'll faint on my wedding day," she complained.

"You wants Mr. Asher to think you gots the smallest waist 'round here, don't you?"

"I would like that, yes, but I wouldn't like to end up in a heap at his feet for lack of air. Now quit pulling and tie it." Caramarena took shallow breaths while Kissie finished the task.

"Miss Cara?" Kissie asked as she worked the ribbons at Caramarena's back.

"Yes, Kissie," she answered without really listening. She looked over at the beautiful silk-and-satin wedding dress that lay on her bed and wished she felt more satisfied about marrying Asher Millhouse. Before today it had been easy to tell herself that she was doing the right thing, that this had to be done for the future of Live Oak. But now that the time had come for her to say the vows, she worried that marrying Asher might not be the answer.

"I knows you likes to hear what goes on 'round here," Kissie said in her unhurried voice.

Caramarena waited a few moments before she answered. She couldn't ask for a better pair of eyes or ears than Kissie's. "Yes, I guess that's true." Kissie lifted the petticoats and hoop over Caramarena's head and settled them around her waist, then tied the ribbons. Caramarena waited for Kissie to speak again, but she remained quiet. It wasn't like Kissie not to come right out and say what was on her mind. "Go on. Tell me what you heard."

Kissie made a long job of tying the petticoats. "Pearl told me Mr. Asher's clothes gots blood on 'em."

"What?" She spun around to face Kissie, the beautiful petticoats swirling around her legs. "Where is he?"

"Oh, not right now!" Kissie shook her head furiously. "She means in de wash. When she washes his clothes there's blood on his shirts and breeches."

Caramarena stood still. Blood. Cypress must have hurt him the other night when they were fighting. Or, did Cypress do something to him on the way to the smokehouse? The hair on the back of her neck bristled. No wonder Asher had spent most of his time the past week in his room and had barely spoken to her. One of her slaves had seriously injured him. And she expected him to marry her and give her a child. No wonder he hated her! Hadn't she told Cypress not to harm him? She'd have Cypress whipped. That would teach him and all the other slaves not to hurt anyone and to mind her orders.

With shallow breaths she demanded, "Kissie, what did Cypress do to Asher before he locked him in the smokehouse?"

"It ain't Cypress, Miss Cara," Kissie's eyes widened, her voice rose in pitch. "He ain't done nothin' to Mr. Asher, I swear. If'n yo' man's hurt, Cypress ain't the one did it."

Caramarena tapped her foot and her small hands circled her waist. Kissie picked up the wedding dress

103

and slipped it over her head. The soft, cream-colored silk slid down the petticoats and fell into luxurious folds at her feet. But Caramarena didn't have her mind on the wedding any more. She didn't trust Kissie to tell the truth when it came to Cypress. Hadn't she seen them in each other's arms? Hadn't she heard how quickly Kissie took up for him and he for her? No, when it came to Cypress, Caramarena wasn't prepared to believe her without question.

Kissie started on the buttons that ran up the back of the dress, while Caramarena worried about what to do. She would be expected downstairs in a few minutes, but she had time to get to the bottom of this.

"As soon as you finish my dress, Kissie, I want you to go find Cypress and bring him to me. I want to talk to him before the ceremony."

"I can't do dat, Miss Cara," she complained. "I gots to finish yo' hair and check to see if Lacy has Miss Bunch all purdy. You don't needs to talk to Cypress anyway. He won't tell you nothin'. I's already asked him. His mouth shut tighter than a turpentine barrel." She finished the last button and faced Caramarena. "It's Mr. Asher you needs to talk to. He'll tell you. Cypress ain't done nothing to him. I knows dat to be de truth."

Caramarena looked into Kissie's eyes. "Are you sure you're telling me the truth, Kissie? You're not taking up for Cypress because you're sweet on him, are you?" Her words demanded the truth.

"No, Miss Cara, dat don't have nothin' to do wid this. I swear. Cypress would rather hurt hisself than hurt yo' man."

The conviction Caramarena heard in Kissie's voice convinced her to turn around and let Kissie tie the satin bow at the small of her back. She took a deep

104

breath and pondered Kissie's gossip. Kissie was right, Asher was the one she should talk to. And—if she found out Kissie was covering for Cypress, she'd have them both whipped.

After a few moments she calmed down, and her thoughts turned in a different direction. She moistened her lips and asked, "Kissie, will I get to see Mr. Asher tonight?"

"I 'spect so. He'll be yo' husband."

"I mean—" She hesitated. "Without—his clothes." Caramarena couldn't believe she was blushing and stumbling over her words. "What I'm trying to say is, if I get to see him without his clothes then I'll know whether or not he's been seriously hurt."

"I don't rightly knows what white folks do, Miss Cara. But Pearl says yo' man bleeding on his chest and on de leg. And if'n Pearl say it, it true."

Caramarena sighed. "Kissie, I've told you his name is Mr. Asher. He is not to be referred to as 'my man.' Understand?"

"Yes'm." Kissie walked over and pulled out the chair in front of Caramarena's dressing table. "But I telling de truth jest the same, Miss Cara. Cypress ain't hurt Mr. Asher. No, he ain't. Something happened when dey's in town. I knows it. Cypress ain't been right since dey come back, neither, but he ain't talking. Lord knows I's tried to get him to tell me what makes him jumpy as a squirrel."

"You think Asher was hurt when they were in Apalachicola?" That possibility hadn't crossed her mind. But what could have happened? Since returning Asher had spent a lot of time in his room, using the excuse that he had to do a lot of paperwork to send to his brothers in London. She'd accepted that excuse without question. "Is Cypress hurt anywhere?" she asked.

Kissie shook her head. "Not dat I knows of. I's telling you Mr. Asher came back from town bleeding. I's sure of dat. But I don't knows why."

Caramarena lifted her skirts, took her place in front of the mirror and looked at herself. The bodice of her wedding gown had a heart-shaped neckline with pearls sewn along the top seam. The sleeves were short and puffy with a small satin bow sewn on the hem of each one. The full, beautiful skirt was lace over satin and dotted with pearls. Fanny and her helpers had worked night and day to finish the dress on time.

Caramarena's eyes were bright and her cheeks had a natural glow. The only thing that seemed to be missing was her smile. From deep inside, she'd find one when the time came. She lifted her shoulders a little higher.

Kissie picked up the hair brush and started arranging Caramarena's hair on top of her head. Fresh flowers from Live Oak's garden would make up her headpiece. Her bouquet was made of pale pink rosebuds.

While Kissie arranged her hair Caramarena pondered all the things the slave had told her. Why did Kissie have to wait to tell her this disturbing news just a few minutes before her wedding? Kissie was good at a lot of things, but today her timing was bad. How could she keep her mind on the ceremony when all she could think about was the possibility that Asher was hurt, bleeding? If that was indeed the case, she'd find out what was underneath Asher's clothes tonight even if she had to rip them off him.

Because of short notice the wedding guests were few, for which Caramarena was thankful. Asher said his vows with little affection. After the priest pronounced them husband and wife, Asher gave her a chaste kiss on the cheek and the small gathering clapped their approval.

Her father had made it through the ceremony looking better than she'd seen him in days. Bunch behaved beautifully, too. She seemed to love the excitement and the companionship of two younger girls who'd accompanied their parents to the wedding.

Caramarena noticed that Asher remained quiet and ate very little from the buffet table. When they danced he was extremely stiff, and he avoided her when she attempted conversation. She was convinced that Kissie was right and that Asher was indeed injured. She had failed to notice anything wrong before now because he'd spent so much time in his room the last few days.

After a short dance and kiss on the cheek her father excused himself and went up to bed. Two families were staying the night and Caramarena instructed Kissie and Ivy to stay up until the last guest had gone to bed. Then she went to find Asher. She was anxious to know what had happened to him. Besides, the guests wouldn't expect the bride and groom to stay up with them.

She found him sitting in a wingback chair talking to one of the guests. She waited until the man excused himself before she approached Asher.

"I think it's time we went upstairs," she said in a soft voice as she walked from behind his chair to stand before him.

"You're in a bit of a hurry to go to bed, aren't you, Caramarena?" he asked in a taunting voice, his gaze dark and brooding.

Caramarena stiffened, but quickly decided to overlook his crude remark. What she asked made her appear forward. He had no way of knowing that what she really wanted was to find out about his injuries.

"Maybe," she managed to say with a smile. She didn't want anyone who might be looking at them to think Asher wasn't being polite. "Kissie and Ivy will handle things down here and see that every guest is settled upstairs before they retire for the night."

"As usual, you've taken care of everything. Was there nothing your father didn't teach you how to do?" he asked.

Caramarena took a deep breath and squelched the urge to put him in his place. She reminded herself once again that he had been forced to marry her, and she had to make allowances for that. It was also apparent to her that he was indeed in pain. His lips had little color to them. His eyebrows were drawn together, forming a frown.

"If you'd like to remain here with your drink a little longer, by all means, please do. Contrary to what you're thinking, I am not eager to get into bed with you. It's been a long day and I'm tired." Her voice was crisp, and her eyes flashed with annoyance.

He chuckled lightly. "No, Caramarena, I will play the part of the dutiful husband tonight and lead you into our wedding chamber."

Asher rose from the chair and took her hand. A thrill of excitement ran up her arm when he touched her, and for a second, when their eyes met, she was sure he felt the same way.

"Why don't we give our guests something to talk about tonight as they retire to their rooms."

He placed his hands to each side of her face and pressed his lips to hers. The kiss was soft at first but with his tongue he gently forced her mouth open and slid it inside, exploring her warmth. Her hands automatically covered his. She swayed toward him. Caramarena's stomach muscles tightened as heat rushed up her cheeks. He tasted of brandy. Someone clapped behind them and yelled a bawdy remark.

Embarrassed, Caramarena pulled away from him and whispered, "You shouldn't have done that in front of our guests. It wasn't proper." However, to the small group of onlookers, she waved and smiled.

"Neither was the wedding, Caramarena," he said softly and took her hand again and headed for the stairs.

His cutting words caused a sharp pain in her chest, but she knew she had to keep up her facade for the guests. She kept a smile on her lips as she said goodnight to everyone they passed. When at last they entered her bedroom, she shut the door and the fake smile was dropped as quickly as an unwanted garment.

Asher went straight to the slipper chair and sat down, holding his side, she noticed.

A lighted candlestick stood on each side of the bed, giving the room a soft yellow glow. The covers had been turned back, revealing crisp white sheets and four fluffy pillows. The windows were open and a gentle breeze fanned the sheers, allowing the night air to cool the room.

Caramarena stood at the foot of the bed and watched Asher. He'd laid his head back and closed his eyes. She could still see a faint trace of the bruise under his eye. The swelling had gone from his lips but now that she looked at him closely she saw that he was pale beneath the dark beard. Curiosity and concern grew inside her, and she softened toward him.

When he looked up and saw her watching him he said, "You know, Caramarena, you are a very beautiful woman. That man who didn't marry you three

109

years ago was a damn fool."

She walked closer so she could see him better. "What kind of man does that make you? You didn't want to marry me either."

He laughed dryly, then winced. "Very good, Caramarena. You're absolutely right. I'm a fool for not wanting to marry you. I admit it."

Somehow that admission didn't make her feel any better. "Would you unlace me or should I ring for help."

"By all means allow me."

Although he tried to hide it, he winced again and held his side when he rose from the low, armless chair. Caramarena turned her back to him and wondered how to best approach the subject of his injuries. She felt his fingers fumbling with the small silk-covered buttons and knew he'd had too much to drink. What she didn't know was if he'd had too much to drink because he had been forced to marry her or if he was trying to ease the pain.

That thought worried her. This might be her wedding night but the marriage bed wasn't on her mind. She had to find out what had happened to Asher before she could think about anything else.

She turned and faced him. "Maybe I should be the one to undress you."

His eyes darkened for a moment before he answered, "Although it's a tempting suggestion, I'll pass. Turn back around and let me finish your dress."

Standing so close to him she could see the pain in his eyes, the tightness in his lips. "Is it because you don't want me to see that you're hurt, that you've been bleeding?"

His eyes narrowed and he took a step back. "I don't know what you're talking about."

His innocent act didn't fool her for a moment.

"Pearl has found bloodstains on your clothing."

Asher swore under his breath. "Do the damn slaves tell everything around here?"

"As far as I know," she said in an anxious tone. Now that he'd admitted he was hurt she wanted to help him. "What happened? Did Cypress hurt you the night—"

"No, no. Cypress didn't do anything but help me. In fact, he saved my life." He turned away and mumbled, "I need a drink."

"I think you've had quite enough for one night. Tell me what happened to you."

He took off his brown silk cravat and threw it on the chair. "It's nothing, forget it. Go to bed."

"Forget it? It's nothing?" Frustration caused her hands to make fists. "Then why are you trying to drink the pain away?"

"I'm not," he said angrily as he unbuttoned his waistcoat.

"Yes, you are," she countered, not willing to back down an inch.

He gave her a hard look. "Mind your own damn business, Caramarena. I didn't ask you to be my keeper."

"You are my business. You're my husband. I know you're hurt, now take off your shirt and let me see how bad it is."

Asher turned cold eyes upon her. Tension filled the air between them. He took a step toward her. "Caramarena, you may expect the slaves, Bunch and your father to obey your every command, but I will not. Is that understood?"

His harsh tone startled her, and she blinked rapidly. "Of course you're right." She cleared her throat. "I apologize. I do forget myself at times." She tried to take a deep breath but the corset was too tight. "May

I please see where you're wounded?" she rephrased softly.

He looked at her in disbelief for a moment, then chuckled. "You're so damned proper sometimes it hurts. All right. Hell, why not? The blasted cut isn't getting any better, and I'm tired of arguing with a woman who doesn't know when she's reached the limit of my patience."

Even with Caramarena's help he winced again when he shrugged out of his jacket and waistcoat. She helped him pull his shirt out of his breeches and unbutton it, showing his chest wrapped in white linen, a dark brown stain seeping through the cloth.

Without comment Caramarena helped him unwrap the cloth, which revealed a red and angry-looking cut about five inches long. The wound ran diagonally across his ribcage.

Caramarena gasped. "No wonder you're in pain. It's infected," she said looking up into his blue eyes. "What have you been putting on it, lye?"

"Don't be ridiculous or funny, Caramarena. I'm in no mood for it. I haven't put anything on it since the first night when my captain took care of it."

"Then that's why it's not healing. If Cypress knew about this he should have made you a poultice. Sit down." She quickly turned back around to him and added, "Please," but didn't wait to see if he obeyed.

Caramarena poured fresh water in the basin and from the chest below pulled out some clean bandages and a small box of ointments and salves.

"Is there nothing that you're not prepared for, wife?" he asked with a smirk when she knelt down in front of him with her box of supplies.

Caramarena ignored the leap in her heart when he called her wife. In any other circumstances it could have been an endearment. She tore off a strip of cloth, dipped it in the water and bathed the laceration.

The water stung but cooled Asher's heated skin. Her fingers were soft yet firm. And he realized, in this instance, he liked her taking charge.

Her half-unbuttoned dress slipped off her shoulder as she worked, showing the firm swell of her breasts. Asher's mouth went dry. He was going to have one hell of a time keeping his eyes and his mind off the fact that he had just married a very beautiful and exciting woman. He didn't know how he was going to get through the next few weeks in the same bed with her. Maybe the fact that his knife wounds hurt like hell would help arrest his desire for her tonight, but he didn't know what he'd do when they healed.

"Bunch often awakes in the middle of the night with imaginary aches and pains," she told him. "I learned a long time ago that it saved running up and down the stairs to have an assortment of medicines up here."

"Doesn't Lacy sleep in her room?" he asked, wondering if it were the brandy finally relaxing him or the soft touch of Caramarena's hand on his skin.

"Yes, but if she awakens, she usually wants me or Papa. And Papa is no longer able to sit with her."

Asher laid his head back and watched with hooded eyes as Caramarena's fingers dipped into the salve and spread it generously over the ugly cut. It hurt and felt good at the same time. The flowers in her hair were wilting. He had the urge to reach up and pull them out and free her golden brown hair. He wanted to see it hanging over her shoulders covering her beautiful skin. It took a moment for Asher to realize that his thoughts combined with the gentle strokes of Caramarena's hands on his chest had his manhood on the rise. He forced his eyes away from

113

her and moved to the edge of the chair.

"You might as well see to this one as well," he said and stretched out his leg. He tugged on the fabric of his breeches, pulling it up and over his boot to reveal an unsightly gash halfway up his leg. At the time of the fight he remembered thinking the cut on his side would give him the most trouble. It gave him no pleasure to have been right.

"My heavens! Asher, tell me what happened!" She looked up into his eyes again. "I'll have Cypress whipped for this."

"I told you Cypress didn't do this."

She placed a hand on his bare knee and asked in a concerned voice, "Then who? Tell me!"

He probably could have refused her if she hadn't placed her hand on his heated skin. Her touch was so soft it comforted him immediately. "All right, dammit," he said, thinking the only thing the brandy had done for him was give him a loose tongue. "When we were in town, I was waiting for Cypress down at the dock." He stopped and picked up her hand and moved it off his knee. It just felt too damn good and gave him ideas of wanting her to slip it higher.

"Go on and finish your task while I tell you the whole story," he said. The dress slipped a little farther, showing the top of her undergarments. He decided it wouldn't hurt to look.

"I talked with my captain on board *Sandor* while Cypress delivered the wedding invitations for you. I told him I would meet him back at the dock at dusk and we'd spend the night on my ship. Darkness fell and Cypress didn't show, but two men did. I guess I looked like easy prey because they pulled out their knives and jumped me. Cypress showed up just in time to save my life."

"Oh, thank God!" she gasped. "Was Cypress hurt?"

He shifted in the chair, groaning slightly. "No—but he killed one of the men."

"No," she whispered this time and her hand came up to cover her mouth. "Oh no, Asher tell me it isn't so!"

"Believe me, he's dead." He rubbed his forehead. "I didn't know whether or not the other man had lived until tonight. I heard some of the guests talking about the two men who were found down by the pier. One of them is still alive but it's going to take him a long time to recover. And naturally the authorities are looking for his brother's killer."

Caramarena moistened her dry lips. "Oh, thank God the other man is alive and that you and Cypress were not killed." She grabbed his hands and said, "You haven't told anyone else have you? No one must ever know about this. They would hang Cypress without question. It wouldn't matter that the man was a thief, or that he attacked you with a knife."

He squeezed her fingers, admiring her strength and her loyalty to the slave. "I know that, Caramarena. I've been in the South many times, and I know how slaves are treated. I've not said a word to anyone."

"Thank you," she whispered.

He grinned. "I couldn't very well turn in the man who'd just saved my life. And I told Cypress not to tell anyone about this, including you."

She shook her head and pulled her hand free as if just realizing they held hands. "Cypress hasn't. If he were going to tell anyone it would be Kissie. They're sweet on each other. I'm sure she would have told me if she knew." She wiped a generous amount of salve down his muscled leg, then reached

115

for a cloth to clean her hands.

"I'm sure of that too," Asher said dryly, remembering that because of Kissie he was now married to the woman tending his wounds. Of all the luck. Why did it have to be that the very slave he wanted to get rid of would be Cypress's sweetheart? He couldn't sell Cypress because that would be no way to repay the man for saving his life. And Cypress would try to kill him again if he hinted at selling Kissie. Damn it, he wasn't having any luck at all in this place.

"Just remember if anyone comes around asking questions—"

She looked up at him. "Don't worry. I know what to do. Your secret's safe with me." She wrapped the leg wound, even though Asher felt it was healing without problems.

"This will need to be done each morning and night until the redness is gone."

"I'm sure you won't let me forget. How long should that be?" He reached for her hand and helped her to stand.

She pushed her dress back up on her shoulder and Asher was sorry to lose the view. "A week at the most. Maybe less if you take proper care of it."

He nodded. "Turn around and let me finish unlacing you. Then I'll step out on the balcony for a while and give you time to get into your nightgown."

Caramarena did as she was told and didn't turn back around until she heard the French doors open and Asher step outside. She didn't know how much time she'd have, so she hurriedly discarded the dress, petticoats and undergarments and slipped a new, white cotton sleeveless nightgown over her head. As she tied the satin ribbon that held the bodice together into a neat little bow, she noticed her hands were trembling. She'd been so concerned for Asher

116

and Cypress she'd forgotten this was her wedding night. The night she'd truly become a woman. Taking a deep breath, she crawled onto the bed and settled back on the pillows.

According to Charlotte the wedding night was the worst. After that, being in her husband's bed was quite enjoyable, her sister had told her. Caramarena folded her hands together in her lap. Well, she already knew she enjoyed Asher's kisses so all she had to do was get through tonight. Her stomach muscles contracted at the very thought of her husband making her a woman and giving her a child.

A few minutes later she watched as Asher walked back into the room. She'd put out every candle except the one by her side of the bed. He'd discarded his shirt and she saw that his chest and arms were very muscular, his hips slim. She wondered what kind of work or exercise he'd done to be in such fine form.

"I thought you might be asleep by now," Asher said when he looked up and saw her staring at him.

"It wouldn't be very polite of me to fall asleep before you came to bed," she answered, thinking she liked the way her husband looked dressed only in his breeches.

No, but it sure would have been easier for him if she were already sleeping. "I thought you told me you were tired. That's the reason you were ready to come upstairs."

"That was a lie. I knew you were injured and I wanted to get you upstairs so I could see if you needed help."

He chuckled but didn't glance her way. He knew exactly how his next comment was going to make her feel, but he said it anyway. "Do you lie often, Caramarena?"

117

She gasped and answered with a quick, "No," paused and added, "Almost never." Her heartbeat accelerated. She didn't want him to think that she lied so easily. "I mean I may have once or twice," she hurried to say.

Asher picked up the nightshirt that Fanny had made him and threw it over his head. Usually he never slept in the things but tonight he needed all the help he could get to keep his hands off Caramarena. As his nightshirt fell to his knees, Asher plopped on the edge of the bed and took off his boots and socks. Then he stood and removed his breeches before looking over at his wife.

Her eyes were luminous with unshed tears. "I didn't mean to lie to you. I didn't really. I am tired—"

Asher reached over, patted her hand and smiled. "It's all right, Caramarena. I'm only teasing you."

She met his gaze with a defiant stare. "If that's true, I don't like the way you tease."

He liked her honesty. Damn, if this was a real marriage he'd love to—but it wasn't.

There was no doubt about it. He wanted her. He loved the way her thick brown hair fell over her shoulders. She looked so prim in her gown with the bow tied so prettily.

"I don't like the way I tease either." He climbed onto the bed and settled beside her.

"Did you intend to leave the door to the balcony open?" she asked.

"Yes, it will make it cooler in here. Do you mind?" He glanced over at her, and she shook her head.

Asher wasn't used to lying in bed with a desirable woman and not touching her. In the dim candlelight he looked at his wife. Caramarena's eyes were a beautiful shade of green, not too dark, and her hair, a glorious, golden brown, flowed over her shoulders. Her full lips had a well-defined shape and seemed to beg to be kissed. She smelled heavenly; she looked good enough to eat, too. He felt her warmth and it drew him. Oh God, he thought, this was going to be harder than he had ever imagined. How could he deny himself this woman for a night, maybe for months?

He closed his eyes and shored up his strength by remembering his father's strap across his back, the angry grimace that never left his father's face, the vow he'd spoken. He opened his eyes, looked over at his wife a second time and said, "Thanks for the healing salve. I feel better already."

Caramarena smiled sweetly. Her heart fluttered and her stomach tensed. This was it. He was going to take her in his arms and kiss her the way he had last week in the gold room. Once he kissed her, she was sure the nervous flutters would disappear just as they had that night.

Asher reached over, and without thinking she closed her eyes. But instead of kissing her lips, he gave her a very chaste kiss on her cheek. Her eyes popped open. Asher then blew out the candle that sat on her nightstand, cloaking the room in darkness.

Already tense, she was grateful for the cover of night, thinking this sort of thing was probably best done in the dark. She waited for Asher to pull her into his arms. She heard him settle himself on his pillows and sigh contentedly.

In the quiet darkness Caramarena stayed perfectly still and waited, thinking at any moment Asher was going to do something—after all, this was their wedding night. The minutes passed and Caramarena's body relaxed as Asher's breathing settled into a regular rhythm. He had fallen asleep. An hour later, she slid down her pillows and lay stiffly beside Asher.

This was not what she expected from her wedding night. Where were the wonderful kisses that had set her on fire a week ago? Where were the sweet words about her beauty, how good she felt in his arms, how much he wanted to love her? Where was the joining of man and woman?

Caramarena wasn't exactly sure what was supposed to happen, but one thing she knew for sure—the perfunctory kiss on the cheek was not going to get her pregnant.

She tried to console herself by remembering that his cuts were causing him a lot of pain. He'd drunk quite a bit of brandy, too. Surely that was the reason he'd fallen asleep so quickly. But another thought kept returning. Asher may have been forced to marry her, but no matter how much she might want it no one could force him to take her in his arms and make her a woman.

Finally convinced he was not going to claim her as his bride, she turned over and fell asleep.

Chapter Eight

The next morning Caramarena presented a happy face to her father and Bunch, but as soon as the guests boarded their carriage her smile disappeared. She stood on the porch and waved as the last carriage started down the driveway, thankful to be out from under watchful eyes.

In all the hustle and bustle of breakfast and good-byes, Caramarena had managed to convince herself that Asher had disappointed her on their wedding night only because he was still angry he'd been forced to marry her. She tried to soothe and reassure herself; he'd get over it in a few days and be a proper husband.

Asher had already dressed and left the bedroom when she'd awakened. When she came downstairs he had remained by her side until the guests started to leave, then excused himself. She couldn't fault him for his manners in front of her family and friends.

"I didn't want them to go away." Bunch said from behind her.

Caramarena turned, put her arm around her sister and smiled. Warm morning sunshine fell across their faces. The skies were a striking shade of blue dotted with floating, white, puffy clouds. Birds chirped in the surrounding live oaks. "You enjoyed playing with those little girls, didn't you?" she asked.

121

Bunch nodded. Caramarena desperately wanted to give Bunch a little niece or nephew to play with. In time, she told herself. It was going to take Asher time to get over the forced marriage. Time to get used to the idea of being married. She just hoped he didn't leave for England until she was pregnant.

"Miss Cara."

Caramarena glanced over her shoulder and said, "Yes, Ivy?"

"Mr. Asher. He in de office and say he want to see you."

Her chest tightened and that angered her. She couldn't tense every time his named was mentioned. "Tell him I'll be right there, Ivy." She looked at Bunch and smiled again. "What are you going to do today?" she asked, tying a ribbon on the front of her sister's dress.

Bunch pouted and shook her head, sending honey blond curls flying across her shoulders. Caramarena knew she was not happy to see her friends leave. "Are you going to help Ivy make sweet cakes or help Kissie cut fresh flowers?"

She shook her head more furiously, brushed away from Caramarena's gentle hand and said, "I don't like you."

Caramarena wanted to calm Bunch before she got too upset. "Well, you don't have to do either one. You can come with me to talk to Asher. We can tell him about your new doll." She reached for Bunch's hand but she snatched it away.

"No! I don't like him." Tears welled up in her eyes, her nose turned red. "I don't like you for sending my friends away. That was a mean thing to do!"

"Bunch, they had to go back home," Caramarena said in a soft crooning voice, trying to explain. "We'll invite them to come again very soon, I promise."

"No! I'm going to tell Papa you sent them away." She spun around and ran into the house, slamming the door behind her.

Caramarena sighed deeply, knowing Bunch would be all right in a little while. She usually got over her temper tantrums very quickly, and she never remembered them.

She touched her hair with her hands. As she'd thought, all the good-bye hugs had pulled wisps of hair from her neatly coiled bun. She smoothed them as best she could and headed for the office, wondering what Asher wanted. As she entered the room she was surprised to find him sitting at her desk. Although she found that odd, she decided not to say anything.

"You wanted to see me?" she asked, walking into the room, her full sunflower-colored dress swishing around her legs.

He pushed the chair back and looked up at her. "Yes, I was hoping you would go over some of the workings of the plantation with me, help me get to know how Live Oak works."

Caramarena stared at him for a moment. He looked more handsome, more relaxed and cooler in the collarless shirts Fanny had made for him. She'd always thought him a handsome man but now she realized he was even more so without those stuffy high-collared shirts and cravats he always wore.

She realized he was waiting for an answer so she cleared her throat and said, "Uh—that surprises me." She walked further into the room.

"Because I want to know about the plantation? This is going to be my home. I should know more about it," he answered.

She moistened her lips and clasped her hands behind her back. He had assumed a businesslike manner and she had to reply in kind. "I thought you'd only

123

stay long enough to marry me, then be on your way back to your travels and your life in England."

His lips widened and she couldn't decide if he were grinning or smiling. "Your father did offer me the option of returning to England immediately after the ceremony, and I do appreciate that—but I've decided to stay here, for a time at least, and get to know Live Oak and how it works."

Thank God, she thought, maybe there would be time for her to get pregnant before he left. But she also felt a twinge of disappointment. He'd said he was staying because he wanted to get to know Live Oak, with no mention of getting to know her better. She could only hope and pray that in time he would forgive her for the reason they married.

"I will be going back into Apalachicola in a few days to see *Sandor* sail."

"You won't go to the docks after dark, will you?" she asked, a worried expression on her face.

"Have no fear about that, Caramarena. I don't like being sliced with a knife."

"Did you dress your wounds this morning?" she asked.

He gave her an appreciative smile. "Yes. I'm happy to report they look much better today."

Nodding, she walked behind the desk and stood before him. "What do you want to know about Live Oak?"

"Everything," he answered casually.

Caramarena wasn't sure what it was but something in his eyes, and the way he'd said *everything* made her uncomfortable. It was the same expression he gave her when he agreed to her father's demand of marriage. He was trying too hard to appear calm and natural. Why was he all of a sudden so interested in Live Oak that he didn't want to sail with his ship? She would

124

have liked to think it was her, but last night had proved that wasn't the case.

He must have picked up on her studying him because he added, "I can't have my wife knowing more about the plantation than I do. Can I?"

"I guess not," she admitted, but still had doubts about his reasons. "However, it's not something you can learn in a few days. I'm not sure where you should start first."

"How about the account books?" he asked, looking up at her, this time definitely grinning.

A smile broke across her face even though she tried to stop it. She thought it amusing that a man should worry that his wife might know more than him. She knew it to be true that most men wanted a wife who took care of their house and children and very little else. Well Asher couldn't take her knowledge away from her, but if he wanted to learn, she'd teach him. It might make him forget about England and stay at Live Oak with her. That thought brought her up short. Did she want him to stay? No. Yes. She didn't know any more. And why did Asher want to learn about the plantation? Could he be thinking he would give up his life in England and live here with her?

Fancy, foolish, notions, she berated herself, and she returned her attention to the matter at hand. If she was going to be his teacher she might as well play the part.

Feeling quite confident in her ability and her position, she said, "All right. The first thing you should learn is *that* is my chair. The one on the other side of the desk will be yours until you can manage the plantation." She enjoyed watching the fleeting moment of shock cross his face. He hid it quickly and that pleased her.

"I do beg your pardon," he said and rose from the

chair, holding it out for her. "The manager of Live Oak should most certainly have this chair."

Quite satisfied, she took the chair and Asher settled himself in a burgundy-colored armchair opposite her. She studied him, trying to decide how best to tell him about the plantation.

"Perhaps first, I should tell you that when Papa started teaching me, I already knew many things that you do not."

Asher hadn't realized just how smart and astute his wife was. She was all softness and beauty on the outside, but she also knew how to put him in his place.

He took a deep breath and made himself comfortable in the chair. Running a plantation couldn't be too different from running a shipping industry, and he certainly knew how to do that. If you had organization, chances were that you'd have harmony. If your workers were happy, they produced.

"I've visited and spent time on many plantations over the last ten years. I think I have a general idea of how they work."

She smiled indulgently, but didn't let her back touch the chair. "A general idea will not get you through one day."

Her tone wasn't boastful, just truthful. He liked that. How a woman who looked so soft and feminine could be a tough businesswoman, too, he didn't know. She would have him in her clutches again if he wasn't careful. She was beautiful, intelligent, desirable, and his wife. Damn, he had to be careful before he made the possibility of an annulment impossible.

"All right," he said. "For now I will agree with you, but I reserve the right to change that when this conversation is over. Prove to me that I don't have enough general working knowledge to run this plantation."

"Certainly." She laced her fingers together and laid

126

her hands on the desk in front of her. "Now, when Papa started teaching me how to manage the accounts, I already knew every slave by name, their age, their occupations, and their status. I also knew how much food it took to feed them for a week and how much cloth to clothe them. I was familiar with what acreage was in fields, woods, swamps and orchards, as well as what crop was to be planted, the best field to plant it in and the time of year to plant. I knew how many bushels of corn to expect from an acre and how long it would take a field hand to pull it. I knew—"

"Hold it." He held up his hand. "You made your point. I do have a lot to learn."

He sat back in his chair and looked at her. It appeared he was going to have to learn the basics before she'd let him get near the account books. And he couldn't start draining the bank accounts until she trusted him. She wasn't going to do that until she was satisfied he knew what he was doing.

Asher already respected this woman, now he truly admired her. She was smart. But he found that all this pulled at his heartstrings. It was quite apparent she loved Live Oak. He'd make it up to her, he told himself. He didn't know how, or when, but somehow he would make it up to her for destroying her home.

"I can see I've got a lot to learn," he said again. "How much work does your father actually do these days?"

"Papa mostly negotiates and signs contracts and checks. For some reason most men do not like dealing with a woman."

"Yes, that's a problem in England as well." He could understand it if most women were as intelligent as Caramarena. She could show up many men when it came to knowing how to conduct a business session. She was a perfect example of how intelligent some

127

women were. And because of that he had to be very careful. She wouldn't be easy to fool.

"One thing you should also know is that we're basically self-sufficient here. We grow everything we eat, we make our own clothes, we have our own iron smith and cobbler as well as our own church. We also have our own laws." She paused, then added, "None of them contradicts the laws of the state." She smiled. "I guess a good way to say it is, for the most part, if we need it we make it. Of course there are always exceptions like furniture and fabrics such as silk."

"I never realized just what a magnificent arrangement the plantation is." His comment had nothing to do with what he was thinking. He was wondering how he was going to stay away from this woman, his wife. She titillated him with her very presence. She smelled good, looked good, and he knew she was eager to become a woman. But—he had to keep his distance. He had to learn the plantation to destroy it, and he couldn't have Caramarena upsetting his plan. His desire for her would be his downfall if he wasn't careful.

"Well, I think it's probably too late today to begin, but first thing tomorrow morning I'll start learning the slaves' names, ages, occupations and status. By status I assume you mean free or bond?"

"It could mean that but that wasn't my reference, no. We have no freemen on Live Oak. By status I meant whether they are house, yard, field or skilled in a trade. For instance, Kissie is a house slave and Cypress is a yard slave. And in case you're wondering, we treat our slaves very well here. We've only had three whippings that I can remember."

Asher's mind drifted back to the past when she spoke of whippings, bringing with it the sting of his father's leather strap on his back. He closed his eyes for a moment. Only three whippings in all her lifetime, when he used to get three a month. He rubbed his eyes, his forehead, his temples. He hated remembering those times.

He looked up at her and caught her watching him intently. Suddenly he had the urge to tell her what he was thinking. He must be going crazy. He cleared his throat. "I see. Well, I should be well enough to ride in a couple of days. I'll start learning the acreage."

"Are you sure the cuts are better? You had a look of pain on your face just now."

Asher saw the concern in her eyes and appreciated it. No wonder he'd wanted to confide in her. She seemed to want to comfort him. "Much better, thanks to your careful ministrations last night. I added more salve this morning. Now, I find that I can move much easier, so it appears that at last it is healing."

"I'm glad to hear that. I see you're wearing your new clothes. How do you like them?" she asked.

Asher looked down at his collarless cotton shirt, then looked up her and smiled. "I don't know how I lived with the others for so long."

She laughed lightly. "I thought as much. I don't know how you survived for almost two weeks in this heat."

He chuckled with her. "Neither do I. It wasn't easy, believe me." The only thing that bothered Asher about the new shirts was that the lower part of his neck wasn't as dark as his face. As hot as the sun was in this part of the world, though, his neck should be as dark as his face in less than a week.

"Oh there you are."

Asher stiffened at the sound of Cantrell's voice. He didn't like Cantrell interrupting his light conversation with his wife, either. He'd stayed as far away from the man as possible the last week. Asher considered himself lucky that Cantrell spent so much time in his room.

"Papa, come join us," said Caramarena, waving him inside. "Asher and I were just talking about Live Oak."

"No, dear. Not now. Hello, Asher."

Cantrell's greeting was toneless but Asher didn't mind. He didn't want the man to be friendly. Asher mumbled a return greeting, and Cantrell turned his attention back to his daughter. "Anything going on I should know about?"

"We received a letter saying the horses we ordered should be here by week's end, and the corn is being stored for the winter."

"Good. You have everything under control. I just wanted to tell you that Ivy has taken Bunch for a walk, in case you looked for her later."

She nodded.

"Now that all the guests are gone I'm going to rest. I'll see you at dinner, Caramarena. Good day, Asher."

He turned and left as quietly as he appeared.

A loving smile appeared on Caramarena's face. "Papa has been so much better the past few days. I think the wedding has been good for him. It forced him to get out and do things and not spend so much time in his room. Didn't you think he was looking better?" She turned her sparkling green eyes on Asher.

Asher wanted to tell her the truth. Her father didn't look any better, in fact he looked worse. But he didn't want to be the one to take the beautiful smile off her face, so he lied. "Yes, he's looking fit," he said, knowing that was what she wanted to hear.

Slivers of moonlight shone through the small curtainless window and fell across the foot of the bed. Night sounds drifted into the room with the wind. A bullfrog croaked, crickets chirped and occasionally an

130

owl would call hauntingly to his mate.

The night breeze felt good to her heated, naked skin as Kissie lay on the cotton-ticked mattress, quietly listening to Cypress's uneven breathing.

"Has dat ever happened to you befo'?" she finally asked when she couldn't bear the silence any more.

"No," he answered solemnly. "I's sorry, Kissie. I guess I's gettin' old."

"Hush yo' mouth! You ain't old. You jest tired. You been working too hard."

His deep sigh let her know he didn't believe her any more than she believed herself. But she didn't believe his explanation as to why he'd failed to complete their union, either.

Kissie raised up and with what little light the moon afforded looked down at Cypress. He was a big man. Smart too. His dark brown skin was shiny and healthy, his firm muscles bulging. His eyes were bright with knowledge and his own self-worth. No. Age had nothing to do with what bothered Cypress. But Kissie had a feeling she knew what had. It had to do with the reason Mr. Asher had been hurt—and it happened in Apalachicola.

She took a deep breath and said, "I wants ta know what happened when you went ta town with Mr. Asher."

"Nothin'," he said too quickly, his eyes darting to her face to find out what was written there.

Kissie hadn't lived forty-four years without learning a few tricks along the way. She put her hands on Cypress's shoulder and the bottom of her feet against his thigh and with one swift push shoved him off the bed.

"What yous doin'—Damn!" he said as he thumped to the wood floor. "Kissie, what you do dat for?" he asked, picking himself off the floor.

She raised up on her knees in the middle of the bed.

"I ain't gonna have no lying darkie in my bed. Get on outta heah and don't show yo' face around my house no mo'."

"What's you mean? Everyone knows I'm yo' man." He finally managed to get to his feet and look down at her.

"I ain't lied ta you and I won't have you lying ta me. Get yo'self on outta heah." She scrambled off the bed and picked up his breeches and threw them at him. His shirt followed, and then one of his work boots hit him on the chest.

"Kissie, stop dis," he pleaded, holding his clothes in front of him as he caught them.

"What happened in dat town?" she demanded.

"I tol' you—"

She let go of the other boot, but he was expecting it this time and dropped his clothes to catch it.

"Kissie, I's getting tired of dis." His voice was low, showing that his anger was barely held in check.

Her skin glistened from sweat. She climbed up on the bed and snapped her hands to her waist, feeling better when she was taller than him. "Get outta heah you lying darkie befo' I calls for help. I don't needs—"

Cypress grabbed her arm, shoved her back down on the bed and pounced on top of her. She squealed and reached up and slapped his face hard before he could pin both her hands.

He grunted from the stinging slap. "Stop dis befo' I hurts you, Kissie."

"Get off me, you lying fool," she bumped and kicked beneath his weight. "Go gets you a woman dat likes lies." She brought her leg up and tried to knee him. She dug her nails into the back of his palms. He groaned and slipped his hands lower on her wrists but didn't let go.

"What got into you?" he asked, panting as he tried

132

to subdue her.

Her breathing was labored as she continued to struggle. She knew she couldn't best him in a fight, but she wanted him to know where they stood with each other. If he couldn't confide in her, she didn't want him.

When she could hold out no longer, Kissie calmed and lay motionless beneath him, giving him false hope. She looked into his eyes, black as midnight, just inches from hers. "I won't have you lying ta me."

Cypress had calmed down, too. "Mr. Asher made me promise not ta tell no one, Kissie."

"Dat don't include me, Cypress. Not if'n I'm yo' woman. He 'spects you ta tell me."

He took a deep breath, his body hard and heavy upon her. "I don't think so. Not dis."

"Then I wants you ta leave." She left him no choice.

"All right. I'll tell. But you gots to promise not to tell another living soul."

At last she was breathing easier. "You knows you don't got to tell me dat." She reached up and touched his cheek with her hand. The beard growth tickled her palm. Her eyes softened.

Cypress held his weight off her by resting on his elbows. "Mr. Asher sent me ta deliver de wedding invites and told me ta meets him at sundown. I has trouble finding one of de houses so I's late. When I got to de dock two white men is all over him. One of de men got a knife and the other wuz holding Mr. Asher so's the other could slice him. Mr. Asher wuz already bleeding so I grabs de man wid de knife and I kilt him."

Fear embedded itself deep in Kissie's heart, and suddenly she was shaking. "No, Cypress, no! Tell me you didn't kill him."

His arms slid under her back and tightened around her. "I didn't mean to, Kissie. It jest happened."

"They's gonna hang you fo' sho'." She circled his neck with her arms, pulling him close, her body trembling with fear.

"I had ta do somethin'. He'd already cut up Mr. Asher and the other was holding him so's he could slash him some mo'."

"What happened to the one holding Mr. Asher?"

"I don't know. I left him lying on de ground, but he breathing when we left."

Tears collected in Kissie's eyes. "Oh, Cypress, you gots ta run away. They'll find out it's you what done it. You knows Mr. Asher don't like you."

He looked down into her tear filled eyes. "He won't tell, Kissie. He told me not ta say a word no matter who be asking. I bet he'd whup me if'n he knowed I told you."

Fear caused Kissie to remain firm. "Dat man'll change his mind de first time you make him mad and he'll tell on you. We can't trust him. You gots ta run."

"Naw, Kissie, you gots to trust me on dis. And I gots to trust Mr. Asher."

He kissed her forehead, then let his lips move down her cheek, wiping the tears with his tongue. He found her mouth and joined it with his.

"Oh, Kissie you is my woman," he murmured softly. "Don't scare me like dat again."

"I's sorry fo' kickin' you outta bed. I knew somethin' was botherin' you mighty bad. I's worried, Cypress. We'll tell Miss Cara, she know what ta do."

He shook his head. "No. Mr. Asher said no one. Now I told you and dat enough ta know. No need ta worry her 'bout dis."

Kissie thought about it for a while and then nodded. "All right. Long as no one comes 'round askin' questions we'll take it ta our grave, but anyone start snoopin' and we gots ta tell her. I won't let nothin' happen ta you."

"I loves you, Kissie," he whispered as he buried his face in the crook of her neck and fit the lower part of his body next to hers.

Kissie felt her heart swell. Although he'd told her many times that he loved her, she'd never responded in kind, preferring to let him wonder. Tonight he needed to know. She gently rubbed the back of his neck and turned her mouth to whisper in his ear, "I loves you, Cypress."

His head popped up and he looked deeply into her eyes. "You mean dat, Kissie?"

She smiled and nodded. "I means it. I loves you."

He kissed her long and hard. His large hand closed over her breast and cupped it gently. Kissie moaned.

After a few moments he raised from the kiss and asked, "Does dis means you gonna marry me and lets me live here wid you?"

"You a greedy man, Cypress." She laughed suggestively as her hand slipped between them and found his manhood. He was hard and ready. "We's gonna take one thing at time. And right now, dis is what I wants." She squeezed him.

Cypress sighed as she guided him inside. Their bodies joined, their tongues tangled, their hands worshiped.

Kissie felt very lucky to have Cypress as her man.

Caramarena wasn't happy and she didn't know how long she could pretend to be. No one could fault Asher, he was a perfect gentleman. For the past week she'd spent many hours with him teaching him about the plantation. He was quick and eager to learn about everything — except her.

She sat at her desk and watched Asher studying.

Earlier, when they'd been looking over the documents together, she had felt his breath fan her cheek, she'd smelled his masculine scent and felt his warmth. For a moment she had desperately wanted to reach over and touch him. But she kept those feelings to herself. Until he made a move, she had to remain quiet.

Each night after dinner he'd read for a while, then go down to the river for a swim, sometimes staying late. He'd quietly slip into the bedroom, thinking she was asleep. She wasn't. She kept waiting for her husband's touch, which never came. He always smelled so fresh after his swim. Sometimes when he turned in the bed a drop of water from his damp hair would land on her heated skin and she longed to feel his cool body next to hers.

Since her wedding night, she hadn't even received a kiss on the cheek. His side had healed so she knew it wasn't pain keeping him from her. She had ceased to worry about getting pregnant; now she worried about getting her husband's attention. Surely it wasn't natural for a man to wait so long to consummate the marriage. She'd given herself many excuses over the past few days. He was still angry. He wanted to reserve the right to annul the wedding. Worst of all was when she suspected he simply wasn't interested in her as a woman.

His only interest in her seemed to be in her knowledge of the plantation. That was the only thing he was hungry for. Each night her hopes sagged a little more as he continued to ignore her. Maybe it was time to admit he simply didn't desire her. But every time she told herself that, she remembered the night he kissed her so passionately. He had wanted her then. She was sure of that. It had to be something else.

"Miss Cara, Mr. Wulpher sent word dat dem ho'ses you bought are here. Dey's puttin' 'em in de corral

136

down by de grain bins."

She pushed back from her desk. "Oh, thank you for telling me, Ivy. I'll go down immediately."

"Yes'm. You be wanting to ask 'em to stay for dinah?"

"No, I don't think so. Just plan on the family." She turned to Asher and asked, "Would you like to come?"

He closed the ledger with a snap. "I wouldn't miss it."

Bunch was sitting on the top step of the front porch when they walked out. She jumped up and showed Asher her doll. "Do you want to hold her?" she asked.

Asher smiled. "I'm not very good with holding dolls, Bunch. I'm afraid I might hurt her."

A pout formed on her lips. "You don't like her."

"No, that's not true," he said honestly. "She's very pretty." He glanced at Caramarena as if asking for help. "We're on our way to see the new horses that are being delivered."

"Can I go?" Bunch asked, excitement lighting her face.

"Bunch, you know you're not allowed down by the corral. You'll have to stay here." Caramarena spoke softly to her sister as usual.

Bunch threw her doll into one of the rockers and said, "I don't ever get to go see the horses. It's not fair, Cara. You get to do everything."

"I've got to check and make sure these are the horses Papa ordered. I won't have time to watch you."

Asher extended his hand toward Bunch. "You can go with me, Bunch. I'll take care of you."

"Asher." Caramarena looked at him, her green eyes sparkling with surprise. What had made him go against her wishes?

"Caramarena, what harm is there in letting her see the new horses? I'm sure she wants to get away from the house once in a while as much as anyone else. Don't treat her like a prisoner."

"A prisoner?" she gasped. "I've never." She tried not to show how badly his comment hurt her. He simply didn't realize how closely Bunch had to be watched.

Bunch recognized a friendly hand when one was extended, so she fit her hand inside his and gave him a beautiful smile. Caramarena knew further argument was useless.

"All right," she conceded, giving Asher a firm look. "But don't let her out of your sight."

The three of them started toward the corral. When they arrived twelve horses were running around in the corral snorting and stomping crazily, kicking up dust.

"Why are they angry?" Bunch asked somewhat fearfully.

"They're getting used to their new home," Asher told her. "They're wild and don't like to be fenced in." He turned to Caramarena. "Why didn't you buy horses already broken?"

"Papa always buys wild ones. He says he prefers them to be broken here so we know what kind of horse we're getting."

She walked closer to the fence and as best she could, with their wild stomping, counted to make sure the right number had been delivered. It was apparent there was one stallion and eleven mares. Just what had been ordered. And the stallion was not happy. He'd stop and paw the earth several times, raising dust, then gallop around the corral again.

She walked over to Mr. Wulpher and Mr. Burrel, the man who had delivered the horses, to sign the release papers. Bunch and Asher followed.

"The horses look fine to me, Mr. Burrel." She looked up at the man. He was a heavyset, bearded man who wore his hat low over his forehead, hiding his eyes.

"Yes, ma'am. We only sell the best."

She smiled. "I can see that." She turned to Mr. Wulpher, who stood watching the wild horses. "Mr. Wulpher, see that hay is thrown in for the horses. Maybe it will settle them down."

"I'll do it right now," he said, tipped his hat and left.

"If you have the papers ready I'll sign them, and you can be on your way, Mr. Burrel."

The man sniffed and pulled his pants up and over his bulging waistline. "I'd rather your pa sign them, if you don't mind, Miss Cantrell," he said nervously.

Caramarena lifted her hand to shield her eyes from the bright sunlight and looked up at the man again. "Papa is resting. I really don't want to disturb him. There won't be a problem with me signing the papers, I assure you."

"Yes ma'am. I'm sure you think it's all proper and legal, but just the same, I'd prefer to wait on your pa. You know how it is," he added, clearing his throat.

Her back stiffened. She lifted her chin a little higher. Yes, she knew how it was, but she didn't like it.

Asher had heard enough. He knew it was embarrassing for Caramarena to be treated this way when she was perfectly capable of signing the damn papers. She was smarter than this man ever would be. He let go of Bunch's hand and stepped forward. "Perhaps I could sign for Mr. Cantrell. I'm Caramarena's husband, Asher Millhouse." The two men shook hands and greeted each other politely.

"Where are you from, Mr. Millhouse?"

"England. London. But Live Oak is my home now." He put his arm around Caramarena's shoulder to emphasize the fact.

"Well, if you're part of the family. I guess it'll be all right for you to sign." He wiped his nose on his sleeve while he thought about it. Finally he said, "Sure, it's

139

fine with me." He reached into his pocket for the papers.

Asher held the papers in his hand for a moment, staring at them. He realized what this meant. This was the start to taking over Live Oak. This would show Caramarena that business people would accept him a lot easier than they would her and give him greater access to the plantation's records.

He quickly signed his name and handed the papers to the smiling man. The sound of hooves splintering wood caused all three of them to turn and look at the corral. The stallion had started pawing the top rail of the fence, and two mares were helping while the others screamed and whinnied their approval. As the wood split away Asher and Caramarena looked for Bunch at the same time. She had wandered away from them and was in the path of the horses should they jump the fence.

"Bunch!" They both yelled her name, and Asher started running toward her.

"Get a rope and collar the stallion!" Caramarena shouted to Mr. Burrel as she lifted her skirts and followed Asher.

Caramarena watched the corral as she ran. Fear for her sister's safety increased when the top board fell away and the stallion leapt over the rest of the fence to freedom, the mares right behind him. Bunch stood frozen in fear as the wild horses charged in her direction. Caramarena screamed for Bunch to run, but she didn't move. Terror filled her at the thought of Bunch and Asher being trampled by the surging horses.

Asher scooped up Bunch on the run as the flank of a passing mare knocked him to the ground. He held on to Bunch and rolled them as fast as he could, hoping to keep them away from the thundering hooves of the mares as they passed by. When he heard the stomping pass, Asher rose to his trembling knees and cradled Bunch in his arms. She was crying softly.

"I'm sorry, Bunch," he whispered and kissed her forehead. He brushed the dried grass from her hair. "I'm sorry, I forgot to look after you."

A swirl of peach-colored skirts settled around him as Caramarena fell on the ground beside them. He looked into her tear filled eyes and knew he'd let her down. He'd endangered Bunch's life. A lump formed in his throat.

"Is she hurt?" Caramarena asked in a frightened voice.

"I don't know," he said, not wanting to give up his hold on the sobbing girl. He wanted to comfort her. He wanted to make it all right. It was his fault.

Caramarena brushed Bunch's hair back so that she could see her face. "Bunch," she whispered in a shaky voice. "Are you all right? Are you hurt?"

At the sound of her sister's voice, Bunch scrambled out of Asher's embrace and flung herself in Caramarena's waiting arms, wailing loudly. Caramarena had seen enough to know that Bunch's arms were scratched and her lips were bleeding.

"I told you we shouldn't bring her!" Fear turned to anger, making her words harsh and accusing. "She can't take care of herself."

"I know." He shook his head. "I'm sorry. I didn't realize how—"

"She has to be watched at all times." Her bottom lip trembled, and for the first time she noticed the expression on Asher's face. He was shaken, too. How thoughtless of her to lash out at him when he risked his life to save Bunch.

"I know I should have listened to you. It's my fault. I—"

"No," she whispered, interrupting him. "I'm the one

141

who's sorry." She held Bunch tighter. "I should be thanking you for saving her life. I didn't mean to speak to you that way. I was just so frightened." Caramarena tried to tell him with her eyes how sorry she was.

Asher nodded. "Let's take her home and get her cleaned up so we can see how badly she's hurt."

Asher grunted when he stood, realizing he had a few bruises himself, then reached and helped Caramarena and Bunch to stand as Mr. Burrel came running over to help.

"Is she all right?" he asked, a worried expression on his round, reddening face.

"She's going to be fine," Asher said. "You and your men take off after those horses."

"Sure thing, Mr. Millhouse."

"I want Papa," Bunch wailed, clinging to Caramarena as if she were drowning.

Asher berated himself as he looked at the frightened young woman clinging so desperately to her sister. Over Bunch's shoulder Caramarena looked into Asher's eyes. "Are you hurt?" she asked in a voice thick with emotion.

He shook his head, wondering how she could possibly be worried about him with Bunch hysterical. He reached over and touched Bunch's hair. "It's all right, Bunch," he said softly. "It's over. Would you like for me to carry you to your Papa?" he asked.

She sniffled loudly but didn't answer. When he touched her shoulder she turned into his embrace and wrapped her arms around his neck. He pulled her slim body up close. Anger tore at him. Caramarena had told him she had to be watched, but he was too damn interested in those papers. Too interested in his plan.

He glanced at Caramarena. Dirt smudged her face and dress and tears glistened in her eyes, making them sparkle like emeralds. He swung Bunch up in his arms, wishing he had four arms so he could carry them both. He turned and headed toward the house, knowing without a shadow of a doubt that he cared what happened to Bunch. Already he felt as if she were his sister.

Chapter Nine

It took the rest of the afternoon and the early part of the evening for Caramarena and her father to get Bunch calm enough to fall asleep. As far as they could tell, she had only minor scratches and bruises which they tended to with loving care.

Caramarena hadn't seen Asher since before dinner when he came up to check on Bunch. With the hour as late as it was she assumed he'd gone for his nightly swim. She had Lacy and Ivy prepare her a bath in her bedroom. While she sat in the round tub she realized she envied Asher's freedom to go down to the river and swim in the cool water. If they had a different relationship she would be tempted to join him. After her bathwater had been carried out she sat in bed, dressed in her white sleeveless nightgown, and thought over the events of the day.

Asher had been wonderful in his rescue of Bunch. Even though he'd been knocked down by one of the horses he'd rolled Bunch to safety. She'd always be grateful for that. Now that she took the time to really think about Asher she realized it was no wonder he had no kind feelings toward her. He'd been caught kissing her and was forced to marry her even after he made it clear he didn't want to. He'd been waiting for Cypress when he'd been jumped by the two robbers and knifed, and now he'd endangered his own life by saving her sister

144

from the runaway horses. How could she expect him to ever want to be her husband and live at Live Oak with her when nothing good had happened to him since he arrived?

She rose from the bed, opened the French doors to the balcony, went out and leaned against the rail. Caramarena felt heavy with guilt. The air was humid, the moon a slice of silver hanging in the dark sky. The damp air caused her long hair to cling to the back of her neck. In the distance she heard the faint sound of one of the slaves singing. His voice, deep and smooth, soothed her more than the warm bath.

As she looked out at the darkness she decided she should tell Asher the truth about the night he'd kissed her. Their marriage certainly wasn't working this way. She wasn't happy and she didn't think Asher was either. She'd tell him about the trap she and Kissie had plotted and how Kissie had carried through with it when she'd seen them kissing. After admitting she trapped him into marrying her, she'd tell him he was free to get an annulment and go back to his life in England. She'd known it wasn't right to deceive him in order to have an heir for Live Oak, but at the time she'd thought it would work and do no real harm. Now she was beginning to like Asher too much to want to treat him in such a manner.

Caramarena closed her eyes and breathed in the hot night air. She'd known Asher only a short time, but it wouldn't be easy to watch him walk out of her life.

She remembered the fear in Asher's eyes when he saw Bunch in danger. His strong arms had circled her and held her close. She saw his hands as they tenderly brushed Bunch's hair away from her face and she saw the kisses he placed on her forehead. With her eyes still closed she remembered what it was like to feel his hands upon her, his arms around her, his kisses. . . .

"How's Bunch?"

Caramarena's eyes popped open and her heartbeat

145

raced as she turned and saw Asher standing in the open doorway. His shirt was off, showing his muscled chest. She liked the way his pants rode low on his hips and the casual way he leaned one shoulder against the door frame. In the shadowed light she could see his dark hair, damp from his swim. The muscles in his arms and chest were pumped up from the swimming. He looked so good she wanted to run and throw her arms around him and be comforted the way she had seen him comfort Bunch.

Silently she berated herself for being jealous of the way Asher held her sister.

She managed to put her thoughts aside. Clearing her throat, she answered, "She's sleeping now. She has an ugly bruise on her hip and a few scratches on her face. Other than that she's fine." Her voice was raspy. He was doing strange things to her insides simply by standing in the doorway, watching her.

"I'm glad," he said.

She leaned her back against the rail and asked, "How about you? Did you hurt yourself when you fell? Did you open the wound in your side?" Her eyes traveled down his torso but darkness kept her from seeing the cut.

"No." He shook his head and gave her a brief smile. "Thanks to you it's healed very nicely."

"Good." She lifted her long hair off her neck and let the night air cool her nape. His constant staring was making her nervous. That and the fact that this was the perfect time to admit her wrongdoing, ask for his forgiveness and give him his freedom.

Asher looked at the slice of moon that hung over Caramarena's shoulder and knew the heat was getting to him. He must be crazy to be standing here thinking about making love to her. For the past week his long swims in the cold river had done a good job of making him so tired he had no desire to do anything but fall into bed and sleep. In the morning, when he was rested and aware that Caramarena lay warm and sweet beside him, he'd

146

rise early, not wanting her to know how badly he wanted her. But tonight, as he looked at his wife bathed in soft moonlight with her long flowing hair, he didn't mind if she knew. He wanted to make love to his wife.

Go to bed!

No, I want her.

She's trouble disguised as a beautiful woman!

No, she's my wife.

It doesn't matter. You'll regret this in the morning!

I know.

Leave her before it's too late.

It already is.

You'll hate yourself in the morning!

I have a feeling it'll be worth it.

Asher walked out on the balcony and joined her by the rail. He knew she'd just taken a bath, because her hair was still damp around the edges and she smelled of sweet-smelling soap. It was intoxicating to be near to her when she looked this beautiful and smelled this good. His hands were itching to touch her soft skin and crush the lush silkiness of her hair between his hands.

He looked into her eyes and said, "I'm sorry about what happened to Bunch this afternoon. I should have listened to you."

"Oh, no! I'm the one who's sorry, Asher. I yelled at you when you'd just saved her life. My only excuse is that fear made me want to lash out at someone."

"You had every reason to be upset." His voice remained soft, his accent heavy. "You were right. You didn't want her to come along because you knew she needed to be watched every minute. I said I would take care of her and didn't. It's my fault. I hope you'll forgive me for failing to understand just how carefully she needs to be watched."

She took a step closer to him. "Asher, I can't let you take the blame for this afternoon. I knew better and you didn't. I can't excuse my—"

He grabbed her shoulders and held her tightly. "None of it was your fault. I should have realized Bunch's limitations. But I didn't. The horses were coming right at her, but she didn't move to try and save herself. It was as if she couldn't see the danger bearing down on her." Suddenly he felt as if he were reliving the whole thing. "I've never been so frightened in my life. It was like I was running but not getting anywhere. I didn't think I was going to get there in time to save her and—I knew I couldn't have lived with myself if I hadn't."

Caramarena's heart went out to him. "I'm not sure she does comprehend the danger of some things. One of the reasons we seldom let her leave the house is that we don't want her to get used to going out. We're afraid she might someday decide to leave on her own and get lost or fall into the river."

His eyes searched hers as his fingers massaged her shoulders. "Tell me about her. I want to understand."

Asher must have realized he was holding her, because he suddenly let her go and leaned against the rail.

She lifted her hair again and brought it all around to fall over her shoulder. "I don't remember too much of the early years. Most of it is what I've heard Papa say. When Mama started labor with Bunch late in the afternoon she and Papa thought it'd all be over in a couple of hours, but the night wore on and the baby didn't come—just the pains. They knew this wasn't normal because Mama already had three children and it had gotten easier with each one. Sometime during the night Papa sent Cypress down the river for the doctor. But from what I'm told there wasn't anything he could do. Mama was so weak by the time he arrived she couldn't help him. Bunch was finally born but the doctor couldn't get her to start breathing. He gave her to Mama and told her the baby was dead. Mama didn't believe him and started shaking Bunch. Bunch started spitting and coughing and crying, then Ma started crying, too. Over the course of the labor

148

Mama had lost too much of her strength. She never got it back. She died a few days later."

"I'm sorry," he said softly.

"Thank you. We all were." She sighed. "We didn't notice Bunch wasn't right until a few years ago. We realized she'd never grown up past the age of five or six. We've tried to teach her things but she doesn't seem to be able to learn past a certain point. For a while we tried to tell ourselves she was spoiled because she was the baby of the family, and we hadn't wanted her to grow up. We don't delude ourselves any more."

"So she's a beautiful young woman in body and a child in mind."

Tears raced to the surface of Caramarena's eyes when she heard the sympathy in Asher's voice. "Oh Asher, I know she'll never be able to marry, and I'll never be able to leave her. I couldn't bear it if anything happened to her. Thank you for saving her life." She threw her arms around him and nestled her face into the warmth of his neck. His hands slid around her waist and she felt immediate comfort.

"Shh—don't get upset again. She's all right, and we're not going to let anything happen to her. I promise."

Asher's heart went out to Caramarena for loving her sister. But it didn't take long for thoughts of comforting to cease and for their place to be taken by thoughts of how much he desired the woman in his arms. She felt so good pressed softly against him. Her hair smelled like a day glowing with sunshine. He rubbed his hands up and down her back, comforting her. Comforting her was all he intended to do, but he couldn't seem to stop himself from kissing the top of her head.

He told himself to push her away and leave her alone, to go to bed, but he stayed, holding her close, brushing her hair with his hand and enjoying how good she felt in his arms. How good he felt.

When she lifted her face up to him he knew he had to

kiss her, if only this one time. But when his lips met hers he knew once would never satisfy his yearning for her.

He would only kiss her once, he told himself again. Just enjoy his mouth on hers, his lips gliding over her soft cheeks and down the slender column of her throat. But then she pressed closer, and he knew he had to see if her breasts were as soft and firm as they looked, so he slid his hand up her ribcage and found a soft swelling mound. Asher moaned softly with pleasure.

Even though it had been weeks since he'd been with a woman he knew that abstinence had nothing to do with the intensity with which he wanted this one. He'd never wanted another woman this hotly, this passionately. Maybe it was because he'd slept beside her for a week and had never touched her. Maybe it was because he knew she was forbidden to him, or maybe he just wanted her that desperately.

The cotton material of her gown was so soft it could have been silk. The smooth fabric let his hands glide over her breasts and back again, each stroke making him grow harder. He moved his lips over hers. They were sweet, and inside her mouth was warm and tasted of oranges. Oh God, how he loved the taste of oranges. He stuck his tongue deeper into the recesses of her mouth, wanting to taste more — all of her. If he remembered nothing else from this night with her he'd always love the taste of oranges.

He felt her soft hands on his back, and shivers of desire coursed through him, weakening his determination not to let this moment with her go any further and make an annulment impossible. Surely he could keep his breeches on. Surely he wouldn't take her nightgown off. Just this loving, just a little more and he'd turn her loose and go for another swim.

"I've wanted you to do this since our wedding night," she whispered. "I've dreamed of your kisses and caresses."

No, he thought. *Don't talk like that. Don't say things that are going to make me want you more. Don't say things that are going to make me forget what I have to do.*

"Oh, Asher, why have you waited so long to come to me?"

"I had to," he whispered in between kisses. "I shouldn't be doing this, Cara."

"It's what I've wanted—what I've longed for."

Caramarena loved the feel of his broad shoulders as her hands spanned his width. She couldn't believe she was actually free to touch him as she'd longed to. She took liberty and ran her hands up and down the entire length of his back, feeling the taut muscles. She then ran them over his shoulders and down his chest, letting the curly hair tickle her palm and make her want to bury her face in the softness and let the hair caress her cheeks.

She gasped with delight as his lips slipped down her neck to the top of her gown. He gently pushed her back against the balcony rail and moved his head farther down until his lips found the peak of her breast through the nightgown. He tried to pull the tip into his mouth. Her stomach muscles tightened and she moaned her approval. This was what she'd wanted, what she'd been looking forward to since their wedding night. This was what she'd felt the first time he'd kissed her. This was the intense desire she'd harbored and nurtured. Now at last, she was free to let it show.

Asher was hurting. He wanted her so badly. He was a fool to think he could kiss her and not take their loving all the way. He wanted her too much. Why did she have to be so damn responsive he lost all control?

She's your wife.

I can't have her!

She wants you to show her how to make love.

No! I don't want to hurt her. I don't want to love her then leave her.

Forget that! You want her. That is all that's important.

No!

Yes!

"Yes, yes, Cara, I've wanted you," he whispered huskily with his lips pressed lightly against hers, coaxing little sounds from her throat.

All in one easy motion he hooked an arm under her knees and the other around her shoulders, carried her into the bedroom and laid her down on the bed.

For a moment as he stood over her reality returned. He couldn't do this, he thought, but then she lifted her arms toward him, her lips slightly parted and he knew she had captured his heart. He wouldn't walk away from her this time. The annulment be damned.

He reached for the hem of her gown and slowly lifted it up — up and over her head and threw it to the floor. She lay on the bed completely unclothed. With coveting eyes he looked at his wife. His gaze started at her toes and quickly slid to her ankles. Her legs were long and shapely. He took note of slim thighs and he briefly glanced at the small patch of hair, then on to her flat stomach and slightly rounded hips. His gaze flew upward to where her waist nipped in and her beautifully rounded breasts and creamy white shoulders lay waiting for him to touch.

She was beautiful. And she was his.

Asher had walked away from many women, but he couldn't turn away from Caramarena. With urgent fingers he unfastened the buttons of his breeches and slipped them down his legs, revealing his swollen manhood. He eased on to the bed beside her, and when her arms circled his bare heated skin he knew without a doubt that this was the only woman he wanted. Their lips met; their tongues explored and played together.

When he first touched her breasts his chest felt heavy with desire. He lightly ran his hand over first one then the other. He cupped one and squeezed it gently. The thrill was as exciting as he'd imagined. He bent his head and covered one rosebud nipple with his mouth and sucked it softly. She moaned her pleasure and he grew harder. He knew by the way she responded that no other man had ever touched her breasts. He was the first.

It was hot but there was no trace of sweat on her body. She tasted of soap. He found that he liked it much better than the heavy cologne. But he was so hot he felt as if he were going to explode. He recognized her untapped sensuality and longed to explore it, release it, drown in it.

His hands roamed over the fine planes of her body and Asher realized her beauty was not the only thing that made Caramarena so special, so desirable. Many things attracted him to her, including how warm and yielding she was in his arms. He was also attracted to her spirit, her intelligence. No wonder he couldn't keep his hands off her and now — now he was no longer going to try.

Over the years Asher had had many women, but right now he couldn't remember one face, not one. None of them had touched him like this woman. He knew this would be her first time and that also pleased him greatly, so much that he felt like it was the first time for him, too.

Their breath mingled. Their hands explored. Their bodies pressed.

"You're so special, Cara. I want you to know this means a great deal to me." He was so excited that he couldn't breathe properly. He wanted it to be good for her, too.

From the way she arched her body to meet his, the way her lips took his and her hands glided over his body, he knew that she felt the way he did. He knew she was ready for him.

He kissed her, knowing the first thrust was going to hurt her, but that it had to be done. He didn't know if it would be easier to take it slow and easy or do it all at once.

All at once, his body told him. With his lips pressed tightly against hers Asher moved his hand between them

153

and his manhood into place.

Caramarena knew this was the moment she'd waited for but she didn't expect the tearing pain. She tried to cry out for him to stop and let her catch her breath but he wouldn't move his lips away from hers. With a few hard strokes he was embedded inside her, whispering her name softly.

"Cara. Did I hurt you?" he asked in a gravelly voice.

"A little." She swallowed hard, her breathing heavy. "Is it over?" she asked, looking up into his eyes.

He smiled down at her. "Oh no." He kissed her tenderly. "I'm just letting you get used to the feel of me inside you. Does it hurt now when I move like this?"

She shook her head.

"Good," he whispered.

Asher slipped his arms under her head and cradled her close and started moving slowly, pumping his hips softly. Caramarena felt the tension building inside her as his belly stroked hers, as his chest stroked her breasts. He continued to kiss her, thrusting his tongue deeply into her mouth. His hands slid up and down her body, touching, caressing, squeezing.

His tempo increased and she found herself moving with him, meeting him. She heard him moan with pleasure and it made her feel wonderful, knowing she could make him feel so good. She tilted her head back, found his lips and thrust her tongue inside his warm mouth. She felt a building of pressure somewhere in her abdomen — no, lower. She moved harder, faster, wanting more, wanting it deeper. Her breath came in short little gasps. Her fingers dug into his muscled back, her legs wrapped around his thighs. She didn't know what was happening, only that it was wonderful and glorious, and then almost as quickly the feeling died away.

She opened her eyes and saw Asher's eyes squeeze shut, his teeth sink into his bottom lip, his body go rigid above her. With one last thrust he rested on top of her.

154

Caramarena smiled.

Asher tried to catch his breath. She was so good, so tight he thought he'd burst before he brought her to fulfillment so that he could find his own release. He kissed her shoulder lovingly and inhaled the scent of their lovemaking. For the first time, he wanted to whisper words of love, to tell her how special it was, but he remained silent. He knew he was heavy but he wasn't ready to roll away from her. Before, it had always been easy to leave the woman but not this time. Not this woman. He wanted her close to him. He wanted to hold her.

When his breathing calmed, he rolled to his side, taking Caramarena with him. "Did I hurt you?" he asked and kissed the tip of her nose.

"Only a little, at first." She smiled.

"I'm glad it didn't last," he whispered and realized he wanted to sleep. How could his body give out on him with this beautiful woman so close to him? Then he knew. Their union had been that complete.

Asher closed his eyes and slept.

Chapter Ten

Pale moonlight shone through the open French doors, bathing the bed with its soft light. A warm breeze drifted across the room. Caramarena lay with her cheek on her husband's shoulder, her hand pressed against the soft hair on his chest, feeling the gentle rhythm of his breathing.

Nothing had prepared her for the joy and pleasure she'd discovered in Asher's arms. Nothing. Why had she thought making love was simply a matter of her husband planting his seed inside her and producing a child? Maybe, if her mother had lived, she would have told Caramarena of the wonderful, glorious feelings that had been in store for her. Why had Asher waited so long to show her how a man loves a woman? How a woman loves a man?

Caramarena let her hand lightly run up and down Asher's chest, finding peace and contentment in the mere touch of him. Occasionally she'd let her hand slip farther, past his navel to the flatter plane of his stomach, wanting to discover everything about him, to leave no part of him untouched by her hand.

There were many things she liked about Asher, and not the least of them was his loving. He was handsome and had a firm and muscular body. He was interested in learning all about Live Oak. Asher had been good to Cypress when he could have very easily had Cypress hanged for killing that man in Apalachicola. And even more importantly, she knew he was very fond of Bunch.

Caramarena sighed contentedly. How many times had she wished for a husband who would want to live on Live Oak and make it his home? And how many times had she wished for someone who would grow to love the place as much as she did?

She smiled when she remembered her fleeting moment of jealousy. Asher had loved her so thoroughly that she now knew he'd held and comforted Bunch as a father holds a child, not as a man holds his lover. She also realized something else. She was in love with him. The thought shocked her for a moment. It wasn't something she'd set out to do. She'd liked Asher the first time she'd met him. Over the past weeks she'd come to respect him as well. And now after their first night as husband and wife she was sure she loved him.

As she thought of all these things her heart filled with warmth and passion. Yes, Caramarena Millhouse loved her husband. She reached over and kissed his bearded cheek, thinking how wonderful, how unexpected, how fortunate she was to have fallen in love with him.

One kiss on the cheek was not enough, she thought, as she looked down at him. The moon and stars gave the room enough light for her to make out his features. He appeared to be sleeping and she didn't want to wake him, but now that she knew she loved him she wanted him to know it as well. Her breasts pressed against his chest as she placed her lips upon his and kissed him. He stirred, mumbled her name, then his arms circled her back and tightened around her.

"I thought you were sleeping," she said in a hushed voice.

"Not any more," he answered, although he didn't open his eyes. His hand started a lazy pattern up and down her back.

"I didn't mean to wake you. I only wanted to kiss you again."

With a gentle hand she smoothed his beard, remembering how it had tickled her skin with its coarseness, deciding she liked it, but also wondering what he'd look like without it.

Asher opened his eyes and caught her staring at him. He reached over and cupped her breast and kissed it.

"What were you looking at, Caramarena?" he asked. His mouth closed over her nipple and pulled it gently into his mouth.

"You," she answered and cradled his head against her. The sucking motion on her breasts made her abdomen tighten and heightened her desire for more. "I was trying to imagine what you looked like without the beard."

She felt his body stiffen, and he moved his head away. "Not much different than I do with it."

Caramarena slipped her leg over his and pressed her body closer to him. "Are you angry I awakened you?"

Asher reached up and brushed her hair away from her shoulder. "No, I'm glad you did. This night shouldn't be wasted sleeping." He ran his hand under her hair, cupped her neck and pulled her face down to his. He kissed her deeply, letting his hands run up and down her back, over her buttocks and up again.

Caramarena sighed and stretched, loving the feel of his hands on her. "I wonder why no one ever told me how wonderful this would feel?"

Asher chuckled as he continued plying her cheeks, neck and shoulders with moist, little kisses. "I'm glad no one did. You may not have waited for me had you known of the pleasures that were awaiting you."

She raised her head and looked into his eyes. "Are you happy I did?" she questioned.

He didn't answer her immediately, and that surprised her, but at last he said. "Right now, I'm very happy you waited for me."

Before she could say anything else he rolled her onto her back and after a few well-placed kisses fit his body firmly into hers.

Asher watched the sky turn from black to purple to light pink. Daybreak was on the rise.

Caramarena lay with her cheek on his chest, her soft body snuggled firmly against him, heating his already warm skin. The night had cooled down to a bearable temperature but his desire for his wife hadn't. He wanted her again.

As he thought back over the events of yesterday and last evening he wasn't even sure how it had all started. Not that the cause was important. He'd wanted Caramarena, and he'd finally let his guard down enough to make her his. He couldn't find it in himself to be sorry about it or try and punish himself. He'd wanted her too badly, and it had been too good to wish it hadn't happened.

Once he found himself in his wife's arms he'd forgotten his reasons for being in Florida and at Live Oak. He'd forgotten the reasons he'd decided to marry Caramarena. He'd forgotten all thoughts of annulment. Lying beside her now, finding her so warm and sweet, it would be so easy to forget about London's cold rainy days and his brothers' smiling faces; but one thing he couldn't forget was the vow he'd made to his father.

Whenever he tried, he saw his father's withered face pinched with pain and aged with bitterness. He felt the

159

sting of the strap on his back and his rage from the slap to his mother's face. Asher knew he had to renew his vow to destroy John Cantrell even if it meant he had to hide, defeat or deny the feelings that were developing for his wife. He had to sacrifice the tenderness, the loving he'd sensed inside her, if he was ever to settle his father's debt.

As the sky grew brighter sleep continued to elude him, but in a way he was thankful for that. It gave him more time to think and plan.

Caramarena was only a woman, he told himself, as she lay nestled so close, her shallow breath fanning him. He'd had plenty of women in the past, and he could have many more in the future, he assured himself. He had escaped falling in love with Elizabeth and, as he remembered, she was one hell of a woman.

But Asher had liked the way his wife responded to his loving and the way she'd loved him. She didn't touch him like a seasoned woman who knew exactly where and how to bring about the maximum satisfaction. Caramarena touched him out of wonder and fascination.

Her innocence and her thirst for discovery of his body had brought him more pleasure than any woman he'd ever been with. Most women were so concerned with pleasing him that they forgot to touch him as if it pleased them to do so. That was what made Caramarena different, special. She wanted to touch him for the joy it gave her. She was still too innocent to know that most women made love to please the man. He'd never known how exciting it was for a woman to touch him as if every little inch of him pleased her greatly.

Asher sighed. Oh yes, the women in the street knew how to make love, but they didn't know how to make him feel loved.

When the sun lifted above the horizon, Asher reluctantly rose from Caramarena's bed. He watched her sleeping as he pulled on his clothes. After a night that should have sated him he found himself wanting to crawl back on the rumpled sheet with her and love her yet again. Caramarena was his wife, he shouldn't have to forsake her bed. But he knew the danger in remaining. He'd already made an annulment impossible, he didn't want to get her with child, too.

His stomach muscles tightened as he walked to the door. He stopped and took a last looking at his sleeping wife. What was he going to do about Caramarena and his feelings for her when he was through with Live Oak?

Caramarena was disappointed to find Asher already gone. Over the years she'd developed the habit of sleeping late. But now, knowing that he was an early riser, she wanted to awaken earlier and find him still in the bed with her. She wanted them to get up and breakfast together.

As she crawled out of bed she realized she was a little sore, but thinking back over the wonderful night, decided it was definitely worth it. She poured fresh water into the basin, wanting to wash before calling Lacy to help her dress. Maybe now she would have the kind of life with Asher she'd dreamed about. He'd made her so happy she didn't want to spend any time away from him. She smiled to herself. Maybe after last night, she would conceive a son for Asher, and he'd want to spend the rest of his life at Live Oak with her and the children they'd have.

Joyous laughter bubbled in her throat. Surely Asher wouldn't want to leave her and go back to England, now. She felt as if she were glowing all over. How could she not love her husband after last night. How could he not love her?

* * *

Caramarena peeked into Bunch's room to see if she was still sleeping, but the room was empty. She hoped that meant Bunch was over yesterday's frightening experience with the wild horses.

She hurried down the stairs and out to the verandah, hoping Asher hadn't yet left the breakfast table. Today would be a new beginning in their life together. She was sure of it.

Asher was seated at the breakfast table but rose when she walked out the door. Her heart constricted. He looked so handsome in his dark brown breeches and white collarless shirt, which he left open at the base of his throat. His hair was attractively combed away from his forehead. As she looked at him she knew she loved him with all her heart.

She moistened her lips and smiled at him. "Good morning, Asher."

"Good morning, Caramarena," he said as he laid his napkin on the table.

Much to her chagrin, his face wore a mask of indifference that chilled her. Caramarena felt a pounding in her ears, and her throat was suddenly dry. It was apparent he didn't feel the same way she did. Her confidence ebbed.

From the far end of the veranda, Ivy started walking toward her with a cup of steaming coffee, but Caramarena shook head. Ivy turned away.

Caramarena took a deep breath and said, "I wish you'd awakened me so we could have had breakfast together." She willed her tone to stay light.

"There was no need for you to rise so early." He purposefully looked away from her when he spoke.

Why? Why, after their wonderful night together, was he acting cold and indifferent? Didn't he feel the same glorious things she'd felt last night?

Asher moved away from the table, turning his back to her. "I'll be going into Apalachicola this morning. I believe I'd mentioned to you that I would need to go back into town when it was time for *Sandor* to sail." When he'd finished speaking he turned to face her.

Cold, emotionless eyes stared at Caramarena. She wanted to cry.

"Oh — I'd forgotten." She stammered over her words, still not convinced he wasn't planning on sailing to England with his ship. She looked away, not wanting him to see how disappointed she was he was leaving so soon, how his attitude toward her broke her heart. Tears wanted to invade her eyes but she refused to let them. Clearing her throat, she looked back at him. His expression hadn't changed. "Yes, surely you must go in and say good-bye to your captain and your men."

"I may be gone for a few days."

Finally their eyes met and for a brief second Caramarena thought she saw a softening in his expression. "Will you — I mean —" Caramarena stopped as Bunch burst through the doorway, her puce-colored skirts swirling about her legs.

"Look, Cara, my bruises need more medicine." She held up her arm for Caramarena to see. "Papa said you'd take care of them for me."

"Of course I will." Caramarena brushed the extra face powder away from Bunch's cheek. "Say good morning to Asher."

Bunch looked over at him and politely held out her hand. "Good morning."

Asher responded with a smile, a greeting and a kiss on her hand. "I think your bruises are the prettiest I've ever seen."

Bunch laughed and turned back to Caramarena.

163

"Do you think my bruises are pretty?"

Caramarena smiled. "Oh yes. They're very pretty." She looked up and smiled at Asher, wanting to thank him for making Bunch feel special. But instead of looking at her he walked over to the table, picked up his cup and drank from it. Caramarena's spirits plummeted farther.

"Bunch, you run back upstairs and get my medicine box while I have a cup of coffee. All right?"

Bunch nodded and eagerly skipped back into the house.

"Asher—"

"Caramarena—"

They spoke at the same time. Their eyes met again.

"I'm sorry," Asher said. "I need to find Lacy and ask her to pack a traveling bag for me. Cypress told me the boat will be by shortly, and that I should be standing on the dock if I expect to catch a ride."

"Will Cypress be going with you?" she asked in a hopeful voice.

"No. It wouldn't be a good idea to send him into Apalachicola for a long time."

"Yes, of course, you're right. I wasn't thinking." She wanted to ask him not to go. She wanted to tell him that she needed him to stay here and love her, but her pride wouldn't let her. She couldn't force him to stay against his will.

"I plan to find out all I can about the two men who jumped me. I'm hoping the surviving man isn't pursuing this." He looked away. "Well, I must hurry. Goodbye, Cara."

Caramarena kept her chin high as Asher brushed past her. She kept her back to the door but heard every footstep he took. When the door opened and closed she squeezed her eyes shut, and her hands made fists. He couldn't bear to look at her. Why? And how could he leave her so easily, so soon? Did last night mean absolutely nothing to him?

Ivy placed a cup of coffee on the table in front of her, but Caramarena continued to look out over the beautiful green lawn. What would she do if Asher sailed with his ship? At one time she'd expected it, wanted it to happen, but not now. Now she knew what it was to have a husband and to love him. If he didn't return it would break her heart.

Later that morning, from a window in her father's bedroom, Caramarena watched the boat Asher was on sail down the river. A sinking feeling attacked her stomach. She wished she knew why he'd been so cold toward her. She wanted to be caught up in his arms and hugged and kissed, and all he'd done was stare at her without really seeing her.

"Well, this is a surprise."

She turned away from the window. "What's that, Papa?" she asked and walked over to where he sat at his desk.

"I see where Asher signed for the horses yesterday." He looked up at his daughter and rubbed his bearded chin. "Want to tell me about that?"

"Oh, I guess I was so worried about Bunch, I forgot to mention it to you. Mr. Burrel didn't want me to sign because I'm a woman. You know we've had that problem before. To keep from having to come back up to the house and disturb you, Asher offered to sign as your son-in-law and Mr. Burrel liked that idea better than me signing." She placed a hand on her father's shoulder. "Why isn't a woman's signature as good as a man's?"

Her father chuckled, something he hadn't done in a long time. "So many men don't think women have a head for business. But the truth of it is most men don't

165

want to think there's a woman smart enough to write her name. It makes them feel more powerful or stronger maybe."

"That's horrible. I'm glad you don't feel that way, Papa," she praised.

He chuckled again. "Don't pat me on the back for it, Cara. Had I a son to leave Live Oak to, I'm not so sure I'd feel very differently from Mr. Burrel."

"Papa! You know if you had had a son he couldn't have loved Live Oak more than I do, or have taken better care of it."

He patted her hand. "Yes, I know that. I'm very proud of you, Cara." He smiled, then looked back at the ledger. "I forgot to ask if Mr. Burrel charged us extra for rounding up the horses."

"No. I think he was so happy Bunch and Asher weren't trampled that he left as soon as the horses were contained."

Her father closed the account book. "Tell me, did you tend to Bunch?"

"Yes. Her scratches don't look that bad today, and she can't be too sore with the way she's moving around. It's amazing that she got over the scare so quickly. I thought we might have trouble with her for weeks."

"That could still happen. She could have a nightmare about it weeks from now. We'll need to watch her closely for a while."

"I know," she answered automatically as there flashed across her mind a picture of Asher crouching on the ground holding Bunch as if he'd never let go. He'd been so gentle, so concerned. She had to find a way to keep him here. She loved him and needed him. Live Oak needed him. And although she tried not to think about it, she could be carrying his child at this very moment. That thought lifted her spirits. Surely

166

with all the interest he'd shown in the plantation and the way he'd touched her last night, he'd come back. He just had to.

"Papa." Caramarena knelt in front of him and took his hands in hers. Her raspberry-colored skirt fanned out around her. "Papa, I don't want Asher to go back to England." Her voice held more desperation than she intended to show.

John Cantrell tilted his head back and looked at her. "I don't believe he is, Caramarena. I'm sure he's going to town for his stated purpose. It seems natural for him to want to speak to his captain and men again before they sail."

It relieved her somewhat to hear the confidence in her father's voice. "I hope you're right." She took a deep breath and asked, "Papa, do you think we could give Asher more to do here at Live Oak? He's used to traveling all over the world and doing many things to keep busy. I'm afraid he'll quickly tire of it here with nothing to do and want to go back to his home."

He squeezed her hands and asked, "Cara, have you fallen in love with your husband?"

Her eyes watered but no tears fell. "I think I loved him from the start. I knew after only a few hours of being with him that he would be a good husband, and he is, Papa. It's so — wonderful." She stopped and blushed, lowering her eyes. "I suppose you know what I mean," she finished softly.

He nodded understandingly. "For your sake, Caramarena, I hope he stays forever."

"It's not only that, Papa. He's been working hard to learn how we do things here. There are still many things he doesn't know but the main thing is that he is interested, and I want to keep it that way. One day I'll be busy with our children, and you'll need Asher to help you."

167

"All right," he patted her cheek and smiled. "Since it seems to be working between the two of you, I'll draw up some papers that will make it possible for him to do business in Live Oak's name. That way, since your sisters don't find time to visit me with their children, you can give me grandchildren to know and love right here. Is that what you want?"

"Oh Papa, that would be wonderful." Joy and anticipation surged through her. "I know he'll stay if we can keep him busy so he won't miss his home and his travels. I'll make him a good wife and be a good mother, Papa."

"I've never doubted that, Caramarena. When a man has a beautiful, intelligent, and loving woman such as you for his wife, he is home. Now you listen to me about this." He pointed his finger at her. "No more fretting that he'll leave. A man knows when he's made a good match for himself."

"Did you ever miss your home, Papa? Did you ever want to go back to England?"

A faraway look entered his eyes before he answered. "No. Never. There was nothing for me in London. Years ago I seized an opportunity that became available to me, and I've never regretted doing what I did. I knew once I left England I'd never look back." He cupped her chin in his weak hand. "That's what you must do now. If you want this man, Cara, you must fight for him."

"That's what I've been doing, Papa."

"I know. And I'm very proud of you. Now before we go downstairs and draw up those papers I have something to tell you."

"Yes, Papa?"

"I'll be leaving for New Orleans soon." Caramarena gasped, but he held up his hand to silence her and con-

168

tinued. "There's a specialist Dr. Johnstone wants me to see."

"Oh, Papa, does he think this doctor will help you to get better?" Her spirits lifted at the thought of her father being well once again.

"I think it's more of him telling me what's wrong with me and how long I have to live."

"No, Papa, don't say that." She reached up and flung her arms around him, holding him close, afraid to let him go.

"Shh—Cara, this isn't news to you. You must be strong now. Surely if there is anything the doctors can do, it will be done. But we have to be prepared for the worst. No tears. Promise me no tears." He pulled her arms away from him.

Caramarena sank her teeth into her bottom lip to keep it from quivering. Her heart was heavy with despair. "I promise. When do we leave?"

"We'll leave at week's end, but, Caramarena, I'm only taking Cypress."

"No!" she whispered passionately. "I want to go and talk with this specialist myself."

He shook his head. "You have to be here to look after Live Oak. One day Asher may be prepared to take over, but not yet. It's too soon and besides, you know Bunch doesn't travel well. Cypress will take good care of me."

"All right, Papa, if you insist." She sniffled but held her tears in check.

"I do. Now let's go take care of those papers."

Asher had wanted to stay on the deck of *Sandor,* where a nice breeze blew. Instead he followed Simon to his cabin. He knew how easily voices carried over water, and he couldn't take the chance any of the men might hear them.

The air inside the small room was as stale and dank as he remembered it. How easy it had been for him to become accustomed to the pleasant smells, fine furniture and spacious rooms of Live Oak.

"Can I pour you one?" Simon asked as he pulled the cork out of a bottle and poured a generous portion of the port into a cup.

Asher shook his head. He didn't want a drink, and he wasn't in the mood for small talk. He had too many things on his mind. "How did things go with Buford?"

Simon settled himself behind his desk and took a sip of his liquor before answering. "Very well. Buford and I have come up with a plan we think will work a sight better than yours," Captain Barclay said, his pipe between his teeth, a small billow of smoke coming from his mouth.

That wasn't exactly what Asher wanted to hear, considering the foul mood he was in. "I'm not used to you changing my plans, but go on. I'm listening." Asher knew the plan he'd come up with wasn't a great one and had considerable risk to his men. Being an honest man, the only thing he'd known to do was hire someone who wasn't honest and let him do the dirty work.

"Remember the area of Florida just round the east bend called Snug Harbor?"

"Yes. It's a haven for pirates." Asher rested his booted foot on his leg.

"Right."

Asher's foot hit the deck with a clomp as he moved to the edge of his seat. "No, it's too risky. Those men are dangerous. I made it clear I don't want any of the men hurt. I just want the turpentine stolen."

"That's what we plan to do, but believe me, Asher, our way will be safer."

Simon had a satisfied smile that worried Asher. He rose from his chair, wishing they'd stayed outside

170

where he could breathe easier. He rubbed the back of his neck and felt the dampness, wishing he'd never started this scheme.

"No, we can't do it. They are real pirates. You can't trust those men not to kill."

"There's one we can trust. Buford has a brother who's taken sanctuary there."

"What?"

Simon picked up his pipe and started stuffing it with tobacco. "He swears it's true, Asher. Sit back down and listen to our plan. Then we'll talk if you have questions."

Asher had trusted this man for the fourteen years he'd been sailing with him. There was no reason not to now. He retook his seat.

"A plague called yellow fever hit Apalachicola a few years back. I've heard it wiped out most of this town plus several others up and down the coast."

"Yes, I've heard of it, too. What does that have to do with getting rid of the turpentine?"

Simon smiled. "So have the men. They've all talked about it at one time or another."

Simon stuck a thin piece of wood into the candle flame. When it lit, he held it to the end of the pipe, making sucking noises until the tobacco ignited. Asher waited patiently for the ritual to end. Years of experience told him not to hurry Simon when he was lighting his pipe. When the captain was satisfied, he blew out the stick and laid it aside.

"Anyway this is our plan. Two days away from Snug Harbor, Buford will come down with a fever. I'll have him quarantined and mention that I hope it's not yellow fever. It'll scare the men so bad they won't mind going into Snug Harbor to let Buford off. We'll anchor for the night, I'll personally see Buford is taken ashore and settled into an inn. But of course, Buford will immediately find his brother and arrange for us to be pirated when we sail the next day. After a visit with his brother Buford will sail to England and state that the fever passed without ill effects."

"Are you sure we can trust his brother not to harm any of our men?" Asher asked, thinking that it just might work.

"I'd say we have a much better chance that things will go as planned this way. In either case, Asher, we're asking a man to rob us. We have to remember that. This way we don't have to worry about anyone, except Buford's brother, double-crossing us. And of course, I'll still voice my doubts of Cantrell's innocence to the authorities when we arrive in London."

The more Asher thought about it the better Simon's plan sounded. He took a resigned breath. "All right. Do it. And send word back to me as soon as you can. I won't rest easy until I know no one was injured."

"You can depend on us. We'll sail at first light. The only thing I need to know is how much of the truth do I tell your brothers. They're bound to ask."

"Nothing except the cargo was stolen outside of Snug Harbor. For now, it's best they know only what the authorities are told. The letter I've written should take care of everything until I return to London."

"Done."

Asher shook his head and rose from his chair. He wasn't worried. He was sick. Now that he'd started this plan he wasn't so sure he wanted to go through with it. It was all Caramarena's fault. He shouldn't have touched her last night. Touched her—hell, he shouldn't have made love to her. He knew it was the wrong thing to do but he'd found it impossible to stop himself. What was really eating at him was the fact that he hadn't wanted just any woman last night. He'd wanted Caramarena.

172

"I guess it's time to say good-bye," Asher finally said.

They shook hands and wished each other good luck.

Asher walked out of the small dank cabin and took a deep breath when he made it to the top deck. How had he lived for years on that ship, with its darkness and musty odor?

All the wonderful smells of Live Oak teased his mind again. Roses, freshness, oranges, Caramarena with her beautiful smile, her brightly decorated home with the finest of everything. But, he reminded himself, the home was purchased with money stolen from his father. He must not forget. He must not forgive.

A few minutes later, Asher walked up the street in search of the tavern he'd visited when he first came to Apalachicola little more than a month ago. While there he hoped to play a game or two of cards, do a little drinking and maybe pick up a woman. Surely that would get his mind off Caramarena. Maybe, too, he could find out some information about the men who'd attacked him. He didn't necessarily like Cypress, but the large buck had saved his life and Asher owed him.

Several doors down on the right he walked into the smoky tavern, with its raucous laughter and loud talk. It was a sharp contrast to the late evening at Live Oak, where it was always so quiet a man could hear himself think.

Although the bar was crowded, he found elbow room and ordered a tankard of ale. The man next to him was bearded, but his skin had a leathery, textured look, as if he had spent a lot of time in the sun. After a few sips of his drink Asher struck up a conversation.

"Are you a stranger in town?" Asher asked him.

"Been here nearly four years. The *Titan* out at the dock, that's my shrimp boat."

Asher nodded. "Maybe I'll take a walk later and

have a look at her."

"You looking for a job?" the older man asked.

"Ah — no. I just like boats," he said letting his eyes scan the card tables, wondering which game he should join.

"It's best you not be walking around the docks after dark. There was a man killed over there three — maybe four weeks ago."

Asher hadn't expected to find information from this man but decided to lead him on. "I'm not afraid. I can take care of myself."

"Can you take care of two men with knives and one of them the biggest darkie you've ever seen?"

"Now wait a minute," Asher felt his anger rise. So the man who'd lived had talked but had obviously lied. Damn! "There was a man killed by two men with knives?"

"It's what the one who lived said." The man finished off his tankard so Asher offered to buy him another, hoping he'd finish the story.

"Thank you kindly," the aging, bearded man said when the barmaid placed a fresh drink in front of him. He took a long drink, then wiped his mouth on his sleeve. "You didn't hear about this?" he asked.

"Only bits and pieces here and there. What really happened?" Asher asked.

"The way Dobson tells it, he and his brother were walking along the dock, just enjoying an evening together when this big darkie and a white man with a knife jumped them. The Negro killed his brother with his hands. Dobson said he wrestled the knife from the white man and cut him a few times before the darkie grabbed him by the neck, too. Dobson's certain they didn't intend to leave him alive. I hear he wishes he was dead because his face was messed up pretty bad. One side of his jaw was broken in three places. Swears

174

he'll get 'em if it's the last thing he does."

Asher digested all the information, including the man's name. He'd tell Cypress to be on the lookout for him. He didn't really think Dobson could track them all the way to Live Oak, but there wasn't any use in taking chances. He'd have another talk with Cypress when he returned and make sure the slave didn't talk to anyone.

"Thanks for the warning. I'll take a look at your boat some other time."

"That'd be the smart thing to do." He finished off his drink and walked away.

Asher rested his elbows on the bar and sipped his drink, visions of Caramarena and their lovemaking dancing through his mind. Oh God, he needed to forget about her, to completely wipe her from his memory. But how could he when so many things reminded him of her? How could he when he still tasted her lips, felt her warm skin and saw her loving eyes?

"Hi, stranger. Want to buy me a drink?"

Asher turned and looked into a set of smiling, dark brown eyes. He quickly scanned the woman's features. She was pretty with reddish brown hair falling across one shoulder, a small, pert nose and well-shaped lips. Her blue satin dress was cut low, revealing a full bosom that would catch any man's eyes.

"What about it, honey? You wanna buy me a drink, or you gonna just look?"

"All right. I'll buy you a drink." He motioned to the bartender and tossed more coins on the counter. "Whatever the lady is drinking," he told the man.

The woman propped her elbow on the bar and leaned against it, making sure her breasts were in full view. "Lady?" she smiled appreciatively. "Where are you from," she asked, moving her shoulders ever so slightly.

175

He returned the smile, satisfied she'd been pleased with his meager compliment. "Nowhere in particular."

She raised her eyebrows and gave him a sideways glance. Most women found his evasiveness frustrating but he knew immediately this woman found it interesting.

"Sounds like you and me have a lot in common." She picked up her drink and sipped it, deliberately wiping her lips with her tongue afterward. She smiled at him again. "It's very good."

"Thank you. I was sure the barman would know what you liked."

"You staying the night in town?" she asked, running the tip of her fingers across the swell of her breasts, inviting him to take a closer look.

Asher nodded as a vision of Caramarena flashed across his mind. She'd looked so tempting when he'd left her this morning. How could a woman be so desirable lying on top of rumpled sheets, her hair tangled about her shoulders? But she was.

He gave the doxy another long look. Before he'd made love to Caramarena he might have been interested.

This whore was pretty and polite, but he was sure she was like any other street woman. If he wasn't interested in spending a few dollars with her she'd move on to someone else. He didn't blame her for that. She had to make a living. Yes, she was a beautiful woman with starry eyes, but she wasn't Caramarena. And somehow Asher knew a whore would never satisfy him again.

"You're very pretty—" He smiled.

"Victoria," she announced proudly.

Victoria? He smiled again. "You're a very pretty woman, Victoria, but I'll be spending the night alone."

She sighed, her eyes already scanning the room for another possibility. "My loss."

Asher reached in his pocket, pulled out a couple of coins and pressed them in her hand. "Now, I'm the only loser tonight."

Chapter Eleven

Caramarena didn't understand her husband. How could he be so warm, appealing and loving one night and so cold now? Since coming home from Apalachicola two nights ago he'd returned to cool politeness during the day and going down to the river every night to swim before coming to bed to sleep.

She was trying hard to awaken earlier, but by the time she dressed and came downstairs Asher was already through with breakfast and in the office, checking the fields, or off to talk with Mr. Wulpher.

This morning she decided to skip breakfast and go directly in to see Asher. She was happy that he took such an interest in Live Oak, but she wanted him to take an interest in her, too. She checked the gilt-framed mirror to make sure her hair was in place. As she looked at herself she decided to pull her half-sleeves lower on her shoulders before continuing on into the office. She had to do something to get him to notice her as a woman again, not merely as part of Live Oak.

Asher glanced up as she walked in. "I'm sorry, Caramarena. I have your chair again. I didn't expect you up so early." He rose and offered it to her.

"No, please keep your seat," she said, but she noticed he didn't sit back down. "I'm trying to get up earlier. I'd like to breakfast with you each morning."

She wanted him to offer to awaken her before he left

the bed but knew that was too much to hope for when he replied, a little too stiffly, "That would be nice."

Caramarena moistened her lips, wishing he'd look into her eyes, wishing he'd give her reason to hope. "I'd like to talk to you about something, if you have the time."

"Certainly." He moved away from the desk as she approached and Caramarena couldn't help but feel that he wanted to get away from her. She took a deep breath, squelching those feelings. If she started believing her husband couldn't bear the sight of her she'd go crazy.

She opened the bottom drawer of the desk, pulled out a sheet of paper and extended it toward Asher. He scanned the document giving him the right to manage Live Oak and his head shot up quickly. At last, he looked her in the eyes. His face was a mask of bewilderment. He glanced back down at the document.

He seemed so stunned it frightened Caramarena for a moment. What if he didn't want the responsibility? What if he thought she was imposing on him? "You don't mind, do you?" she asked, her voice a little shaky.

"No." His answer was soft and raspy. His eyes seemed to be glued to the paper.

Caramarena wasn't so sure he meant that. Had she misread his interest in Live Oak? He'd spent time surveying the land, getting to know the slaves, reading the operation's books. But now he didn't seem pleased.

She walked closer, and he backed away. His rejection stung like a needle but she hid it with a rush of words. "I know it's a lot of responsibility, and you haven't been in the family very long. But as you discovered the other day most men don't want to do business with a woman—"

"Cara, it's all right, really," he interrupted and looked at her once again. "It's just unexpected."

Caramarena didn't know why but when he called her Cara she felt warm all over. He said it so softly it was like the sun on a cool day. Why didn't he show her more of this side of him? She mentally shook herself. This was not the time to give herself false hope. "Are you sure?"

He gave her a smile. "Of course I'm sure. I'm just stunned, that's all." He laid the paper on the desk. "Tell me, what made your father decide to do this?"

This was a subject she didn't want to talk about. Caramarena sighed and walked away from the desk. "Papa is going away for a few days. He has—business to conduct in New Orleans." Caramarena found it easier to lie to Asher than to admit her her father was so sick the doctor was sending him to a specialist. She turned her back on him so he wouldn't see her squeeze her eyes shut and send up a brief prayer. The doctors had to find out what was wrong and make him better. They just had to.

She tried to hide her worry with a false smile and turned back to Asher. "Papa is pleased that you've decided to stay here and that you've taken such an interest in Live Oak. He would like you to take care of any problems that may arise in his absence." Her voice softened. Her eyes searched his face for understanding. "Are you sure you don't mind?"

"I'm sure." He glanced down at the paper again before asking. "How long will he be gone?"

"A month or two, maybe a little longer. He's not sure. Cypress is going with him."

Asher nodded and leaned a hip against the desk. "I'm glad to hear that Cypress is going with him. When I was in town I heard talk. The man he beat up is looking for a large Negro. It's only a matter of time before someone tells him Live Oak has such a slave. He just might recognize him."

Caramarena took a step toward him. "If he accuses Cypress, we'll simply deny it."

"Would the authorities accept a slave's word over a white man's?" he asked.

"Probably not. Although they should when he's the kind of man who was trying to kill you," she answered with conviction. "But none of that matters. We protect our own."

"I've noticed. Well, maybe it won't come to that." He took a deep breath. "Tell me, when does your father leave?"

"Tomorrow. It's a long journey. I just hope Papa doesn't get too tired."

"Don't worry about him. I'm sure he'll be fine."

There was an edge to Asher's voice that stiffened Caramarena's back. Perhaps he thought she worried too much about her father, which she probably did, but Asher didn't know just how sick her father was.

"Well, if you'll excuse me I need to go talk to Cypress about something," she said.

Asher didn't speak and Caramarena didn't leave immediately. She looked at him. She wanted him to take her in his arms and hold her, to comfort her and tell her her father was going to be all right, that he'd take care of Live Oak, that he would love her and give her children. When he didn't look at her she turned and walked away.

When Caramarena left Asher felt as if his heart went with her. He sat back down in the chair and rubbed his eyes until they ached. It would have been so easy to have lost control again and have taken her in his arms and held her, kissed her, loved her.

He chuckled ruefully. How innocent she was to simply walk in and give him what he needed to complete his destruction of Live Oak. How easy it would be now for him to bleed the bank accounts dry with risky investments. With no money coming in from this year's harvest Live Oak would be in ruins come next spring.

But that thought brought Caramarena's face to mind. God, how he fought with himself to stay away from her. Swimming in the evenings until he thought he might drown, using every last drop of strength from his body just so he wouldn't reach over and touch his wife. If he touched her he'd have to have her. Rising early in the mornings when his body was still tired, when all he wanted was to pull Caramarena close to him and love her once again.

This couldn't go on. He propped his elbows on the desk and let his head drop into his hands. As soon as her father left tomorrow, he'd move into another bedroom. He had to. If he didn't remain cold and distant toward her he'd never be able to carry through with his plan to destroy Live Oak, as his honor demanded.

Whenever he found himself wanting to abandon his plan all he had to do was take a moment and remember the years he spent in his father's house. Asher raised his head and reached for a piece of paper. He'd get to work and get the job done. The sooner, the better.

But when he tried to concentrate, another thought ate at him. What was he going to do about Caramarena?

He rose to look out the window at the beautiful live oak trees which were heavy with Spanish moss. One thing was for sure, after delivering Live Oak into his hands so innocently, Caramarena would never forgive him for what he had to do. At one time, Asher had hoped he might make Caramarena understand that Cantrell had ruined his father's life and made a miserable existence for his wife and their children. Now he knew that was false hope, sprung from that one beautiful, haunting night in her arms. He sighed heavily. He had to forget any notion of building a life with her, and continue with his original plan to place her and Bunch in another house.

He didn't like the way that made him feel. But now that he'd found John Cantrell he couldn't let him go unpunished. He'd promised his father and he'd already sent word to his brothers that he'd found the man. He didn't want to give up Caramarena, but if that's the way she wanted it, he'd see that she and Bunch had enough money to live comfortably.

He stuffed his hands in his pockets and continued to look out the window. He'd lost all desire to study the account books. If he wasn't careful John Cantrell would get the best of the Worthys again. He couldn't let that happen. But Asher feared he was falling in love with Caramarena.

Kissie sat in the shade of the back porch mending a doll dress for Bunch when Cypress walked up carrying a tub filled with sweet corn. His smile grew wide as he approached her. "Good morning, Miss Kissie," he said, setting the tub down, then grinning up at her.

"What you doin' callin' me Miss Kissie?" she asked, forcing herself not to show him how pleased she was.

"I did it 'cause I knew you'd like it." His grin widened. "You did, didn't ye?"

Kissie couldn't hold it in. She lifted her chin and gave him a wide smile. " 'Course I did."

Cypress wiped sweat from his forehead with his shirt sleeve. "It sho' be a hot one taday, Kissie. I gots ta shuck dis corn fo' Ivy. Wants me ta sit by ye whiles I do it?"

"No I don't," she said huffily. "I don't wants Miss Cara to see you near me again."

"She didn't mind me kissin' you. Far as I know she

183

didn't tell nobody. Ain't no one whupped us yet."

"Don't make no difference. Miss Cara don't want to see us kissin'." She went back to her sewing.

"Did she tells you dat?" he asked, slapping at a fly buzzing about his head.

Kissie jerked her head up and glared at him. "She don't have ta. I knows white folks don't wants ta see us kissin'."

Cypress chuckled lightly. "Why we talkin' bout dis? I weren't gonna kiss you. I just gonna sit by you and shuck dis corn fo' Ivy."

Kissie stopped sewing and laid the dress in her lap. She looked down at Cypress and said. "I don't wants you ta go away wid Mr. John."

His smile faded. "I gots to go. Mr. John, he's too sick to go a long ways by hisself."

"I knows dat." Her voice turned huffy again. Fear kept her from being gentle. "I done lost two husbands, Cypress."

"I knows dat." Suddenly his eyes lit with surprise. "Does dis mean you gone marry me, Kissie?"

She picked up the dress and needle. "It means ifs you goes off and gets yo'self in trouble we ain't ever gone marry."

"I ain't lookin' fo' no trouble. You knows I don't like it. I's gonna miss you, Kissie."

Kissie softened. She would miss him too. She didn't want him to leave her.

"I'll see you tanight. You come to my do' same as always."

"I be there." Cypress grinned, picked up the tub and walked toward the barn.

Kissie sighed contentedly. Cypress was a good man. She didn't want to tell him for fear something would happen to him, but she intended to marry him before too long.

184

The door opened and Kissie turned around.

"Kissie, I've been looking for you," Caramarena said, walking over and sitting down on the top step beside her. Her green dress matched the color of the grass. "I need your help."

Kissie continued working the needle but started shaking her head. "I don't likes it when you talks like dat, Miss Cara. I can't helps you no mo'. Don't go talking ta me."

Caramarena remained calm. "Put that stuff away, Kissie, and look at me."

"No sir, Miss Cara. I's gots to finish dis befo' Miss Bunch comes out here screamin' for her doll dress."

Caramarena grabbed the mending from Kissie's hand and hid it behind her back. Kissie's eyes rounded in shock.

"I—I didn't mean to jerk this away from you, but this is important. I don't have time to play games with you. Now will you listen to me?"

Kissie brushed at her apron and nodded.

"Good." Caramarena took a deep breath and set the sewing down on the far side of her skirt. "I come to you, Kissie, because I know that you've been married. I can't talk to Papa about this. And you know I'd go to my mother if she were alive." She reached over and grabbed one of Kissie's hands. "You will help me, won't you?"

Kissie smiled. " 'Course I will. Whats you need?"

Caramarena laced her fingers together and folded them in her lap. She looked out over the lawn. "I can't get Asher to notice me."

"Whats you mean—notice you?"

"Kissie, don't make me say it. You know what I mean." She looked down at her hands. "I want him to pay attention to me." She closed her eyes as Asher's loving flashed before her mind. "I want him to kiss me,

185

hold me, touch me. I want—" She stopped and opened her eyes. "He reads for a while after dinner, then goes down to the river for a swim, then just crawls into bed and goes to sleep. He doesn't kiss me goodnight or anything. He just turns his back and goes to sleep."

"Humm." Kissie placed a finger on her pursed lips. "Dat man ain't right in de head, Miss Cara. You done gots a husband ain't no good."

Caramarena sighed, shaking her head. "That's not true, Kissie. He did love me one time, one night. I thought it wonderful, glorious, but I—I guess I didn't know enough to please him. He hasn't touched me since."

"Naw, dat can't be so, Miss Cara. Men don't wants you to know anything. Dat is not at first." Kissie seemed to ponder the problem for a little while, then asked, "What you does while he's swimmin'?" she finally asked.

"I do needlework—"

"What's you wearing when he comes ta bed?"

Caramarena moved nervously. "Well, Kissie you know what my nightwear looks like."

"Dos you wear it ta bed?"

"Of course."

"No wonder he turns his back. You all wrapped up in dat long gown. A man would smother tryin' ta find ye. When he comes in tanight you be laying on dat bed naked and he won't turn off de light, I promise you dat."

"Kissie," Caramarena gasped. "I couldn't possibly do that. What kind of woman do you think I am?"

Kissie stretched her arms up and over her head and yawned to show her lack of interest. "You asked me, and I told you. Why you want ta ask me things all de time when you never listen ta what I say? Now gimmie dat doll dress."

186

Caramarena felt a little rebuffed. "I don't listen to you because you usually want me to do something crazy like sit in bed naked and wait for my husband to come home." Caramarena stuffed the dress back in Kissie's hands.

"Don't sound crazy ta me," she informed Caramarena.

"There has to be another way. I simply can't do that." She shook her head to emphasize her point.

Kissie rubbed her chin thoughtfully. "Wells, how 'bout you joinin' him in de river."

"Join him in the river? Kissie, you know I can't swim."

Kissie laughed, a deep husky sound that irritated Caramarena. Kissie was teasing her and she was in no mood for it. "Be serious, Kissie," she demanded.

"Oh Miss Cara, I can't help ye. You too young. You don't know enough."

Caramarena was desperate. "Kissie, I'm not that young, but I am inexperienced. What can I do to make my husband want to kiss me and touch me?"

Kissie reached out and caressed Caramarena's cheek. "You so pretty, Miss Cara, I don't knows whats wrong wid yo' man. Maybe dey is somethin' we can do." She pondered for a moment. "If you too proper to sit naked in de bed maybe I can get Fanny to sews you a nightgown dat makes you look naked."

Caramarena almost laughed. "What?"

"Now wait a minute," Kissie said. "She gots some cloth dats so thin I swear yous can see right through it."

"Is it tulle?"

"Hows I know de name of it? May be. I don't never gets to wear any of dat fancy cloth she gots."

Caramarena remembered Asher's deep kisses, his strong arms and gentle touch. It was worth a chance. She took a deep breath and rose. "All right, let's

187

go talk to Fanny and see what she can do."

Before Kissie opened the door Caramarena touched her arm and asked, "Are you sure it will help?"

"No sir, I's not."

Caramarena felt like stomping her foot in frustration. "Then why are we doing this?"

Kissie's eyes rounded. " 'Cause you wants your husband ta notice you, but you don't wants to be naked to do it." Kissie smiled. "Maybe if we gets you almost naked you'll feel better about it and it'll get Mr. Asher's attention, too."

Chapter Twelve

"I want Papa!" Bunch wailed and threw her dessert spoon on the table.

"Now I told you three times yo' Papa done gone ta do his business in town," Kissie said in a gentle voice but felt like jerking Bunch up by the arm and shaking her until her teeth rattled in her mouth. "Now you eats yo' lunch so Miss Cara will be proud of you."

"No!" Bunch folded her arms across her chest and shook her head furiously. "You can't make me."

Kissie pulled on the kerchief that covered her hair. She was hot and tired and getting too old to suffer the whims of spoiled little white girls. "I's not gone try to makes you eats dat food. Don't matter ta me if'n you gets hungry befo' dinner."

"Psst!"

Kissie looked around and saw Lacy standing in the doorway motioning for her to come. Kissie looked at Bunch's pouting face, then walked over to Lacy. "You wants to try and feed her?" she asked the older woman.

Lacy shook her head. "We gots big trouble."

Kissie tensed. "What you mean?"

"Mr. Asher jest come up de stairs and told me ta move his clothes into another bedroom. He ain't gone sleep with Miss Cara no mo'."

Kissie's hand flew to cover her mouth and stifle her cry of alarm. "Lord in heaven! Dis gonna kill Miss

Cara." Kissie looked back to see if Bunch was watching them. She was still pouting. "Did you tell him you can't do no such thing like that widout Miss Cara's tellin' you?"

Lacy's eyes widened. "I'm not gonna tell him no such. Yous tell him. I'm gone move his clothes like he said."

"First her Papa gone away and now dis." Kissie shook her head commiserating with Caramarena. "What dat po girl gone do? Where's Miss Cara now?"

"Fanny called her up to the sewing room for a fitting."

"Oh no! Oh me! Dats my fault. Dat po', po' chile."

"What's wrong, Kissie? Are you sick?" Bunch pushed away from the table and walked over to join the two women.

Kissie put a hand on her shoulder. "No, chile, I's fine, but I somethin' ta do. Go with Lacy and she'll cut you a big piece of sweet bread."

"You gone tell her?" Lacy asked.

Kissie nodded, thinking she'd like to kill the bastard for hurting Miss Cara.

Caramarena looked at herself in the full-length mirror and gasped with surprise. She couldn't believe the masterpiece Fanny had created. Kissie had been right. The tulle was so fine you could see through it. Fanny had made a simple sleeveless design with no ribbons or lace. The heart-shaped neckline was cut low over her breasts and the material fit snugly. It was almost like being naked.

"Oh, Kissie come in and look what you and Fanny created." She ran to her and took both her hands in hers. "Surely Asher will not ignore me if I have this on." Caramarena twirled around for her. "Well, don't just stand there, say something."

Kissie slowly shook her head. "Mr. Asher jest asked Lacy to move his clothes into another bedroom."

Caramarena stood perfectly still, afraid to move. Surely she hadn't heard Kissie right. Should she ask her to say it again? No, she couldn't bear to hear it a second time. She felt light-headed and faint. Taking a deep breath, she tried to get hold of herself. She'd never fainted in her life. No, she wouldn't break down in front of the slaves.

She had to keep her chin up and her dignity. She had to keep her sanity. She willed her breathing to slow down, the tears to stay behind her eyes.

"Well, no matter," she said in an even tone. "This is a beautiful gown. I—I'll wear it anyway." With that said, she lifted the hem and pulled it over her head and handed it back to Fanny. "Have Lacy put it with my nightclothes." Her fingers trembled as she slipped on her chemise, her day corset and petticoats and, at last, her dress. Kissie remained in front of the door watching Fanny help her dress. A ringing started in Caramarena's ears and her head pounded with pain. She needed to be alone.

She swallowed hard and spoke again. "Kissie, I'll wait here until everything of Asher's has been removed, then come get me. I'd like to lie down for a little while."

"Miss Cara—"

"Please, Kissie, just do as I say." She didn't know how much longer she could hold herself together. Her husband didn't want to share the same bedroom with her. She folded her hands across her chest as a sharp pain of rejection sliced through her. How could he do this to her? How could their one night together have been so wonderful for her and so obviously wretched for him?

191

Dinner was a horrible affair that night. Bunch was irritable and Asher was silent. Caramarena's head continued to throb. One thing she'd decided as they struggled through the meal was that tonight when Asher came back from his swim she would ask him what was wrong with her. She wasn't pregnant and with Asher in another bedroom there was no chance of it. But having a child didn't seem as important as it once had. Now she wanted Asher.

Whatever the reason — another woman, the fact that he'd been tricked into marrying her or because she simply hadn't pleased him — it had finally driven him from her room.

As soon as possible after dinner, she sent Kissie and Ivy to their cabins and Lacy and Bunch up to bed. She knew Asher always came into the house through the warming room, so she waited there for him.

"Cara, I'm surprised to find you still up," he said as he opened the door and stepped inside.

Caramarena openly stared at him for a moment. He was so handsome with his damp hair brushed away from his forehead, his white shirt held in his hand and his breeches riding low on his hips.

"I wanted to talk to you." Her voice was too high. She had to calm down or she'd never get through this.

Asher leaned against the built-in cabinet, which was filled with crystal goblets. "All right."

This wasn't going to be easy but had to be done. "I — I don't understand why you moved out of our bedroom." There, it was said.

He dropped his shirt on the countertop and held up his hand. "Look, Cara, I really don't want to discuss this."

She stood her ground, knowing she couldn't go on this way any longer. "We have to. I don't want to be

4 FREE BOOKS

4 FREE BOOKS

TO GET YOUR 4 FREE BOOKS WORTH $18.00 — MAIL IN THE FREE BOOK CERTIFICATE T O D A Y

Fill in the Free Book Certificate below, and we'll send your FREE BOOKS to you as soon as we receive it.

If the certificate is missing below, write to: Zebra Home Subscription Service, Inc., P.O. Box 5214, 120 Brighton Road, Clifton, New Jersey 07015-5214.

FREE BOOK CERTIFICATE

4 FREE BOOKS

ZEBRA HOME SUBSCRIPTION SERVICE, INC.

YES! Please start my subscription to Zebra Historical Romances and send me my first 4 books absolutely FREE. I understand that each month I may preview four new Zebra Historical Romances free for 10 days. If I'm not satisfied with them, I may return the four books within 10 days and owe nothing. Otherwise, I will pay the low preferred subscriber's price of just $3.75 each; a total of $15.00, *a savings off the publisher's price of $3.00.* I may return any shipment and I may cancel this subscription at any time. There is no obligation to buy any shipment and there are no shipping, handling or other hidden charges. Regardless of what I decide, the four free books are mine to keep.

NAME

ADDRESS   APT

CITY   STATE   ZIP

TELEPHONE
(   )

SIGNATURE   (if under 18, parent or guardian must sign)

Terms, offer and prices subject to change without notice. Subscription subject to acceptance by Zebra Books. Zebra Books reserves the right to reject any order or cancel any subscription.

GET
FOUR
FREE
BOOKS
(AN $18.00 VALUE)

ZEBRA HOME SUBSCRIPTION
SERVICE, INC.
P.O. Box 5214
120 BRIGHTON ROAD
CLIFTON, NEW JERSEY 07015-5214

married for the rest of my life to a man who can't stand the sight of me."

His gaze met hers. "Cara, that's not true and that's not fair," he said angrily.

Caramarena remained stiff, holding her pain inside. "What's not fair is for you to move out of our bedroom and not tell me what I did wrong. I deserve an answer."

"Nothing," he said firmly, his eyes never leaving her face. "You haven't done anything wrong."

"Are you still angry you were forced to marry me?"

"No."

"Is there another woman?"

"No!"

She took a step toward him. "If I didn't please you it's only because I didn't know how. If you'd teach me—"

"No, dammit!" He rushed toward her and grabbed her arms and brought her so close to him his lips were almost touching hers. "You pleased me." His voice was raspy. The fury in his eyes turned to tenderness. "You pleased me as no other woman ever has, but I can't continue sleeping with you."

"Why?" Her heartbeat was racing wildly. She desperately needed to understand.

"Because I can't stand not touching you. I had reached my limit."

She dropped her hands to his chest. Hope rose within her. If he wanted her, what was the problem?

"Asher, you can touch me. I want you to. I thought it was wonderful. I—"

"No!" He turned her loose so suddenly she almost fell. "I can't touch you again, Cara. And I can't tell you why so don't ask. Just believe me when I tell you it has nothing to do with my feeling for you."

"But it must," she challenged. "It's my bed you're leaving."

193

"It doesn't! Damn it! It's the only thing I can do under the circumstances. Now leave it alone."

"I don't understand. Asher, help me to understand."

He rubbed his forehead and paced back and forth across the small room. "You will one day. Caramarena, the only thing you need to know right now is that what I did today has nothing to do with the way you loved me. That night was — wonderful for me too," he said passionately. "Listen to me. There is no other woman, and I wasn't forced to marry you against my will. I agreed, remember?" She nodded. "If things were different, I'd take you upstairs right now and make love to you all night long. But I can't. It's not that I don't want to. I've been through hell trying to keep my hands off you, I have to force myself not to look at you because I want to kiss you every time I do. For now, just accept things the way they are. Believe me, it's what's best for both of us."

A wave of nausea swept over Caramarena, weakening her. "I don't think I have a choice."

"You don't." He picked up his shirt, then turned and strode out of the room.

Caramarena sat in a rocker on the front porch, adding a column of figures. It was late September but the cooler days of approaching fall hadn't come to northwest Florida. It was more pleasant outside in the late afternoon than in the office, so she'd come out to finish her work. Asher was looking after most of the everyday running of the plantation, but there were a few things she still took care of. They'd continued with their ever-so-polite routine for more than a week now. In spite of her resolve not to, she found herself wanting to talk to Asher about his decision again. She'd believed him when he'd said the problem wasn't her, but what was it? What or who was keeping him from her bed?

"Miss Cara," Lacy called as she walked up the front steps to the large verandah.

"What is it, Lacy?"

"Do you know where Miss Bunch is? I needs to get her ready for dinah."

"I haven't seen her in the last hour. Have you checked with Kissie?"

"Yes'm. She ain't seen her. Ivy neither." Lacy leaned against the large Doric column and picked up the hem of her apron, twisting it between her fingers.

Caramarena smiled and said, "She's probably upstairs playing with her dolls." She went back to her figures.

"Yes'm," Lacy said, but made no move to go in the house and look for her.

Suddenly a chill ran up Caramarena's back. "Have you already checked upstairs?"

"Yes'm."

"Every room? Every closet?" The woman nodded. "The cupboards in the cookhouse and the warming room?" Her voice was getting higher and Lacy just kept nodding. Caramarena tried not to let her imagination run wild. All right, think, she told herself. Where would Bunch go to hide? "Did you check with Jank to see if she wandered down to the barn?"

"Do you think she went down there?"

"Well, I don't know." She snapped the book shut and rose from her chair. "She may have because she's been looking for Papa. You go see if Jank's seen her. I'll re-check the house. Don't just stand there, Lacy. Hurry!"

Caramarena sped into the house calling Bunch's name. Kissie and Ivy met her in the gold room. "We's already helped Lacy look behind every chair and under every bed, Miss Cara. She's gone," Kissie offered in a shaky voice.

"Nonsense. She has nowhere to go." Her heartbeat accelerated and her breath was choppy but she wouldn't allow herself to think that Bunch might have wandered away from the house.

"We checked everything, I swear on de Bible," Ivy proclaimed.

"Well, we'll do it again. You might have missed her. I'll take the first floor. Kissie, you take the second, and Ivy you take the third. Is Fanny in the sewing room?"

"No, she's sewing for us taday," Kissie said.

"Make sure you search that room carefully, then meet me back here as quickly as you can."

Caramarena felt as if her heart were in her throat. She hurried as fast as she could but still checked behind each chair and sofa and inside every cupboard, calling her sister's name.

Frantic with worry, Caramarena rushed back into the gold room. Kissie was waiting for her, twisting her hands together. "I can't finds her nowhere, Miss Cara."

"Kissie, I'm beginning to think she's wandered off." Tears of frustration filled her eyes.

"She knows better dan dat."

The front door opened and they ran to see if Bunch had come home. Lacy was empty handed. "Jank says he ain't seen her. He's outside de do'. Wants ta know ifs you want him ta help look."

Ivy came running down the stairs and joined them on the front porch. Caramarena had to calm down and think. "Kissie, you and Ivy go get everyone and bring them here."

"All of dem?"

"Anyone who's old enough to walk and look for Bunch."

"I do dat fer you, Miss Cara." Jank offered.

Caramarena knew he wanted to take advantage of Cypress's absence to take over his duties. She tried to smile. "No, Jank, I want you to come with me to the river."

"No, Miss Cara," Kissie said. "You don't needs ta go."

"You lets Jank go," Ivy said.

"I can't let you go down to dat river, Miss Cara," Jank complained.

"Stop it, all of you." Her hands made fists. She felt as if her insides were shaking. She knew they were only trying to spare her feelings. She appreciated it but she had to go. "Be quiet and listen to me. You're wasting my time with your blubbering." She put her hand over her mouth and tried to calm the rising fear.

"Maybe Mr. Asher took her wid him," Kissie said, immediately filling Caramarena with hope.

"Naw. I saw him and Mr. Wulpher ride away. She weren't wid 'em," Jank said.

"Where is Asher?" Caramarena asked. "Did you hear where they were going?"

"Over to de north field to check de cotton."

That was at least two miles away. She turned to Kissie. "Go get Asher and Mr. Wulpher. Run!" Kissie took off, her bare feet kicking up dust. "Ivy, you go get the rest of the slaves. I don't care what they're doing, tell them to stop and come immediately and wait for me here. Lacy, you stay here in case Bunch shows up. Ivy, don't just stand there, take off!"

"Come on, Jank." Caramarena picked up her skirts and hurried down the steps. She didn't pause as her feet hit the ground. She ran toward the river, Jank right beside her.

"I wish you'd let me handle dis, Miss Cara. If'n she in de river I don't wants you ta see her."

Caramarena looked over at Jank but didn't break her stride. "Stop that kind of talk! I don't want to hear it."

197

"Yes'm!"

Her heart was pounding as they neared the river. She didn't slow down until she reached the dock. She stopped to catch her breath, then slowly walked toward the end of the pier. Sweat ran down her cheeks. Her hands clutched her dress so tightly the material had turned hot in her hand. When she reached the edge, her eyes scanned the water from side to side and back again. When she was sure she didn't see Bunch floating in the water she let her shoulders drop, and a dry heave escaped from her trembling lips. Thank God! She knew that finding no body didn't mean Bunch hadn't fallen in the water. She could have been swept downstream. But somehow not finding her here gave Caramarena new hope.

"You wants me ta walk de bank?" Jank asked.

Her chest was tight, her head was throbbing. "Yes, downriver. Don't forget to look for tracks along the way." She was shaking so badly she could hardly stand. "I'll go back and send others to help you. We need to cover both sides before dark."

Jank scratched his head. "If'n she fell in de river she might be forty miles away by now."

Caramarena closed her eyes. "Jank, please don't say things like that. Just go. I'll get help."

Caramarena started back to the house again, running. Her skirt slipped from one of her hands and tumbled around her legs. Her foot caught the material, and she fell, sprawling to the ground. The jolt winded her for a few seconds, and she moaned from the pain that raced up her side. She crawled to her knees, then to her feet and was on the run again.

Several field hands were already gathering on the front lawn. In a state of near-panic Caramarena sent them immediately to help Jank. She ordered a reluctant Lacy in to check the house once again. She was

198

getting ready to go looking herself when she saw Asher and Mr. Wulpher riding up on their horses. At once she felt a sense of hope. Asher would help her find Bunch. She rushed off the porch to meet him.

Asher brought his horse up sharply. Jumping down, he pulled her into his arms.

"Oh, Asher I don't know what to do. We can't find Bunch."

"Kissie said Bunch has run away."

She looked up at him, her heart hammering so fast she could hardly speak. Her whole body was tense and rigid. "I don't know if she's run away, or lost, or hurt. I only know we can't find her anywhere."

"You're sure she's not in the house?"

She nodded. "Jank and some of the others are already . . . searching the river bank." She choked on the last words and Asher pulled her closer, pressing her face against his chest. Comfort issued from him and she let herself relax against him.

"Don't worry, Cara. We'll find her. Mr. Wulpher," he said over her head as he continued to hold her, "Saddle the rest of the horses and get some of the men out looking immediately." He pointed to two young women who'd joined them. "Go check every corner of the turpentine mill."

Caramarena sent up a prayer of thanks because Asher had taken over. If she hadn't been so worried about Bunch she would have buried her face in his shoulder and cried.

"Cara," he lifted her chin, forcing her to look at him. "Does she have any favorite places away from the house?"

She shook her head. "No. We never let her leave the house by herself. She's never been farther than the barn where we took her a couple of weeks ago."

"All right." He turned to the other slaves who had

gathered in the yard around them. "You three take that direction. Check every bush and tree. You two go to the barn and look under every pile of hay. And the rest of you check your own houses. Don't overlook any place!"

Caramarena listened as Asher sent everyone looking for Bunch. Lacy came out of the house. "I can't find her, Miss Cara. We done looked three times. I told you she ain't in there."

"She's got to be somewhere," Caramarena pleaded, coming out of Asher's arms.

"Lacy, stay here with Caramarena and don't leave her."

"No, Asher, I'm going to look, too," Caramarena protested. "I can't stay here another moment. I'm going crazy."

"I know, Cara. But you need to be here. When we find her you're the one she's going to want. We don't want to have to waste time looking for you too. Lacy, you make coffee. Plenty of it. Start gathering lanterns in case we need them."

"Yes sir, Mr. Asher." Lacy hurried inside, leaving Asher and Caramarena alone.

The sun was low in the western sky; it was less than an hour to sundown. For a moment he just looked at his wife. He knew there would be no comforting her if anything had happened to her sister—sweet, beautiful Bunch. The thought of what Caramarena must be going through tightened his chest. He had to find Bunch.

Caramarena had felt so good in his arms he wanted to pull her close once again. He knew she needed the comfort he could give, but he also knew he had to go look for Bunch. He didn't want to leave her in case one of the slaves brought bad news, but knew he had to.

He grasped her shoulders and squeezed them. "Don't worry, Cara, we'll find her." He brushed a

200

strand of stray hair away from her face and wiped a smudge of dirt from her cheek. "How did you get so dirty?" he asked and gave her a teasing grin, hoping it would take some of the worry lines out of her face.

She looked down at her dress, wiped it with her hand and whispered, "I don't know. I think I fell when I was coming back from the river."

Asher's heart went out to her. Even with dirt smudged over her face and dress she was beautiful. With the tips of his fingers he lifted her chin and bent down and kissed her lips tenderly. He wanted more but knew there was no time.

He turned and picked up the reins. "Ring the bell if someone finds her."

Caramarena nodded. Asher climbed on his horse and rode away.

Darkness fell. Caramarena and Lacy lit lanterns, poured coffee for those who returned and sent them back out to continue searching. She knew there would be little chance of finding Bunch in the faint light of a half moon, but she couldn't give up and leave Bunch in the darkness alone.

Numbness covered her as the night grew long and no word came of Bunch. She had to force herself not to think of what might be. She knew that every person was doing everything possible, but it just wasn't enough. Jank's horrible words kept coming back to her with every group that returned empty-handed.

Late into the night Caramarena had Kissie and Ivy stop looking and prepare buttered bread spread with peach preserves for the slaves as they came in. No one complained of the skimpy dinner after a full day's work in the fields.

The moon continued to rise in the sky as midnight came and went, leaving them with a new day. Caramarena kept her vigil on the front porch, watching for anyone who came back, hoping and praying that someone would find Bunch safe and unharmed. But not one had found a trace or track.

Close to sunrise, Asher came back for coffee. He took Caramarena's hand and said, "Why don't you sit down and try to rest. Every time I've come back you've been standing by that column."

"No, I can't. I keep thinking that if I went out I could find her. I might look some place they've missed."

"No. You stay here." His voice was firm.

Caramarena grabbed his shirt sleeve. "Asher, I'm going crazy doing nothing but waiting here. I need to be out looking, too." She couldn't keep the agony out of her voice.

"Think, Cara. What would we do if we found her and brought her home and you were gone? No, you're much more important here."

She rubbed her forehead. She knew he meant to soothe her fears but it wasn't working. "I can't get what Jank said out of my mind. I keep hearing it over and over again. I think I'm going to start screaming."

Asher pulled her into his arms and held her close to his chest. "What did he say to you?"

"No, it's too awful I can't repeat it."

"Tell me, Cara." He spoke softly.

She looked up into his eyes. "He said—if she fell in the river she could be forty miles downstream by now. Oh God, Asher, do you think that's true?"

"No, no, of course not." He rubbed his hands up and down her back trying to calm her. "The fool didn't know what he was saying. She probably didn't even go toward the river. They haven't found any tracks leading downstream." He pressed her head against his shoulder. He couldn't bear to see what this was doing to her. He had to find Bunch for Caramarena. He had to.

She pulled away from him. "But what if she did! What if she's in the water? What if she drowned?"

"Cara, stop this, or you will drive yourself crazy. We don't know that she went anywhere near the river. Wait a minute—I had a thought. Is anyone looking up the river?"

"I—I don't know. I told Jank to look down river on both sides of the bank."

"Damn! I think that's the only place we haven't looked. I'll take some men and go along the upper bank.

She grabbed his shirt and pleaded, "Let me go too."

"No. If we find her I'll send someone right away. I promise."

It wasn't a long walk to the river but Asher didn't want to take the time to walk it. He mounted his horse and shouted for some of the slaves to follow him.

The sky was light with the first threads of morning. Asher was tense with fear. If they didn't find her somewhere upstream, he knew that what Jank said was probably true. They'd covered every inch of three miles in every direction. She couldn't possibly have had time to wander farther than that before they started their search. When he reached the river some of the slaves were coming back from searching downstream and they joined him in his search along the upper bank.

An hour later Asher heard one of the slaves calling and he spurred his horse toward him.

"Mr. Asher, Mr. Asher, I found her!"

Asher stopped the horse at a clump of briar bushes. He swung his leg over the saddle, dismounting as quickly as he could.

"Over here," the dark man called. "I don't think she wants me near."

Asher fell to the ground on his knees as the slave held the lantern close. Bunch's eyes looked wild. Blood streaked her face and arms. Her hair and dress were grotesquely tangled into the thorny vines. She was humming an eerie, throaty sound.

"Bunch, everything is going to be all right now. We're going to take care of you," he said softly. She didn't stop humming. She looked at him, but he didn't think she recognized him.

Asher turned to the slave. "Take the horse and get Cara here as fast as you can. Have someone bring back a wagon to take Bunch home." The slave started to leave, but Asher grabbed his sleeve. "Leave me the lantern, and bring something to cut these damn briars with, too."

Compassion welled up in Asher as he looked at the young woman who was tangled among the briars, unable to move without the thorns tearing her flesh. How had this happened to her? Had she fallen into them, or gotten scared and run into them? He brought the lantern closer to see if there was any way he could free her. No. Most of her hair and dress would have to be cut away.

"Bunch," he said softly. "Everything's going to be all right."

She continued to stare at him with wide eyes, humming that deep groan. The briars were so tangled he didn't know where to start, but he had to do something. He couldn't sit quietly and do nothing while she suffered. He reached to try and free her dress. His first tug on the material caused her to start screaming and thrashing.

"Bunch, no! Be still! It's all right. I'm not going to hurt you. Stop!" He shouted, trying to make her hear him over her screams. "I'm trying to help! You're only hurting yourself more."

The thorns cut into his hands as he tried to grab her and hold her still. That wasn't working so he reached into the bush of thorns, around her back and pressed her face into his chest, hoping the physical contact would soothe her. It did. She stopped screaming and thrashing and started sniffling softly.

"It's going to be all right, Bunch," he crooned. "Help is on the way." Thorns cut into his hands, arms and shoulder. One was piercing his cheek but he didn't move for fear of setting her off again.

"We'll have you cut out of here and in your own bed in just a few minutes," he whispered softly. "See how much better it is when you're still?"

Asher continued to hold Bunch, calming her with soft words, wishing the slave would hurry. Thank God he'd found her for Caramarena. He hadn't let his wife down this time.

At last he heard the approach of a horse and breathed a sigh of relief.

Chapter Thirteen

"Cara, you need to get some sleep." Asher laid a gentle hand on Caramarena's shoulder as she sat on Bunch's bed.

She shook her head. "No, I can't leave her."

Asher glanced down at the bed where Bunch was resting peacefully. Kissie and Caramarena had washed her cuts and scratches and plied them with ointment, then given her a little laudanum to help her sleep. Looking at her now, with her pretty face relaxed in sleep, he could forget the terrified expression she'd worn when he first found her.

It had been no easy task freeing her from those thorns. Her dress had to be cut away from her body and her shiny honey blond hair had to be cut to the length of a boy's.

He knew her wounds would heal, and he could only hope she'd get over this experience as easily as she did the one involving the runaway horses.

His gaze moved to his own hand, resting on Caramarena's shoulder. It was marred with deep burning scratches. He knew how much pain Bunch must have been in when he found her. Dammit! If she'd never wandered away from the house before, what had made her do it yesterday? Maybe Caramarena was right. Maybe she was looking for her father, or maybe she just wanted to know what lay beyond the house.

And what about Caramarena? Her emotional pain had been just as bad as Bunch's physical pain. Both of them could end up scarred from this incident.

"Cara, listen to me." He moved from behind her and knelt down in front of her, taking her hands in his. "When Bunch awakens, she's going to be in a lot of pain. She's going to need you, then. She doesn't need you while she's resting peacefully. You should get some sleep now. She'll sleep for several hours and so should you."

She shook her head. "I can't leave her," she said again. "I feel so responsible for what happened to her. Papa trusted me to look after her."

"Look at me, Cara." He grasped her chin and forced her to face him. "You take excellent care of Bunch. No one could question your devotion or your love for your sister. Now, I don't want to hear any more talk like that." His tone softened. "You can leave her now. She'll be all right. She's not going anywhere."

Her voice was barely a whisper as she looked into his eyes and said, "No, it's my fault she got lost. I —"

"No," he said firmly. "It's no one's fault. She has a mind of her own. If she'd decided she was going to look for her father no one could have stopped her. She would have found a way to sneak away from all of you. Don't blame yourself."

"But I know she can't take care of herself. I know she doesn't understand any of this."

"Maybe she knows it now. I don't think she'll start out on her own any more. This has probably taught her a valuable lesson. All we need to do now is thank God she's all right and hope she doesn't have any lasting effects."

Caramarena relaxed a little, then looked down at the hands that held hers so tightly, giving her strength. Startled, she rose from the bed and stared at him, her wide eyes filled with concern.

"You have scratches all over your hands—and your face. I was so worried about Bunch I didn't notice you were hurt."

She reached up and touched his cheek. Her hand was warm and soft and comforted him at once. At that moment he realized he wanted to hold her. He wanted to lie down beside her and feel her warmth and rest with her.

He swallowed hard as his thoughts begged to remember the night he made love to her. No, he wouldn't think about that. "I'm all right," he whispered huskily.

"Did Kissie put something on these scratches?" She picked up his hands and looked over them.

He shook his head. "I washed them. They'll be fine."

"That will never do. You need something on these immediately."

Asher pulled his hands out of hers and grasped her shoulders. He smiled. "You've done enough doctoring for one day. I'll be fine, but I'm worried about you. You need to get some sleep." *And I need to lie beside you and hold you.* He took her hand in his, kissed her palm and felt her breathing hasten. His touch seemed to do for her what her touch did for him.

Their gaze held for a sweet moment, then she said, "Nonsense. I'm not the one who's hurt." She reached into the box of medicines that sat on the table by Bunch's bed and pulled out a small tin of salve. "Sit down and let me take care of these or they'll end up infected the way your knife wound did."

Asher didn't argue with her again. The scratches were burning and he knew the ointment would help.

208

"If you insist on doctoring me, you might as well get them all." He pulled his shirt out of his breeches and over his head, revealing more scrapes and cuts. He'd gotten most of them when he'd first reached Bunch and had to hold her to calm her down so she wouldn't continue to harm herself.

As she bathed his scratches in the soothing balm, Caramarena's eyes watered for the first time since finding Bunch. Asher knew she was going to fall apart if she didn't get some rest.

"There, that feels better already," he said. He picked up a cloth from the bedside table and handed it to her. "Now wipe your hands. You're going to bed."

With the back of her hand, she wiped away a stray tear before she accepted the cloth. As she cleaned her hands she turned back to look at Bunch. "I think she'll be all right as long as she doesn't develop a fever. Some of the scratches are deep. But I believe we got all of the thorns out." She touched her sister's forehead.

"Does she feel feverish?" Asher asked.

Caramarena shook her head. "No, she's cool." There was a knock on the door and Asher turned to see Kissie standing in the doorway holding a tray.

"I broughts Miss Cara some hot tea."

Asher saw his opportunity to get Caramarena out of the room and took it. "You're just in time to sit with Bunch, Kissie." He took hold of Caramarena's arm. "You drink the tea to keep you awake while you watch Bunch. Cara's going to lie down for a couple of hours." He ushered his wife toward the door. "If Bunch wakes you're to come get us immediately."

"Asher wait—I—"

"No arguing, Cara. You're going to get some sleep if I have to hold you to the bed."

Caramarena looked up into her husband's eyes and found she was too tired to argue any more. "All right." She turned back to Kissie, who was taking her place at Bunch's bedside. "Come get me the minute she wakes up."

"Yes'm."

Kissie watched Mr. Asher and Miss Cara walk out the door before placing the tray on the nightstand. She reached and cupped Bunch's cheek tenderly. "I's shore glad dey found you, Miss Bunch. You gave us a mighty big scare."

Sighing, Kissie eased into the chair by the bed, then reached over and poured tea into the delicate china cup. After letting it cool for a couple of minutes she picked up the cup and sipped the lukewarm liquid.

"Mmm," she mumbled aloud. It was no wonder white folks liked to drink out of fancy little cups. Sure made tea taste better than her tin cups.

Caramarena was surprised that Asher followed her into her room and closed the door behind them. He hadn't been in her room for two weeks. A nervous flutter started in her stomach when she faced him. She wasn't certain why he'd come in with her, or if he intended to stay. She took a deep breath, deciding to make light of the tense situation. "You don't have to hold me to the bed." She smiled at him. "I promise to get some rest."

He just looked at her for a moment as if he wanted to say something. She didn't know if he was trying to talk himself out of what he wanted to say or trying to get the courage to say it. "Turn around, I'll unfasten you," he finally said.

Caramarena did as she was told, finding it soothing to have Asher so close even if she didn't know his intentions. She was too tired and too emotionally drained to question him.

While he worked at the buttons on her dress and ribbons on her corset, Caramarena remembered how gently he'd talked to Bunch while he cut her hair and her dress, leaving both among the thorns. She remembered how he lifted Bunch from amidst the briars and placed Bunch in her arms. She remembered how he held them both close as the wagon carried them to the house.

Asher had her in a constant state of confusion. Why was he so gentle and caring at times like this and so cold and wooden at others?

Caramarena allowed Asher to help her step out of her dress, petticoats and corset, leaving only her chemise. She sat on the edge of the bed while he took off her shoes and stockings. She found comfort in every little thing he did for her. With gentle hands he pulled the pins from her hair and ran his fingers through the length of it several times before easing her back against the pillows.

When that was done, he walked over to the windows, loosened the tiebacks and let the drapery panels fall together, shutting out the morning sunlight and darkening the room.

With the darkness came the fears that had been with her all through the night. Even through the room was warm a chill shook her body. Caramarena didn't want to be alone.

She rose from her pillows and looked at her husband. "Asher, don't leave me," she whispered softly.

He strode back to the bed and smiled at her. "I don't intend to." He reached down and took off his

211

boots and socks, but left his breeches on and lay down on the bed beside her.

Caramarena closed her eyes and breathed a trembling sigh of relief. He wasn't going to leave her.

"Come here, Cara," he murmured. "Lay your head on my shoulder so we can both rest."

"What about your cuts?" she asked, not wanting to hurt him, yet knowing she wanted nothing more than to be in his arms at this moment.

He reached over and touched her cheek. "They'll feel much better if I'm holding you."

Caramarena looked into Asher's eyes and believed he wanted to hold her as much as she wanted him to hold her. Whatever was keeping him from her bed, he had put it aside for now. That pleased her. She scooted closer, gently laid her head on his broad shoulder and placed her arm across his chest.

Asher moved a little and fit his body next to hers. His skin was warm, his warmth comforting, his comfort healing. Asher's arm came around and grasped her shoulder, holding her close. He bent his head and rested his cheek against the top of her head. All the tension Caramarena had experienced throughout the night eased out of her body and she fell into a restful sleep.

A few minutes later so did Asher.

Kissie lit a lantern in her small one-room house and sighed heavily. She'd spent the last five nights at the big house in Bunch's room. For the first three days Bunch had been too sick for her or Lacy to leave at night and for the last two she'd just been too spoiled.

She felt sorry for the young woman because her mind wasn't right, but she did get tired of catering to that girl's every wish. It was a shame Bunch wasn't as bright as Miss Cara.

Kissie rubbed her neck and shoulders and looked around the room. A narrow bed stood against the far wall, the covers neatly arranged. A square table and two chairs set in one corner and a short chest which held her few clothes in the other. Her rocker was in front of the window where she liked to sit and listen to the sounds of night after the day was finished.

The house wasn't much, but it was her home and had been for close to twenty years. The place seemed empty now, and Kissie knew it was because Cypress was gone. The thought of him brought a smile to her lips and a low chuckle in her throat. Neither one of her husbands could make her as mad as Cypress could and neither had ever made her feel nearly as good.

As she glanced around the silent room she realized just how much she missed Cypress. She missed his sneaking up behind her in the middle of the day and stealing a kiss. She missed his coming over and talking to her about the day's events. She missed him staying the night with her and she missed their loving.

Right now she wanted to feel his strong arms around her. But Cypress was gone and it would probably be a few more weeks before he returned.

Kissie walked over to her chest and pulled out a worn but clean nightgown. She sure hoped Cypress didn't get into any trouble while he was gone. Mr. John might be too sick to take care of him the way Mr. Asher had.

While she undressed, getting ready for bed, she thought about Miss Cara and Mr. Asher. He sure wasn't turning out to be the kind of husband Miss Cara was wanting. Although, by what he did for Cypress, Kissie knew him to be a good man. If only he'd sleep with Miss Cara long enough to get her with child, Kissie thought, she might even learn to like him.

With her nightgown on, Kissie walked over to her rocker and plopped herself in it, kicking her shoes off so she could rest her feet. She really hadn't liked Mr. Asher when he first came to Live Oak, but little by little that was changing. He'd done right by Cypress when he'd killed that white man in Apalachicola. And he'd saved Bunch's life—twice. But she sure didn't like the fact that he didn't sleep with Miss Cara. No, she didn't like that at all. Miss Cara wasn't going to get pregnant by that man unless he got in the bed with her.

Mr. Asher had slept with Miss Cara for a few hours after they found Bunch. But Kissie had sense enough to know he didn't touch her. It was written all over Miss Cara's face when she got up that afternoon. Kissie didn't know how that man could keep his hands off a woman as pretty as Miss Cara. He sure was a strange one. She never would understand white folks. Never would.

She leaned her head back and closed her eyes. She was tired. Bunch would run the legs off a dog. Kissie must have gone up and down the stairs fifty times for that girl today.

Kissie didn't know how long she'd been rocking and thinking when she heard a soft knock on her door. At first her heartbeat increased thinking it was Cypress, but she remembered he was gone. It was probably Ivy wanting to talk before she went to sleep.

She opened the door and was surprised to find Jank standing there holding a rose in his hand.

"Jank, what you doin' at my do' dis time a night?"

214

"I brung you dis here rose, Kissie." He smiled and held it up toward her.

Kissie shook her head. "I ain't takin' dat rose. Anybody finds it in heres and days think I stole it outta de garden."

"Don't nobody ever come in yo' house, Kissie. Take dis rose. It smells pretty like you does."

Kissie looked down at Jank smiling up at her. Jank was a few years younger than Cypress, but not nearly so big or so handsome or so strong, and if that rose meant he'd come calling, he wasn't smart as Cypress either. But it also meant he wasn't afraid of Cypress. That thought forced her to take a second look. She didn't know of many men who weren't afraid of Cypress. She relented and reached for the rose.

"What you want, Jank?" she asked as she carried the pink rosebud to her nose and inhaled the sweet scent.

The whites of his eyes shone brightly in moonlight, and he kept the smile on his lips. "I's hopin' you'd let me come in and sit wid ye for a spell."

"And do what?" Kissie decided not to give him any slack. Everyone knew that Cypress was her man, so for Jank to be at her door meant he was trying to change that. Cypress wouldn't be happy if he knew Jank had stolen a rose for her.

"Jest talk, Kissie," he hurried to say. "I jest wanted to talk to ye fo' awhile. I knows Cypress is yo' man. But he ain't here and I is."

"Dat don't matter. What you doing at my do' if'n you know Cypress is my man?" Kissie liked Jank all right and she was quite pleased he'd stolen the rose for her. But the fact remained she wasn't interested in anyone but Cypress. She thought it was best to make

215

sure Jank knew that right from the start. She wouldn't have to stop anything if it never started.

"I told you, Kissie. I jest wanted to talk."

"No, dat ain't all you wants. I knows better. Dis rose sho' is pretty but I can't take it, Jank. You go gives it to one of de younger girls. Deys plenty of 'em whats got dere eyes on you." She tossed the rose back to him and he caught it between his hands and his chest. A thorn must have nicked him because he let out a high-pitched yelp.

"I wants you ta have it, Kissie. I picked it for ye." Careful how he held the stem, he extended the rose to her once again.

His big dark eyes shone with tenderness and Kissie hated hurting him. "You go find one of dem young girls. I too old fo' you, and besides, I don't want Cypress killing you over one rose. It ain't that pretty. Now go befo' someone see you at my do' and tells my man. Go on gets."

Jank lowered his chin to his chest turned and ambled away from her house. She watched him until he was out of sight. It gave her a right good feeling to know Jank was sweet on her.

Kissie leaned against the door frame and looked up at the beautiful sky. The round moon lung low. The stars twinkled and sparkled as if they were trying to talk to her. She missed Cypress more at that moment than any other time. She wished he was standing behind her, with his strong arms wrapped around her waist, with her pulled tight against his wide chest. She sighed and walked back in and closed the door. Cypress had been gone three weeks, but to her it seemed like three years. She sure did miss that big man when he was gone.

216

* * *

Caramarena awoke feeling more refreshed than she had in a week. It was the first time she'd slept through the night since Bunch had gotten lost. Her days were very tiring because she spent them helping Lacy and Kissie care for Bunch's every little whim. She hadn't been outside the house in a week so she decided today she'd take a ride.

As Lacy helped her dress she remembered the day she and Asher had lunch under the large live oak on the bluff before their wedding. Maybe she'd ask Asher if he'd like to have a picnic with her today. They had to start trying to build a better life together.

She hadn't been alone with him since the morning Bunch was found. That morning he had stayed with her, holding her until she went to sleep, but she was alone when she awakened. He hadn't been back to her bedroom. They'd both been too busy to see each other during the day with Bunch taking so much of her time and with him managing the plantation. Once or twice he'd asked a question but for the most part he'd taken care of everything without her help.

"Miss Cara," Kissie said, sticking her head in Caramarena's room.

"Oh Kissie, I want you t—"

"I's sorry ta interrupt, Miss Cara, but Mr. Wulpher is downstairs and he's says fo' you ta come right away. He says deys a big storm on de way and de cotton still in de field."

Caramarena froze for a moment. It was late in the season for a hurricane, but they had been known to come as early as May and as late as December. She remembered a bad storm when she was a little girl. The hard rain and fierce winds had destroyed their cotton crop that year, several trees had been uprooted and parts of the roof had blown off the house.

"Where's Asher?" she asked.

"He be with Mr. Wulpher in de office."

"All right. Good. Tell them I'll be right down." She turned back to Lacy. "We won't worry about my hair right now, Lacy. Don't take time to put it up. Just finish buttoning my dress as quickly as you can."

A few minutes later, Caramarena rushed down the stairs, holding up the skirt of her spruce-colored dress. She'd taken only a moment to brush her hair away from her face and left it to hang down her back.

Asher and Mr. Wulpher were standing in front of the window when she entered the office. "Good morning," she said to both of them.

"Miss Cara, there's a storm on the way," Mr. Wulpher said, holding his hat in front of his round stomach.

Her eyes lighted on Asher briefly before her gaze darted back to Mr. Wulpher. "A storm or a shower?" she asked, wanting to be sure he wasn't blowing this out of proportion.

"Looks like a full hurricane coming up the Gulf. A man on a passing boat just stopped to tell one of the slaves who was on the dock. He said the wind was already high in Apalachicola with the seas up. Said he left before the rain started, but they're already boarding up the windows in town and heading for higher ground. It sounds like this may be a bad one, and we've still got cotton that needs picking."

Caramarena's heart started beating faster. It wasn't unusual to still be picking this late in the year with as much cotton as they planted. Light rain didn't hurt cotton bolls that had just opened, but a storm with high winds and hard rain would flatten the stalks to the ground and ruin the crop. She turned to Asher.

218

"How many fields are left to pick?"

"Four—totalling about one hundred acres."

Caramarena winced. Losing that much cotton would cut into their profits. How could they get three weeks of work done in only a few hours? Oh God, she hoped the man was wrong and that it was only a small storm and not a hurricane.

"Mr. Wulpher, go immediately and put everyone in the fields. From the youngest to the oldest. Shut down the mills and put all of the mill workers in the field, too. Start with the fields closest to the barns and as soon as a wagon is filled have it taken to the barn and emptied."

"Yes, Miss Cara. I know what to do."

His tone was a little hard-edged and that angered Caramarena. "Then why are you standing there, get to it," she snapped.

Mr. Wulpher looked from Caramarena to Asher, then popped his hat on his head and hurried from the room. She knew the problem. Mr. Wulpher was like most men. He would rather take his orders from Asher.

"I'm not as well versed as Mr. Wulpher, Caramarena. I don't know what to do. You'll have to tell me."

You can hold me and tell me everything is going to be all right, she thought, but said, "You can help Mr. Wulpher get the slaves organized. The ones who work the mills and gardens won't be happy about being sent to the fields. They'll have to be pushed."

Asher nodded. "Is that all?" he asked as if he expected there to be more that he could do. "I mean is there anything else I can do for you?"

It was on the tip of her tongue to tell him that she needed to feel his arms around her, if only for a few seconds. But if he didn't know what she needed right now, she wasn't of a mind to enlighten him.

She lowered her lashes and swallowed hard before shaking her head. "Excuse me. I've got to find Kissie," she murmured softly, and she hurried from the room.

Caramarena found Kissie, Ivy and Lacy in the cookhouse talking about the approaching storm. Two other young girls who helped with the cooking were with them. Caramarena's back stiffened.

"Why are you in here and not in the fields?" she demanded. "I told Mr. Wulpher I wanted everyone out picking that cotton."

"We ain't field hands, Miss Cara." Kissie complained. "We don't knows notin' 'bout pickin' cotton."

"I gots to take care of Miss Bunch, Miss Cara. She ain't well enough to leave on her own yet," Lacy said in the same lazy tone of voice Kissie had used.

"And I gots ta cook fo' you so you don't go hungry. You two get on outta heah and get down to de cotton fields like Miss Cara told ye," Ivy said to her two young helpers, and they stumbled over themselves to get out the door.

For a moment Caramarena wondered if she'd been too good to the three women standing in front of her. She was very fond of each one, but today, like it or not, they were all going to the field.

"Lacy, you're to go get Fanny to stay with Bunch. She's older than you are and probably can't pick as fast as you can." She held up her hand and said, "Don't argue with me. I don't have the time or the patience to listen. Ivy, you can forget about cooking for now because we don't have time to eat. I know there's plenty of bread, butter and preserves and that will be sufficient until later. In the afternoon you can put on a big pot of pea soup. Enough for everyone.

But for now, you're going to help out in the field with everyone else."

Caramarena took a breath and turned to Kissie. "I agree that you're not a field hand, Kissie, but for today you'll have swallow your pride and be one."

Caramarena stood with her back straight, her chin high and slowly looked at the shocked expressions on the faces of the women. Not one of them had expected her to make them work in the fields.

"You're wasting time. I will personally check each one of your bags and they had better be full. Now go!" she said firmly, not wanting any of them to give her any more trouble about this.

With their dark eyes rounded in surprise and their egos severely wounded, all three women hurried out the door.

Caramarena hurried back upstairs to see Bunch before she went to the fields. Mr. Wulpher could push the slaves and keep them working but she was needed to push Mr. Wulpher. If Asher had more experience she was sure he'd do it for her.

Still dressed in her nightclothes, Bunch sat in the middle of her bed playing with one of her dolls. Most of her scratches had healed nicely but Caramarena was sure there were some that would leave scars.

"Good morning, Bunch," she said in a light voice. "You're looking very pretty today. How do you feel?"

"Baby has a tummyache. Can you make her all better?" She extended the doll toward Caramarena.

"Oh, I don't know. Let me see." Caramarena eased down on the bed beside her and took the doll in her arms. She pretended to look the doll over carefully before laying it on her shoulder and patting its back. "I think she does have a tummyache. Maybe you should let her stay in bed today."

221

"I will," Bunch said as she took the doll from Caramarena and placed it on one of the pillows.

"Bunch, listen to me. I don't want you to be frightened but there's a storm coming. Everyone is going to have to go out to the fields, including me."

Bunch grabbed Caramarena around the neck and held tightly. "Don't leave me, Cara. I don't like storms. Don't leave me!" she pleaded.

"Bunch, stop this. Turn me loose and look at me." Bunch did as she was told. Tears had welled up in her eyes. She'd had so much attention for the past few days that she expected someone to be with her at all times. "I'm not going to leave you alone. I've asked Fanny to come stay with you. Will that be all right?"

Bunch pursed her lips and wiped her eyes with the back of her hand. "Will she play with me?"

"I'm sure she will. But she doesn't have a doll. Do you have one she can borrow?"

Bunch nodded.

"Good. I've got to go. You get your dolls ready, and Fanny will be up in a few minutes. All right?"

Bunch nodded again and scrambled off the bed, her nightgown clinging to her legs. "I have plenty in here," she said as she threw open a trunk and started pulling out dolls.

Caramarena stayed in her morning dress but quickly changed from her soft slippers to sturdy boots. She also took the time to twist her hair into a knot at the back of her neck and pin it.

The sky was gray and a light breeze blew as she headed to the west field at a brisk pace. As she walked she sent up a brief prayer that the storm would dissipate before it reached them. Losing so much of the crop might hurt them.

In the distance she saw the large field of cotton dotted with darkies. The tall ones were down on their knees to pick while the shorter ones stooped. One of them hummed a familiar tune. She smiled. Live Oak had good slaves. She couldn't remember the last time one of them caused trouble.

Of course, Cypress had killed that man in town, but that wasn't his fault. He'd saved Asher's life. That incident had been more than two months ago. Surely if they were going to hear anything about it they would have by now.

As she topped a sloping hill she spotted Asher and Mr. Wulpher standing at the far end of the field and hurried over to them.

"Miss Cara," Mr. Wulpher called to her as she approached. "I was just telling Mr. Millhouse that of fifty-three slaves we have forty-nine working. One, of course, is with Miss Bunch up at the house. Two of them are just too young to work, they're still babies. I left them with the mother of one of the babies and told her she'd have to feed both of them," the overseer boasted as Caramarena looked up at him.

"Yes. That would be Hannah. I'm glad you let her stay. She hasn't been well since she had the baby. Thank you, Mr. Wulpher for getting them in the fields so quickly."

Caramarena glanced over at Asher. His eyes weren't on her. He was watching the darkies in the fields as if he'd been mesmerized by the sight. He didn't look natural and it gave her an uneasy feeling. What was he thinking about?

Asher looked out over the field of beautiful white cotton bursting from the dark brown shells and knew he didn't want the approaching storm to destroy it.

223

Was he going crazy? He'd just spent the last week depleting John Cantrell's bank accounts without so much as a blink of an eye, but now it put a knot in his chest to see how everyone worked to pick the cotton before the storm hit.

Writing bank drafts for risky business ventures in Pensacola was one thing, but to stand by and watch the wind and rain destroy what he'd watched grow for the last two months made him feel sick inside.

He didn't understand these new feelings. He didn't understand them at all. The money in the bank was Cantrell's, but Asher felt as if the cotton was his own. He was the one who'd been out to check on it twice a week. He was the one who'd told the slaves to hoe the weeds, chop the dead stalks and carry water to dying plants.

Yes, dammit, this was his cotton. His! He wouldn't let nature take it without a fight.

Asher turned to Mr. Wulpher. "Give me one of those cotton sacks, and take one for yourself."

"W-what do you mean?" the portly man asked, stumbling over his words.

"We're going to pick cotton, Mr. Wulpher." For a brief moment Asher let his gaze stray to Caramarena. He knew he had some decisions to make concerning her, too. Right now the cotton had to come first.

"I-I have to watch the slaves, Mr. Millhouse." Mr. Wulpher drummed his fingers on the band of his hat. "They won't work if I don't stand watch over them."

"Yes, they will." Asher picked up two of the burlap sacks and handed one to the older man. "Get to it."

"Surely you don't mean—"

"Yes, I do," Asher interrupted him. "Don't let me have to speak again."

Mr. Wulpher's face flushed, and his eyes widened

with indignation. He turned to Caramarena. "I think you need to speak to your husband, Miss Cara. He obviously doesn't know how we do things around here."

Pride filled Caramarena. "No, you're the one who's mistaken, Mr. Wulpher. My husband has spoken."

Mr. Wulpher looked from one to the other, snorted a couple of times, then headed for the cotton field, snapping the sack against his leg as he went.

Asher turned to Caramarena, and he saw something shining in her eyes. Love. It was love and it made him warm all over. He'd known his wife loved him, but he hadn't wanted to admit it. He still wasn't sure he wanted it to be so. But he'd have plenty of time to think about it while he picked the cotton.

He turned away from her but she touched his sleeve. "Wait. I'll go with you." She reached for a sack but he grabbed her arm and stopped her.

"No. You stay and make sure the wagons get to and from the barn as fast as possible. You'll also need to send someone around with a bucket of water in a couple of hours. You stay here and take care of those things."

Tears of joy wanted to fill Caramarena's eyes but she held them off. "Oh, Asher you don't have to pick," she said huskily, her face glowing with all the love she was feeling.

"Yes, I do," he responded huskily. "I have to."

Without thinking, Caramarena placed her hands on Asher's shoulders and reached up and kissed him on the lips. When she started to back away Asher surprised her by scooping her up in his arms, returning the kiss. But instead of a brief sweet kiss like the one she gave him, his was hard and demanding, forcing her lips apart and her mouth open. Once he'd tasted

225

her, he slowly let her go.

For a time they just looked at each other. So much needed to be said but there was no time.

"Keep those wagons moving," he said; then he walked over to a row of cotton and fell to his knees.

The whole field went quiet as all the slaves looked up to see the overseer and Asher picking cotton. One of the men started singing a song with a quick tempo and soon others joined him as the field came alive with activity once again.

Caramarena's heart swelled with love for her husband. He must love Live Oak. Why else would he pick cotton? Her father would be so pleased when she told him what Asher was willing to do for the plantation.

Even though she wasn't carrying Asher's child now, she suddenly knew that someday she would. Asher loved Live Oak enough to work beside the slaves. Maybe some day he would love her.

She smiled. Tonight she would tell him how much she loved him—then she would show him.

Chapter Fourteen

By early afternoon the sky was bleak and threatening with puffs of gray clouds that moved swiftly across the sky. The wind blew hard and thunder rumbled in the distance. Asher had insisted they all keep working until the rain started.

Caramarena was surprised at how much everyone picked. They worked hard and fast. Some of the men had bets going to see who picked the most sacks by the end of the day. Seeing Asher and Mr. Wulpher in the fields seemed to make the slaves work harder than they ever had. It was as if the participation of those two men had made all the slaves realize how important it was and they rallied to get the job done.

One of the young girls did nothing but walk up and down the rows with a bucket of water, letting each one drink their fill. Caramarena knew, too, that they were working faster because there was no hot sunshine sapping their strength.

At midday she'd sent Ivy up to the cookhouse to prepare large pots of pea soup. As soon as the first batch was ready, she let the slaves go up four at a time for a piece of cold bread and a bowl of hot soup. Asher and Mr. Wulpher had taken their meal right beside the others.

At one point late in the afternoon, when Kissie came to the wagon to empty her sack, she paused to talk to Caramarena. "You knows when dat man first came here I didn't likes him one little bit."

"Are you talking about Asher?" Caramarena asked with a smile on her face.

"Mmm—he's de one." Kissie reached up and retied the dark brown kerchief that covered her hair. "But nows I think he be a fine man. Taking care of Cypress de way he did, saving Miss Bunch, and now here he is in de fields working as hard as any of us. Yes sir, he sho' enough a fine man."

Caramarena laughed. She was happy that Kissie had finally admitted to Asher's good points. "I've always known he was a good man, Kissie. I sensed it right from the first."

"Not me. I always thought he wuz hiding something. He wuz always so quiet. And I didn't like the way he were looking at me and Cypress."

"He was outnumbered, Kissie, and forced to marry when he didn't really want to." She looked away wistfully. "I'm sure that can do strange things to a man."

"Wells, I's better get back to de field befo' Mr. Asher comes afta me." She turned away, still mumbling, "Yessir, you knows how to picks de best husbands."

A short time later the wind increased, blackness covered the sky and the rain started. It was light at first but in a matter of minutes it turned into large stinging drops. Caramarena's hair and clothes were saturated in a few seconds. The slaves started throwing their half-filled sacks on top of the wagons and heading for their cabins. As soon as a wagon was full Caramarena shouted to the driver to hurry to the barn.

By the time there was only one wagon left, Caramarena was shaking from the chill of the cold, hard rain. She spun around when a hand touched her shoulder. Asher was standing before her, rain pelting his face and running down it. His hair was flattened to his head and his shirt was clinging to his chest. He squinted his eyes against the force of the rain.

"You go on to the house. I'll finish up here." He had to shout for her to hear him over the wind and rain.

She shook her head. "I'll stay and help," she responded.

"No!" He brushed his hair away from his forehead and tried to wipe the rain from his face. "We're almost through. You go on back to the house and check everything there. I'll be up in a few minutes."

Caramarena's shivers prompted her to agree. She turned and started toward the house, her heavy, wet skirts twisting and clinging to her legs.

When she made it to her room she changed into a warm cotton robe and left her hair hanging down her back to dry. She ate a bowl of soup while she visited with Bunch, who was still content to spend most of her time in her room. Caramarena had told Kissie, Ivy and Fanny to go straight to their homes in the slave quarters, assuring them she and Lacy could take care of Bunch through the night.

A short time later, when the thunder grew louder and the lightning started, Bunch became agitated. Caramarena gave her some milk laced with laudanum so she'd sleep through the storm. She then went to Asher's room, picked up some towels and his robe and went to wait for him in the warming room.

Within a few minutes Asher came in, dripping wet. His hair was plastered to his head, and rain droplets ran down his face. His clothes clung like a second skin to his frame. A puddle formed at his feet as he stood in front of the closed door.

229

"I brought some towels and your robe. The coffee's still hot. I'll get you a cup while you change."

Caramarena turned her back on Asher and took a deep breath. Why was she so nervous? Because she was expectant? Because she'd sensed something in Asher's kiss that morning that hadn't been there before? Because she didn't want to be alone tonight?

A loud crash of thunder sounded and Caramarena jumped. She was supposed to be pouring Asher a cup of coffee, not nursing her neurosis. She heard him changing behind her. When she thought enough time had passed for him to be covered she turned around and found him standing in the same spot, tying the black sash of his burgundy-colored robe.

She moved forward and handed him the coffee.

"Thanks," he said and sipped the warm liquid. "I sent Jank up to check the shutters again. Did he do it?"

Lightning flashed lighting the room and thunder rumbled immediately behind it, rattling the window-panes.

"Yes. All is safely locked up." Caramarena folded her hands across her chest, trying to ward off the chill that threatened her. "The last time we had a storm this bad we lost a few shutters, part of the roof, some trees and an entire cotton crop. This time we won't have lost an entire parcel. We managed to get quite a bit of the cotton picked."

"Not enough," he said. "We only covered about ten acres with a light sweep."

"Asher, that's extremely good."

The coffee was all right, but what Asher really needed was a good stiff drink of brandy. He was having a hell of a fight with himself. He was tired and irritable. Part of him wanted to grab Caramarena and kiss her while he carried her all the way up the stairs—wanted to kiss her and not stop kissing her until morning. The other half was telling him to be sensible, to leave things as they were between them and get the hell back to England as fast as possible.

While he picked the cotton he'd decided it would be best to wait until he'd settled things with his brothers before he asked Caramarena to come to him and be his wife. But now, with her standing before him looking so beautiful, so desirable he wanted to take the time the storm had given him and love her.

"I've kept some soup hot over candles," she said. "Will you have a bowl?"

He shook his head but his eyes didn't leave her face. "I'm not hungry." That was a lie. He was hungry for her. Sipping his coffee, he watched her.

He hadn't touched her in weeks, but tonight, knowing the way he felt today when Live Oak was threatened by something other than himself, he didn't want to resist Caramarena's allure. There were many reasons why he shouldn't touch her, but he was forgetting them one by one.

The expression on her face told him she was nervous. Hell, he was, too. He was trembling for want of her, yet wondering what in damnation he was supposed to tell her. As he'd worked in the fields it was easy to tell himself that he'd leave for England as soon as the storm was over, settle things with his brothers and come back and make a home with Caramarena. After today he knew he didn't want to destroy Live Oak. But now he found the temptation to make love to her overpowering. He didn't want to wait the months it would take to sort out the whole story.

Lightning flashed again and he realized they were standing there looking at each other. Obviously, neither of them knew what to say. "How's Bunch?" He reached down and picked his sopping wet clothes off the floor.

Caramarena quickly took them from him and laid them on the table. "She's sleeping soundly."

"Through this?" he asked, pointing toward the window. The wind howled and the rain slashed fiercely against the panes.

"When the lightning and thunder started she became frightened. I knew she wouldn't be able to sleep through it so I gave her some laudanum."

Asher opened one of the cabinets, looking for the liquor. Maybe if he had a drink it would relax him enough so that he'd come to his senses and go to his own room.

"I don't think it's a good idea to give her so much of that, Caramarena."

"Oh, I don't give her a lot," she defended herself. "I didn't want her upset again so soon after her accident."

"She's got to learn to rely on her own strength," he answered.

The next door he opened revealed an assortment of liquor bottles, and he found himself shaking his head and chuckling lightly. What a fool he was. Telling Caramarena that Bunch had to rely on her own strength when he was looking for support in a bottle.

"Is something wrong?" she asked.

He looked over at her. Damn, she looked good with her hair flowing over her shoulders. The sash of her robe was pulled tight about her waist, emphasizing her gently rounded hips. He wanted to touch her. He wanted to hold her and make her his.

"No. Nothing's wrong." He turned his attention back to the cabinet, selected one of the bottles and poured a generous portion into the empty coffee cup. When he noticed that Caramarena was still watching him he asked, "Will you join me?"

Caramarena shook her head, suddenly feeling cold. She didn't know how much more of this she could take. The way Asher was looking at her a few minutes ago she would have sworn he loved her and wanted to take her into his arms and to his bed. But now she wasn't even sure he wanted to be in the same room with her.

She was going crazy with Asher's love-hate feelings for her. Why had he kissed her so passionately that morning only to reject her again now? The ache inside her made her shoulders droop. She wanted to tell him to go away and leave her alone. She wanted to scream at him to make up his mind. Did he want her or didn't he?

She turned away sharply when he put the cup to his lips. If he wanted the whiskey let him take it to bed with him. She was tired of wishing for something that wasn't going to happen.

"Cara, wait! Don't go yet."

Caramarena stopped, but didn't turn around. She wasn't sure she wanted to hear what he had to say. The strain of the day and the storm had her tense enough already. She didn't need Asher adding to it.

His cup hit the counter top with a clatter. "I'll walk up the stairs with you and check the shutters."

Asher would have laughed if he hadn't been so damn scared about what he should do. Couldn't he have come up with something more original than checking the shutters? He placed his hand to the small of her back and picked up the candle to light the way. Caramarena held herself rigid as they walked toward the stairs, but he didn't blame her. He hadn't exactly been the loving husband. If only she knew how he'd fought with himself over the last few weeks.

The storm continued to rage outside but the one going on inside his gut had the hurricane beat. Today his life had taken a different direction and would be forever changed. He didn't want to destroy Live Oak. He wanted to work it and make it even more prosperous.

But what about his brothers? Simon should be arriving any day with the letter to Parker and Winston he now wished he had never written. He wished he hadn't stolen the turpentine, either. Now it was too late.

If he hadn't sent that letter he wouldn't have to explain any of this to them. He wouldn't have to tell them he'd found Cantrell. He wouldn't have to worry about going back to England to tell them that he'd fallen in love with his wife—Cantrell's daughter.

Asher opened the bedroom door for Caramarena and she walked inside. He followed and shut the door behind him. Lightning brightened the room for a split second and loud thunder followed, piercing the air and rattling the windowpanes again.

"Would you like me to close the draperies?" he asked as he set the candle on the bedside table.

"No. I'm fine," she said, but didn't look him in the eye. "Storms don't frighten me." She turned her back to him. "If you'll excuse me, I'll say goodnight and get under the covers. I think the rain is making me feel chilled."

Instead of leaving he walked to where she stood at the end of the bed and grabbed her arms. He turned her around to face him and pressed his lips to hers in a fierce kiss.

Caramarena was so shocked at first she couldn't do

234

anything but let Asher grind his lips against hers. There was no emotion, tenderness, or feeling in the kiss. She felt as if he were trying to punish her for something. All of a sudden his brutish action made her angry, and she pushed at his chest, trying to pry her lips from his. With one arm around her back he held her to him and with his other hand he held her head so she couldn't force her lips away from his.

"Let me go!" she managed to say when she finally twisted her face away from his.

Asher let her go as quickly as if she'd been a hot poker. He lowered his head in his hand and rubbed his eyes. "Damn! I'm sorry, Caramarena. I don't know what came over me." He felt lower than a snake. Why would he want to hurt her like that?

She scraped the back of her palm across her lips. "Just please go to your room."

He didn't move.

"Go to your room," she said again, her voice shaky this time.

He deserved to be treated like a naughty boy. He'd deliberately hurt her. How could he tell her he was angry with her because he'd fallen in love with her and he no longer felt the need to ruin her father? How could he tell her all the things she needed to know before he took her in his arms? He couldn't tell her. Not now. It would take a long time to explain and even longer for her to understand. Tonight she would be his. Tomorrow, he would decide what to tell her about himself, why he was at Live Oak and why he'd decided to marry her.

"No, Cara. I don't want to go away. I want to spend the night with you." His voice was husky with emotion. His gaze caressed her face.

Her stomach quickened at the thought, but her

235

good sense took over. She brushed her hair from her shoulder to her back. "You have an odd way of showing it. I don't like your boorish behavior."

Asher slid both hands through his damp hair and pushed it away from his forehead. His robe parted, showing his chest. "I'm sorry." He looked into her eyes, knowing she didn't have one reason to sympathize with him. "I've had a hell of a time with this marriage right from the start. There are things you don't know. Things I can't tell you at this time, but, Cara, I now know that I want to be married to you. I want to be your husband."

"No. I don't think you know that yet. I think you're still unsure." She couldn't keep her bottom lip from trembling or her voice from shaking. "Don't come to me until you are certain you want to stay, Asher. I'm tired of you treating me kindly one day and not speaking to me the next."

"I'm sorry. I know it wasn't easy for you. It was my way of trying to cope with what I was feeling for you."

Asher looked at his wife and knew he loved her more than he hated John Cantrell. He was startled for a moment when the truth of what he'd just realized hit him. But he also knew he could never have the kind of life with her she wanted until he'd spoken with his brothers and they'd settled between themselves the problem of the vow. Honor demanded that he consult with them. And to do that, he had to go to England. But could he tell her all that? No. Not right now.

Not tonight. He wouldn't even think about it again. His brothers and the vow be damned. Right now he was going to make love to his wife. Tomorrow would be time enough to plan.

He moistened his lips. "I thought about a lot of things today while I worked in the field." He spoke

236

softly. "But the most important thing I discovered is that I love you." Closing his eyes for a moment he pushed aside all the complications that admission brought with it. There, he'd said it. It felt good. Right.

He'd told her, but he could see in her eyes that she wasn't ready to believe him. She searched his face for confirmation. He had to prove it. Tonight Cara would be his wife, the only person on his mind.

He reached down and with the tips of his fingers tilted her chin up and very softly pressed his lips to hers, then lifted his head. He looked into her shining green eyes. "I love you, Cara. I didn't want to, tried my best not to, but I won't deny it any longer. I want to be your husband. I want you to be my wife."

"Are you sure now, Asher?" she questioned him in a soft voice. "Have you settled those problems you had?"

He shook his head. "No, but right now they don't seem so big, or important. Right now the only thing that matters is how I feel about you and how you feel about me."

"I love you," she whispered. "I have for a long time."

His arms tightened around her. It felt good to hear her admit that. "Then all the other things will work out. They won't be easy, but I swear to God and to you, I'll settle them."

He bent his head and took her sweet lips with his once again. Tonight she would know just how much he loved her and how desperately he'd wanted her.

After a long satisfying kiss Asher pulled on the sash of her robe and slipped it off her shoulders, leaving it to fall and settle around their feet. He pushed her hair out of the way and kissed the back of her neck.

He untied his robe and let it fall to the floor, then in one fluid motion lifted her chemise up and

237

over her head and flung it away.

Asher took a step back and looked at her. The candlelight gave her skin a soft glow.

A smile eased across his lips. "You're so beautiful," he whispered. "Did I tell you how happy I am that you waited for me?"

"I think you told me that the first time we made love, but I'm not sure I believed you."

"It's true," he answered.

He reached around her and brought her long golden brown hair over her shoulders, the length falling below her breasts. "I remember how the first few days I was here I longed to see your hair down like this, lying against your skin. I wanted to touch it like this. I've wanted to touch you so many times."

Asher took the fullness of her hair in the palm of his hands and crumpled it. He buried his face in its lushness, inhaling deeply the provocative scent of rainwashed hair. He moved closer and took the ends and rubbed them against his bare chest, letting the silkiness excite him.

Lightning streaked across the room and bathed them with its light, its energy, its magic.

"Oh, Cara, come here."

Letting go of her hair, he wrapped her in his arms. He kissed her hard, wanting to take her essence into him. He'd been waiting weeks to hold her like this again, and he wasn't going to hurry the night no matter how badly his body ached for the quick release. He wanted to make love to this woman as if he'd never had any other lover. When she was in his arms like this he wondered why he had denied himself for so long. How could he have put his duty to his father above his duty to his wife? He loved her, wanted her, needed her.

While he kissed her passionately, his hands explored her body, sliding low to cup and shape her leg and back up to sink his fingers into her hair. His lips left hers and rained moist, hot kisses along her cheeks and neck. She trembled and moaned softly and it made him cherish her all the more. Her skin was soft, yet her body firm. Asher knew by the way she touched him that she was enjoying this as much as he.

By the time he picked her up and laid her on the cool sheets, their bodies were fevered with sweat. He ran his tongue between her breasts and caught the moisture. There wasn't anything about her that he didn't want.

"Oh God, Cara, I don't know how much longer I can wait." His voice was raspy, intense. "I've wanted you too long."

"I love you," she whispered back to him.

As he entered her his body shivered from the sheer delight that coursed along his spine all the way to the top of his head. He remained poised above her for a few seconds and let the glory of the moment wash him. Lightning flashed and he saw love in Caramarena's eyes. He started moving slowly, doing what he knew would make Caramarena enjoy lovemaking as much as he did.

Her hands tightened on his buttocks, her body stiffened, she whispered his name. It was over quickly for both of them. Asher rolled to his side and cradled Caramarena in his arms, suddenly afraid to let her go, feeling he might lose her forever.

The thunder and lightning, the wind and the rain continued on into the night and so did their lovemaking. The storm of passion and the storm of nature calmed by morning, both taking a bit of the past with them and both leaving the promise of a new day.

For the next two days, while the storm slowly moved away from Live Oak, Caramarena and Asher spent as much time together as possible.

They took time to look over the plantation and found that the rest of the cotton had been beaten into the ground, part of the roof was missing from one of the barns, and several small trees had been uprooted.

Between Kissie, Lacy and Ivy, Bunch was kept occupied and Caramarena only had to go to her a couple of times a day.

In the early hours of morning on the third day, while Caramarena slept with her cheek pressed against his shoulder, Asher made his plans.

It was already early November. Most of the ships that were sailing for England had already left, but Asher felt sure he'd find a delayed one in Charleston. He decided to travel by land to Charleston and find a ship heading east. What he had to say to Parker and Winston couldn't be explained in a letter. They would have a hard time understanding that he no longer wanted to destroy Cantrell or Live Oak. He wanted to explain that Cantrell was a sick old man. And that with his plan, George Worthy's inheritance would once again be returned to the house of Worthys.

Leaving this time of year he'd be forced to spend the rest of the winter in England. He hoped to find comfort in the fact that it would be better than living with this deceit between him and Cara.

He'd settle the business of the vow with his brothers, then return and settle the ownership of Live Oak with Cantrell. He'd tell the old man the whole story and insist he give up all control of the plantation. He was certain Cantrell would agree that Caramarena should never be told any of this. Asher had a feeling Cantrell would rather give up Live Oak than Caramarena's respect.

Asher rubbed his bearded chin. He was going to shave the damn thing off as soon he left Live Oak. When he came back to Caramarena he'd have nothing to hide. And that led him to his hardest task. Telling Caramarena that he was going back to England.

"Cara, Cara. Wake up, love," Asher whispered and kissed her on the cheek.

Caramarena slowly opened her eyes and saw Asher bending over her. She reached up, put her arms around his neck and kissed him soundly. "Mmm— that's a very nice way to wake up."

"I love you," he said huskily.

Caramarena smiled. "I love you, too, Asher." She started to kiss him again, then realized he was up, dressed in his English clothes and sitting on the side of the bed. Fear pebbled her skin, chilling her.

She sat up in bed quickly, thinking she'd overslept again. "Why didn't you wake me so we could dress together?" she asked, rubbing the sleep from her eyes, trying not to wonder why he was dressed so formally.

"It's still early." He paused and took her hand in his, squeezing it gently. "I have to go away, Cara."

Denial flashed in her eyes. She brushed her hair away from her shoulder and pulled the sheet up to cover her breasts. "What do you mean? Are you going into Apalachicola?" She asked the question, but in her heart she knew the answer before he spoke.

"No." He rose from the bed, walked over to the window and looked out.

That one word seemed so final. Something was

wrong. But what? They'd been so happy since the storm. The clothes—it had something to do with the reason he had on his English clothes.

"No," she repeated, afraid to ask questions, afraid of his answers.

He glanced over at her. "I have to go back to England, Cara."

She started shaking her head before she repeated the word. "No!" Her hands trembled and her head felt heavy. "No, you can't. Not after the last two nights. Not after you said you loved me. Asher, this isn't funny." Her words sounded dry and brittle in her throat. Her chest was too heavy for her to breathe properly.

"It's not a joke. It's true."

"No, please, Asher don't do this!" She dropped the sheet she had clutched tightly against her breasts and covered her face with her hands. "Don't even say things like this." She yanked her hands down in anger and turned glistening eyes upon him. "I don't understand any of this. You're not making any sense. How can you just tell me you're leaving? I love you. You told me you love me."

Asher stood perfectly still and stared at her. "I do love you," he finally said.

She shook her head. "No, no you don't. I can't believe you're doing this. You told me you wanted to be my husband. You wanted me to be your wife. You lied to me." Her last words were a mere whisper.

He rushed to the bed and grabbed her shoulders. His eyes stared into hers. "You are my wife. I do love you. Remember when I told you something was keeping me from your bed? That is still between us, Cara. I have to go to England to settle it. I can't do it from here."

242

"If that's all, tell me what it is. Asher, Bunch and I will go with you," she pleaded.

"I wish it were that simple. Believe me, I do. But it's not." He squeezed her arms tighter. "I can't tell you. You can't go with me. You're going to have to trust me to decide what's best in this." His voice lost all emotion. He turned her loose and moved away from the bed.

"Asher, please don't do this to me. Tell me what's wrong. I want to help you." Tears fell from her eyes and she quickly wiped them away, not wanting him to see how badly she hurt.

"I wish I could. I have to go back for a short time. Once I have this problem settled I'll return to you and our lives will be different. I promise you that much. I'll come back to you."

"It doesn't mean anything to me anymore. I can't believe anything you say."

He flinched.

"You won't come back. I know you won't. You never wanted to marry me. You were forced to marry me and now you're leaving." She took a deep breath. She had to calm herself or she was going to completely fall apart.

Asher stared at her from the other side of the room. "I wasn't forced to marry you, I married you because I wanted to. And I will come back to you, Cara. I meant it when I said I loved you."

She dried her eyes with the back of her hand again and sniffled. She had to do something to stop the pain. She swallowed hard and took a different approach, one she hoped would give her back her dignity.

She brushed her hair away from her tearstained face and lifted her shoulders. "Asher, if you leave me now, I don't want you to come back."

He looked deeply into her eyes. "You don't mean that."

"Yes, I do." Her lips trembled but she held firm with her statement. "If you can't tell me what this problem is and let me share it with you, then I don't want you to come back to me. We don't have a marriage."

"Cara, there are things you don't know about me." His voice rose in pitch and he took a few steps toward her. "Things I'm not free to tell you because they involve other people. If I don't get this settled it could very well destroy lives, and yours would be one of them. I can't take that chance."

She rose up on her knees, not bothering to cover her nakedness. "You're talking in riddles, Asher. Can't you see that by leaving me you'll be destroying my life? What could hurt me more than this? Share it with me."

"Cara, I have to—"

"Don't call me that!" she screamed. Caramarena cupped her mouth with her hand, appalled at her behavior. She was acting like a childish shrew but she was powerless to stop herself. This was her life Asher was manipulating.

As she stood on her knees in the middle of the bed, her hand covering her mouth, she took the time to really look at Asher and saw that this was hurting him, too. He didn't want to go. Why?

She was hurting too much to make it any easier on him. "Only people who love me can call me Cara," she said in a softer, more controlled voice.

His face masked the emotion he'd let slip for a brief time. "I do love you," he said.

Caramarena sat back on her heels, calmer than

she'd been moments before. He was so handsome standing in his English clothes—cravat, waistcoat and ruffled shirt. Caramarena closed her eyes and moaned in pain when she realized she hated the sight of them. They represented his life away from her, away from Live Oak.

She lifted her head and looked into his eyes. "No. I don't believe anything you've ever told me."

"How can you say that after the last two days?" His pain showed in his face and his voice.

"How can you leave me after the last two days?"

"It's not easy," he admitted.

"Then stay," she whispered.

"I can't, Cara. But I do promise I'll return." He turned and walked out of the room.

Caramarena fell face down on the bed and wept.

shut down.   room in
tucked up   pillow
intended   to   grown
to see him sleep, Caramarena
her hand   . As   w

Chapter Fifteen

Four days after Asher left Caramarena's father came home. He asked immediately why Bunch's hair was so short but Caramarena put him off, wanting him to go straight to bed to rest a couple of hours before dinner. After his nap Caramarena had a tray brought to his room and she and Bunch joined him there for dinner.

Caramarena was eager to talk with her father about the specialist but knew she should wait until Bunch was in bed to ask the questions that burned on her tongue. When John asked about Asher, Bunch at once said Asher had gone back to England. Caramarena promised to tell him about it later. She was thankful when he didn't pursue it in front of Bunch.

Bunch also told her father about getting caught in the briar patch, but now she didn't seem to remember it as a frightening experience. Caramarena was glad Bunch told the story with little fanfare because her father didn't get too upset.

Soon after the dinner trays were carried away Bunch fell asleep on the foot of the bed. Caramarena helped Lacy carry her to her room, then went back to talk to her father. She knew he was tired from the long journey, but she didn't want to wait until morning to hear what the doctor in New Orleans had said.

When she walked back in his room he'd turned the

lamp down, leaving the room in semidarkness. He lay propped up against his pillows with his eyes closed. His hair and beard had grown long in his absence from Live Oak. She made a mental note to have Kissie trim both tomorrow. As she stood in the doorway watching him, she realized she didn't really want to know what the doctor told him.

Taking a deep breath she walked over to his bed and sat down on the edge. His eyes fluttered open. She smiled and picked up his hand and kissed his knuckles. "I'm so happy to have you home again. We all missed you."

"It was a long trip. I'm glad to be home."

"Are you too tired to talk?" she asked, rubbing the top of his hand.

He shook his head. "No, but I wouldn't mind having a sip of brandy. Why don't you get a little for both of us."

It wasn't easy but she kept the smile on her face. If her father wanted her to have a little brandy he didn't have good news. She walked over to his desk and poured a small amount of the amber liquid into two crystal glasses. Maybe she did need something to help dull the pain. She didn't know if she could bear to hear she was going to lose her father so soon after losing Asher.

She settled herself back on the bed beside him and handed him one of the glasses. A sinking feeling attacked her stomach.

John lifted his glass for a toast. "To your smile, Caramarena. I hope it's found and returned to your face where it belongs." He tipped his glass against hers, the fine crystal making a high tinkling noise.

Caramarena looked away and sipped the brandy. It burned her tongue and throat but she liked the sweet taste and it warmed her immediately. She took another sip before lowering her gaze to her father's face.

Drawing her eyebrows together she asked, "What kind of toast is that? I haven't stopped smiling since you returned."

He shook his head. "Your lips are moving but you're not smiling."

She reached up and touched his face. "You're wrong, Papa. I'm so very happy you're home."

"But so very sad Asher is gone."

"Yes." There was no need to lie. She couldn't fool him. "Now, tell me what the specialist said."

"I'm the oldest. I get to ask the first question. Why did Asher leave for England? I believed him to be quite content here when I left."

The tightness in her chest increased. It had been there since Asher left, but a direct mention of him overpowered her, affecting her breathing. She took another sip of the strong brandy and looked at her father. In the dim light he was ghostly pale. Dark circles had formed under his eyes, and she could tell by the way he was breathing that he was very tired. Still he wanted to hear about her problems. Her heart went out to him.

It wouldn't do her father any good to know she had been completely devastated by Asher's departure. She tried smiling again but realized he was right, it wasn't reaching her eyes. The smile withered on her lips.

The first day Asher left she had done nothing but stand at the office window and watch the river below, thinking it had all been a bad dream or a horrible mistake, and she'd see the boat bringing Asher back to Live Oak. Back to her.

She didn't sleep at all that night as her emotions ran the gamut. She loved him, hated him, then loved him again. But by the end of the third day she was thinking more rationally. If he said he must go to England to clear up an important matter she had to believe him and live with it. She also decided she had to accept his declaration that he would one day return to her. She had to believe that or she would slowly go insane.

"There's really nothing to tell, Papa," she finally said. "Asher had pressing business to attend to in London so he left earlier in the week. He promised to return in the spring."

"Do you believe he will?"

She cut her eyes around to her father. "I have to believe that. I can't live with anything less."

John sipped his brandy, then laid his head back. "Mmm — it's very soothing. Now, did Asher tell you what this business was all about?" he questioned.

She shook her head. The brandy and the warm night had her too hot. She set her glass on the table beside the lamp and answered, "Only that he and I couldn't have complete happiness until he settled some problems in England. He was really vague about the whole thing. I suppose it has something to do with his brothers, their shipping company or his life back in England."

"And how do you feel about that, Cara?"

She sighed. "I think you know. I'm not happy about it. I tried to get him to tell me what was wrong but he wouldn't. He wouldn't change his mind about going."

John patted her hand. "I think it's for the best, Cara. He may have debts to settle. It's best he go ahead and do it. Think about it. If you had gone to London and decided to make it your home wouldn't you want to come back here and say your good-byes and make sure everything was settled?"

Caramarena licked the brandy from her lips with her tongue. "I suppose so. But, Papa, I keep remembering that he didn't want to marry me."

"Don't believe that, Cara. Asher is a strong man. I couldn't have forced him to marry you even with a gun pointed at his head, if he hadn't wanted to. Take my word for it. He wanted to marry you or he never would have done it."

Maybe her father was right. Caramarena remembered the night she visited Asher in the smokehouse. Asher wasn't a weak man. She was sure of that. And he'd as much as admitted that whatever was taking him back to England had kept him out of her bed. But why wouldn't he tell her what that was? Why must he keep it a secret?

"I think you may be right. In any case, he's gone and I can't bring him back by wishing it were so. I've already tried that." She looked down, then back up at him quickly. "Now, it's my turn for questions. Tell me what the specialist had to say."

He held up his hand and sipped his brandy. "Not yet. I want to hear about Bunch's accident. How did it come about that she wandered so far away from the house?"

"You don't play fair, Papa. You can see that Bunch is all right and is suffering no ill effects from being lost. It's my turn to get some answers. I've been waiting patiently since you returned."

"Well, we have some good news and some bad news," he finally said. He swirled the brandy around and looked into the glass as if searching for something.

Caramarena's chest tightened more. "You're stalling, Papa. Tell me what he found out."

"I'm going to die, Cara. There's nothing to be done about it."

"Oh, Papa, no!" She reached up and hugged him close, almost spilling his drink.

"Careful now. Here now, none of that. Sit back." He finished his drink and set the glass on the table beside hers. "Take your drink and finish it."

"I don't want it," she whispered huskily, forcing the tears to stay in her eyes.

"Go ahead and drink it. I insist. You'll sleep better." He reached for her glass and handed it to her.

Caramarena put the drink to her lips and finished it off as her father had. It burned all the way down. Heat rushed up her neck and cheeks. She coughed and cleared her throat but didn't speak. She didn't think she could.

"Now, the good news is that I'm not going to die right away." He patted her hand affectionately.

She wiped her eyes, telling herself the tears were from the burning brandy. "What do you mean? What are you saying?"

"It seems I've some kind of sickness that's incurable. I don't remember all the details about it but apparently it has attacked my blood and weakened it. They've only recently given it the name leukemia. It's not something that will take me quickly, Caramarena. I'll continue to have good days and bad days and slowly get to where I can't get out of the bed at all. Judging from how long I've been ailing with this, the doctor expects, I should have another year or two ahead of me."

"Oh, Papa, no! Please tell me this isn't true." Her heart was so heavy she thought she'd burst into tears.

"Cara, don't make this harder for me by crying. Please, dear. I expect to be around for the next couple

251

of years. Maybe longer. Even if I'm bedridden, you, Bunch and your children can come in and sit with me and read to me. So it won't be so bad."

"What about the pain, Papa?"

He rubbed the palm of one hand. "That will most likely get worse as the sickness progresses but there are medicines to help me bear the pain. The main thing is that I should be around long enough to see you give me a grandchild. I'd like to see that happen, Cara."

"I hope so, Papa. I should know in a month or two if I'm carrying Asher's child."

The thought of giving her father a grandchild brightened her spirits for the first time since Asher left. She and Asher had had three wonderful days of making love. Surely this time she would be pregnant. She wanted to present Asher with a son when he returned in the spring.

Talking with her father had made her feel better about Asher returning, or maybe it was the brandy that had soothed some of her fears and given her a languid feeling.

"Let's write to Charlotte and Catherine and ask if they can come for Christmas this year. I'd like to see them and their children."

"Are you sure you'll be up to having so many in the house, Papa?" she asked.

"Yes, I'm sure. I'd like them to come while I can still make it down to dinner once in a while. I know they can't visit often, I'd like them to come this year."

"All right, Papa. We'll write the letters the first thing tomorrow."

"Good. Now I'm tired. Go and let me get some rest. We'll talk more in the morning."

She reached over and kissed his forehead. "Good

night, Papa." She rose from the bed.

"And, Cara, let's keep this news between the two of us. No use in upsetting anyone else."

She nodded, not trusting herself to speak.

Kissie hurried away from the big house, hoping to find Cypress waiting on her doorstep when she arrived at her cabin. She'd missed him terribly and wanted to spend some time with him. Mr. John had taken a late nap and that had put supper off, which meant she stayed at the house later than usual.

But there was no sign of Cypress as she walked up to her door. She stood on the first step for a few minutes looking around, thinking he would come walking up any second.

A half moon shone in the cloudless sky and thousands of stars twinkled at her. The night air had just enough of a crispness to make it feel good. She stood, watched and listened to the quiet sounds of night.

When a few more minutes had passed and Cypress didn't show, an uneasy feeling hit her, and the crisp air that had felt so good a while ago suddenly chilled her.

She opened the door to her cabin and went inside. She lit the lantern, thinking Cypress may have been waiting too far away to see her and was watching for a light to show in her window. Why hadn't she thought of that?

Feeling more confident that he was on his way, she poured some water in a basin, took off her dress and washed her body. After putting on her best nightgown she fluffed the pillow and straightened the sheet even though it didn't have a wrinkle in it, then went to the rocker to wait for her man.

Kissie watched the moon from the curtainless window, its silvery brightness adding light to the darkened room. When the minutes continued to pass, worry turned to anger. What or who was keeping Cypress from coming to her after being gone for two months?

She continued to sit and rock while contemplating what she should do. Finally deciding that he wasn't coming to her, she decided to go looking for him. In haste, she threw the nightgown off, put on a fresh dress and walked back out into the night.

About a quarter of a mile down the trail she came to the small cabin that Cypress shared with five other men when he didn't stay the night with her. The door was open to let the cool night breeze inside. She heard sounds of sleep coming from inside. One man snored loudly and another was breathing deeply.

She started to turn around and go back. If Cypress didn't want to come to her it shouldn't matter. But it did. She knew she'd get no sleep until she found out what was wrong. She reached up and knocked lightly on the door frame

"Cypress, you in there?" she called softly.

A couple of moments later Cypress appeared in the doorway. "What's you doing here, Kissie?" he asked in a surprised voice.

"Do you wants to talk here where everyone can hears us or you gone take a walk wid me?" She barely kept her anger in check. To think that he was here all along and hadn't made an attempt to see her caused her temperature rise.

"I'll walk wid ye, Kissie."

He was bare-chested and barefoot. He tied the rope holding his pants up as he came down the steps.

"Why you come looking for me, Kissie?"

That question angered Kissie even more. Why did

she have to come looking for him? He'd been gone two months. They'd only gotten a glimpse of each other when he brought Mr. John up to the big house earlier that afternoon.

"Why do you think?" she snapped crossly when all she really wanted to do was wrap herself around his wide chest and be cradled against him.

"I don't know," he answered calmly.

About half way to her cabin, Kissie stopped, closed her hand into a fist and let it fly at Cypress's jaw. His head snapped back, and he grunted, but before he realized what was happening she caught him under the eye with another punch.

"What de matter wid you!" He grabbed her wrists, but she struggled free and attacked him again.

"You black darkie! I won't be treated dis way!"

"What you talking about!" he asked as he tried to catch her flailing arms. One fist hit its mark and jerked Cypress's head back again.

Cypress got mad.

He grabbed Kissie by the shoulders and shoved her up against a tree so hard she groaned from the pain in her back. He caught both hands, held them above her head and pressed his lower body against hers, grinding her back into the tree.

"Turns me loose, you black-eyed darkie!" she demanded, although her voice lacked the strength that it had earlier.

"Nows you stop dis fighting me and tells me what ails you," Cypress demanded. His nostrils flared with each breath and the white of his eyes shone brilliantly against his dark face.

"Whats de matter wid you, Cypress?" Her words were slurred with emotion. She stopped struggling. "Why didn't you come ta me tonight?"

255

He looked at her for a long moment but made no move to loosen his hold on her wrists, or to move his body away from hers. His face softened. "I didn't thinks you wanted me to."

Tears welled up in Kissie's eyes and she would have kicked herself if she could have for letting the weakness show. "Why?" Her bottom lip trembled. "You been gone two months and you didn't thinks I wanted ta see ye? You didn't wants ta see me!"

"Casey told me Jank been calling on you whiles I gone. I thought you wants him fer yo' man."

"Jank!" she yelled. "Dat boy ain't been calling on me. He knows I'm yo' woman." Her words were spoken like an oath.

"Casey swore he saw you take a rose from Jank, Kissie. I knows I could break Jank's neck wid my bare hands fo' taking my woman. But I decided I already kilt one man, and I didn't want ta kill another."

"So you were gone just let me go. You weren't even gone ask me what happened?"

He turned her loose and took a step back. Sweat had beaded on his forehead and he wiped it away with his hand. "Weren't nothin' I could do but kill him. I 'spect I don't needs to kill another man, Kissie."

"You were gonna let him *have me!*" Kissie reached up to slap Cypress again but this time he saw it coming, grabbed her hand and shoved her up against the tree again. The bark scratched her back, causing a burning pain, but she continued to thrash and try to struggle out of his grasp.

"You better have a mighty fine reason for hitting me dis time, woman. Nows, I tired of it."

"Damn your soul, Cypress." A tear rolled down her cheek. "I can't believe you'd give me up so easy. Gets away from me rights now. I hates you."

256

"I'm sorry ta hear dat, Kissie."

A sob broke from her lips and she lowered her head to his chest. "I thought you loved me!" she cried.

"I thought you loved me!" he countered quickly. "I didn't know you's gone take up with Jank the minute I got my back turned."

"I didn't," she said softly, the fight gone out of her. "He came calling twice but I never let him inside, Cypress. I never did. I gave him back dat rose he stole from Kiss Cara garden and tole him I was yo' woman."

Cypress moved his face a little closer to hers. "You mean that, Kissie?" His voice was husky with emotion.

"Course I do. I ain't never lied to you, Cypress, and don't reckon I gone start now."

He bent his head and kissed her tenderly on the lips. "I's shore glad to hear dat, Kissie. I didn't want ta kill Jank." He kissed her again, harder, and his arms circled her back, protecting her from the tree.

"Hush your mouth. I don't wants you killing no man. Can't blame Jank for trying. But you shoulda asked me. You suppose ta fights fo' me."

"I's don't want no other man touching you, Kissie. Not if you's my woman."

"You the only man to ever touch me that I weren't married to. I told Jank I don't want no roses from him. I don't care if he did steal 'em special for me."

"I bout went crazy when I thought I lost you, Kissie." His hand came up and cupped her breast, finding the nipple underneath the thin material of her dress and rubbing it between his thumb and forefinger. "I knews if I weren't careful, I be killing Jank befo' de night's over."

"Let's don't think bout him no more, Cypress.

You's my only man."

"And you's my woman, Kissie." His lips met hers in a long passionate kiss while his free hand caressed, squeezed and molded her breast.

"Mmm—dat sho' do feel good, Cypress. I's missed you mighty bad."

Her words encouraged him and he kissed her harder, thrusting his tongue deep into her mouth, pressing his manhood against her soft belly. She ran her hands up and over his wide chest, loving the feel of his naked skin beneath her palms. His exploring tongue heightened her hunger and she slid her hands between them, wanting to feel his hard shaft. With nimble fingers she untied the rope, slid her hand inside and grabbed him. He gasped and kissed her harder, deeper.

Cypress pulled at the buttons on the front of her dress and freed her breasts. He bent his head and sucked a dark brown nipple into his mouth.

"I's missed you, Kissie. Missed you," he whispered against her lips. "I gots to have you, right now. I can't wait no longer fo' you."

His breath was hot and gusty upon her face. With his free hand Cypress lifted Kissie's skirt and quickly shoved his breeches off his hips, leaving them to fall and gather around his bare ankles. He slipped his hand low and eased his finger inside her warm moistness to see if she was ready for him. It had been too long. They were both ready.

Kissie grabbed his buttocks and squeezed tightly as he drove himself inside her. She moaned her pleasure, spreading her legs to give him better access.

Cypress grabbed the tree and held tight as he pumped until he heard her little cry of satisfaction, then he smiled and released his seed inside her.

"Oh, Miss Kissie," he breathed her name softly a few moments later. "You de best."

Finley Dobson stared out of his bedroom window at the half moon hanging low in the cloudless sky. It wasn't unusual for him to be awake at this late hour. He seldom slept until the wee hours of the morning.

He'd been in constant pain since the night he and his brother had tried to rob that Englishman down at the docks. It had taken months for his jaw to heal enough so he could eat a decent meal. With so many teeth missing he'd never enjoy a good side of beef again. He'd lived on soup so long he'd lost a lot of weight and muscle.

Even though he was getting better he knew he'd never catch the eye of a pretty wench like he once had. That black buck had left one side of his face disfigured for life.

If that wasn't enough to make him go looking for the bastard, he still had his brother's death to avenge. Hell, they weren't going to kill the white man. They'd just wanted to scare him into handing over his money. Bringing out the knives had caused many men to hand over their wallets without a fight. It wasn't their fault the Englishman started one.

He couldn't expect any help from the sheriff. The sheriff had too many unanswered questions about that night. Like why did the black man and the white one kill his brother and leave him for dead but not take the money in their pockets? And another man reported a robbery that same night but said it was two white men who attacked him, not a white man and a Negro.

No, it was best to leave the sheriff out of this. He

asked too many damn questions. Finley would find the men on his own. He had the time, and he had some leads.

He'd already found out that the ship that was in the harbor that night was named *Sandor*. The woman he was paying to take care of him had told him the ship had sailed about a week later. She also found out that the owner of the ship had married one of the daughters from Live Oak. And everyone knew that Live Oak had one of the biggest bucks around.

He grunted as he shifted to another position, the pain never quite leaving his body. He would pay a visit to Live Oak as soon he was able to get around by himself.

At the thought of killing the Negro he tried to laugh but it hurt too bad. He'd get the son of a bitch that did this to him, even if he had to kill a few extra darkies along the way. Wouldn't matter to him. He'd gladly put a few of them out of their misery.

He had a few coins put back from what he and his brother had stolen over the last year so he'd last in this town long enough to find the man he was looking for. Even if the white man had sailed with the ship, he'd find the darkie. He wouldn't rest until he killed him.

Chapter Sixteen

"It was a hell of a trip," Asher told his brothers, Parker and Winston, as they gathered in the paneled office at Parker's home on the east side of London.

"You were foolish to leave so late in the year," Winston admonished him. "It serves you right."

"I'm a little too old to be reprimanded," Asher told the middle brother, giving him an annoyed glance as he seated himself in one of the blue velvet-covered wingback chairs.

Winston pulled on the tail of his expensively tailored wool coat and peered down at Asher with stern eyes. "Obviously not when you pull foolhardy stunts like this."

"It may not be the safest time of year to travel, but it's by no means impossible." He gestured with his hands. "I'm living proof, am I not?"

"Enough of this picking at each other," Parker said, handing Asher a glass of brandy. "You're home safely and that's all that matters." He gave the other glass to Winston, who remained perched in front of the fireplace, letting the small fire warm his back.

Winston took the drink but didn't back down. "That's part of his problem, Parker. You've always been too easy on him."

"Someone needed to be. Papa never was." Parker turned away and picked up his own drink. He lifted his glass in a toast and said, "To your safe return."

Asher lifted his glass and nodded before carrying the drink to his lips. Over the rim of his glass he watched his two older brothers. Parker was taller than Winston but not quite as tall as Asher. Of the three brothers Winston was the one who looked most like their father. He was even developing a slight roundness in his midsection, but Parker, who was four years older, was still handsomely fit. Only a showing of gray hair at his temples gave testimony to the fact that he was almost forty.

All three brothers had blue eyes and brown hair. And even though Parker had just indicated he'd been easy on Asher, he hadn't. He'd tried to control him, but not in the outward verbal way of Winston.

No, Parker was quiet, subtle and had a way of making you change your mind while making you believe it was all your doing. That was one of the reasons Asher had started sailing with their ships. Parker was trying to make Asher into the man he wanted him to be, not the man Asher wanted to become.

During this visit, he had to keep in mind that Parker was the one he had to worry about even though he knew Winston would be the one to show his anger and outrage.

Asher sipped the brandy again. It was good and strong, and it warmed him immediately. "Tell me about the company. Are the revenues still strong?"

Parker laughed and rested his haunches back against his desk, allowing Winston to take the chair opposite Asher. "You should know. You're the one who visits and charms the wealthy planters in America, keeping them immensely happy with us. Your personal contact with our clients is no small reason we've done so well the past few years, Asher."

262

His oldest brother did know how to make one feel important and appreciated, Asher thought. "Thank you for your vote of confidence, Parker, but I think your idea of going to the smaller, faster ships was the turning point in our business."

"Please brothers dear," Winston remarked sarcastically. "I'm bored to tears. Can we cut short the mutual praise for a bit and hear about John Cantrell?"

Asher's stomach tightened. It wasn't going to be an easy story to tell, and he'd just as soon put it off for a while. "First, let me ask if *Sandor* arrived safely."

"Oh, yes, some weeks ago," Parker hurried to tell him. "I'd forgotten because the matter of the pirates robbing the cargo has been turned over to the insurance company. That's something else we should discuss. I couldn't get Simon to talk. He's very dedicated to you, Asher."

Asher heard the pique in Parker's tone and smiled. It delighted Asher when Parker tried to remain calm when all he really wanted to do was lash out the way Winston handled things.

"I'll see he's amply rewarded for his loyalty," Asher said and put his drink to his lips again.

"Yes, do tell us, Asher, how it happened that the only cargo that Captain Simon Barclay has ever lost to pirates was Cantrell's. And I do believe he mentioned to the insurance investigators that he heard one of the pirates mention the name Cantrell." There was amusement in Winston's voice, although his face held a mock expression of horror.

Asher ignored Winston and sipped his brandy. He liked the way it warned him. The voyage had been long and cold. Many times he'd wished for a sip of brandy or a ray of sunshine to warm him during the long voyage.

263

"Is it true that the pirates didn't harm any of the men?" he asked, wanting to make sure Simon hadn't somehow forgotten to mention any wounded men in his letter.

"Not a one." Winston said proudly. "Barclay's one of the best captains around. It appears the old man knows when to fight and when not to. He returned with his full crew, save the one they dropped off in Snug Harbor because of a fever."

Asher smiled again. At least that was one less thing to worry about. "That's good to hear." Simon and Buford had done an excellent job. He'd see they were well paid.

"Come, Asher. You're too damn slow. Tell us how you found Cantrell after all these years. And how you're sure he's the man you've been looking for." Winston wasn't long on patience or temper and both were beginning to show.

Asher felt as if a knife was twisting in his stomach, and he didn't like that feeling. The brandy hadn't helped calm him as he'd hoped and he knew the reason why. This visit was too important.

He had to tell his brothers that he'd fallen in love with Cantrell's daughter. And it wasn't going to be easy to convince these two that their debt to their father would be paid by Asher gaining control of a plantation in America. He knew them well enough to know they'd want it destroyed and for Asher to remain in London.

"How I found him isn't important. But short of coming right out and asking him, I'm sure he's the right man. All the facts I've discovered about his past coincide with what we know of him."

"How did you manage to invade his home without arousing his suspicions?" Winston asked eagerly.

"Surely your name caused him a moment of hesitation, if not more."

"I had a friend issue a letter of introduction, and I only used Millhouse. They know me as Asher Millhouse. I grew a beard before I arrived. I didn't bother altering the shipping documents since the company was given the name Three Sons several years after Cantrell left for America."

Asher reached up and touched his chin. He still had a tendency to want to reach up and scratch even though the damn irritant was no longer there. What would Caramarena think about him without his beard. She'd not remarked about it one way or the other. Except once after they'd made love. She told him she wondered what he looked like without it. Well, when he returned, she would no longer wonder.

Winston's laugh broke into Asher's musing about his wife. "I wish I could have seen that. You with a beard. It must have added ten years to your age."

"I wouldn't know," Asher countered. "I found the thing a damn nuisance."

"So tell us about Cantrell. Your letter was much too short. What else have you done to him? You must have completed your task or I assume you wouldn't have come home."

Winston knew how to cut through the unimportant details and get to the meat of the matter. Asher rested his elbow on the chair arm and rubbed his eyes. Suddenly he was tired and warm and wanted only to go to bed and sleep for a while. Maybe he wasn't up to facing his brothers with the truth yet.

He finished off the brandy and handed the glass to Parker. He held up the glass to ask if Asher wanted another, and he shook his head. His sight was already getting fuzzy. If he had any more to drink, he'd surely fall asleep.

"As I wrote to you, Cantrell has a plantation named Live Oak in the upper regions of Florida. He's been there since leaving London. What was it? Twenty-eight, twenty-nine years ago?"

Parker nodded. "Close enough. You'd never been to this area, is that right?"

Asher nodded. "The port is small by most standards, but busy from what little time I spent there. All the plantations up and down the Apalachicola River send their cargo down the river to the Gulf of Mexico, so I decided to stop and see if there might be some business for us."

"And you asked around as usual and found that he was nearby?" Winston helped him along.

"Yes, thirty miles up the river. Apparently he bought Live Oak and married shortly after moving there. His wife is deceased but he has four daughters. Two are still living at home." A picture of Caramarena and Bunch flashed across his mind. He loved both of them but not in the same way. Caramarena as a precious lover. Bunch as a treasured sister.

Thoughts of Caramarena reminded him of the day he left her on the bed, her sparkling emerald eyes heavy with tears. She couldn't possibly know how difficult it was for him to leave her that morning, or that he would have to fight to save her from knowing the wrong her father had committed so many years ago.

"Go on, Asher. I grow weary with your lapses."

Asher straightened in his seat. "As I wrote to you, I had very little trouble securing the contracts from Cantrell, although I had to make them attractive for him. After that was accomplished I fully intended to come home and through a series of accidents and piracy leave Cantrell without any money from this

266

year's harvest, and hopefully the next."

"And why didn't you?" Parker asked.

Asher swallowed hard and looked his oldest brother in the eyes. "I married Cantrell's daughter."

Winston gasped, then swore. Parker's expression remained passive for a moment, then as if he realized the power of Asher's comment, his face split with a satisfied smile.

"You better have a hell of a good reason for this treachery—this outrage, Asher!" Winston's face reddened as he talked, and he jerked to the edge of his seat.

Parker remained unruffled. "Maybe you'd better start at the beginning."

"That's the long and short of it," Asher said, hoping to forestall telling them the truth—that he'd fallen in love with John Cantrell's daughter. "I married her."

"Come, Asher, please!" Winston complained. "Must we drag every word from your mouth. We grow old waiting for you to speak. Why did you marry this—this woman!"

Winston hadn't changed, but then neither had Parker. As always his oldest brother was content to let Winston rile him with his badgering and sit back and wait for Asher to give in and tell all. He might as well tell the whole story.

"Even though Caramarena is a very beautiful young woman—" Asher's voice softened when he spoke of his wife. He couldn't help it. "My only thought when I married her was to try, as her husband, to be privy to the financial matters of the plantation. Especially since her father is ill, and Caramarena manages most of the day to day operations."

"Cantrell is ill?" Winston asked.

"Yes. I don't know what's wrong with him or how

267

bad it is. Only that he has very little strength and tires easily. I suspect he'll never be well again."

"I don't give a damn about his illness. Go on with the details of this marriage."

Winston's tone was making short work of Asher's temper. He moved restlessly in the large chair. "Caramarena has nothing to do with what her father did thirty years ago. And no, I won't go into details of the marriage because it's none of your damn business. The only thing you need to know is that I was successful in depleting Cantrell's bank accounts to a pittance of what they were when they were made available to me." Now was the time to tell them. "But now I find that's not what I want."

"Bravo, Asher, you've done well," Winston praised him, lifting his glass in a salute. "But what do you mean? What more could you possibly want?"

Asher remained quiet. Both he and Winston looked at Parker, who'd been very quiet through the entire discussion. "Well, tell us," Winston said. "What more could any of us ask for than the destruction of the man's life?"

Parker sipped his brandy but didn't take his eyes off Asher's face. When he removed the glass his lips remained wet with the brandy. "Winston, you never listen," he admonished, and the shortest brother had the nerve to gasp in outrage. Parker fixed his cold blue eyes on Asher and said. "Asher wants our acceptance of his new American bride."

"What!" Winston rose from his seat and looked down at Asher. "This can't be true!" he exclaimed and quickly plopped down in the chair again.

Although it didn't show on the outside, Asher's stomach felt as if it were twisted in knots and his chest was heavy with apprehension. He remained seated, appearing calm. "That's not all of it, Parker. I'm in love with Caramarena, and I want to make Live Oak my home."

"Goddammit—Asher you can't be serious," Winston shouted angrily, jumping out of his chair again.

Parker turned to Winston. His only outward display of anger was the flaring of his nostrils. "Calm down, and watch your language. This is my home, not a gaming house. And for heaven's sake, stop popping in and out of that chair!"

Winston pulled on the tail of his coat and stiffly said, "My apologies," before fixing his stern gaze on Asher.

"I'm very serious," Asher answered calmly. "I admit that when I first married her I only wanted to see John Cantrell's plantation destroyed. I didn't plan to fall in love with her. I didn't want it to happen."

"Then why did you?" Winston asked, his tone accusing.

Asher would answer any question about Cantrell or Live Oak but none about Caramarena. He remained silent.

"Well, you can forget any foolish notion of living in America on a plantation that was bought with our father's money, Asher. We won't stand for it."

"I'm not eighteen anymore, Winston." He spoke to his middle brother but knew the one he had to convince was the one who was remaining quiet—listening, thinking and planning. "You can't tell me what I can or can't do." He looked at Parker. "I want to exchange my investments in Three Sons for yours and Winston's share of Live Oak."

Winston swore under his breath again. He picked up the brandy decanter and poured himself another drink. Parker moved away from the desk for the first time and stood with his back to the fireplace.

"And what about the vow we made to our father on his deathbed?" Parker asked. "Do you consider it paid because you emptied Cantrell's bank accounts and bedded his daughter?"

Asher came to his feet and drew himself dangerously close to Parker. "Leave Caramarena out of this or we'll no longer be fighting with words."

Parker didn't flinch. Asher didn't expect him to. He knew Parker was testing his strength and conviction where Caramarena was concerned. Parker wanted to know just exactly what he was up against, and Asher didn't want to leave his brother any doubt that he'd lose to Caramarena.

"To live up to the vow I made to my father would destroy my life. I'm not prepared to do that for a man who never had a kind word for me. But because Live Oak was purchased with Papa's money and I did make the vow, I'm prepared to return his money to the Worthy family and consider the debt paid."

"What about Cantrell?" Parker asked.

Asher stepped back. "I expect that before long Cantrell's sickness will consume him and he'll be living in hell with our father. I'll consider that a just punishment."

Parker moved away from the fireplace and over to the window. He turned back to look at Asher. "Give us some time to think about all this," he said.

"Why the hell should we!" Winston exploded, his eyes wide with anger. "Even though he was the one always looking we had an agreement between us that we'd get the son of a bitch who stole Papa's money and cut his balls off. Damn it, why couldn't Asher have just bedded the wench and let it go at that!"

Asher grabbed Winston's shirt front and shoved

him up against the desk, but it was Parker who spoke.

"Winston, either clean up your gutter language in my home or get out! After thirty-five years you'd think you'd know when and where it's appropriate."

Winston looked into Asher's smoldering eyes and mumbled a quick apology. After calming down a moment, Asher let go of his shirt and stepped away. He didn't want to fight with his brothers about this.

Winston took a deep breath and downed his drink, then set the glass on Parker's desk with a bang. "You're right of course, as usual, Parker." He straightened the cravat Asher had just rearranged for him and sighed deeply. "I think I'll take your advice and go visit someone who actually likes my gutter language. I've got to do something to work off this frustration before I put my hands around his neck." He gave Asher a hard look before turning to Parker. "Talk some sense into him, will you." He turned and strode out the door, closing it soundly behind him.

"Don't think too badly of Winston, Asher." Parker tried to smooth the rift between the two. "He'll calm down. We haven't had time to get used to the idea that you're married, let alone to the fact that you're married to Cantrell's daughter and seem to be happy about it."

"I just want Caramarena left out of this. We'll talk of her father but not her. This point is not negotiable."

"That will be difficult, Asher. She's the one keeping you from completing your destruction of Cantrell. If it weren't for her, would you want a plantation in America?"

Asher didn't answer. There had to be some reason he'd kept returning to the planter's homes year after year. Maybe he was so willing to keep Live Oak because he'd always wanted a plantation in America but

271

never would admit it to himself. But would Parker understand his fascination with plantation life?

He looked over at Parker. "Don't you think that it will destroy Cantrell if I go back to him and announce that I've come to claim Live Oak for the Worthys? And if he puts up a fight, I'll tell his daughters about his sordid past."

"Perhaps," Parker said too calmly. "But if Cantrell realizes you're in love with his daughter he may call your hand. If he does—are you bluffing or will you tell your wife the truth?"

Parker was too damn smart. Asher rubbed his eyes and sighed with fatigue. "I really don't know the answer to that right now. I'm tired, Parker. Can we continue this discussion in the morning—after I've rested?"

"Yes, I think that's an excellent idea. In fact, maybe we should let this news sit for a week or two. No need to try to settle everything the first day you're back. Tell me, should I have a bed prepared for you here or will you take the carriage to your town house?"

"I'll go home," Asher answered. "I think I may sleep two days straight."

Parker rested a friendly hand on Asher's shoulder as they walked toward the door. "I don't believe I had the opportunity to tell you that Richard Bassett was thrown from his horse shortly after you left last spring."

"No. How is he?"

"He's not. He lived for a time but there was nothing to be done for him I'm afraid."

"And Elizabeth?" he questioned as he remembered the beautiful woman who had once stolen his heart. The woman he'd once thought about marrying.

"She's doing well. As you know, Asher, she didn't

272

marry Richard for love."

"I know she had feelings for him," Asher defended his former lover.

"Mmm—feelings for the money in his pockets no doubt."

"Parker—"

"No need to say it, Asher. My remark was in poor taste. As you know, I've always liked Elizabeth. I would have been quite happy for you to have stopped your wandering and marry her. She couldn't wait forever, you know."

Parker opened the door and they walked out into the dimly lit hallway. It was much colder than the office and Asher pulled his coat tighter around him. How could he miss those scorching days in Florida?

"As soon as it's out that you've returned the invitations will start pouring in. I've no doubt you'll see Elizabeth at someone's house."

"Is she receiving guests during her mourning?"

"No, but it's been almost a year now and she has started attending selected gatherings."

Asher pursed his lips as they stopped in the foyer. "I should call on her and offer my sympathies."

"No doubt about it. It's the proper thing to do," Parker agreed and handed Asher his overcoat. "I'll go to the back and send the carriage around."

Asher couldn't help but notice that Parker was once again sporting that satisfied smile he wore so well. Parker could go to hell, Asher thought. There was no way he was going to desert Caramarena for Elizabeth. No way in hell.

His first week in London went quickly as Asher caught up on the internal business of Three Sons

Shipping. All of his days were spent at the office and at night he went home to a warm dinner which his housekeeper always left prepared for him. By the end of the week he'd received an answer to his request to visit Elizabeth and offer condolences. Sunday afternoon at tea time was the appointed hour for the visit.

It was a blustery late January day as he stepped out of the carriage in front of her London house. The fierce wind whipped at his coat and hat as he hurried to the door. He promised himself he'd never complain about Florida's heat again. It was preferable to the bitingly cold days of a London winter.

A maid answered his fervent knock and showed him inside. He gave her his coat and hat, then rubbed his hands together for warmth as she led him into the parlor to see Elizabeth, who rose from her chair when he entered. Asher stopped to stare at her, a smile coming to his face. Her dark brown hair was pulled back in a chignon but instead of it making her appear severe and matronly she was striking, graceful, more mature-looking than the last time he saw her.

"My, my, Elizabeth. You are more beautiful than I remembered." His voice was husky but he hadn't intended it to be. He found that after all this time he was glad to see her.

She laughed lightly and held out her hand. "Asher, you haven't changed. Only you would know how to give me sunshine on such a dreary day. I had a child less than a year ago. Surely it shows."

He strode over to her and took her offered hand. He was surprised at the tingle it sent up his arm to feel the pressure of her warm hand in his. His gaze left her face and traveled over her breasts. They were fuller, rounder than he remembered, and beautiful enough to cause a rise in his manhood. His gaze roamed down to her waist, which still looked small to him. The only thing that showed she'd become a mother was the heaviness in her breasts. A pain started deep in his chest. He wanted to see Caramarena like this, a beautiful mature woman whom motherhood had blessed.

"All the changes have been for the better," Asher answered when he realized he was staring. He cleared his throat. "My sympathies, Elizabeth. I always liked Richard. He was a fine man." His words seemed trite but they were all he had to offer.

"Thank you, Asher. He was a good husband. I'm happy he didn't suffer long. And I'm more than pleased he left me with a son to fill my days."

"A son." Asher smiled. "Then you are very lucky."

"Come let's sit down and have tea."

They settled themselves on the small camel back settee. The skirts of her plum-colored dress fanned out and covered his knee. She didn't bother to move it and Asher didn't either. Somehow that made him feel closer to her than he actually was. He watched as she poured the steaming tea into a delicate china cup and handed it to him.

"A confection?" she asked and picked up a tray filled with delicious-looking biscuits and tarts filled with sugared cream and fruits.

"Not now, thank you."

"How long has it been since we've actually talked, Asher?" she asked as she poured her own tea.

"I don't believe we've been alone like this since before your marriage."

She nodded, her brown eyes sparkling. "I think it was when I told you that if you had no plans to marry me, then I was going to accept Richard's proposal. Wasn't that it?" she asked with a smile gracing her finely shaped lips.

Asher grinned. She knew damn well it was. "It doesn't appear you've regretted your decision."

"No. Have you?"

He shook his head without hesitating. He'd loved this woman who sat beside him now—but not enough to marry her. Not as much as he loved Caramarena. For Elizabeth he wouldn't give up going to sea. For Caramarena he was willing to give up the sea, his family and his country. Everything.

"Elizabeth, I want you to know that when we became lovers I really thought we'd marry some day."

"So did I."

She looked away for a moment and Asher wondered if she were telling the truth. But why would she lie about that? Of course she expected him to marry her.

"That was one thing that always made Richard so special," she continued when he didn't speak. "He never minded that he wasn't my first lover. He never mentioned it. He seemed happy just knowing he had a much younger wife to stand beside him at parties and to give him sons. Richard was certain I was going to give him a son."

"Did he—"

She looked back at him. "No. The baby was born six weeks after he died."

"I'm sorry," he said again, knowing it wasn't going to help one damn bit.

"You know, I think we could have been happy together if you'd stopped traveling long enough to marry me."

He smiled and set his tea cup on the table. "It's true that you are the only woman in London who caught my eye—ah—that is to say the only one I ever considered marrying, but I knew I couldn't settle down to a

276

home life when there were too many things in the world that I hadn't seen. I wasn't ready, Elizabeth."

"And now? Are you still content to sail around the world sampling all life has to offer? The good, the bad and the forbidden?"

Her smile held a teasing quality and he was grateful for that. He didn't want their conversation to get too maudlin. If they both weren't careful it would.

Asher leaned back against the settee and stretched his arm across the top. "Now, Elizabeth, I'm a happily married man."

He knew the news shocked her, although she hid it well. Her eyes blinked rapidly, giving away her surprise. It pleased him that she so graciously tried to remain settled.

She set her cup down, but not before it rattled in the saucer. Smiling she said, "I have to hear about this woman who finally got you to the altar, Asher. No one told me. Who is she? Where does she live? Tell me about her."

"Her father owns a rather large plantation in America. The state of Florida to be exact."

"Oh, yes, I remember, you were always so fascinated by the land you called the South with its beautiful women, spacious homes, and—slaves, I believe."

"You're showing your claws, Elizabeth," he said but his tone held no level of rebuke.

"Now that I think about it, I'm not surprised you married an American," she said, ignoring his slight reprimand. "Tell me what she's like and don't tell me she's young and beautiful. I'm sure of that."

He nodded, grinning. She was taking this well. But if he remembered correctly, they'd discussed Richard much the same way three years ago. If only his brothers had taken this attitude the whole business of Cantrell and Live Oak could have been settled quickly and painlessly.

"Very beautiful," he agreed. "Her coloring is similar to yours but her hair is not as dark. More of a golden brown. Some may even call it blond. She might be a bit taller but not much. Her eyes are the color of a smoky emerald." As he said that he remembered they weren't smoky the morning he left. They were bright with anger, confusion and tears.

"And you're happy with her? Happy you married her?"

"Yes," he said with conviction. "She's very intelligent. She manages the plantation because her father is ill. She also takes care of her sister, a lovely younger woman who's simpleminded and can't be left alone. Caramarena is wonderful with her, gentle and kind yet firm when she has to be."

"Caramarena." Elizabeth spoke her name softly and smiled. "Even her name is lovely. And—it seems her virtues are far above the price of rubies."

Asher grinned again. It was too much to ask for Elizabeth not to show her claws. He found he really didn't mind. She was a stimulating woman. If she married again he hoped the man appreciated her humor, her honesty.

"Would you want me to have a wife I couldn't brag about?" he asked.

She sank her teeth into her bottom lip and appeared to ponder the question.

"Bitch," he said softly.

She smiled. "Occasionally."

"Tell me, will I get to see your son today?" he asked, deliberately changing the subject. Elizabeth was still a heady woman.

"If you'd like. He's sleeping, but we can go in qui-

278

etly." She rose from the sofa and so did he. "Tell me, when will you bring your wife to see me?"

"I won't. She's still in America. I came back to tell my brothers about Caramarena and to settle some business affairs. I'll be returning to Live Oak in a few weeks. I plan to live there with her."

"That bit of news must have made Parker and Winston two unhappy men." A smile played about her lips but never lighted on her face.

"I'm sure you can imagine their reaction," he remarked dryly.

"Well, there's no reason we can't have another visit or dinner before you leave, is there?"

"None at all," he answered. "It always has and always will be a pleasure to be in your company, Elizabeth."

Asher didn't want her thinking he was afraid to be with her. She was beautiful, and he enjoyed their banter. But he was no longer interested in her as a lover. She wasn't Caramarena and even though his body might tell him he wanted this exciting woman, he knew in his heart he didn't.

Chapter Seventeen

"Well, what do you think?" Winston asked as he fidgeted with his cravat. "He's been here three weeks and he's showing no sign of weakening. He's trying to sell some of his holdings here in London, and any day I expect him to come into the office and announce he's taking the next ship back to the wife he seems to hold in such high regard."

"Don't you hold your wife in high regard?" Parker asked, looking up from the papers stacked neatly on his desk.

Winston snorted. "Yes, but she's our own kind. There's a difference, you know."

"Not as far as Asher is concerned. And you'd do well to remember it. Condemning her will only make Asher rise like Hercules to her defense."

Winston made a fist and smacked it into the palm of his other hand. "We should have realized this would happen if he continued those damn jolly rides around the world with Barclay. Somebody needs to knock some bloody sense into that hard head."

"You're not the one to do it, Winston," Parker said in a tired voice as he rubbed the back of his neck to ease the ache that had been there for days.

Winston placed his hands on Parker's desk and bent toward him. His eyes bulged with indignation. "And I suppose you are. Asher has made it clear he wants to live in America with his sloven wife. And I don't see you doing one little thing about it."

Parker laughed which caused him to start coughing. He'd had a heaviness in his chest for several days and the cough wasn't getting any better. In fact it was worse. He knew he should take a few days off and stay in bed until he was over it, but he hated to appear weak.

"Are you all right, Parker?" There was genuine concern in Winston's voice as he straightened.

"Yes, I'm fine." Parker cleared his throat and wiped his mouth with his handkerchief. The coughing was probably the reason his chest hurt so much. "But you won't be if Asher hears you speak that way about his wife. And I'm sure she's not sloven. Unlike you, Asher has always insisted his women be clean."

"You're right. How about, she's a clean, conniving bitch. Will he like that any better?"

Parker went back to the papers before him. "Your prattle tires me, Winston. Either say something constructive or go away and leave me in peace to do my work."

"He's been over to see Elizabeth twice," Winston said as casually as if he'd been speaking of a spring day. "Did you know that?"

Parker looked up and eyed his brother suspiciously. "Are you having him followed?"

Smiling Winston pulled on the tail of his coat and sniffed loudly. "Let's just say — I have my way of knowing things and leave it at that. What do you make of it?"

"Nothing." Parker pushed his chair back. "They were lovers once. They could be again, and it wouldn't matter a damn. He'd still leave her and go back to the American woman because he had the

281

chance to marry Elizabeth years ago and didn't take it. He may bed her, but she won't be able to keep him here when he gets ready to leave."

"I suppose you're right," Winston conceded reluctantly, pulling on the loose skin under his chin as he thought about what to say next. "But what about you, Parker? Are you doing nothing to change your brother's mind?" There was scorn in his tone.

Parker coughed again, holding his chest to keep it from hurting so badly.

"Have you had that cough seen to?" Winston asked, worry returning to his voice.

Parker nodded and when he could speak he said, "As far as Asher goes, Winston, I'm thinking. Something that might do you some good as well. Why don't you try it?"

Winston gave him a rude gesture and walked out of his office without further comment.

Parker put the papers aside, and lay his head back against his chair and closed his eyes. Even breathing had seemed to be a chore for the last couple of days. He did need a rest but right now he was too busy keeping Asher and Winston away from each other's throats.

Winston was going about this the wrong way. They wouldn't break Asher. He was sure of that now—but what about his wife? What kind of woman was she? Was she as in love with Asher as he was with her? Probably not. Maybe she was the one they should go after. But how?

He thought back over all he knew about Asher's trip to Florida and an idea formed. Asher said she was running the plantation because of Cantrell's illness. Surely by now she'd realized he'd bled the accounts? He wondered what she thought about that after he left. What would she think when she discovered the cargo had been stolen?

Parker opened his eyes and stared at the closed door. What if Caramarena found out Asher was behind it all? That's it! Why hadn't he thought of it before. Asher's wife was the one they needed to go after.

If Asher was laying the blame of the piracy on Cantrell why couldn't someone else lay it on Asher? He could see that it was done. All he had to do was send a messenger to Live Oak and drop a few hints. Maybe he'd even tell the whole damn story. Didn't Asher's wife have a right to know the truth about her father and her husband?

A prick of conscience struck him. Well, he wouldn't think about that part. For now he'd simply think about what would happen if someone made it to Live Oak before Asher and implicated him. That should make his little American wife think twice before she welcomed him back into her home, her arms or her bed.

Parker felt certain if Asher stayed with his American wife they'd never see him again. Breaking up the family between two countries would be Cantrell's last bitter legacy to the Worthys. No, Parker wouldn't let that happen.

It meant nothing to him that Cantrell was a sick old man. He wanted him to know that George Worthy's sons had found him and that they intended to take what was rightfully theirs. Asher was thinking with what was between his legs, not his brain. He fancied himself in love with Cantrell's daughter.

Parker tried to laugh but his chest hurt too much. Well, Caramarena wasn't the only woman in the world. Asher would forget her soon enough once she banished him from her bed.

Caramarena paced back and forth in front of the fireplace in her office. She found she had trouble concentrating these days. At last the holidays were over and Charlotte and Catherine had left with their children, husbands and maids. Now she had time — too much time — to think.

Today she was worrying about the bank accounts again. What had Asher done? What could he have been thinking by running their accounts so low? She hadn't worried so much about it at first, knowing in the spring they would receive payment for the turpentine. But today she'd received a letter stating that the shipment had been stolen by pirates and that the insurance company was investigating the incident. She knew how long insurance companies took to settle such matters. They'd be lucky to be paid by the end of the year.

Whenever Caramarena started to get angry at Asher she remembered the child she was carrying and she couldn't stay mad for long. Thinking about the little one growing inside her always brought a smile to her face. Asher had given her an heir for Live Oak, a child to love and care for.

She pushed the drapery panel aside and looked out on the bleak February day. No, she couldn't stay angry with Asher. She loved him too much. She would make the money stretch until they could harvest another crop and sell it.

The biggest problem that lay ahead of her now was how to keep her father from finding out about the low bank accounts and the stolen turpentine. She didn't want to upset him. The visit from his grandchildren had been good for his spirits, but it had also weakened him considerably. If he asked to look at the account books she'd simply have to lie and tell him that everything was fine and he needn't worry about anything. But if it came down to it, could she come right out and tell him the money for the turpentine shipment had been received when it hadn't?

Maybe after she told him about the baby he'd be so happy he wouldn't think about the accounts. She'd missed her monthly in December and January and now it appeared she was missing February's as well.

Caramarena let go of the drape and wrapped her arms around her stomach. Yes, now that the third month had passed she was sure it was safe to tell her father. She hadn't told him because she didn't want to get his hopes up only to discover, her monthly to come around three weeks later, that she was wrong.

Tonight she would share the good news with her father and Bunch. She walked to the chair behind her desk and squeezed her eyes shut. If only Asher would hurry back so she could share this wonderful news with him. If only Asher hadn't invested their money in a sawmill in Pensacola, she would be free from worry.

But as she thought that she knew it wasn't true. She'd never be free from worry until Asher returned. He had promised to return in the spring, and at times she was sure he would but at others she was just as certain he wouldn't. She hadn't received any correspondence from him since he left. Whatever had taken him to England might keep him there.

She'd thought about writing to tell him about the baby, but in the end she decided against it. If he came back, it had to be because he wanted her, not because of duty.

A knock on the door frame snapped her head up. "Yes, Kissie, come in," she said softly.

"We can't do a thing wid Miss Bunch. She done throwed her cooked peaches on de floor and made a big mess." Kissie threw her hands up in the air to make her point.

Caramarena sighed and rubbed her forehead. Sometimes she got so tired of settling every little thing that came up. She longed for Asher to come back and help her with the plantation. The bank accounts were the only thing he'd messed up and she could teach him how to take care so that he didn't overspend.

Bunch had been in a foul mood ever since Charlotte and Catherine had left with their children. She knew that Bunch got bored easily with no one to play with. She was just a child and wanted constant attention. Maybe it would help if she had Fanny make her a new doll. Yes, that should do it.

"Kissie, ask Fanny to make her a new doll. And — this time tell her to make it a boy doll."

"What you want Miss Bunch to hab a boy doll fo'? She ain't no boy!" Kissie's eyes widened.

"I'm perfectly aware of that, Kissie. Just tell Fanny to make the body the same. Just put boy clothes on it. That way she can pretend she has a brother and that should keep her occupied for a few days."

Kissie shook her head in bewilderment. "I'll tell her. Maybe Miss Bunch will wants to help her pick out de clothes fo' de boy doll."

Caramarena smiled. "I think that's an excellent idea. Now was there anything else you wanted?"

"Yes'm." She walked farther inside, scratching behind her ear. "I's hoping you could ask Mr. John — to give me and Cypress permission ta marry."

Caramarena rose from her chair and hurried to Kissie's side. "Of course I will! This is wonderful news." Caramarena reached over and hugged Kissie briefly, something she didn't do often. "I'm so happy for you. Tell me, when were you thinking of doing it?"

"Well, Cypress said it'd be better ta do it soon— befo' planting time. It be hard fo' de field hands ta come when dey starts planting."

"Don't worry about that, Kissie. You go ahead and pick a day you like and I'll see everyone gets the day off. I'll tell Cypress he can have a pig roasted, and I'll have Fanny make both of you new clothes."

Kissie smiled broadly. "Thank you, Miss Cara. But we gots plenty of clothes. You always been good 'bout dat. And you don't have ta give us no pig."

"Of course I do," Caramarena said excitedly. "You need a wedding dress and Cypress needs a new suit. We'll get Fanny started as soon as she finishes the doll for Bunch."

"You sho' is a good woman, Miss Cara."

Caramarena blushed and turned away. "I'm glad you think so," she said softly.

Kissie eyed Caramarena with a sideways glance. "Can I speak mys mind?"

"You usually do without even asking." Caramarena looked back at her and smiled.

"Has you told Mr. John you wid chile yet?"

Caramarena gasped and her hands closed around the skirt of her dress. If Kissie had guessed others probably had, too. "Oh, Kissie, how did you know? I didn't think anyone suspected."

"Lord a mercy! How you think you can hides somethin' like dat from me? I sees you every day!"

"Well." Caramarena shrugged her shoulders slightly. "I'm not showing yet. I haven't gained any weight. And I haven't been sick to my stomach like some women."

"Don't you think I knows when you gets yo'

287

monthly and when you don't?"

Caramarena laughed lightly. It felt so good to talk with someone about it. "Of course you do. I've just tried not to get too excited about it in case it wasn't true. And I've had a lot of things on my mind recently. I guess I wasn't thinking clearly."

"Well, has you told anyone?"

She shook her head. "Not yet. And you're not to tell anyone either, including Cypress. I was just thinking about telling Papa and Bunch tonight. I'm at least three months now and I think it's time."

"It past de time. Dis what you been waiting fo'. You gone make Mr. John so proud." Kissie's face fairly beamed with happiness.

"Yes," she said softly and turned away. But it would have made her so much happier if Asher were with her. *Please let him come back to me,* she prayed silently.

"Miss Cara—"

Caramarena spun around quickly. "No, Kissie. I know what you're going to say and I don't want to hear it. Not right now. If Asher comes back it will be because he loves me and wants to make Live Oak his home. Not because of duty to his child." She sighed. "Now. Take Bunch to Fanny and get started on that doll. We have a wedding to plan!"

"What does the doctor say?" Asher whispered outside Parker's bedroom.

"Parker definitely has a lung fever," Winston answered. "He'll be in bed for a long time even if he pulls through. Which I'm beginning to doubt. He's been sick for some time and never would admit it."

"Yes, I'd noticed the constant coughing has been going on for more than two weeks, but he told me he

288

was taking medicine for it. Dammit, why did he let it get this bad?"

"I'm certain it wasn't by choice, Asher. You know how important it is to him to always be the strong one. He won't admit he's wrong and he won't admit he's sick."

"Where's Harriet?" Asher asked, noticing that he'd seen nothing of Parker's wife since he'd arrived.

"She's resting in another room. Apparently she was up with him all last night and needed to get some sleep before she found herself in Parker's state." Winston sighed. "Well, we best go in. He's been asking for us. He'll probably rest better once he's talked to us."

Winston opened the bedroom door and they stepped inside. The room was hot. Too hot, Asher thought. A fire blazed in the fireplace. Only one lamp was lit, making the room dark. A maid sat in a chair beside Parker's bed wiping his forehead with a cloth. Winston waved her away and moved the chair so they could both kneel down beside Parker.

The whiteness of Parker's face shook Asher. Large beads of sweat dotted his forehead even though he'd just seen the maid wipe it. His lips were too pale. A tremor shook Asher. He didn't want his brother to die.

He knew the sweating was good. If he could keep sweating until the fever passed maybe he would be all right. Asher noticed that his nightshirt and sheets were drenched. He'd see that the maid changed them before he left. It wouldn't do Parker any good to sleep on wet bedclothes.

"Parker?" Winston spoke his name softly and Parker's lids fluttered up. His gaze darted wildly from Winston to Asher as if he was attempting to focus. Finally he gave them a little smile.

289

"I'm—glad you came." His voice was a soft, gravelly whisper.

"Of course we came. Did you doubt we would?" Winston asked, but didn't expect an answer.

Parker shook his head and wet his dry lips.

"Do you want some water?" Asher asked, and he nodded.

Asher lifted Parker's head a little and helped him drink a few sips. Parker was still very hot. That worried Asher.

When Asher took the glass away from his lips Parker spoke again. "Tell me you—you won't leave Winston until I'm well."

Asher knelt beside him again and took his hand. He could tell there was no strength in it. "Don't worry. I promise I won't leave until you're better. And you will be better soon," Asher assured him.

Parker gave his head one shake. "I'm—not so sure. I—I feel like hell."

Asher smiled. "Well, at least that kind of language lets me know you still have your wits about you."

Cutting his eyes around to Winston, Parker said, "Asher will help you in the office until I'm better. Be—be patient with him. He h-hates paper work."

Winston chuckled and patted Parker's leg. "I'll try not to make him too miserable."

"We better go," Asher said. "Rest is the best thing for you. We don't want to tire you."

Parker's hand shot out and grabbed Asher's sleeve. "If I don't m-make it I want you—"

"No! Don't say it, Parker. Don't even think it," Asher said in a desperate tone.

Parker's eyes watered and Asher regretted speaking so roughly, but he couldn't let Parker start thinking that he may not make it. The will to live would do more for Parker than several bottles of medicines.

"But I—I want—"

"No." Asher spoke softer this time. "You're going to live, Parker. And I refuse to let you think otherwise. Now close your eyes and rest. We'll be back in later to check on you."

Parker closed his eyes and a few moments later Asher and Winston rose from the floor. Before he joined Winston outside the bedroom, Asher told the maid to let Parker rest for an hour, then to change his bedding.

Winston grabbed his arm the minute the door closed. "Why the hell didn't you let him speak? He could very well die you know and then we'd never know what he wanted to say." Winston's fingers cut into Asher's flesh, and his tone was mean.

"I know." Asher gave Winston a hard look and jerked his arm out of his brother's grasp. "But if he gives us what he believes to be his deathbed statement right now, he'll have no reason to get better. He'll think he can die with all of his affairs in order. This way he has a reason to live! He didn't get to say what he wanted to."

"You better hope you're right."

In his usual fashion, Winston pivoted on the ball of his foot and stalked down the stairs. Asher leaned against the wall and rubbed his eyes. What was he going to do if it took Parker a long time to get well, or if, as Winston suspected, he didn't get well? Either one would put off his trip to the states and back to Caramarena. He squeezed his eyes shut. Damn, he missed her. He missed holding her, loving her, talking to her.

But what was he to do? He had to promise Parker he'd stay. And he would.

291

Caramarena probably needed some more money by now. He'd hoped to be back by April, but he doubted he'd make it now unless Parker had a remarkable recovery. He'd send a letter to their bank in Charleston instructing them to put more money into Live Oak's accounts. He'd also write Caramarena and explain that Parker's illness had delayed him. He'd promised her he'd be back in the spring, and he hated like hell breaking that promise to her.

In the meantime, he would continue to sell his holdings in England so that when he left London this time there'd be no reason to return.

Chapter Eighteen

Kissie pressed the palm of her hand to Pearl's fevered brow and looked up at Lacy. "She got any of de other symptoms?" she asked in a hesitant voice.

Lacy's eyes grew bigger and her lips pouched out. "She's gots 'em all. De stomach pains, de runs, everythin'. But dat ain't de worse, Kissie. Dey's mo'."

Cold fingers of doom crawled up Kissie's back and she shivered. "What's you trying to tell me, Lacy?" she asked, even though she was afraid to hear the answer.

"Jank and Fanny done come down wid it, too. Jest dis morning I hear two of de field hands are feelin' poorly taday and Mr. Wulpher, too."

"Oh, Lord have mercy!" Kissie covered her mouth with trembling hands and shook her head. "Miss Cara gone kill us if de yeller fever don't gets us first."

"What's we gone do, Kissie? I don't want ta gets de fever. I don't wants ta die. I ain't ready ta die, Kissie. I gots to see—"

"Shut yore mouth!" Kissie said harshly and gave her a hard smack on the arm. "You get holds of yo'self right now. Don't matter what you want. We gots ta think of Miss Cara and her babe."

Kissie looked down at Pearl stirring restlessly on the cot and shook her head again. Suddenly Kissie was sick with fear. "I knows I shoulda told Miss Cara two days ago when Pearl got sick. I knows I shoulda told her."

Lacy picked up the hem of her apron and wrung it in her hands. Her lips trembled and her eyes darted from Pearl to Kissie and back again. "We didn't know it de fever, Kissie. Didn't too many of us get it de last time. How we know it de yeller fever?"

"I told ye ta be quiet and let me think." Kissie folded her arms across her chest and nervously patted her hands against her arms.

Pearl continued to move restlessly in the bed, moaning in her fitful sleep.

"Dey's only one thing dat's important," Kissie said, as much to herself as to Lacy. "We gots to keep Miss Cara from getting dis fever. It'll kill her baby fo' shore."

"How's we gonna do dat, Kissie? We's can't tell dis fever ta stay away from Miss Cara and her babe. It won't listen ta us."

Kissie looked over at the babbling woman. Lacy took a step backward as if fearing Kissie would hit her again. She'd twisted her apron into an unsightly knot and her bottom lip was red from where she'd sunk her teeth into it.

"I's gone go tell Miss Cara right now not ta come out of de house no mo'."

"You wants me ta tell her fo' ye?" Lacy asked with a tremble in her voice.

Kissie gave her another mean look and snapped her hands to her waist. "Now why I want dat? I's been taking care of her since she was born and I'll continue till I's die. You takes care of Pearl and go sees about Jank, too. Don't come back to de big house. We done took enough fever there."

A groan issued from Kissie's throat as she whirled around and left the slave quarters, heading for the big house. She'd never forgive herself if Miss Cara lost the baby. She'd never forgive herself.

Caramarena sat on the front porch stitching a rose on the collar of a tiny dress. She was hoping her baby would be a boy but had decided to have a few gowns ready that would only be right for a girl. The hot sun of midday had passed and the shade of the late afternoon made the spring heat bearable. April was usually one of her favorite months but this year the days had been extremely hot for so early in the year.

Now that she was well into her fifth month she found she became tired more easily, and by the end of the day she was ready for dinner and bed. She'd marveled at the changes in her body as her baby grew and reshaped her form. Her stomach had rounded and become very tight. Her breasts were larger and frequently ached, and her ankles would swell if she spent too much time on her feet. She enjoyed each little change she noticed as her child continued to develop.

She and Bunch and her father had had many wonderful conversations about the coming baby, but Asher was never far from her thoughts. She'd hoped he'd be back by now. He'd had time to make the round trip if he hadn't tarried long in London. Every chance she got she looked out the window to the river below, hoping to catch sight of a riverboat, praying one would stop and Asher would come running toward her with outstretched arms. Each day she was disappointed.

She hadn't even received a letter from him. Mail coming from England wasn't reliable, she knew that. Too many things could happen to keep a letter from reaching its destination. Asher had to know that her life wouldn't be complete, her happiness always diluted until he returned.

The slaves were busy caring for the corn they'd planted in March and getting the cotton they'd picked last fall ready to be loaded on ships.

She didn't have the time or the strength to watch over the slaves as she'd had last year, but Mr. Wulpher seemed to be doing a good job with them.

Everything was going as well as she could expect, especially since they had very little cash on hand. She'd cut back on every expense that wouldn't arouse her father's suspicion. She could always sell some cattle or hogs but she was afraid her father would have to be notified if she did that, so she was biding her time, hoping the insurance money would not be as late as she feared.

"Miss Cara, I gots ta talk to ye," Kissie said breathlessly as she burst through the front door and out onto the porch. "I's been looking all over de house fo' ye."

"I thought you'd remember that I like to sit out in the fresh air when it's not too hot." She smiled. "Sit in the other chair and join me for awhile."

"No, ma'am."

Caramarena laughed lightly. "Kissie, if I give you permission to sit on the chair it's perfectly all right. You don't have to be afraid."

"Yes'm, I knows. But I's don't wants ta say what I

came ta say sittin' down." She folded her hands in front of her and squeezed them until her knuckles turned light brown.

A close look at Kissie told Caramarena she was definitely upset about something. She started to speak when she saw Cypress striding anxiously toward the porch. His long gait brought him quickly to stand beside Kissie.

"I couldn't let you do dis alone, Kissie," he said. "T's yo' husband now, and I's gone stand by ye."

She gave him a grateful smile. He took her hand and closed it inside his.

Caramarena felt the first stirring of uneasiness. She rose from the rocker and met the two slaves on the steps. "What's wrong?" she asked in a husky voice.

Neither of them spoke for a moment and the feeling of fear increased.

"Kissie, Cypress tell me what's wrong." Her voice was stronger this time. More demanding.

"It de fever, Miss Cara." Kissie cut her eyes around to Cypress for support. He nodded to her. "Jank, Pearl and two mo' already real bad. I's so sorry, Miss Cara. I shoulda told ye when Pearl first took sick but I didn't know it de yeller fever! It ain't been round here in three or fo' years." Tears started rolling down Kissie's cheeks before the last words were spoken.

"No," Caramarena whispered, remembering the horror of a few years ago when they'd lost eight slaves. Whole towns along the coast and up and down the river had been wiped out.

She dropped the dress she was holding and took a step toward them. Maybe they were wrong! Maybe it wasn't yellow fever but something else.

297

"Kissie, how do you know it's yellow fever? Perhaps it's a stomach sickness."

Kissie shook her head. "I don't think so. Dey sho' is sick."

Caramarena tried to think but her mind simply wouldn't work. "H-how long have they been sick?" she finally asked.

"Pearl wuz de first. She been sick 'bout three days."

"Oh, Kissie, you should have told me!" she wailed. "We could have sent for Dr. Johnstone."

"I didn't wants ta worry you wid de baby coming and all. I's hoping Pearl gone get all right. She been real sick befo' same as we all has. I didn't know, Miss Cara. I didn't know." Kissie lowered her head.

"Don't blame Kissie, Miss Cara, she only did whats she thinks best fo' ye. Pearl could jest had a stomach sickness."

Caramarena looked up at Cypress. She softened her voice even though her heart was beating wildly. "I don't blame her, Cypress. We all do what we think's best." She placed her hand on her forehead and tried to think. "Go for the doctor immediately, Cypress. And tell him to bring extra medicines—all he can spare. He can confirm whether or not it's the fever, and he'll know whether or not it's only on Live Oak."

Cypress took off running and Caramarena hurried down the steps after him calling, "Cypress, take a horse." He turned back to wave that he'd heard but kept running. Next she turned to Kissie. "Go inside and get my medicine box and meet me at Pearl's cabin."

"No, Miss Cara you's gots to think of dat baby!" Kissie cried. "You gots to get in de house and don't come out. We'll takes care of Pearl and de others fo' ye."

Kissie's words brought Caramarena up short. Kissie was right. She had her baby to think about now. For a moment she'd forgotten she was pregnant. But how could she not go and see to the sick slaves? They were her responsibility. Caramarena's breathing increased so fast that she felt light-headed. She made it up the steps and leaned a hand against one of the great stone pillars for support.

"You all right, Miss Cara?"

Caramarena heard Kissie, but for a brief time she felt that if she moved she would fall, so she remained still and quiet. When the worst of the weakness passed, she looked into Kissie's fearful eyes, hoping to find an answer to her dilemma. She was torn between checking on her slaves and taking care of her baby. Kissie was right. She was strong. She might live through the fever if she got it—but the baby wouldn't.

"You gets inside rights now and takes care of Miss Bunch, Mr. John and dat babe. You can't helps dem dats got it. I'll come ta de back do' and lets you knows when de doctor comes."

Caramarena didn't move.

"You go on and gets inside de house now, Miss Cara," Kissie said again. "Me and Cypress gone take care of dis for ye. You keeps Ivy in de house to help you. We won't let no one else go in 'cept de doctor when he gets here."

Caramarena started slowly backing up. "I have medicines. Laudanum will help them rest, make them feel better."

"I'll come to de back door and you give it ta me. Gone on, now gets in de house," Kissie encouraged.

When Caramarena's back hit the door she felt behind her for the handle and opened it and rushed inside. When the door shut she fell against it, trembling. She felt faint again. What was she going to do?

The slaves needed medicine to make them feel better, to take away the pain and suffering, but Kissie didn't know how to administer it. Neither did Cypress. But what about her baby? Yes, she had to think of the baby. Live Oak's heir.

First she had to calm her breathing and gain control of herself. She was letting fear and confusion rule. She'd get nowhere as long as she allowed that. She covered her face with both hands and breathed deeply into her palms until she started breathing normally again. Then slowly she removed her hands and opened her eyes. She was better: still afraid, but now able to cope.

She would go to her father. He was far wiser than she. He would tell her what she must do. On shaky legs and with heavy feet, she climbed the stairs to her father's room.

Through the open doorway she saw him dressed in his nightshirt and robe, sitting at his desk writing. Her heart constricted. It wasn't fair that he should be burdened so when he was no longer able even to dress for the day and walk down the stairs.

Tears collected in her eyes, but not for her father. She was ashamed of herself for not having the courage to deny her child and go help the slaves. She wanted to hear her father tell her she must, then she would go.

On wooden legs she walked quietly into the room. "Papa," was all she said, before running to him and falling on her knees and burying her face in the folds of his cotton robe, her slender shoulders shaking with sobs.

"Cara, dear what is it?" he asked in a worried voice as he stroked her hair, comforting her.

She couldn't answer him. She had to cry and get it all out before she could speak. Once she stopped, she knew she would have to assume the role of the strong one. When she did that, tears wouldn't be allowed.

After her sobs died to sniffles and her sniffles to an occasional whimper, Caramarena raised her head and accepted her father's handkerchief. She blew her nose and brushed the loose strands of hair away from her wet face. Taking several deep breaths, she calmly said, "It's yellow fever. Four slaves already have it."

John Cantrell squeezed his eyes shut and muttered a damning oath.

Caramarena continued in a soft voice. "Kissie just told me, although she's known for a couple of days. She was hoping the sickness would turn out to be something else and didn't want to worry us. I know I should go to them and help ease their pain and suffering."

His eyes popped open and she voiced her fears aloud. "I'm worried about my baby, Papa."

She felt the tremble in his hand as he grasped hers. "And you should be. I won't hear of you going to them. As far as I know I'm still the master of this plantation. I'll go take care of the sick."

Using the arm of the chair for support, she rose from the floor. Her skirts felt heavy around her swollen stomach. "Papa, you can barely get out of bed in the mornings. How do you plan to make it down the stairs and to the slaves' quarters?"

"I'll do what I have to, Cara." He stood and puffed out his chest as he tightened the belt of his robe.

This wasn't what she'd expected. She'd wanted him to tell her it was her duty to see to the sick so she wouldn't have to take the responsibility of them. "You're too weak, Papa!" she exclaimed, taking hold of his arm. "You can't do this."

He shrugged off her constraining hand. "Nonsense! This is just the sort of thing I've needed to get my blood going again. Get me your box of medicines, Caramarena."

"Papa! No. You're not well enough," she pleaded, trying to grab his arm once again. "You'll do more harm than good if you get the fever as well."

He brushed her aside. "You know the slaves can't take care of themselves, Caramarena. They don't know how. I've been exposed to the fever many times and have never fallen ill. No reason to think I will this time."

John kept his head straight and his shoulders back as he walked with purpose out the bedroom door, but after only a couple of strides he was holding on to the wall as the burst of energy faded from his weakened body.

Caramarena wanted to cry. It hurt to see her father, once so strong, so capable, unable to walk more than a few steps.

She slid up under his arm and he caught hold of her shoulder. She could feel his chest moving with fast, excited breaths. Underneath her palm his heart beat rapidly.

"You can't make it, Papa," she said firmly as they looked downstairs.

"With your help, I can make it, Cara," he insisted, already winded.

She wet her lips and looked up at him as she held his trembling body close to hers. "I might get you down the stairs but you'd be too weak to help anyone."

He looked at her, then down the curving staircase. His shoulders sagged. "I guess it's foolish to try."

Nodding, she said, "Let me help you back into bed."

It taxed Caramarena's strength to get her father back in bed, although she tried not to show it. She was so proud of her father for wanting to help care for the sick.

"Maybe if I had Cypress carry me down the stairs," John suggested as she placed extra pillows behind his back.

"He's gone after Dr. Johnstone."

"Well, we'll just have to wait until he gets here," he said. "I don't want you going down there. They'll have to manage by themselves until the doctor arrives."

"If the fever has hit the town he may not be able to come."

"We'll see." He folded his hands together in his lap, his fingers working nervously.

Caramarena smoothed his hair back with her hand. "Papa. I need to go to them. Laudanum will help them rest so they won't tire themselves out. Like you, I've been exposed and have never had the fever."

"It's too risky this time, Cara. You're all I have left to take care of Bunch and Live Oak."

"That's not true," she admonished him. "You have two other very capable daughters."

303

"I'm no fool, Cara. They'd sell Live Oak and split the money and put Bunch away. They've never cared for her the way you do. They don't have the patience with her that you have."

"Stop fretting, Papa. I—"

"No! Caramarena, I forbid it." He grabbed her arm with both hands as if to keep her from walking away. "You must not risk your child for the slaves. They're not worth it."

"Papa, I can't let four people, and possibly more, die in agony when I have medicines to make them feel better. That's not right, Papa."

His eyes took on a faraway look. "Sometimes we do things that aren't right in order to have a better life. I had to make a decision like that once, Cara." He paused. "And I've never regretted it."

"What are you talking about, Papa?"

Looking into his daughter's eyes, he opened his mouth to speak but shook his head instead. "I was so much younger then, so much stronger. After all this time, I guess it's better left unsaid."

She smiled at him and patted his hand. "You can tell me about it when I have more time."

"Cara—"

"Shh—Papa as we were talking I had an idea. I'll go downstairs and show Kissie how much laudanum to give to Pearl and Jank. I'll tell her exactly what needs to be done. That way I won't have to go inside the cabins."

He smiled. "Yes, show Kissie how to care for them. She's the smartest of them all. Show her!" He grabbed her hand and squeezed it desperately.

Caramarena swallowed hard. She'd never seen her father so militant. "All right, Papa." She pulled her

304

hand away from his, and he fell back against his pillows.

"Find Bunch and bring her to my room. We'll keep her in here with me until this is over."

"Yes, Papa," she whispered and hurried from the room.

Caramarena called Kissie into the kitchen and showed her how to administer the laudanum and other medicines to help ease the symptoms of the fever. Kissie was nervous, so Caramarena promised to stay by the back door in case she forgot what to do.

By late afternoon Cypress arrived with Dr. Johnstone. He confirmed that it was yellow fever. He also told them that several plantations up and down the river had been hit by the sickness. All he could do was leave more medicine and say that he'd check with them again on his way back down the river.

Caramarena held up well until three days later when her father showed signs of having the fever. She moved Bunch back into her own room and labored through the night, washing her father's fevered body, holding the chamber pot when he retched. The next morning his fever was worse.

"Miss Cara, I brung Mr. John a cup of tea."

"I don't think he'll keep it down, Ivy," she said, rising from the chair beside her father's bed. Caramarena rubbed her back. It ached from bending over the bed most of the night.

"I sent word ta Kissie. I know she'd want ta know bout Mr. John." Ivy held a glass out to Caramarena. "You best drink dis milk, Miss Cara. You lookin' poorly."

"Thank you." She hadn't realized how thirsty she was until she started drinking. She finished off the milk before bringing the glass down from her mouth.

"Miss Cara, I come as quick as I could." A breathless Kissie hurried into the bedroom and went to stand beside Caramarena and Ivy. "What we gone do about Mr. John?" she wailed.

A chill ran up Caramarena's back when she looked at Kissie. Her dress was damp and beads of sweat lined her forehead and upper lip. The whites of her eyes had turned a dirty shade of yellow. Suddenly Caramarena noticed Kissie was swaying. She was sick! She was going to faint!

Caramarena called out to Ivy and together they caught Kissie in their arms and lowered her to the floor.

"Oh my! Oh my! What we gone do, Miss Cara? Kissie done gots de fever, too." Ivy rose from the floor and backed away, frightened.

"Stop complaining, Ivy and go get Cypress." Caramarena tried to calm herself and still her quaking stomach. She couldn't lose control now.

"I can't go down there where all dat fever is, Miss Cara. I gots ta stay here and takes care of you and Miss—"

"Stop blubbering, Ivy, and get Cypress before I take Papa's razor strap to you. Now get going!"

Ivy's eyes rounded in shock. "What's you gone do if I goes down there and gets de fever? Won't be no one round ta help ye!"

Caramarena rose from the floor. "You'll wish you had the fever when I get through whipping you if you don't go get Cypress right now. Go!"

At last, Ivy turned and Caramarena heard her run down the stairs, mumbling to herself.

Caramarena turned around and looked from her

father, lying so still in the bed, to Kissie on the floor and held her tears at bay. She'd had her cry in her father's arms when she'd first heard about the fever. She'd tried to protect herself and her baby. Now she had no choice. There was no one else to care for her father and the slaves but herself. She took a deep breath. She was mistress of Live Oak, and she would take care of her own.

Caramarena had Cypress put Kissie in one of the bedrooms upstairs so she could tend to her and her father. Thankfully she and Cypress had shown no signs of getting the fever. Ivy appeared to still have good health so she told her to look after Bunch and keep soup hot for the sick.

Pearl and Jank were the first slaves to die from the fever and from then on they buried at least one a day. Caramarena divided her time between the slave quarters and the second floor of the house. It was difficult for her to leave her father when he was so sick, but the others needed her attention, too. Cypress continued to beg Caramarena to rest and take care of herself, but she knew she couldn't until the fever left them. She tried to slow down but the sick needed constant care.

Cypress and Caramarena worked hard to save Kissie and the other slaves. Kissie was strong and at the end of a couple of days showed signs of improvement, but a lot of them were just too weak to withstand the high temperatures. Such was the case with her father.

By the end of the week Caramarena stood in front of her father's bedroom window watching Cypress dig a grave beside her mother's. Tears rolled down her cheeks and her chest heaved with racking sobs. Each time the shovel hit the dirt she felt as if

307

it were hitting her heart. Now more than ever she needed to save her baby, but she already feared she'd waited too late to rest. She'd developed cramps in her stomach and lower back.

Caramarena managed to stand beside Bunch at her father's gravesite and read the Twenty-third Psalm. As soon as she closed the Bible she bent and picked up a handful of dirt and threw it in on the pine box.

Later that night Caramarena sent Cypress to find Dr. Johnstone. But it was too late.

Her baby was born three months too soon.

Asher had been staring at her all night. Watching her tempting lips as they smiled so prettily at him. Watching those dark and beautiful eyes tell him she'd welcome his advances if he were so inclined. Watching Elizabeth fill his wineglass yet again when he knew he'd had too much already.

She extended the glass toward him. The crystal caught the lamplight and sparkled invitingly. The ruby red wine seemed to be calling to him, but he shook his head and declined the drink.

"I should be going," he said, and thought that his voice sounded different, slow and heavy. He massaged the back of his neck and thought how he'd like to lay his head back and close his eyes and sleep.

It'd been too easy to spend time with Elizabeth during Parker's illness and recovery.

Elizabeth moved closer to him, laying her arm on the sofa behind him and pressing her breasts against his arm. "Don't go yet. The night is still early," she whispered softly. "And I don't want to have to spend the rest of the night alone."

Asher looked down. Her black dress was cut low, revealing the full swell of her beautiful breasts. His mouth went dry, and an ache started in the pit of his stomach and spread to his manhood. He wiped his lips with the back of his hand and swallowed hard.

Caramarena was on the other side of the world, and he hadn't seen her for six months. Half a year, damn it! He was hungry for sex. Slowly his gaze traveled back up to Elizabeth's face. Her eyes were hot with desire, her lips formed a provocative pout. Did he want this woman or Caramarena? Or was he so damn drunk or so randy he'd take any woman right now?

Yes, that had to be it. He hadn't been this long without a woman since he had his first many years ago. He tried to shake his head and clear his rambling thoughts, but he wasn't certain he accomplished it. With the pads of his fingers he rubbed his eyes, trying to clear his head and his mind of the lascivious thoughts. He was married, and he loved Caramarena.

He felt Elizabeth's hand on his chin, pulling his face toward her. When he focused on her face, her eyes looked glassy.

"I know we've had too much to drink tonight, but maybe that's what we've needed to get past the barrier that's been between us since your return," she whispered.

Her tongue came out and wiped those delicious looking lips. Asher's breath grew shallow. His gaze fell to her breasts again. They were full, white and he wanted to touch them. He wanted to taste them.

Who would ever know?

Caramarena.

How will she know what I do in England?

As if sensing his dilemma, Elizabeth reached over and pressed her lips to his. Asher's manhood was already hard, just waiting for the least provocation to jump to life. She tasted of wine. Sweet wine. It was good. He dipped his tongue inside her mouth and licked all of the wine from her mouth. She moaned her pleasure, catapulting him into the pit of passion.

His hand slid up her midriff and found her breast. He tried to distinguish the shape but the velvet dress and corset hindered him. With eager fingers his hand slid beneath her clothing and pulled her breast free of its bondage. It was heavy, full, ripe. His thumb and forefinger found the nipple, and he rubbed it slowly back and forth. How could he not taste her after feeling how heavy her breasts were with milk?

His mouth left hers, and he kissed his way down her chin, over her chin, under her chin. All the way down her neck. When his lips hit the swell of her tight, firm breast he trembled. This was so new, so exciting. At last his lips closed around the nipple and he pulled it into his mouth.

Do you want Elizabeth or Caramarena?

I don't know.

Think!

No!

You can't have both.

Right now I want this woman.

What about tomorrow?

No, I don't want to think about tomorrow, only now.

Caramarena.

No! Dammit, leave me alone! I'm hot. I'm hard.

You're betraying Caramarena!

The bland taste of mother's milk flowed into Asher's mouth, and he stiffened. What was he doing?

"Goddamn!" he swore softly and pushed away from Elizabeth.

"Asher, no!" Elizabeth cried behind him as he jumped off the sofa. "Come back! Please don't stop."

He ran both hands nervously through his hair and moved away from the small settee. How had he let things go so far? How could he come so damn close to betraying Cara.

Dammit! he was a man, not a saint. He couldn't help wanting her because she was beautiful and exciting—and it had been so damn long.

But you're supposed to be strong enough to say no.

Taking a deep breath he turned and faced her. "I can't, Elizabeth, I'm married."

She grabbed his shirt front, digging her nails into the expensive cloth. "It doesn't matter," she answered in a shaky voice. "I want you to stay—if only for tonight." Her eyes implored him, her chest heaved with unfulfilled passion. "Asher, finish what you started," she whispered.

He took hold of her wrists and pulled her hands away. He still felt the effects of the wine. Damn, he wished he hadn't drunk so much. This had taught him something good to know. If he could resist Elizabeth who was so desirous, so tempting, so willing, he could resist all other women.

"I can't." His eyes turned hard and cold. "I love Caramarena. I don't want to betray her trust. It's not right for you to tempt me so."

"Asher, I don't understand. We were lovers for a time before. I'm not asking for forever. Only tonight."

"I know," he softened. "Elizabeth, you're beautiful, ever so tempting. I'll always be attracted to you. Always. But only as a beautiful woman. I now know my feelings for you don't go any deeper than that. I wish it could have been different for us." He wiped his hand down his face and breathed deeply. He'd never liked to disappoint a lady.

"I'd better go."

Elizabeth stepped back and lifted her chin. "You won't be back, will you." It was a statement, not a question. Her eyes were filled with disappointed resignation.

"No."

She straightened the bodice of her dress and smoothed her skirt, lifting her shoulders a little higher while doing so.

Asher remained quiet while she regained her aplomb.

"Well, Asher, all is not lost. It's a meager consolation at best, but it's immensely satisfying to know that your body still wants me even if your heart does not."

He followed her gaze to the front of his breeches. The protruding bulge was difficult to hide. When he looked back up at Elizabeth she was smiling.

A wide grin spread across his face. "You're one hell of a woman, Elizabeth."

Chapter Nineteen

The next morning Asher made an unannounced visit to Parker's home before going to the office downtown and found Parker sitting in the parlor by the fire, looking over some papers.

"Asher, this is a pleasant surprise," he said in a weak voice as Asher strode into the room.

"It's a surprise for me to see you out of bed." Asher's brows drew together to form a frown. "How long have you been coming downstairs?"

Parker didn't meet his eyes but started neatly stacking the papers in his lap. "Just the last day or two. It's slow, but I am regaining my strength."

"After six weeks I'd think it was about time." Asher didn't try to hide his irritation. It had crossed his mind the past week or two that Parker was much better than he let on.

Ignoring his brother's foul mood, Parker asked, "Did you come here for a particular purpose, Asher?"

"Yes." He moved to stand directly in front of Parker. "I've come to tell you I'm going back to America. I should be ready to leave by the end of the week."

Parker's head snapped up and his eyes widened. "You promised to stay—"

"I promised to stay until you were well enough to go back to the office," Asher interrupted angrily. "At the rate you've been going you'll never recover. I think you've been playing at being sick in order to keep me here."

"How can you suggest such a thing?" he asked indignantly. "It's only been six weeks. I was very ill. I almost died if you'll remember."

"Yes, I remember." Asher's tone softened. He did love his brother, and he knew he had been seriously ill for a time. But not anymore. "That is the only reason I've stayed as long as I have. Parker, by the first of next week you should be well enough to go to the office for an hour or two each day until you build your strength again."

Parker laid the papers on the floor and rose from his chair. "All right. Maybe I'm a little better than I've pretended to be. But why is it wrong for me to try and keep you here where you belong? America is not your home. London is! If you must stay married to your American wife bring her here to your homeland to live." The challenge Parker issued with his words was also in his eyes.

Asher looked away from Parker to the glowing red coals in the fireplace. Their warmth seemed to give him strength for what he had to say. "You're wrong, Parker. London is no longer my home—Live Oak is. I want to live there with Cara."

"And John Cantrell." Parker spit the name from his lips as if poison had been placed on his tongue.

"Yes!" Asher said, his voice rising in pitch. "But I plan to tell Cantrell that we know of his bloody little secret, and that if he doesn't sign Live Oak over to me I'll tell Caramarena the whole sordid story."

"Save your breath. We've talked of this before." Parker paced in front of the small settee. "Cantrell will call your bluff without a moment's hesitation. Any

314

fool can see you love the woman. One look at you and Cantrell would know that you don't have what it takes to hurt her. Because of his daughter, you will be at Cantrell's mercy rather than the other way around. Dammit, Asher, I can't believe it's come to this!"

"That's not true. I will tell her," Asher said with conviction. "In fact, maybe I should tell her anyway so that we'll have no more secrets between us. It's been a hell of a way to live."

"Oh, do tell her, Asher. I agree completely. It's the best thing to do." Parker smiled and walked over to the small sofa and sat down.

Asher knew the argument was draining Parker's strength, but this had to be done. He also knew Parker had a point. If he told Caramarena about her father's past he'd risk losing her for good. He knew that, but could he live with this secret between them for the rest of their lives?

"I don't want to argue with you about this. I can see you're not up to it."

Parker sighed. "You force it upon me, Asher. Don't you realize that this will give Cantrell the ultimate victory over our father? Over us. His last laugh on George Worthy will be that he separated his sons." He hung his head low. "I can't believe you're willing to let him win again."

Asher settled himself on the settee beside his brother. Parker was saying all the things he expected him to say. And he understood every one of his objections. He had only one thing to refute the words.

"Cantrell has nothing to do with my going back to America. It's Caramarena. My wife. I love her and I want to be with her. I want to live with her on Live Oak and make it *our* home. I promise you one way or another Cantrell will sign the plantation over to me."

"That's big talk for the youngest brother," Parker said with a touch of humor to his voice.

"Will it make you feel better if I promise to bring her for a visit in a year or two?" he asked when he sensed a weakening in Parker's attitude.

"No," Parker said gloomily, and then, as if another thought struck him suddenly, he glanced at Asher and said, "I thought perhaps Elizabeth might be fitting into your life again. You've spent so much time with her since you've been back."

A guilty feeling washed over Asher as he remembered last evening. He hoped he managed to keep any emotion from showing on his face. Today he was glad he'd had the strength to resist Elizabeth last evening.

"Elizabeth and I are just friends, Parker. That's all it's been. That's all it will ever be."

"So you expect me to sit calmly by and watch you walk out of our lives and not try to stop you?" Parker didn't keep the note of dissatisfaction out of his voice.

Asher smiled. "Not try and stop me? Parker, come now. Own up to your machinations. You've held me up more than two months with your illness and playacting. I'd say you've done a damn fine job of keeping me here."

Parker cut his eyes around to Asher. "Not good enough, brother mine. Not good enough."

Asher started running as soon as he jumped off the riverboat that brought him to the dock at Live Oak. The late June sun had burned down on his head during the thirty-mile river ride and fear had hammered in his chest.

When he'd boarded in Apalachicola the captain of the boat had told him that Live Oak and several other

316

plantations along the river had been hit with yellow fever. The man didn't know who had lived, or who had died. Half way through the journey he'd given the captain a five dollar gold piece and told him to stack his trunks on the dock.

His boots crunched rhythmically in the dirt and sweat broke out on his forehead as he ran. He started calling Caramarena's name as soon as he neared the house. Taking the front steps two at a time, he made it to the top quickly and rushed inside.

Ivy met him in the foyer, twisting the hem of her apron in her hands. She looked like a small, frightened animal. "Ivy," he said breathlessly. "Where's Cara?"

She didn't speak for a moment and fear consumed him. He shook. "Ivy?" he said her name again, a question in his voice.

Finally in her high-pitched voice she answered. "She down in de fields, Mr. Asher. Dat's all I's know."

Thank God she was alive. A feeling of relief bathed him, making him weak and he leaned against the door frame. Out of the corner of his eyes he saw Bunch slip around the corner. She was holding a doll.

"Bunch," he smiled, and started toward her, but she backed away. A little, fearful sound issued from her mouth. She didn't remember him. His heart continued to hammer loudly. He tried to calm his breathing. Caramarena and Bunch were still alive. He could handle anything else.

"I don't guess she remembers me," he said softly, glancing back at Ivy.

"It's be de beard, Mr. Asher. Yous don't have it on yo' face any mo'."

Asher reached up and touched his cheek. He'd been

317

so long without it, he'd forgotten that he'd once had one. Of course the change in him would frighten Bunch. He was a stranger to her. She didn't like things that weren't familiar.

He turned back toward her. "It's me, Bunch. Asher. I shaved off the beard, but it's still me. Do you remember now?"

Like a darting rabbit she ran past him and threw her arms around Ivy's rounded frame. "She ain't been right since Mr. John died," Ivy said, brushing a kind, dark hand through Bunch's honey-colored hair.

"Cantrell's dead?" He said feeling no sorrow for the man's death, except on behalf of Caramarena. She would have taken it hard. He knew how much she loved her father. He wanted to hold her and comfort her. He had to find her, but then remembered to ask, "Who else, Ivy?"

"Mr. John, he died quick, and dat Mr. Wulpher wuz sick for a long time befo' he died — Jank and Pearl and po' Lacy. Dey's all gone. I reckon Miss Cara lost more'n half of us."

"Half! My God, Ivy, I've got to see her."

He should have been here. Dammit! he should have been here to help her through this. He had to find Cara. He had to hold her and comfort her.

"Do you know what field she went to?" he asked.

Ivy shook her head. "She don't tells me nothin' but to watch Bunch and do de cookin'."

"What about Kissie?"

"Miss Cara says we so short-handed dat she has ta put her in de field pulling de corn. Miss Cara been pulling de corn, too," Ivy told him.

Anger at himself built a large knot in his chest. How could he have been playing around in England when Cara needed him so desperately?

318

"I'll find her," he said determinedly.

He looked at Bunch again. He wanted to touch her, to tell her he was going to make it up to her and Caramarena. He reached his hand out to caress her cheek but she squirmed away from him. What could he expect? He'd been gone almost eight months. He'd have to win her trust again.

Asher turned and strode to the door, furious that Cara was actually doing the work of slaves. He jerked the door open and turned back to Ivy, who hadn't moved from her spot in the large foyer.

"Have a tub of warm water waiting for Miss Cara in her room when we return."

Anger continued to eat at him as he stood on the porch. Caramarena could be almost anywhere. No. Ivy said Cara was pulling corn. He knew which fields should have been planted with corn. He'd check those first. Maybe he'd stop by the barn and saddle a horse to cover the distance faster. He might find Cypress there, too. Surely he'd know which corn field Cara was in.

Long strides took him toward the barn. It was late afternoon but still very hot. As he walked he untied his cravat and stuffed it in his jacket pocket. Just as he was about to go into the barn he saw someone walking slowly toward the house.

"Caramarena," he whispered. At least he thought it was Cara. He shaded his eyes with his hand and looked again. It was difficult to tell with the sun bonnet covering her hair, its brim hiding her face. Her dress hung loosely from her shoulders.

"Cara," he whispered again, and started running toward her.

The sound of his approaching steps caused the woman to stop and look his way. He'd hoped to see

319

joy and happiness light her eyes, but all she did was stare up at him as he stopped before her.

His first thought was to pull her to him and hold her but the passive, blank expression on her face stayed him. Something was wrong. This was not the Cara he'd left behind.

"Cara, it's me, Asher," he said, wondering if she had trouble recognizing him without the beard. "I know I look different, but you do know who I am, don't you?"

She nodded. Dark circles framed her dull and lifeless eyes. Her lips and cheeks were pale and dry. She'd lost a lot of weight, and she looked as if she'd been through hell. My God, he realized, she had. She lost more than half of the slaves to the fever and she'd been do the work of field hands. He wanted to pick her up and carry her to her room where she could rest, but he was afraid to touch her. She was too cool, too distant.

Asher didn't know what to say, so he said what any idiot would. "I'm back."

She didn't answer but continued to stare at him with that blank expression. She reached up, pushed the bonnet away from her face and let it fall down her back. He noticed her hands were rough and reddened. Damn, he hated himself all over again.

"You don't look well, Cara. You look tired." Another idiotic thing to say.

"No, I'm fine," she answered in a soft voice and started walking toward the house.

Asher's heart ached. She wasn't glad to see him. He didn't blame her. But it hurt. He wanted to hold her and tell her he was going to make it up to her. That he wasn't going to leave her again. Ever.

"Cara, I'm sorry I wasn't here when the fever hit." He knew that wasn't going to help now, but what else could he say? Dammit! what else could he say?

Her pace was slow but she continued to walk as she said, "It's best you weren't here. You probably wouldn't have lived through it."

That rankled. He'd have had as good a chance as she had. "I should have been here," he mumbled again as if trying to come to grips with the fact he hadn't been. How did a man ever live down this sort of thing?

He knew he should tell her he was sorry about her father, but he wasn't, and right now he didn't want to lie to her. But he was sorry for the pain it caused her. She needed—deserved to be comforted. He reached out and touched her arm, stopping her before she reached the front steps.

"Cara," he spoke her name softly, waiting for her to look at him. When she did, he continued. "I'm sorry about your father. I know how difficult it must have been for you to lose him."

She made no attempt to answer him.

"I want you to know I'm back to stay. I promised you I'd be back, and I won't be leaving again."

"That's nice."

She turned to walk away. Without really thinking he grabbed her arm and swung her around to face him. "That's nice! I've been gone for eight months and you tell me it's nice that I've returned." His voice softened when he realized he had no reason to take his anger out on her. "Cara, I know you've been though a lot but—"

"A lot!" she interrupted, fire springing to her eyes. "I lost Papa and—and—" she faltered, unable to finish her sentence.

Asher wanted so much to hold her but something told him that wasn't the thing to do.

321

"Cara, did you get my letter telling you my brother was ill and I—"

"Your brother was ill!" she interrupted him again, her voice louder. "I buried twenty-seven people while you were gone. Over half my people!" Her bottom lip trembled and her voice shook. "After you left I discovered we had little or no money left in our bank accounts. We didn't get any money from the turpentine because your ship was pirated. I still owe the doctor for the medicine he gave us during the fever. We're working day and night to try to get the corn in before it dries so I'll have enough money for us to live on." Her gaze locked on to his. "Pardon me, Asher, if I'm not exactly thrilled to have you back."

Asher had never felt so helpless. He deserved her rancor. "Cara, I sent word to my bank in Charleston to replenish the money I took from Live Oak's accounts before I sailed to England. The monies should have been made available to you within a few weeks after I left."

"Well I guess they didn't get the message." Her voice sounded tired this time, not angry. She rubbed her forehead and Asher once again noticed her hands were scratched and reddened from work they weren't used to. He had so much to make up to her.

"Cara, I have no excuses. I should have been here."

"Go away, Asher. I'm too tired to talk any more."

Asher placed one hand on her back and the other he hooked under her knees, lifting her off the ground before she had the chance to complain.

She gasped. "What are you doing?"

"I'm taking charge. Something I should have done a long time ago." He bounded up the steps and kicked the front door open. "I told Ivy to have a tub of warm

322

water waiting in your room. You're going to get a bath, a bowl of soup, and then you're going to bed and you're to stay there until I say you can get up."

"How dare you think you can just walk in and take over my life. I've got to get the corn harvested and—"

"From now on that's my job. Yours is to manage the house." He took the stairs as if she weighed no more than a small bundle of clothes.

"What gives you the right to come back into my life and start issuing orders, Asher Millhouse?" she demanded, but the fact that she was being carried in his arms made the words lose their strength.

"I'm your husband. That gives me all the rights I need." He let her down in the middle of her bedroom beside the tub of water Ivy had placed in the room. "I'll be back up in a few minutes with a tray."

"I told you to go away, Asher. I don't need you." Her eyes seemed to back up her words although her voice lacked conviction.

Asher knew what she said to be true. She was a strong woman and very capable of taking care of herself and Live Oak without one bit of help from him. She'd proved that many times. He wasn't going to admit that to her, but he would make another admission. "You may not need me, Cara, but I need you." He strode from the room, closing the door behind him.

Caramarena let her face drop into her hands. "Thank God, he's home," she whispered.

Caramarena was at her dresser brushing her hair when Asher came in carrying a tray of steaming food. Part of her wanted to rush into his arms but another part of her didn't trust him not to leave her again.

323

She'd been through too much pain to welcome him back so easily.

Through the mirror she watched as he set the tray down on the night table then turn back the coverlet on her bed. She also noticed that he'd changed from his English clothes to one of the lightweight shirts and for some strange reason that made her feel better.

She breathed deeply, put down her brush and placed her hands in her lap. She felt so empty. She'd felt that way since losing the baby. Her hands moved upward and her fingers splayed over her stomach. Her baby. Asher's baby. Their little girl was lost to them forever. She squeezed her eyes shut and pressed her hands hard against her abdomen. If only the pain of loss would go away. If only she could go back and change . . .

"Cara?"

Startled, she jumped and opened her eyes. He was standing behind her but looking at her reflection in the mirror.

"Come to bed," he said.

Caramarena didn't have the strength or the will to argue. She rose from the stool and walked over to the bed. Asher pulled the sheet up over her legs as she leaned against the pillows. He placed the tray on her lap, and she looked down on a steaming bowl of chicken and potato soup, a large slice of buttered bread and a glass of water.

The soup smelled wonderful and looked delicious but Caramarena hadn't regained her appetite since losing the baby. She ate only enough to keep her going.

"Am I going to have to feed you?" Asher asked from the side of her bed.

She looked up at him and was struck with how

handsome he looked. Of course, he'd shaved the beard. Yes, she vaguely remembered noticing it missing when she first saw him. But he was one of those rare men who looked just as handsome with a beard as he did without one. She wanted to smile but couldn't find it within herself to do so.

Asher must have realized what she was thinking because he rubbed his cheek and chin. "If you don't like me without it I can always grow it back," he said.

She lowered her eyes without comment. She needed to do some thinking and she couldn't do it with him staring at her. She picked up her water glass and emptied it before bringing the glass down from her lips. Working in the field drained all the moisture from her body and always left her thirsty. Next she picked up the spoon and sipped the broth, leaving the hunks of white meat and potatoes in the bowl. She felt Asher's eyes upon her but didn't look up until she'd eaten all the broth. She picked up the tray and extended it toward him.

He looked at the bowl with the vegetables and meat still in it. "Well, it's a start," he said. "You lie down and rest. Try to sleep. I'll be up to check on you in a little while."

Caramarena did as she was told and slid down in the bed. She knocked all the pillows off the bed and rolled to her side, bringing one knee up to her stomach. She should have told Asher about the baby. She should have told him she was glad to have him back but the words wouldn't come. He'd been gone so long she'd decided he wasn't going to return. How could he expect her to just open up to him as if he'd never left?

She closed her eyes. Maybe he didn't. She should have told him about the baby.

Later when Asher checked on Caramarena she was asleep. He wanted to stretch out on the bed beside her and pull her into his arms and just hold her. He knew he'd feel better if he could touch her. Even if it took the rest of his life he'd spend every day trying to win Caramarena back.

He walked out to the cookhouse and told Ivy to set the table in the dining room for him and Bunch. The sooner Live Oak returned to the normal way of doing things the better everyone would feel. When he came out of the cookhouse Kissie was waiting by the door. The fever had taken its toll on her as well. She was also thinner and her cheeks were hollow. He'd never liked the slave, but he'd always admired her loyalty to Caramarena.

"How are you, Kissie?" he asked.

"I's fine, Mr. Asher. I sent Miss Cara to de house. She ain't got no business out in dat field all day. She ain't gots over losing—" Kissie's eyes rounded in shock and she clamped her mouth shut.

"It's all right, Kissie. I know she lost her father to the fever. And I know how difficult it must have been for her. You don't have to worry about her now. I intend to take very good care of her."

"Yessir," she said and nodded. "I 'spect you will." She pulled on the handkerchief she kept tied around her hair.

"Cypress? Is he all right?"

Nodding again she said, "Yep. He's didn't gets de fever. Wouldn't none of us made it if'n it weren't fo' him and Miss Cara. Deys done took care of us all," she praised. "Cypress had ta take over po' Mr. Wulpher's job cause Miss Cara didn't have no money to hire another overseer."

Asher tensed. He'd write a letter tonight and find out why the money wasn't deposited as instructed. Kissie was staring at him so he said, "I'll see Cypress is rewarded."

"Yessir, dat be mighty fine of ye."

"Ah—I haven't seen Lacy."

Kissie started shaking her head before he finished. "Lacy, Fanny, Pearl, Jank. Deys all dead. We sho' had lots a good workers ta bury, but weren't none of 'em as sad as digging de grave fo' Mr. John and—" She stopped, once again before finishing her sentence.

"It's all right, Kissie. I know how you felt about Mr. John. Have you been sleeping in Bunch's room?"

"No sir. Me and Cypress got married. I sleep wid him. Bunch been sleeping wid Miss Cara. Ivy, she been staying in de house wid 'em, though. We ain't left 'em alone."

"I see. Well," he said, "Tonight I'm sleeping with Cara so it looks like Ivy will have to sleep with Bunch."

A broad smile eased across Kissie's dark face. "I's sho' glad ta hear dat, Mr. Asher."

Asher smiled at her before he walked away.

While he was waiting for Ivy to call him for dinner Asher wrote a letter to his bank in Charleston to find out what had happened with the draft he'd ordered. He felt sure the bank must not have received his letter. The mail system probably wasn't as reliable in America as it was in England, but it'd been impossible for him to personally go to the bank and make the arrangements before he'd sailed to London.

The meal was strained as Asher tried to talk to Bunch, watching every word he said, not wanting to upset her. He tried to regain her confidence in him by asking simple questions about the food.

"Cara's tired," she said when they'd been quiet for some time.

Asher was encouraged. It was the first time she'd spoken without being prompted by a question from him.

"Yes, she is. She's been working very hard. She's sleeping right now."

Bunch nodded.

Maybe this was a good time to tell her he would be sleeping with Caramarena tonight and she'd have to return to her room and settle for Ivy. He laid his napkin down, pushed back his chair and asked, "You're not afraid of me, are you, Bunch?"

She shook her head.

Very slowly he rose and walked over to her chair and knelt down beside her. "It's upset you, hasn't it, the changes here at home?"

"Cara says Papa has gone to heaven. I miss him." She wrinkled her nose.

"I'm sure you do. He was very good to you, wasn't he?"

She nodded, and he saw some of the stiffness leave her body.

Her eyes rounded and sparkled. "Cara was going to have a baby for me to play with. But the baby came too early and didn't live."

Asher's chest tightened. He swayed on his knees. Surely Bunch didn't know what she was saying. For the first time in his life he felt faint, as if he couldn't breathe. He grabbed hold of Bunch's hand and realized his hands were cold and trembling.

"Bunch, are you saying that Cara was pregnant?" His voice was raspy. "Was she expecting a baby?"

She nodded again and pulled her hand out of his. "I watched her stomach grow this big. She let me touch it once, and I felt the baby move."

A chill ran up his back. "W-when did she have the baby?" he asked, trying to keep the pain out of his voice, out of his expression.

Bunch sank her teeth into her bottom lip and rolled her eyes upward. "When she started having pains. Kissie wouldn't let me stay in the room. I wanted to."

"I'm sure you did." Suddenly Asher wanted to be alone. No, he wanted to be with Caramarena. Sick brother or not, he never would have stayed in England so long if he'd known she was expecting their child.

Bunch was watching him so he said. "Thank you for telling me about the baby."

He started to rise but she spoke again so he remained on his knees. "Cara said you gave her the baby. Will you give her another one so I can play with him when he's born?"

He smiled. Her innocent question tore at his heart. "Yes, I'll give her another one. Just as soon as she gets her strength back. She's too weak right now to carry a child. Will you help me watch over her and see that she gets plenty of rest?"

She nodded.

"Good. When she's better I'll see what I can do about giving her a baby."

She giggled. "I'd like that. Cara said I could hold him and rock him."

Asher looked up and saw that Ivy had come into the room. He saw in her eyes that she also grieved for Caramarena's baby. He gave his attention back to Bunch. "I'll be sleeping with Caramarena now. That means you will have to go back to your room. Ivy will stay with you. Will that be all right?"

"Cara lets me sleep in the bed with her," she argued.

"That's because you were taking care of her until I could return. And I'm very grateful you did. But now it's my place to sleep with her and Ivy will stay with you. All right?" he asked again.

For a moment he thought she was going to get upset, but finally she nodded. He rose. "Ivy, have someone else clear away the dishes and you help Bunch get ready for bed."

"Dey ain't nobody else ta work in de house, Mr. Asher. Miss Cara didn't have de money ta buy no mo'—" She paused. "Kissie—she can work in de house but Miss Cara sent her to de fields—"

Asher held up his hand. "I know," he said even though he still didn't understand why a field hand couldn't work in the house. "As of tomorrow Kissie is no longer in the fields but back to taking care of Bunch and Caramarena. And you pick out someone to take Lacy's place. Train her to work in the house. Make sure Bunch likes her. I'm going up to check on Cara."

He'd planned on sleeping in his old room but now he knew he couldn't leave Caramarena alone tonight. He had to hold her. No wonder she'd looked so lifeless when he'd first seen her. She'd been expecting his baby and trying to live through yellow fever all the time he'd been dancing Elizabeth around London. What a fool he'd been to stay. He'd make it up to Caramarena. He didn't know how, but he would.

He opened the bedroom door, stepped across the threshold and closed himself inside. Pale moonlight shone in the room, outlining the bed. He walked farther into the room until he could see the bed, then slowly discarded his clothes as he watched Caramarena sleeping. He wanted to tell her how sorry he

330

was that she'd lost the baby. He wanted to tell her that it hurt him, too. He wanted to tell her that he loved her. But all that would have to wait. He didn't want to wake her.

Carefully he climbed onto the bed and gently tugged on her arm. She murmured something he didn't understand and willingly turned into his arms. She was warm, soft, his.

Asher's arms tightened around her and he kissed the top of her head. God, she felt so good, so right, so womanly. Tonight his feelings for her weren't of a sexual nature. His desire for her this night was to comfort and be comforted. He would never leave her again no matter the reason. Never! Because of Parker's illness he'd missed so much. He wanted to hold her tighter. He wanted to kiss her and let her know he was close.

He wanted to cry.

Chapter Twenty

Caramarena awoke to bright sunshine lighting the room and a wonderful warmth against her back. As she shrugged off the last vestige of sleep she thought Bunch must have inched too close in the night and was now snuggled tight against her. But then she realized something heavy lay across her stomach. Without moving her head she lowered her gaze and saw a man's arm thrown over her, then she remembered. Asher had come home. Asher!

Quickly she rolled over and found him staring at her with his blue eyes. In that moment she knew she loved him and wanted him, but she wasn't ready to admit that to him, or to forget what she'd been through while he was gone.

"Good morning," he said and smiled at her.

"What are you doing in my bed?" she asked, her voice still raspy with sleep. With the back of her hand she wiped her eyes, trying to clear the lingering threads of a deep sleep.

"It's *our* bed, Cara." His voice was firm, possessive.

She picked up his arm and removed it from around her, then brushed her hair away from her face. "You can't just walk back into my life as if you'd only been gone a few days. Too much has happened."

"I know. I admit that I thought it was possible when

I first arrived, but now I know it's going to take time for you to heal from all that you've been through. But, Cara, I'm not leaving." He stuffed his arm under his pillow, then laid his head on top of it. He looked into her eyes and said, "Not this house, not this bedroom, not this bed."

No, she thought, she didn't want him to be understanding. If he were too kind she'd break down and cry. She'd been fighting it too long to give in to tears now.

"Asher, I can't—pick up where we left off."

She turned to get out of bed but he grabbed her arms and held her to him, forcing her to stay.

"Caramarena, don't run away from me. I'm not asking anything from you. Look at me." He lifted her chin with the tips of his fingers. "Open your eyes and look at me. That's better." He moistened his lips, and a muscle twitched in his jaw. "I love you. That's all that's important right now. Just remember that. Everything else will be all right with time."

Asher's hands were firm but gentle on her arms as he held her. His words were firm but kind as he spoke. His tone was stern but sincere as he soothed her mounting fear. Yes, she needed him to comfort her for the loss of their baby, her father and the slaves who died.

"Everything's going to be all right, Cara," he said again. "I'll never leave you again."

Asher was being too understanding, and Caramarena was too close to tears to hold them in any longer. They trickled down her cheeks although she made no sound. Her heart ached, knowing what she had to tell him.

"No, that's not true. You don't know everything." Her grief was too great to deny. "Asher, I—I lost our baby," she said in a thick voice, filled with emotion, no longer able to withhold the knowledge from him. She squeezed her eyes shut and more tears poured from beneath her lids.

With the tips of his fingers Asher wiped the tears from her face. "I know, Cara. Bunch told me last night. I'm so sorry. I should have been here for you. I'll never forgive myself for not being here." His voice was a hushed whisper.

"It was my fault," she whispered.

He pulled her close and buried her face in his chest. "No! Don't say that."

"It's true," she mumbled, raised her head and looked at him. "I had to help the sick ones, Asher. I had to help Papa, Kissie and the others. I knew I wasn't resting enough, I knew I wasn't eating, but there was so much to do, so many to care for that— I—"

"Cara! Cara, don't go through it all again." He cupped her face with his hands. "You did exactly what you were supposed to do. And I'm so proud of you. Losing the baby wasn't your fault. Don't ever let me hear you say that again."

"But I—"

"No, you did the right thing. You had no choice but to help the others. I should have been here to help you, but—we're not going to live the rest of our lives thinking about what might have been. We'll have other children. Are you listening to me?" She nodded. "I love you more now than ever before. When you're better I'll give you another baby, and I promise I'll be around to take care of both of you. But I'm not going to rush you, Cara. All right? I know you need time to get over all that you've been through."

She nodded again and moistened her dry lips. With

334

the back of her hands she wiped her face dry and sniffled. She felt better now that Asher knew about the baby, now that she knew he didn't blame her for losing the baby.

"I've got to get up. There's so much to do."

"Absolutely not," he said firmly as she tried to pull out of his arms. "The only thing you're going to do for the next few days is get your strength and your weight back. And to do that, I order bed rest. I'll take care of everything else."

"Asher, I can't. The corn—"

"Can wait until I go into Apalachicola and hire some workers. If it dries before it's pulled, we'll use it for seed and feed." He kissed her forehead.

Caramarena wanted to sit up but found she had very little strength. She gave him a sideways glance. "What do you mean, hired workers?" she asked.

He looked lovingly at her and smiled. "Caramarena, I didn't grow up owning slaves the way you did. I'll do things a little differently. We'll keep those slaves we have, but we won't be buying any more. I have plenty of money to hire all the workers we need. I know there are many other things we need to discuss but we'll do that later. Come closer. Lay your head on my shoulder and go back to sleep. You need more rest. I'll stay here with you until you go back to sleep."

Realizing she was still tired, she did as she was told and laid her head on his shoulder. His body was warm and inviting. It was comforting to hear the rhythm of his breathing in her ear. So many nights she'd lain awake wanting to be this close to him again, wanting to be held this way by Asher. Now that he was here she was going to let him take over. She snuggled closer, burying her nose in the warmth of his neck.

"You don't have to worry about anything from now

on. I'll take care of everything. Go to sleep."

Caramarena threw her arm across Asher's chest and sighed contentedly. Asher would take care of everything and she could rest. He was right, they still had many things to discuss, but they would do it later. Right now her eyes were too heavy.

After spending a third day in bed Caramarena was feeling better but Asher insisted she have dinner in her bedroom at least one more night. She'd enjoyed the pampering for a time, but now that she was getting her strength back she was ready to vacate the bed and get back to her normal duties. She decided to tell Asher as soon as he had returned from his swim and said good night to Bunch.

Caramarena closed her eyes and rested against her pillows and thought of Asher. He'd been so understanding and attentive the last few days. He'd told her he wasn't going to rush her into doing anything, and he hadn't. A kiss on the forehead or cheek when he started to leave for the day was all she'd received.

It had been two and a half months since she'd lost the baby. Her breasts and stomach had gone back down to their former size. With her eyes still closed she laid her hands on her breasts and let them slide down her body to her stomach. She wondered if there were any physical signs left to show she'd once been pregnant.

The baby. She tried not to think about the little girl that never cried. She had known there was no hope for a six-month baby but still she'd prayed for its life.

Now she knew why Dr. Johnstone wouldn't let her see her daughter. At the time she'd cried, begged, and pleaded until he'd made her drink something to put

336

her to sleep. The baby had already been buried when she awakened. He said she would get over it quicker if she didn't look at the baby. Maybe he was right, because even now she couldn't bring an image to mind of what the baby must have looked like.

"Cara, are you all right?"

Startled, her eyes popped open. Asher was standing over her with a concerned look on his face. Her hands, lying on her stomach, had clutched her gown into an unsightly wad.

"What's wrong? Are you hurting?" he asked.

She moistened her lips. "Oh, no, I'm fine. I was just — resting." She gave him a smile and smoothed the wrinkles from her nightgown.

"You looked as if you were in pain."

She glanced up at him. He'd left his shirt and boots off and was dressed only in a pair of tanned breeches. She thought him especially handsome with his hair slightly damp from his swim.

"No, Asher. I'm fine, really. In fact, I was just trying to decide how to tell you that I plan to get out of this bed tomorrow and resume some of my duties."

"Oh, you do, do you? And what made you come to this decision?"

He slipped his pants down his legs and threw them across the slipper chair before sliding into the bed and under the sheet beside her.

Caramarena caught a quick glimpse of his naked body and the sight of him made her heartbeat increase. He'd slept naked beside her the past three nights but for some reason tonight she felt different. Tonight the thought of his nakedness made her breath grow short and her chest heavy. Tonight she felt good, expectant.

No, she told herself. She needed more time. She

337

wasn't ready for him to love her. But if that were true why did her hands itch to caress his broad shoulders and back? Why did her stomach contract with wanting? Why did she feel empty and in need of filling?

She straightened the blue bow that held the front of her nightgown together. She had to do something to keep her thoughts off Asher, so she answered his question. "One of the best ways for me to get my strength back is to start doing little things."

"All right. Tomorrow you can start doing little things like sitting out on the porch and watching Bunch play."

"You're trying to make an invalid out of me," she complained, and glanced over at him. "All I needed was a little rest."

"I want to take care of you." His eyes turned serious and he picked up her hand and held it in his. "Cara, I want you to know I've sent a letter to Charleston. I want to find out why money was never taken from my accounts and deposited into Live Oak's. I had no idea the money had not been replaced."

"Asher, that's not important now. I've told you it doesn't matter."

"It matters to me. It wasn't my intention to leave you penniless when I sailed for London."

"I was always sure of that, Asher." She smiled and covered his hand with her other one. Instead of being warm and comforting tonight his touch set her on fire with desire and made her think of kisses and caresses and loving words. She thought of how much she'd missed him and how she'd longed for him to return to her.

Asher looked at her hand covering his, then said, "Cypress is doing a good job overseeing the slaves. They all like him and work hard for him. I'm thinking of leaving him in charge of them. What do you think of that idea?"

"I think he will do very well." She slowly, softly, rubbed the top of his hand, letting the fine hair tickle her palm. She wasn't ready to say good night so she kept talking. "When Mr. Wulpher died there was no money to hire another overseer so I told Cypress to handle the slaves. I'm glad he's done a good job and pleased that you approve of my decision."

"I've never doubted any decision you've made concerning Live Oak."

His husky voice touched her and she looked up into her husband's questioning eyes. At that moment, she knew she wanted his loving tonight. But there was something that still had to be settled between them.

"Asher, I — tell me — the reason you had to go to England. Is everything cleared up now? Are you free from whatever took you back there?"

He looked away from her searching eyes briefly, then turned back to her. "Most of it, Cara. There could still be some repercussions from it. I want to tell you all about it. Everything. You have a right to know, but not tonight. Will you trust me that this isn't a good time to tell you but know that I will tell you the whole story one day soon?"

When he had that gentle look in his eyes how could she not believe him? And he'd promised her he would return to her and he had.

She continued to caress his hand, sometimes sliding her hand up his arm. "I remember that you said you'd written that your brother was ill. Is he better now?"

"Yes." His voice remained husky.

"Will you have to go back to England?"

"No." He smiled. "Never without you. I said good-bye to my brothers and told them if I returned it

339

would be for a visit and with you beside me. This is my home. I told you when I returned that I wasn't leaving, and, Cara, I won't."

"Do you mean that, Asher?" There was a plea for a promise in her voice.

"I promise." He bent his head and kissed her tenderly.

His lips were soft, moist and ever so good and pleasing. It seemed as if she'd been waiting an eternity for his lips to caress hers and she wasn't going to hurry it. She opened her mouth and shyly stuck her tongue into his mouth, wanting to taste more of him, wanting to be a part of him.

Asher moaned as a piercing stab of desire shot through him like hot coals and hardened his manhood. His arms slid around Caramarena like bands of iron, entrapping her in their strength. He kissed her roughly for only a moment, bruising her lips beneath his in an effort to sate the desire bubbling inside him. When he realized he was thrusting his hips toward her, wanting to find that softest part of her and invade its warmth, he pushed away from her.

His breathing was ragged gasps. He closed his hands into fists to keep himself from reaching for her again. "No, Cara. We have to stop." He wet his lips, finding the taste of her lingering on his tongue. "I can't take too many of your kisses. They make me want more."

She laid her hand to the side of his face, and felt the clean-shaven cheek for the first time. She smiled. "I want more than kisses, too, Asher. I want you to love me."

He shook his head, even though his heart said yes, even though his eyes said yes, even though his whole body said yes. "It's too soon. I don't want to hurt you.

340

You're not well enough."

"There's nothing wrong with me." Her heart was pounding, afraid of being rejected by him yet again. "Are you making excuses, Asher?"

"I'm worried about you." He swallowed hard. "I don't think you're ready."

Caramarena slid her hand around his neck and gently tugged to bring his face closer to hers. "Do you love me, Asher?"

"Yes."

"Do you want to kiss me?" She moved a little closer.

"Yes!" he rasped.

Her lips brushed against his as she asked, "Do you want to make love to me?"

"Hell, yes!" he answered and once again took her lips with his in a hard, bruising kiss as he pulled her slim body to him and rolled her to her back. His lips left hers, and he looked down into her eyes. "Cara, I don't know if I have the strength to be gentle tonight. I want you so badly. I've been too long without you."

Caramarena slid her arms around his neck and shoved her fingers into the back of his hair. She fit the lower portion of her body against his swollen member.

"If you get too rough I'll let you know."

Asher started with her eyes and kissed his way down to her lips, taking time to let his tongue play with hers, sipping her sweetness. He left her lips long enough to snuggle his nose into the curve of her neck and shoulder and smell her cleanness. His tongue darted out and he licked her soft skin and pulled it into his mouth to taste her. His hand inched down to her breast and he felt the nipple harden at his touch. She moaned softly and arched toward him as her hands gently pulled his hair. Asher loved the way his wife responded to his caress.

341

"Cara, I love you," he whispered. "Damn, I've missed your touch, your taste, your scent. Thank God you're all mine."

"I didn't think you'd return," she murmured between passionate kisses.

"How could I not when I love you so much?"

Caramarena stroked his back, hips and buttocks, exploring his muscular body with her hands. A light film of moisture coated his heated skin. She pressed closer and realized her nightgown was keeping her from feeling the hair-roughened skin of his broad chest and flat stomach. With eager hands she grabbed the cotton gown and pulled. Asher realized what she was doing and helped her yank the unwanted garment over her head and toss it aside.

He raised up and sat back on his knees, holding his weight off her legs. "Let me look at you. I've missed you."

"No, don't," she whispered, suddenly feeling exposed. She folded her arms across her chest.

"Cara, don't be afraid," he said softly. "I know it's been a long time, but I want to see you." He held out his arms. "Do you like to look at me?"

Her gaze left his handsome face and traveled down his muscular chest to where his manhood stretched out before him. He was beautiful. She looked back to his eyes and saw his love for her. He hid nothing from her.

"I hope I please you half as much as you please me."

He gently lowered first one arm and then the other, taking time to caress the length of each. He stroked her firm breasts, her waist, her hips and her breasts again as he took in the sight of all of her, loving her with his eyes, his touch, his heart.

"You have no reason to hide from me, Cara. You

342

are a beautiful woman in every way." He dipped his head and covered a nipple with his lips, pulling it into his mouth and sucking.

Caramarena's abdomen tightened and her fingers dug into his back as chills of desire swept across her. How could such a natural act fill her with the need to feel him deep inside her? She closed her eyes and enjoyed her husband's mouth, lips and tongue bathing her breasts with his passion. She moaned and squirmed until she could no longer stand the pain of his arousal fitted next to her but not inside her. With hands that knew what they wanted, she wedged a space between their thighs and found his pulsating shaft. She tested its satiny length and its rigid hardness with her hands. She shivered with anticipation.

Asher tensed above her and mumbled his approval as he continued to suckle her breasts and shape her waist and hips with his hands.

It seemed natural for Caramarena to guide the pink tip to her womanhood and massage that part of her that so ached to be touched. It felt wonderful. She trembled with pleasure as she caressed herself with his penis. Tension mounted. Sweat collected on her body. Her breaths became gasps. When she could hold off no longer she guided him to the place he most wanted to be and buried him deep.

She heard him swear and answered with a desperate, "Yes."

Asher moved slowly at first, then suddenly rapidly. Caramarena cried out when the pleasure became so intense it was almost painful. She lost the fight to prolong her climax and grabbed hold of his hips to thrust him in deeper, hold him in tighter as his movement eased her over the edge. A moment later Asher poised above her and released his seed, his love inside her.

343

Asher rolled to his side but didn't retreat from her body which held him tight as a well-fitted glove. He tried to kiss her again but he was too out of breath. He managed a quick, "I love you," and she reciprocated in kind.

They lay quietly for a few minutes with only their breathing breaking the silence.

"Damn, I'm glad to be home," Asher said when he had recovered enough to speak. He raised up on his elbow and looked down at his wife.

Caramarena reached over and kissed him. "You don't know how happy it makes me to hear you say you're home to stay."

He smiled. "I'll have to say it more often because all I want to do is make you happy." He kissed the tip of her nose. "I didn't hurt you, did I?"

She shook her head and stretched her arms up over her head and sighed. "It was wonderful."

"Yes, it was." He grinned. "And it was only the beginning. I have so many things to teach you about lovemaking. We've had so little time together, and tonight I find myself wanting to make up for all the time we've lost."

Caramarena laughed lightly. "I think we can manage that. I seem to remember a few things you taught me before you went away." She slid her hand between them and gently cupped the soft sack beneath his manhood.

He trembled.

The fire started and there was no putting it out.

Finley Dobson had been watching the main house at Live Oak for the better part of two days. There was a large oak tree on a bluff overlooking the house which made it easy for him to watch from behind the cover of the tree. He was certain as the ill-set bones in his jaw that the two men he wanted were the two men he'd seen coming and going from the house to the barn and fields.

He'd made his first trip to Live Oak some months back, but yellow fever had hit the area before he could do anything. He'd been hoping the fever would take the whole damn plantation, but a few were spared, including the big buck named Cypress and the Englishman named Millhouse.

The big buck spent a lot of time around the barn late in the afternoon after Millhouse went in to dinner. The first part of his plan was to sneak into the barn and wait for the Negro to return and then knife him. If he didn't have any problems with the buck, then he'd slip into the house and kill the Englishman. He should be back to his horse and on his way to Pensacola before anyone could send the slaves after him.

Dobson left his horse tied to a branch of the live oak and started his careful walk to the barn. In a plantation as big as this it was fairly easy for him to slip unnoticed into the barn and hide in a dark corner. Then he remembered most of the slaves had died of the fever, but still he praised himself for his cleverness.

Once he'd settled himself where he felt adequately hidden, he pulled his knife from his gun belt and looked at it. The long blade glinted in the semidarkness. He ran his finger over the sharp edge and smiled. Perfect, he thought.

He then pulled out the new gun he'd bought back before the fever hit. He checked it once again to make sure it was ready to fire, carefully replaced it in the holster and settled back against the boards to wait for his prey.

Through a crack in the barn siding he watched the sun sinking lower in the azure-colored sky. Everything was going according to plan. By the time he'd killed the buck and the Englishman it would be dark and difficult for anyone to follow him. He reached up and rubbed his jaw, feeling the jagged bone that now mis-shaped his face.

Once this day was over he could live with his disfigurement a little better, knowing the two men who caused it were dead. He took a deep breath and puffed out his chest, quite pleased with himself.

A few minutes later Dobson was rewarded for his patience. He watched as the barn door swung open and the unsuspecting Negro ambled in carrying a tub filled with corn.

Dobson's stomach rumbled with hunger. He'd been so caught up in his plan of murder that he'd forgotten to eat. Maybe he'd stop in a little town along the way to Pensacola and have a victory dinner.

He smiled as he quietly, slowly rose to his feet, pulling the long-bladed, shining knife from his belt.

The buck was humming, which made it easier for Dobson to sneak up on him. He'd practiced walking quietly and it was paying off. As he neared the buck's back he realized just how tall the bastard was and experienced a moment of doubt. He'd have a hell of a time reaching up and slitting his throat. It was too late to back down now, and besides, justice was on his side, he told himself as he lunged for the slave, jumping on his back and slicing the knife across his throat.

The dark man made a gurgling sound and fell to his knees, clutching his throat, before falling face down in the dirt. A stream of blood ran from his neck and puddled.

Dobson looked at the dying man for a moment, watching the blood ooze from under his body. He wiped his nose on his sleeve and sniffed, then reached down and wiped the blade of his knife on the buck's pant leg. The slave was still twitching but with the way he was bleeding it would be only a matter of a minute or two before he was dead. A light chuckle rumbled in Dobson's chest as he stuffed the clean knife back under his gun belt and took a satisfied breath. Now all he had to do was get into the house without being seen. After that, the rest would be easy. If he couldn't get Millhouse with the knife, he'd use the gun. What he had in mind should upset their dinner quite nicely.

He decided to walk up to the front door as if he were expected. If anyone called to him he'd simply say he was passing through and ask for directions to the nearest town. He forced himself not to watch his back as he walked up the steps. His confidence soared when he made it all the way to the front door without a problem. From here on he'd be more careful. Once inside the house he couldn't very well say he'd lost his way.

With one hand he pulled his gun from the holster and with the other he turned the door handle. Slowly, he opened the door and peered into the large foyer. It was empty, so he stepped inside and quietly closed it behind him. Despite his earlier feeling of confidence, his courage waned somewhat now that he was inside. He didn't like the feeling of being trapped. He heard a door close upstairs and quickly scooted to the safety of the stairwell and waited. His blood ran hot and fast, his breathing sounded loud and raspy in his ears. If it was the Englishman coming down the stairs he'd step out and say, "This is for killing my brother," then shoot him right between the eyes. But by the light steps he knew it was a woman approaching him.

He saw the green skirts before the woman sailed by him, leaving the scent of perfume in her wake. Within a matter of seconds he realized how she could help, so he reached out and grabbed her around the neck. She tried to scream but it was more of a whimper because of the pressure he put on her throat. She struggled against him, kicking and gasping for breath as her fingers tore at his arm. He pointed the gun at her ear and barked, "Quiet! Or I'll blow your head off."

She went still in his arms, and he dragged her back toward the door and leaned against it, waiting to see if anyone had heard her. Now that he had one of the women Millhouse was sure to show his face.

"I don't want to hurt you. I want the Englishman. Millhouse, where is he?" he whispered in a gravelly voice.

She made a sound and he realized he was strangling her. He let up on the pressure on her throat. She gasped and coughed, struggling for air. Her chest heaved and she tried to move away, but he jerked her back against him again and repeated harshly. "Where's the damn Englishman?"

"Not home, yet," she managed to say.

Dobson tensed. "You're lying!" He held her neck tighter. "I saw him heading this way."

"No! — I swear, he d-didn't come home." She pulled on his arm, trying to free herself, trying to breathe.

Didn't too many women lie with a gun barrel sticking in their ear. "You his wife?" he asked.

She nodded.

Well, this just might work out better than he planned, Dobson thought. He could take her up the bluff with him to where his horse was tied. When the damn Englishman came looking for her, he'd shoot him, jump on his horse and ride hard. That way he could be miles away before anyone started out after him. Yes, he liked that idea much better.

Out of the corner of his eye Dobson saw a darkie walking out of a doorway. She screamed before he had a chance to stop her.

Dobson pressed the gun farther into the woman's flesh and said, "Quiet! Or I'll shoot her!"

Caramarena grabbed the arm that cut off her air supply and pulled with all her strength. "Kissie—do as he says," she managed to say between gulping breaths.

Kissie covered her mouth with both her hands and stared wide-eyed at her mistress.

The cold barrel of the gun dug deeper into Caramarena's ear, cutting the tender flesh, but she dared not cry out. She trembled with fear and her chest felt as if it was going to explode. For some reason this madman wanted to kill Asher.

The man moved away from the door, dragging Caramarena with him. "Open it!" he told Kissie, and she quickly obeyed. He motioned for her to go out on the porch ahead of them, and again Kissie did as she was told.

"You see that bluff up there?" He took the gun away long enough to point with it. Kissie bobbed her head furiously. "That's where we're going. As soon as we're out of sight, you find that Englishman and send him after us. You understand me, girl?"

Kissie nodded, then said, "Don't takes Miss Cara. I'll go wid ye if'n you lets her go." She started toward him and he pulled back the hammer on the gun.

Caramarena squeezed her eyes shut waiting for the

349

blast in her ear.

"Stay where you are," he bellowed. "Do as I say or I'll drop her where she stands."

"I'll do it. I'll do it. Jest don't hurts Miss Cara," she said in a trembling voice, rubbing her hands together nervously.

Caramarena opened her eyes but her legs were so weak she could hardly stand. If the man wasn't holding her she'd surely fall down. She was more afraid for Asher than herself. She wanted to tell Kissie not to go after Asher, that this man wanted to kill him, but he held her so tightly she couldn't speak.

He started backing away from Kissie and maneuvered them down the steps while keeping his eyes on her. As soon as they could no longer see Kissie he whirled her around and pushed her forward and told her to run. She picked up her skirts with one hand while he grabbed the other and wrenched it behind her back, pushing her up the small incline.

A few moments later she heard Kissie screaming sorrowfully in the distance below. A chill of foreboding crawled up her back. Now she knew who this man was and why he wanted to kill Asher. The man from the dock had come for revenge. Each time a foot hit the ground she heard, "Stop him. Stop him. Stop him!"

Caramarena stumbled but he yanked her up. Wrenching her arm again, he pushed her forward. She cried out in pain but continued to run until she was cruelly shoved against a tree. Her head hit the trunk, grazing the flesh, stunning her. She turned around quickly and looked at her assailant who was peering down the slope to see if anyone had followed. She wiped her eyes and face with the backs of her hands and tried to calm herself. She couldn't think until she regained control.

"What do you want?" she finally managed to ask in a shaky voice.

He glanced back at her and said, "Quiet, bitch, or I'll kill you, too."

Caramarena trembled with fear. The look in his eyes told her he meant it. But she couldn't just stand quietly by and let this man kill Asher when he came up the bluff. She heard shouting and more screams from below and knew word had gotten around that there was a violent man with a gun loose on the plantation.

The man's back was to her. She could push him down the hill, she thought, but as if he sensed what was on her mind, he turned around and grabbed her around the throat once again. Caramarena struggled with all her strength, kicking his legs. She managed to sink her teeth into the meaty part of his arm. He let out a yell before hitting her head with the handle of the gun.

Blackness and twinkling stars appeared before her eyes. She groaned.

"Don't go out on me, bitch!"

He shook her and Caramarena cried out from the piercing pain that filled her head. Something warm was running down the side of her face. Through the haze of dizziness she heard Asher call her name. Asher! She couldn't black out. This man wanted to kill Asher. She had to save him.

Fear for her husband's safety renewed her strength to fight the man who held her. But within a matter of moments he had her tight around the throat with the gun once again at her head.

Asher bounded to the crest of the slope and stopped. He looked from Caramarena to the man

351

holding a gun on his wife. Asher had never experienced such fear. His whole body trembled. What if he made a mistake that would cost Caramarena her life? He swallowed hard, trying to think. A cut on her forehead was bleeding and a red bump showed underneath her eye. He wanted to kill the bastard for hurting Cara.

His chest heaved from the running and his breath was shallow. "Let her go," he said in a deadly quiet voice.

"Or what?" The man laughed loudly, his chest shaking with each gusty breath. "You'll kill me?" He laughed again. "Look who's holding the gun."

"What do you want?" Asher asked, stalling for time while he tried to form a plan.

"An eye for an eye. You and that buck of yours killed my brother, caused me months of pain, and left me looking like this." He sneered. "It ain't a pretty sight, is it?"

The man pulled the gun away from Caramarena and shoved her with one hand as he pointed the gun at Asher with the other. He'd misjudged the length of Asher's legs and his distance from him. Asher kicked his leg and knocked the gun away as it fired. Dobson stumbled backward but managed to slide the knife away from his belt as Asher charged him. The blade caught Asher along the ribcage, crossing the scar he'd received from his last fight with this man.

He heard Caramarena scream but didn't take his attention off the killer as he cupped the man's wrist with both his hands. The knife was suspended in the air, caught between the two.

Caramarena tried to watch their movements as she looked on the ground for the gun, praying that Asher would best the older man. She heard a groan and her

352

head snapped up. The man jerked upward and his eyes grew wide and cloudy. His mouth gaped open. Asher stepped back, and she saw that the man still clutched the handle of the knife which was embedded deep in his stomach. He stumbled backward and fell to the ground. His eyes remained open but there was no movement in his face.

Caramarena shuddered and rushed into Asher's arms. He held her close, whispering words of comfort. "It's all right. He's dead. Are you hurt? Did he hurt you?"

"No, I'm fine," she said.

He didn't believe her. He brushed hair away from her forehead and saw a deep cut near her hairline. "You're bleeding."

"So are you."

Asher looked down at his shirt and Cara's dress which was now covered with blood. "Yes, but that's the last time that bastard will knife anyone."

She peeled the slit material aside and looked at his wound. "Thank God it's not deep. If we get something on it you should be all right."

Asher took hold of her arms and held them tightly. He'd give up anything he owned if what he was about to say wasn't true. "Cara." He looked into her eyes. His chest heaved. "He got to Cypress first."

Caramarena started shaking her head and trying to free herself from his arms. She couldn't breathe. She felt as if someone was standing on her chest.

"I'm sorry, Cara. It looks bad. He may not make it."

"No! No! Asher tell me it isn't so! I've lost Papa and the baby. I can't lose Cypress! No!" She fell in his arms sobbing but just as quickly pushed away again. "Where is he? Has someone sent for Dr. Johnstone?"

"The barn, and yes, Casey is on his way."

353

Tears streaming down her face, she tore away from Asher's reaching arms, picked up her skirts and ran down the slope. She heard Asher's feet stomping behind her, but she didn't stop. She had to get to Cypress and tell him everything was going to be all right. She wouldn't let him die. She wouldn't!

When she made it to the barn she had to push the other slaves out of her way to find him. Kissie knelt on the ground, cradling Cypress in her arms, his head resting against her breasts. Blood covered both of them.

"Oh, Kissie," she wailed and fell on her knees and circled them both in her arms.

"He's still breathing, Miss Cara, but we don't know what ta do," Kissie wailed.

Caramarena rubbed the tears from her eyes and said, "I'll take care of him."

She tore several strips of cloth from her petticoat as she spoke orders for a pan of water. She knew when Asher knelt beside her but she didn't take her eyes off Cypress. After wiping away most of the blood she could see where the knife had struck Cypress low on his throat, missing the jugular, but tearing across the collarbone and stopping high on the chest, leaving a gaping wound.

Caramarena winced. Asher was right. It was bad.

Chapter Twenty-one

It took two weeks for the house to settle down after the brutal attack on Cypress. He lingered at death's door for several days and Caramarena was sure that Kissie's love for the man was the only thing that pulled him through the dark hours. During that time, Caramarena spent many hours by the graves of her father and her baby. She had just been getting over their deaths when Finley Dobson had showed up, bringing old memories back to haunt her days and nights.

When Cypress improved, Asher insisted she and Kissie return to their normal duties. He also suggested that the two of them needed to get away from Live Oak for a day and asked her to plan a trip into town. And he was right. Planning for the visit stirred a little excitement in her.

Caramarena sat in her office writing notes to some of the people she wanted to visit when they took their trip into Apalachicola next week. She especially wanted to see the families who had children Bunch liked to play with. And she was hoping to cheer Kissie by taking her shopping for new fabrics for the slaves' clothing.

She was just finishing the last note when Kissie came in and announced there was a man to see her.

Wary of any stranger she asked, "Did he state his name and business, Kissie?"

"He says he from de insurance company 'bout dat missing shipment of turpentine."

"Oh, yes, by all means send him in," she said, but Kissie didn't leave. She remained in the doorway, pulling on her kerchief. Caramarena's heartbeat increased. Kissie was acting strange and too many things had happened for her not to pick up on it. She rose from her chair. "What is it, Kissie?"

"Wells, dis man, he seem ta think you name is Worthy. I told him you ain't Miz Worthy. He done come ta de wrong place."

"Oh, is that all." Caramarena breathed a little easier and smiled. "I'm sure he's simply mixed up our name with some of his other clients. I'll take care of it. Did you tell him you'd send for Asher?" she asked.

She nodded. "Says he wants to speak ta you. Not Mr. Worthy."

"All right. I'll take care of it. You can send him in."

A few moments later Caramarena greeted the handsome, well dressed man as he entered her office. "Mrs. Worthy, it's nice to meet you. I'm Bradford Hallaway."

His accent was British, heavy like that of her husband and that made her smile. "Mr. Hallaway, I'm delighted, but I'm afraid you've made a mistake. My name is Millhouse. Maybe I'm not the person you're looking for."

He smiled. "Did this plantation contract with Three Sons Shipping last fall to carry turpentine to England?"

"Yes."

"Then I have the right person."

"In that case, please sit down. Would you like some refreshment?"

He promptly sat on one of the chairs and said, "No, thank you I'm fine. Your husband is one of the owners of Three Sons Shipping, isn't that correct?" he asked.

There was something about his air of confidence that

356

bothered Caramarena. She walked around her desk and sat down. "Yes, that's correct. Now, how may I help you?"

"Well, of course, the first thing we'd like to do is clear all interested parties who may have had direct access to the cargo—which I believe was loaded on *Sandor* in September of last year. Your—ah—maid told me that Mr. John Cantrell is deceased. Is that correct?"

Caramarena stiffened. There was no hint of condolence in the man's voice and that bothered her immensely. "It is. Yes."

"And he contracted with Three Sons in August for several hundred barrels of turpentine. Is that correct?"

"Yes. I believe I just said that." She didn't mind answering his questions, but she didn't like him treating her as if she didn't know what she was talking about.

"And Asher Worthy made the transaction on behalf of Three Sons, is that correct?"

"No." She didn't like this man or his manner of speaking to her. She placed a false smile on her face, determined that this man refer to their correct name. "My husband's name is also Millhouse."

"Mmm . . ." He put a finger to his lips and moved to the edge of his seat. "That's one of our problems with this case. The contract was signed by Asher Millhouse when, according to his brothers, his name is in fact Asher Millhouse Worthy. His brothers are Parker and Winston Worthy. Do you know of any reason why your husband would be using a different name for this particular transaction—the only cargo that *Sandor* has ever lost to pirates?"

Something told Caramarena that this man knew more than he was letting on and it angered her as well as upset her. But she decided she must remain firm in her husband's defense. "No. You must be mistaken, Mr. Hellman. You've obviously mixed up your clients.

357

It's a very easy thing to do. I know my husband's name." She gave him another false smile and he had the confidence to return it.

"You're very clever, Mrs. Worthy. You've made your point by mispronouncing my name. Tell me, do you know of any reason why your husband would have not wanted the turpentine to reach its intended destination."

Caramarena cleared her throat. "I don't think I'll answer any more of your questions, Mr. Hallaway. I believe I'll send for Mr. Millhouse. I'm sure he will be happy to speak with you about your concerns."

He rose from his chair. "That won't be necessary for now. You're the one I came to talk to today, Mrs. Worthy."

Caramarena lifted her chin and shoulders a little higher as she stood up. "Why? If you think my husband had something to do with the cargo being pirated, why don't you stay and ask him about it."

This time a genuine smile appeared across his face and those icy fingers of fear crawled up Caramarena's back. She suddenly had a feeling this man wasn't from the insurance company investigating the missing turpentine.

"I know what happened to the cargo and so does your husband. You're the one who doesn't know. Oh, don't take my word for it. Ask your husband if he had anything to do with it. And while you're at it, ask him what his full name is. I think you'll be surprised with his answers."

Caramarena's skirts rustled as she hurried from behind the desk. "I want you to leave," she demanded. "I don't think you're with the insurance company at all. Kissie!" she called, and Kissie appeared in the doorway. "Show this man to the door."

"No need to call your bodyguard. I can find my way

out, Mrs. Worthy." He winked at her before turning away.

"You want me ta get Mr. Asher?" Kissie asked before following the man.

Shaking her head she said, "Just watch him and make sure that he leaves Live Oak."

Caramarena paced in front of the fireplace in the gold room the rest of the afternoon while she waited for Asher to come home. Several times she contemplated sending Kissie after him but always decided she wasn't ready to see him. Mr. Hallaway had been too sure of himself for there not to have been any truth in what he said about Asher's surname, but why would he implicate Asher in the piracy? That was lunacy.

When she heard his familiar call from the foyer she stepped to the doorway and looked at him. Her stomach felt nervous and jumpy. She loved him so much. Why would he lie about his name?

"There you are," he said and walked toward her. "Did you have a good day?" he asked as he pulled her into his arms.

"Yes." Her smile was a little shaky but Asher didn't seem to notice. His kiss was gentle, loving, promising. When it ended naturally she moved away from him and walked farther into the room.

The late afternoon sunshine made slatted patterns on the wall and bathed the room with a golden glow.

"Caramarena, what's wrong? I can tell you're upset about something. Is it Bunch or Kissie?" He followed her into the room and took hold of her hand. "You're trembling, Cara, tell me what's wrong."

"There was a man here today." She looked into his eyes and found warmth and concern. Her fears vanished. How could she believe a stranger over her husband? Asher loved her. He wouldn't have lied about his name or anything else.

"Go on. What man? Who was he? What did he want?"

"Nothing," she said, and turned her back on him. "I'm just being silly."

He took her arm and forced her to face him. "You've never been silly a day in your life. Come sit down and tell me what happened today." He led her to the gold-striped settee.

"It was nothing really. A man named Mr. Hallaway said he was from the insurance company and he wanted to talk with me about the piracy."

"Why didn't you send for me?" His words were cautious.

She moistened her lips and looked into his blue eyes. "He wanted to speak to me. Asher, I don't think he was really from the insurance company. He—he insisted your name is Worthy."

She saw the affirmative answer in his face before he made a sound. No! her mind screamed.

He squeezed her hand. "Cara, it's true. I'm Asher Millhouse Worthy."

Caramarena shook her head but found no words. The only thing she could think was that he'd lied to her. From the moment they'd met he'd lied. If he was untruthful about his name, he could have lied about the missing turpentine, too. And about loving her? No! she screamed inside. She didn't want to doubt her husband. She didn't want to distrust him.

"I can explain, Cara." He tried to take her other hand but she pulled it away. She didn't want him to touch her.

"Cara." He said her name softly. "What else did he tell you?"

He knew. It must be true. Her throat felt as if it had

360

been dried with cotton. "Do you know what happened to the turpentine? Were you involved in the piracy?"

"Let me explain," he said calmly.

But Caramarena wasn't calm. "Explain! How can you explain away so many lies, so much—deception." She swept away from the sofa, away from Asher. She felt as if her world were coming to an end. She turned on him in anger. "Asher, I've been your wife almost a year, and I don't even know your real name! How long were you going to keep if from me?"

"I planned to tell you—"

"When!" she interrupted, unable to stay quiet.

"When you were better. You were in bad shape when I returned, Cara."

"And whose fault was that?" she asked in an unnaturally high-pitched voice, outraged. All that'd happened the past few months came crashing down on her. "You left me with a false name, only pennies in the bank, and you stole the turpentine so we couldn't be paid. Asher, how could you do this to me? Why!" Her last sentence was a mere whisper.

Asher stood still, his gaze fixed on her face. "None of it was done to hurt you, Cara. It all started a long time ago. Let me explain."

"No!" she screamed. "I don't want you to call me Cara ever again. I told you only people who love me can call me that." Her throat ached and her chest was so heavy she felt as if it were pulling her down. "I want you to leave! I don't want to hear any more lies from you. Just go away!"

He calmly started toward her, but she backed away. "Sit down and listen to what I have to say."

She shook her head and sniffed back the tears that threatened. "I want you to leave Live Oak. This is no longer your home. Now!"

"I'm not going anywhere and neither are you until

you listen to me." He grabbed her arms and Caramarena screamed and started struggling against him.

"Stop! Cara, I don't want to hurt you. Let me explain, damn it!"

Asher knew by what little Caramarena had told him that Parker and Winston had to be behind this. They were trying to destroy his relationship with his wife and by the way Cara was fighting him they'd succeeded.

"Let me go!" Caramarena screamed again.

Asher heard another scream and looked up in time to see Bunch coming at him with her doll. He turned Cara's wrist loose and threw up his arm to keep the doll from hitting him in the head as Bunch attacked him, too.

"What's goin' on in here?" Kissie demanded from the doorway. "What you crazy white folks hittin' each other fo'? Stop dis!"

Caramarena managed to pull her other hand free from Asher's grip as Bunch pelted his back with her small fist. Caramarena grabbed Bunch and held her away from him.

Asher wiped his mouth with the back of his hand, then brushed his hair away from his face. He'd never seen Caramarena so hot with anger. He'd strangle Parker and Winston if he ever saw either of them again.

"I want you to leave Live Oak," Caramarena said again, between gasping breaths.

"Like hell," he told her angrily. "This is *my* home. Dammit, I'm not leaving."

"Don't hurt Cara!" Bunch screamed out at him.

"Kissie, take Bunch to her room," Caramarena said, her voice calmer now.

"No!" Bunch screamed again. "I want to stay. Asher's being mean to Cara."

"Bunch, Asher and I aren't going to fight any more. I promise. You go with Kissie. I promise to be up in a few minutes. Now do as I say."

Bunch stuck her tongue out at Asher and marched over to Kissie.

"You sho' yous wants me ta leave you wid him?" Kissie asked without bothering to look at Asher.

"I'm not going to hurt Caramarena," Asher said to reassure Bunch and Kissie, although right now he felt like strangling her for being so unreasonable.

"I'll be fine, Kissie. Take Bunch away, please," she said.

After they walked out Caramarena turned cold eyes upon Asher. "You have lied to me for the last time. I should have never married you. I've had nothing but misery since I met you. I want you to leave Live Oak."

Her tone and implication set Asher's temper to boiling. "Now who's lying?" he asked sarcastically. "I believe you've suffered more than misery at my hands, Caramarena. Shall I name the nights you've lain beneath me enjoying the pleasures I've given you?"

Caramarena gasped and her eyes widened in shock. "I can't believe you'd mention that at a time like this. You won't make your faults any less by pointing out mine, Asher."

Asher was immediately sorry for his rude remark, but dammit, she had it coming. If she'd just sit down and listen to him he'd tell her the whole sordid story.

"You're no longer welcome at Live Oak. I want you to leave," she said again.

Her arrogance almost got the better of Asher. For a moment he wanted to blurt out just what kind of man her father really was and wipe that smug look off her face. He opened his mouth to tell her but stopped himself in time. He loved her too much to hurt her that way. It would be best to tell her later. In the frame of mind she was in right now, he doubted she'd believe him.

363

He tucked the tail of his shirt back in his breeches and combed through his hair with his hands again. "I promised I wouldn't leave you, and I meant it. This is *my* home. You are *my* wife, and I'm not leaving."

For a fleeting moment he thought he saw admiration in Caramarena's eyes and that gave him hope.

"Very well then, I'll have Kissie move your things into another bedroom."

"You can move me into another bedroom, but I won't leave the house." He took a deep breath. "I'd really like to explain everything. When you're ready to calm down and listen to what I have to say, let me know."

"I won't, Asher. I can't trust you to tell me the truth." She whirled and walked out.

Asher turned and jammed his fist into the back of the small settee, knocking it over.

When Caramarena refused to speak to Asher for three days he told her he was going to Pensacola to check on the sawmill he'd invested in before leaving for England a year ago.

While he was gone Caramarena looked over the bank account books and saw that they had more money than they ever had. Asher had certainly made up for emptying them last year. But why? She'd know by now if she'd given him the chance to explain. Now that she'd had time to think about it she was certain that it was all connected to the reason he had to return to England. But what? She decided she'd ask him as soon as he returned. She'd been childish and foolish for not letting him explain everything the other day.

Caramarena was in the office still looking over the books when she heard a loud knock on the front door. She hadn't gotten over the frightening experience when

Cypress was nearly killed.

Asher wasn't expected back from Pensacola until late tomorrow. She opened her desk drawer, pulled out the gun she'd placed there weeks ago and hid it beneath the folds of her skirts as she went to the door.

She peered out the window first and saw Kissie standing on the porch talking to a man who looked vaguely familiar. He was dressed in English-style clothing. Her hand tightened around the gun. She'd hear no more stories about her husband until she talked to Asher.

With the gun still hidden she stepped outside and said, "I'm Mrs. Worthy. What can I do for you?" She was surprised at how natural the name sounded on her tongue.

"Caramarena, I knew I'd know you anywhere." He took a step closer and she drew the gun up and pointed it at his chest.

"Don't come any farther until you've identified yourself," she warned.

The man looked flustered for a moment but eventually took off his hat and smiled. He was shorter than Asher by several inches and his hair was thinning, but there was no mistaking the smile.

"I'd consider it an honor. I'm Winston Cambridge Worthy, one of Asher's older brothers."

Caramarena let the gun drop to her side, feeling like a fool and a terrible hostess. "Oh my, I'm so sorry. Please come in. Here, Kissie, take the gun. Get Mr. Worthy something cool to drink. I do apologize." She took hold of his arm and walked him into the house. "You must think I'm a terrible person."

"Not at all. I take it Asher's not here. Surely you don't greet guests with a gun when he's home."

She led him into the gold room. "How right you are, Mr. Worthy. Asher is away on business and—one of our slaves was seriously wounded by a madman a month ago. I'm afraid we've all been a little on edge because of it."

"I can understand why you're so cautious. Do call me Winston. And I'd like to call you Caramarena. We are family."

"I'd like that." She smiled, but inside she prayed Asher would forgive her for greeting his brother with a gun in her hands. "And by all means loosen that shirt, Winston. You Englishmen do like to choke yourselves with all that clothing."

Winston laughed. "No, really I'm fine, however I do know why Asher damned the heat."

"Kissie will be here with some refreshment for you soon. Tell me, is Asher expecting you?"

"Maybe—maybe not." Winston pulled on the collar of his shirt as if he were suddenly uncomfortable.

His answer confused her but she didn't say anything because Kissie came in carrying a tray with a pitcher of orange juice and two glasses on it. "Thank you, Kissie. That will be all."

Caramarena could see by the look in Kissie's eyes that she didn't trust Asher's brother. She also noticed the pearl handle of the gun protruding from her dress pocket. Maybe Kissie was wise to be so cautious.

She handed the filled glass to Winston and said, "Asher has gone to Pensacola, and I don't expect him back before late tomorrow or possibly the day after."

"It's too bad that I'll miss him," he said, but Caramarena didn't hear any remorse in his tone.

"Oh surely you can stay after coming all this way. I won't hear of you leaving before he returns."

"No, really I can't stay. I hired a driver to bring me here and the man's waiting to take me back to Tallahassee for the night. From there I'll travel back to Charleston. I'll be there a couple of weeks if Asher wants to make the trip up and talk." He finished his drink and set the empty glass on the tray.

"Let me fill it again for you," she said.

"No. That was very refreshing. If you don't mind I'd like to tell you what I came to say to Asher. In fact, I think I'd rather tell you. I've no doubt Asher will be mad as a wild boar and I'd just as soon he have time to cool down before he comes looking for me."

Caramarena thought his comment strange but decided to listen to what he had to say. "If you're certain you can't stay, I'd be happy to pass along your message."

"We received Asher's letter telling us of your father's death and his decision to tell you everything. But by the time his letter reached us Parker had already sent Hallaway to inform you about Asher's real name and his part in the piracy of *Sandor.*"

Caramarena was trying hard to understand what Winston was talking about, but she was having a hard time of it. One thing she was sure of, Asher's brothers had sent Hallaway to make sure Asher was found out. She held herself very still and listened.

"Naturally we were hoping it would make you throw him out and he'd change his mind about staying in America and come back home to London. He'd told us he would tell you about your father but we didn't believe he'd take the chance of losing you. It was apparent he loved you and wasn't going to give you up."

The fine hairs on the back of Caramarena's neck stood out. What did his comment about her father mean? Before she had a chance to ask he continued.

"Anyway, we decided we didn't want Asher angry with us for life, so Parker sent me on this mission to make peace with Asher—and with you too, of course. We've decided to make amends for any trouble we might have caused by giving Asher our interest in Live

Oak, and we'll let him keep his interest in Three Sons." Finished, he smiled.

Caramarena had no idea what Winston was talking about and she had the feeling she didn't really want to know. Unknowingly, he'd said too much without saying enough. How could Asher's brothers have any interest in Live Oak? She swallowed the lump that rose in her throat and affected her breathing.

"Winston. I'm afraid I'm not clear on some things." She smiled. "Would you please start at the beginning and explain the whole story to me."

She saw in his eyes that he realized his mistake in telling her so much. He shifted in his seat. His eyebrows lifted. "You don't know anything I'm talking about, do you? Damn Asher's soul. He didn't tell you, did he?"

"Well, that's not entirely true," she said, trying bluff him. "We did have a man come here and pretend to be from the insurance company. That's when I found out that my husband's surname is Worthy, not Millhouse. I also found out that he had something to do with the piracy of *Sandor*. What I don't know is the reason for any of this."

Winston held up his hands. "Oh no. I'm not going to tell. I've said far too much as it is. From Asher's letter we assumed you'd know the whole story by now." He rose from the settee and pulled on the tail of his coat. "I really must be going. Tell Asher I'm in Charleston, staying at our usual hotel. He can get in touch with me there."

Caramarena touched his arm. She couldn't let him leave now. Not before she knew what had happened. "Please, Winston. You must finish the story."

"No, Caramarena," he said firmly and shook off her hands. "If Asher hasn't told you he has a good reason. I'll just be saying good-bye."

"Kissie!" Caramarena called. Kissie appeared in the doorway and leveled the gun at Winston's chest.

"You makes a move and I's cuts you down likes a bear!"

"What's the meaning of this?" Winston said indignantly.

Caramarena remained calm. "Sit back down, Winston. I believe you have something to tell me."

He pulled on the tail of his coat again. "Absolutely not! Asher will kill me."

"Would you like to take your chances with Asher or a woman whose husband was almost killed by a white man a mere month ago?"

Winston looked at Kissie. The whites of her eyes were glowing against the dark pupil. She pulled back the hammer of the gun to prove Caramarena's point.

"This is madness!" His gaze darted from Caramarena to Kissie. "All right, goddammit, I'll tell you." He cleared his throat. "Pardon my language. And I believe I will loosen my shirt."

Caramarena realized she was holding her breath. She let it out with a sigh. At last she'd get some answers. "Good. Now sit back down. Kissie, stay where you are."

"I ain't goin' nowhere, Miss Cara."

"I've heard that slaves are dedicated to their masters. I guess this is proof. Would she really pull that trigger?"

"Without battin' an eyelash," Kissie answered from behind him. "You wants ta live? Yous better tell Miss Cara what she be wanting ta know."

Winston grunted. "Well, I'm glad to know that Asher will be living in a perfectly civilized world," he complained in a irritable tone. "I've no idea why he wants to live in this godforsaken place. It's hot as hell here."

Caramarena smiled. It appeared this complaining and swearing man was the real Winston. The polite gentleman who'd greeted her at the door had vanished.

"You have a story to tell, Winston, and a man waiting for you."

He pursed his lips. "Very well, but I have to warn you, Caramarena, that you're not going to like it. I'm certain that's the reason Asher hasn't told you. I wish you'd wait and let him explain."

"I don't want to wait. I want to hear it from you."

Winston cut his eyes around to Kissie one more time as if to assure himself he had no choice. The gun was still pointed at him. "It all started about thirty years ago—oh hell, I'll tell it as briefly and as painlessly as possible. Your father, John Cantrell, worked for my father, George Worthy. When still a young man Cantrell embezzled a large sum of money from my father and absconded with it."

"What!" she gasped. "You're lying."

"With a damn gun pointed at my head?" He sniffed. "I think not." His confidence improved when he saw how shaken she was. "Well, Caramarena, it's up to you. Do you want to hear the rest of it?"

Chapter Twenty-two

The next morning Caramarena awoke early after getting little sleep. Her heart was still heavy from the horrifying story Winston had told. She didn't want to believe that her father had stolen another man's money. The very thought of it brought her physical pain. But even though she tried to deny it, in her heart she knew it had to be true. It all fit together too well. From the beginning Asher hadn't wanted to marry her, and from the beginning she'd known of his keen interest in Live Oak. And why not. It had been purchased with his father's money.

She was the encroacher. Not Asher.

Caramarena was quiet as Kissie helped her dress. She left off the cumbersome hoop and petticoats and insisted on wearing one of her lightweight, older dresses. For what she had to do today she needed as little clothing as possible.

When Kissie finished with the buttons Caramarena turned to her and said, "Kissie, I've decided to leave Live Oak."

Kissie cocked her head to one side and placed her hands on her hips. "What you talkin' bout, Miss Cara?" she asked gruffly.

"You heard what Winston said last night. This plantation was bought with stolen money. Why Papa would do such a thing I don't know. I think he tried to tell me before he died. And looking back, I believe there were other times he wanted to tell me but couldn't bring himself to say it. I hate to admit it, but I'm glad he didn't tell me. I don't think I could have—" She couldn't bring herself to say more. She closed her eyes briefly and took a calming breath.

When she was in control of herself again she continued. "In any case, Live Oak belongs to Asher and his brothers. Not me. Not the Cantrells. I don't want to give up this place. It's such a part of me that I . . . But now I know I don't belong here. And it hurts me to say it, but I never have."

"Yous talkin' crazy, Miss Cara. Dis yore home." She pointed to the floor with a long slender finger. "I ain't gone let no fine-dressed Englishman take yore home even if'n his name is Mr. Asher. No sir. Not me."

Caramarena wouldn't be persuaded. "No, it's not my home any more. I have to leave today. I can't stay any longer. I want you to pack a light bag for Bunch and me. We'll borrow one of the wagons and go to Charlotte's house in Georgia. She's closer than Catherine."

Kissie's hands made fists and anger lit in her eyes. "Stop dis, Miss Cara. We's can't go all da way ta Georgee in de wagon. Mr. Asher be mad fo' a week if'n we tries it. 'Sides, you know Cypress ain't in no shape ta travel dat fer."

Caramarena put her hand to her lips and held back the sobs that wanted to burst from her chest. Through sheer willpower she held her voice steady and said, "You and Cypress won't be going with us, Kissie. Unlike me, you belong here. This is your home." She turned away and sought control of her voice. "Live Oak never really belonged to Papa and now it doesn't belong to me. When I think about all the times I wanted an heir for this place it makes me want to cry. I can't do that." She squeezed her eyes shut and her bottom lip trembled. "When I think of all I've gone through, all the dreams and plans I had for something that was never really mine I just want to—"

Kissie grabbed her shoulders and spun her around. "You listen ta me. Dis yo' home cause you Mr. Asher's wife. He don't want you leavin' him and goin' ta Georgee. He love you."

She pushed away from Kissie, not wanting to be touched, feeling as if her father's past had made her dirty. If only he were alive so she could talk with him, understand why he did it.

"I'm not sure of that any more. How could he love me knowing what my father did? How could he love me knowing I wanted to throw him out of his home." She laughed bitterly. "No wonder he was so adamant about not leaving. This is his home. Not mine!"

"I ain't gone listen ta dis no mo'. I's gone gets yo' medicines and fix you a toddy. You in bad shape."

"No, Kissie. I'm fine." Caramarena lifted her chin and her shoulders. It was time to go. "You've got to accept the fact that I'm leaving, and I need to leave as soon as possible. I can make it to the MacCarols before dark if I don't tarry. I'm sure they'll put us up for the night. From there I can travel on to Tallahassee tomorrow and take the stagecoach to Charlotte's home."

"No sir. No sir." She shook her head firmly. "I can't let yous take no wagon to de neighbors. Mr. Asher whup me fer sho' if'n I lets you leave."

Caramarena took a deep breath. "I'm going, Kissie."

"Then I's comming, too. I'll gets Ivy ta look afta Cypress until he be ready ta travel." Kissie stood with her feet spread apart as if she were expecting a fight.

"No. You can't go." It hurt Caramarena deeply to have to be so harsh. "You belong to Live Oak. I can't have Asher coming after me because I've stolen one of

373

his slaves. I won't do that. Enough has been taken from him."

Kissie's eyes watered and her full bottom lip stuck out, quivering slightly. "I belong ta you and Bunch, Miss Cara. Don't make me stay. I don't wants ta lose you. I done lost two husbands and po' Cypress ain't where he can walk yet."

"Kissie, don't!" Caramarena threw her arms around the older woman and embraced her tightly. "You know how much I care for you and Cypress, don't you?" She felt Kissie's head bob up and down and heard her sniffle.

"Listen to me." Caramarena forced Kissie to look at her. "You have to understand that I can't take anything that belongs to Asher. Papa and I've taken far too much as it is. But when I get to Charlotte's I'm going to ask her to buy you and Cypress for me, and then I'll set you both free. You'll be free to stay with me or go wherever you please. Would you like that?"

Kissie wiped her nose with the back of her hand. "You set us free?" she asked.

Caramarena nodded. "It's a promise."

A slight smile played on Kissie's lips, then she chuckled. "Ah—we's don't have nowhere ta go, Miss Cara. Gets nobody ta take care of us."

"Then you can stay with me. A free man and woman. Not as slaves."

Kissie rolled her eyes around a moment, then stuck out her bottom lip. "If'n Mr. Asher don't come afta you that'll mean he be mighty mad. He may not sell me."

Caramarena's heart constricted. "I think he will if you're all I ask for. Kissie, I wish so many things had been different. I wish there was more that I could do for you and the others."

Kissie nodded. "So do I, Miss Cara. So do I."

* * *

Asher dismounted at the barn and gave his horse's reins to the slave who'd taken Cypress's place. He spoke gently to the young man because he still acted as if he were afraid of Asher. He took his gloves off as he walked toward the house and realized he actually missed seeing Cypress around. They'd met under less than desirable circumstances but Cypress had been brave and loyal, and Asher hated like hell that Dobson had almost killed him.

The trip to Pensacola had done him good. He'd decided he had to tell Caramarena the story about her father whether she wanted to hear it or not. He'd tie her down and make her listen if he had to, but once and for all they were going to clear up the twisted, secret past that stood between them.

"Cara," he called when he stepped into the foyer. He wasn't surprised when she didn't answer. She hadn't spoken to him for three days prior to his leaving, so why should he expect her to come running to greet him now?

Damn it! He was tired of the silent treatment. He strode into the gold room and then into the office but saw no sign of her in either place. In fact the house seemed unusually quiet. Ivy would be in the cookhouse preparing dinner but there should be some noise from Kissie, Bunch or Caramarena.

When he made it back to the foyer an uneasy feeling crept up his spine. "Cara!" he called again and took the stairs two at a time. He burst into her room and found Kissie dusting the furniture with a white cloth. Without really looking around he knew Caramarena was gone from the room, from the house, from Live Oak.

Kissie looked up at him with her big black eyes and sorrowful expression.

"Where is she?" he asked, his voice deep and throaty.

"She gone."

375

Asher tensed. Damn! He hadn't meant to drive her from her home. "When did she leave?"

"Dis morning. Afta she talked wid dat fancy-dressed man who says he be yo' brother."

"What man?" His throat was so dry he could hardly speak. He walked farther into the room, his muscles taut. He was almost afraid to hear the answer. "What man, Kissie?"

"Dat man named Mr. Winston. He come yesterday. He told her all de bad things her Papa did, stealing dat money and buying dis here house."

"My God! I'll kill him." Asher's hands made fists, and he kicked the chair leg and sent the chair sliding across the floor. His heart was hammering so fast he thought he might lose his breath. "Where did she go? Who's with her?" he managed to say.

"Jest her and Bunch gone on de wagon. She told me I had ta stay here cause I belong ta you now."

Asher suddenly felt so weak he leaned against the bedpost. He took deep breaths and found a bitter chuckle rumbling around in his throat. There was no woman he wanted to belong to him less than he wanted Kissie. And if he couldn't get Caramarena back he'd sail back to England and beat the hell out of Winston and Parker.

"Where's she heading?" he asked when he felt calm enough to speak again.

Kissie stood by the dresser twisting the dusting cloth in her dark hands. "She gone try ta make it to de Mac-Carols house tonight. I's told her you be mad. But she say dis ain't her home no mo'. She says you don't want her."

Asher gave her a hard look. "The hell I don't! Kissie, make sure Caramarena and Bunch's beds are turned down. It'll be late, but we'll be back." He strode out of the room and hurried down the stairs.

376

In the barn Asher picked out the best horse and fitted him with the lightest saddle. He had some hard riding to do and he had to have a horse that would hold up.

Within five minutes of entering the barn, Asher was riding out at a fast canter. He knew if he pushed the horse too hard the animal would give out before he found Caramarena. So he had to bide his time and keep a steady pace, a slower pace than he wanted.

He estimated that it was about three hours past noon when he left Live Oak. That meant Caramarena was at least five to six hours ahead of him. If she were taking it slow and easy he should catch up with her before dusk.

Asher stopped twice to water his horse while the late September sun beat upon his head. He'd become numb with the fear that he might have lost Caramarena forever. She'd loved her father very much. He wondered what she was feeling, what she was thinking. Winston's news had obviously put her over the edge. He had to get her back. He had to.

As the sun dipped low in the western sky Asher saw a dot moving ahead of him. His heartbeat sped up and he spurred the horse faster. He drew nearer in a matter of minutes and assured himself that what he saw was the wagon carrying Caramarena and Bunch. Relief made him weak.

"Cara!" he called and spurred the horse again.

Once again Caramarena thought she heard someone approaching but her neck was sore from twisting around to see if Asher were coming after them. It was foolish of her to think he'd come after her even if he made it back to Live Oak today. No, he'd wanted the plantation. Not her. It had been Live Oak from the very moment he arrived in Florida.

"I want to go home, Cara," Bunch complained for the hundredth time and pulled again on Caramarena's arm.

"I told you —" This time Caramarena was certain she heard a horse approaching. She pulled on the reins and stopped the horses as Asher came galloping up beside the wagon.

They simply stared at each other for a moment.

"Don't hurt Cara, Asher," Bunch told him in a fussy tone, clutching her doll tighter.

He cut his eyes around to her. His breathing was hard. "I'll never hurt her, Bunch. Never again."

Caramarena couldn't take her eyes off him. His hair was wet with sweat and his shirt clung to his damp skin, but he'd never looked more handsome to her. She'd hoped and prayed that'd he come after them but now that he had, what did it mean? Could he forgive her father? Could he forgive her?

Asher wiped his forehead with the back of his hand and said, "I need to talk to you, Cara."

"Asher I don't —"

"Damn it! Why didn't you give me the chance to explain before you left?" His horse snorted loudly and Bunch jumped from his harsh tone.

"Don't yell," Bunch complained.

Caramarena was going to tell him he didn't have to explain anything, but he cut her sentence short. She rubbed the back of her neck and down her shoulder. She was tired from sitting in the wagon all day. She wanted him to tell her that the past didn't matter, and they could put it behind them and start all over again. She wanted him to say he loved her and wanted her to come back to him and be his wife and the mother of his children.

She took a deep breath. "I didn't think you'd want me to stay after the things I'd said to you," she said softly, looking up at him with love in her eyes.

He gave her an incredulous look. "You didn't think I'd want you to stay?"

She held the leather reins so tight they cut into the palms of her hands. "Asher, what my father did was unforgivable, and—and I tried to throw you out of your own home! I wouldn't blame you if you hated me and never wanted to see me again."

His expression softened. "Cara, I don't hate you. One of the reasons I hadn't told you the whole story is because I was afraid you wouldn't forgive me for keeping the truth from you, for deceiving you. Dammit, Cara, I didn't want to tell you about your father because I knew how it would hurt you. When I returned from England and found he had died, I'd hoped the past could be buried with him."

"I want to go home, Cara," Bunch said again and pulled on her arm. "Let's go home."

"Shh, Bunch," she reprimanded.

When Caramarena looked back at Asher he was watching her with a loving expression on his face. "Cara, will you come back home and give us the chance to talk?"

Caramarena winced inside. She'd hoped he'd come after her because he loved her. Not because he wanted to explain about her father. "I can't undo what my father did. Will talking about it change anything, Asher?" she asked.

His horse snorted again and tried to move up to where the team was but Asher held him back. "Not some things. It won't change the past, and it won't change the fact that I love you, Cara."

Caramarena's breath caught in her throat and she closed her eyes for a moment, savoring the words she most wanted to hear. "Oh, Asher, I was hoping you loved me enough to come after me."

Asher jumped off his horse and climbed on the running board, lifting himself up to the seat. He reached across Bunch to grab Caramarena's hands. "Cara, I love you and I don't want to live without you."

She smiled and squeezed his hands. "And I love you with all my heart."

"Move! You're hurting me," Bunch complained and pushed against Asher's shoulder.

They ignored Bunch and continued to stare into each other's eyes.

"I've got a lot of explaining to do," he admitted.

"I think your brother told me most of it."

"I'm sorry Winston had to be the one to tell you. I know how much you loved your father and at first I wanted to keep it from you, but then I realized we shouldn't have any secrets between us. I knew I had to tell you even if it meant you'd hate me for doing it."

She nodded. "Asher, I'm sorry Papa stole that money. I never had any idea."

"I know that, my love."

"I'll repay your brothers—"

"Shh." He shook his head. "Take my word for it. They won't want any payment."

"I just wish I knew Papa's reason for what he did. I think I could accept it better if I knew why."

"With both our fathers dead now we'll never know all that was between them." He smiled. "But we've got the rest of our lives to try to figure it out," he whispered. His hands slid up to her face. Their lips met in a sweet, soft kiss.

"No," Bunch complained again. "You're hurting me. Move, Asher. I want to go home."

"I think she's tired," he whispered against Caramarena's lips, and she nodded. "Let's take her home," he said.

They made it back to Live Oak late that night. After putting a sleepy Bunch to bed Caramarena took a

380

wipe-off bath from the basin while Asher took a dip in the river. When her bath was finished she went to her drawer for a nightgown and saw only one, the one Kissie had designed and Fanny had made. All her others were still packed in the trunk that sat on the wagon in the barn.

She pulled the gown free of the drawer and held it against her. Fond memories of Fanny, Lacy, and all the other slaves who lost their lives to the fever filled her mind. Loving memories of her father and her baby were there, too. In time she would come to terms with all that had happened to her in the last year. The important thing was that she had Asher to help her through it. With her husband beside her she could get through anything.

Caramarena slipped the sheer gown over her head, opened the French doors and stepped out on the balcony. The sounds of night, the frogs, the crickets, the nightbirds all beckoned her, soothed her, cleansed her. This was her home. No one could take it away from her now. Asher had made it so.

The half moon draped her with silvery light. The sultry heat of summer was gone and in its place a cool breeze fanned her streaming hair.

"Cara?"

She turned and saw Asher standing in the doorway dressed only in his breeches, the way she liked him best.

"My God! You're beautiful. What do you have on?" He walked onto the balcony and took her hands, turning her so the moonlight filtered through the sheer material, giving him a glimpse of his wife's desirable body, giving him a glimpse of heaven.

She went into his arms and hugged him tightly. "All my other nightgowns are packed in the trunk which is still sitting on the wagon." Caramarena laughed, a soft lilting sound that wafted on the air. "I'll have to tell you

381

the story behind this nightgown someday."

He ran his hand up and down her back, pressing her breasts against his chest with each movement. When he held her like this he wondered how he could have ever wanted another woman.

"Mmm . . . someday we'll talk about a lot of things, but not tonight. Cara, I love you. I almost went crazy when I found out you'd left. Please don't leave me again."

She raised her head and looked into his loving, blue eyes. "I love you, Asher. I don't plan to leave you or Live Oak again. You're both mine."

Asher smiled, rubbing his hands over her shoulders and down her back. "It feels wonderful to have you in my arms again. I love you so much."

Caramarena kissed his neck and breathed in his clean scent. "Asher you don't know how I felt when I thought I'd lost you and Live Oak. Do you really think you can forget about the past and leave your life in England behind?"

He reached down, picked her up in his arms, carried her to the bed and laid her down. He looked at her lovingly, feeling he was the luckiest man in the world. "I already have."

She smiled and reached for him. Asher crawled in the bed beside her. His hand covered her breast and massaged it as his gaze swept up and down her length.

"As for the other nightgowns—leave them in the trunk." He bent his head and kissed her.

Caramarena thrilled to his touch.

THE LIVES AND LOVES OF THE WEALTHY
AND BEAUTIFUL

DESIGNING WOMAN   (337, $4.50)
by Allison Moser

She was an ugly duckling orphan from a dusty little town, where the kids at school laughed at her homemade dresses and whispered lies about her fortune-telling grandmother. Calico Gordon swore she would escape her lackluster life and make a name for herself.

Years later she was the celebrated darling of the fashion world, the most dazzling star the industry had seen in years. Her clothes hung in the closets of the beautiful and wealthy women in the world. She had reached the pinnacle—and now had to prevent her past from destroying her dreams. She had to risk it all—fortune, fame, friendship and love—to keep memories of her long-forgotten life from shattering the image she had created.

INTERLUDES   (339, $4.95)
by L. Levine

From Monte Carlo to New York, from L.A. to Cannes, Jane Perry searches for a lost love—and discovers a seductive paradise of pleasure and satisfaction, an erotic and exotic world that is hers for the taking.

It's a sensuous, privileged world, where nights—and days—are filled with a thousand pleasures, where intrigue and romance blend with dangerous desires, where reality is *better* than fantasy. . . .

FOR WOMEN ONLY   (346, $4.50)
by Trevor Meldal-Johnsen

Sean is an actor, down on his luck. Ted is the black sheep of a wealthy Boston family, looking for an easy way out. Dany is a street-smart kid determined to make it any way he can.

The one thing they all have in common is that they know how to please a woman. And that's all they need to be employed by Debonaire, Beverly Hills' most exclusive escort service—for women only. In the erotic realm of pleasure and passion, the women will pay any price for a thrill. Nothing is forbidden—except to fall in love.

Available wherever paperbacks are sold, or order direct from the Publisher. Send cover price plus 50¢ per copy for mailing and handling to Pinnacle Books, Dept. 615, 475 Park Avenue South, New York, N.Y. 10016. Residents of New York and Tennessee must include sales tax. DO NOT SEND CASH. For a free Zebra/ Pinnacle catalog please write to the above address.

PINNACLE BOOKS HAS
SOMETHING FOR EVERYONE —

MAGICIANS, EXPLORERS, WITCHES AND CATS

THE HANDYMAN   (377-3, $3.95/$4.95)
He is a magician who likes hands. He likes their comfortable
shape and weight and size. He likes the portability of the hands
once they are severed from the rest of the ponderous body. Detec-
tive Lanark must discover who The Handyman is before more
handless bodies appear.

PASSAGE TO EDEN   (538-5, $4.95/$5.95)
Set in a world of prehistoric beauty, here is the epic story of a
courageous seafarer whose wanderings lead him to the ends of
the old world — and to the discovery of a new world in the rugged,
untamed wilderness of northwestern America.

BLACK BODY   (505-9, $5.95/$6.95)
An extraordinary chronicle, this is the diary of a witch, a journal
of the secrets of her race kept in return for not being burned for
her "sin." It is the story of Alba, that rarest of creatures, a white
witch: beautiful and able to walk in the human world undetected.

THE WHITE PUMA   (532-6, $4.95/NCR)
The white puma has recognized the men who deprived him of his
family. Now, like other predators before him, he has become a
man-hater. This story is a fitting tribute to this magnificent animal that stands for all living creatures that have become, through
man's carelessness, close to disappearing forever from the face of
the earth.